FEAST
OF
SAMAEL

A Devil's Trials Novel

Stephanie Gluck

Cover art, illustrations, and formatting
by Etheric Tales & Edits
etherictalesnedits.com

Editing by Laura K.

ISBN Paperback: 978-0-6454075-1-8
ISBN eBook: 978-0-6454075-0-1
ISBN Hardback: 978-0-6459347-4-8

For Don and Barbara,
who believed in me decades before I believed in myself.
&
For Mr. Puff and Ira, always

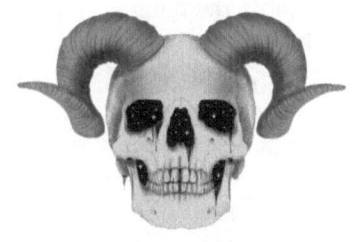

Chapter One

A shiver of warning curled down my spine. I shouldn't have been alone in the dark.

The wind wailed through the alleyway—a stark warning for those wandering in the fading light. The sound seared against my soul and left goosebumps raised against my skin. I had superstitiously heeded this warning in the past, but tonight, I chose to ignore it.

There was a makeshift crate table a few meters ahead, and it creaked with the force of the wind. It wasn't unusual to hear whispers in the wind. If ghosts were real, Ilrea would be their home. A place where lost souls came to die. Apprehension tickled at the back of my neck as it so often did once the last rays of daylight slipped away. Danger and trouble lived in the shadows, and both were hungry creatures that only went bump in the night.

It was easy to ignore the danger in a situation when the pay-off felt large enough.

I huddled deeper into my jacket and tried not to think of the rumours from that very morning of a body found carved open, sliced from throat to pelvis for the most valuable assets a poor man had—his organs. Although, the chancellor's men officially claimed he had died of the chill long before his organs were stolen, and that the danger should not become a cause of unrest.

The nights in Ilrea were cold and exposed the residents to a chill—one which would settle in their chests and claim many lives, but I was determined that my own would not be included in those numbers, not if I was quick and lucky. Hunger twisted and curled in my stomach—a gnawing monster that was hard to dismiss but couldn't be satiated just yet. It was enough to make me brave the cold... and the monsters of Ilrea. With a heavy sigh, I stepped around the corner and bits of rock bounced off the worn toe of my boot. Broken glass crunched as it shattered beneath my heel and mixed into the gravel. Another few months and these boots would be worn so thin that the sharp edges would prick right through them.

"Hello, Boyd." My voice was raspy and out of place in the quiet night. It grated against the air like my vocal cords were protesting at the concept of speaking at all. They were the first words I had said all day, unless a grunted goodbye at my mother this morning counted. Which it didn't because she hadn't heard me. I didn't need to hold a conversation to lift silver from a pocket, and very few people seemed interested in holding a casual conversation with me.

The man seated at the crate straightened his back, his broad shoulders rolling and settling into place. He was old, with greying hair that had balded in the middle of his head, leaving shiny skin behind. I watched as his beady eyes flicked up and down my body in quick and brutal assessment. As per usual, he found me lacking compared to his usual gamblers.

"Octavia." His tone was short, and it offered the impression that I had ruined his evening. There was a fair chance that was true. Then he flashed a smile. His rotted teeth sat crooked in his mouth. They were his worst feature, and vile enough to give me nightmares. The heavy lines around his eyes lifted, and for a split second, he appeared to be a much younger man.

"Come to pay up, 'en? The old men don' wait long for their coin." My silver ringed fingers slid deep into my pockets, and each hand curled around the contents within. Slowly, I balanced the weight of the objects in my hands and prepared myself for his disappointment. The cold air burned in my lungs as I drew a deep breath. It was nothing more than a hopeful yet futile attempt at fortification for human interaction.

I lifted my hands from my pockets.

"Nah, Boyd. This is all I got." I tried to sound nonchalant, like I wasn't bothered that I didn't have what he wanted. The hammer of my heart inside my chest said otherwise.

The pointed edge of my chin jerked in a flippant movement, and I flashed the contents of my pockets at him. As my heavily ringed fingers curled open, I turned them skywards—an offer to the moon for luck. Not that the moon had been a token of my fortune in the past. In fact, the full moon never brought me much luck, but there was little else for me to pray towards these days.

He wouldn't like this. I had known as much before I walked into the alley. Boyd expected me to turn up with so much more. It took guts to approach his table, and few did it without full payment. I had never been a rational thinker when it came to the cards. I hadn't played at any table for two nights now, though, and the urge to do so felt like ants beneath my skin. Itchy and distracting until I could think of nothing else. I had approached him out of pure compulsion, not self-preservation.

Inside my left palm sat five fat silver coins, each stamped with the stark symbol for Pride—a preening peacock. In my right hand were two emerald dice. The numbers were scratched and scuffed from overuse, and one corner was chipped slightly, so they rolled just right. They were my lucky dice. With them in hand, I was certain I would win often. With them, it felt like my hastily muttered prayers were answered with a touch more favour.

My toes flexed inside of my boots and wiggled as apprehension flickered through me. I swayed forward onto the balls of my feet restlessly. It granted the momentary illusion of extra height—something I desperately need as a woman in this world. A rueful smile twisted onto my lips, and I steadied myself for his reaction.

Even before I spoke again, a thrill lit through my veins. It was a thrill that had the tips of my fingers tingling in anticipation, and the beat of my heart quickened in hope. Just at the sheer thought that Boyd might agree to what I had to say.

My tongue darted out to wet my lips, and the offer flowed out breathlessly after it. "Double or nothing?" It was my favourite bet of all time. There was something I couldn't resist about placing it all on the line. Luck only truly showed itself when I risked everything for nothing.

"No." He hadn't even pretended to consider the offer. "Pay up, missy."

"Aww. C'mon, Boyd. You know me, I—"

"You owe us over a hundred coins. Due tonight, ain't it?" He stood and consulted a watch he didn't wear, even though his skin had lightened where it once sat. "October fourteenth, it is."

The makeshift table creaked, and the crate threatened to fall apart with the force at which he knocked into it. Boyd was old as sin, but he was solid enough to make a mess.

A playing card fluttered down from the tabletop. It landed on my toe and I squinted at it in the darkness. It was the queen of clubs, and there was an old bullet hole in place of her face. Fantastic. An ominous sign on an already bad night. My throat bobbed, and within seconds, I had backed away from Boyd.

I knew I shouldn't have come here, not to Boyd, and not without enough coin to keep him appeased. Hindsight was clearer than foresight, however, and I commonly had very little of the latter. The main problem was that, too often, I felt that I won more at his table than any other; even though I always lost just as much, or more, than I earned. A hundred coins of debt had built up quicker than I would have liked to admit. It seemed like nothing, though, when I needed the win more than anything else in the world. It was the only thing that released the coiled tension and the unforgiving need in my soul. A solid win with enough to take home was the only way I felt worthwhile in this community.

"Nah. C'mon, Boyd. Boyd? *Boyd.*"

He withdrew a knife from his belt—its blade short, stained with blood. "Two more days, Boyd," I breathed, panic high in my voice. "I got you. I swear… just give me two—"

The table gave way as he stood on it. The wood cracked loudly, the noise echoing through the alley. I glanced over my shoulder and wondered if it would bring help.

The table would have never held his weight as Boyd was a thick man, well-padded from the spoils of the game, so by the time he stepped back down onto the ground, I had spun on my heel and ran off as fast as I could.

Another gust of wind barrelled down the alleyway with me, raising a foreboding feeling in the pit of my stomach. It felt like the universe was laughing at me for being so foolish.

If I held any singular advantage on Boyd, it was that I was small and fast. However, I had made one fatal mistake… I turned my back on the enemy. Rule number one of surviving: always know how far the danger is from you.

"You get back here, missy!" Boyd bellowed. "Before I come for yer blood!"

I could hear the crunch of broken glass beneath his clumsy steps. Blood pounded in my ears. Although I knew there was space between us, I could have sworn that I felt the heat of his dirty breath on the back of my neck. It was revolting, both in thought and feeling.

It urged me to move faster as a shiver rippled down my spine.

"Two days! Please, Boyd, two days," I shrieked, sounding like a fabled banshee. My chest burned for air as I fled for the edge of the alley.

One foot after the other, I just had to keep going and clear the alley to be free of him. The mouth of the alley loomed ahead. There was a whistle in my ear again, but this time, the ghosts of Ilrea had not come to laugh. This time, his dirty little knife sailed past my shoulder.

My breath caught at the proximity. As it spun past me, it nicked against the soft flesh of my collarbone. A grunt spilled from my lips at the sudden, sharp pain. The air rushed from my lungs as I tripped over my own feet and pitched forward. In a pathetic attempt to regain lost balance, I waved my arms and staggered left towards the stone wall.

It didn't help, and I cursed fate, fortune, and the moon as I tumbled head over heels and hit the ground hard.

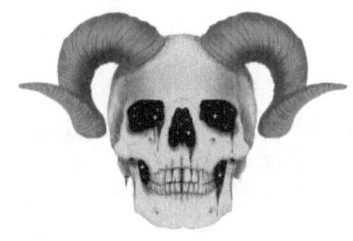

Chapter Two

My knees, palms, and chin bore the brunt of the impact, and my momentum sent me skidding forward. Loose rocks buried into my skin.

"Owww," I groaned weakly. I was too out of breath to whine properly. Pain seared my hands and knees. I lifted my head, flexed my fingers, and blinked through the sting. My teeth bit hard into my lip, and I squinted against the sharp, hot tears that prickled at the corner of my eyes. It was only as I turned my head that I realised the knife was right there. The dirty blade sat an inch from my outstretched fingertips. Maybe Lady Luck had granted me a single smile, after all.

Normally, I was not one for violence. I would run from a fight before I participated in it, but Boyd had already drawn my blood, and my attempt to run had failed. I couldn't stop my thoughts of the man and his missing organs, too. I couldn't stop imagining myself in his place—cold, dead, and missing everything vital. A loud groan escaped from my gritted teeth, and I lunged forward as best that I could to wrap my fingers around the hilt of the knife. It was small and smooth in my hand and its handle was worn with use.

As quickly as possible, I rolled, and my back scraped against the loose stones. I had barely raised the knife from the ground when Boyd appeared in the corner of my tear-blurred line of vision.

"Where do you think yer goin', missy?" He bore down on me, too far inside of my space for comfort. His heavily lined face was hard with stark disapproval and fury, which reminded me of one important fact. He may have been old as the devil himself, but he was still dangerous.

"Boyd, please," I was not above begging to save my life.

Wildly, I lifted the knife higher and jerked my arm outwards. It was a messy and blind attempt to settle the blade in the expanse of his gut. There was enough of it spilling from his belt that I figured I could manage to hit some part of him.

"Oi!" In an abrupt move, he brought his foot down right onto my wrist, ending my attack well before I managed to get any momentum. His weight crushed my bones. A loud gasp tore from my throat, and the knife slid free of my grip as my fingers spasmed with pain.

"None of that now, missy!" he barked.

"Please," I whimpered and begged again to retain my place in the world. Or all my appendages, depending on Boyd's mood. He might not kill me right now, but he wouldn't hesitate to remove my entire hand as a lesson.

Ilrea was a void on the earth, and my life was a mess, but that didn't mean I was ready to leave it over a measly hundred-something coin.

"Ya got twenty-four hours. Ya hear me?" Boyd growled, as he finally relented. "You'd best be havin' me coin ready by this time tomorrow night."

A sigh of relief heaved from my chest, and it crossed my mind that if he wasn't so foul, I might have kissed him for his mercy.

"Yeah, yeah, of course, yeah, I'll—" I fell silent as Boyd crouched closer and crowded over me. He was close... too close now, and his rotten breath spilled across my face. It was a struggle not to recoil away. I pressed my tongue up against the roof of my mouth and mentally counted to ten to stave off a gag.

I tried to remain still so as not to agitate him further. Not that I had anywhere to go while his heel cut off the blood supply to my wrist and kept me effectively pinned to the gravel. I didn't know if it would be worse to lose my hand to the tip of his knife, or because he stood on it too long. Either way, I was already losing feeling in my fingers.

"If ya don't bring me the coin," Boyd spat his ultimate threat, and no small amount of saliva flew across my face. This time, I did recoil. "I'll be takin' it outta ya organs, missy. They'll be fetching good devil-coin, they will."

My head scraped against the ground as I managed to nod. His weight shifted. I couldn't bite down the whimper on my lips as the pain in my fingers flared when the blood rushed back into them. Boyd straightened. His rotten teeth flashed at the sound of my distress. His boot finally lifted completely from my wrist a second later, and I closed my eyes in sweet relief.

With everything I had left, I prayed for him to turn and walk away... no such luck, or at least never my luck. Boyd was a revenge man through and through, and he didn't let me go without some sort of lesson. He swung his foot sharply, and it slammed hard into my ribs. The power of his kick forced the air from my lungs with a loud grunt, and the crack of my ribs reverberated through my body. I whimpered as I realised the damage he had done. I curled into a ball on the dirty ground and cradled my arms around my screaming ribs. I stayed like that long after Boyd wandered back to his shattered table. I remained there, still and on the ground, to try to avoid further notice until he had packed up his cards.

Boyd strode right past me to the mouth of the alley. As he passed, he dropped three items. Two worn emerald dice and the damaged playing card. I was filled with a sweeping sense of relief at the sight of my lucky dice. They landed by my scraped-up face, and it took all my willpower not to flinch as they bounced.

Once his footsteps disappeared, I slowly reached for them. The cubes were tucked against my sore hands—the shape of them familiar and reassuring. It was with tremendous effort that I pulled myself to my feet a few moments later. Every movement felt jarring to my broken ribs. I pocketed the die, and the card, with the intent of keeping them safe.

After a moment to simply catch my breath, I took stock of myself. My olive-toned skin was dirty, as always, with a layer of grime that never seemed to wash off properly under cold water. Angry grazes had raised across my palms, and the blood on my pants told me that my knees had been ravaged by the ground as well. My ribs ached with a sharp and searing pain that jolted through my body with every drawn breath. I pushed at them gingerly and decided that they were probably broken. There was very little I could do except live with it until they healed. Blood dripped from the edge of my chin and smeared along my collarbone from the nick of the knife. Absently, I rubbed at the bright blood with the back of my hand and succeeded only in smearing it further.

There was not much I wouldn't give for a hot bath, and after tonight, I would need one. A wipe down with a wet rag wasn't going to properly clean my wounds. As I explored the knife wound with the tips of my fingers, a hiss of pain slipped over my lips. It hurt, but it seemed shallow enough that it might stop bleeding on its own. I hoped that I wouldn't need to find a needle and string. Sewing wounds was a skill I had learned a long time ago, but I always managed to do a miserable and painful job of it, and it left behind rough but healed scars. More blood stained my pants as I wiped my fingers against them.

With care, I tucked my collarbone-length dark hair behind my ears. Without a piece of ribbon or string, it was the best way to keep the ends away from the ravaged skin of my face. The movement exposed the line of tarnished metal rings that run through the holes in the cartilage of both of my ears—six in each. The pain of each hole reminded me that I was alive. Once I had started piercing through them, I hadn't been able to stop. Not unlike playing cards.

I breathed out a heavy sigh. The night felt like a waste now. All I had wanted was a game or two, just enough to settle my urges and my nerves.

Slowly, I flexed my aching fingers, each one lined with two or three of the same tarnished, thin, twisted metal circles. It was a laughable attempt at homemade jewellery. I glanced over at them and inspected the bruised skin of my wrist. I could see the dirty imprint of Boyd's boot.

"Come on, Octavia," I tried to amp myself up as a feeling of dread settled in the pit of my stomach. "One hundred coins and twenty-four hours. Not impossible odds." Just highly unlikely, but it was easy enough to ignore that truth.

As I hobbled to the mouth of the alley, my gaze was drawn upwards to the sky. I squinted at the stars in a brief attempt to find a tumbling one and wish on it for a little more luck since it would be the only way I would meet Boyd's deadline, and while I knew of many lucky concepts, few seemed to be on my side. It was too late for many others to be out now. Most of the people who lived in Ilrea had better sense than to stay in the dark and find shelter to wait out the night. That meant there was no point in collecting coins for my debt tonight. There was no chance that I could steal a hundred coins in a day, either. Even I could admit that I wasn't that good. Especially not when most of Ilrea was broke and grovelling, and the few good targets took days of planning to rob.

Even though I should have gone home for the night, six blocks later, I found myself sitting cross-legged in front of another shoddy table.

The cloth on top of *this* crate was a blood-stained shirt, the logo faded beyond recognition, but still, I frowned at it like I could make it what it had been. My eyes lingered on the old blood for a second and then bounced up to the man who ran the game. I didn't know him, and that was for the best. If I didn't know him, then I didn't owe him. There were already too many dealers that held a tally of my debts.

"Place your bet," the dealer demanded.

His gaze flickered quickly over my piercings and the stack of metal rings on my fingers. His upper lip curled with faint distaste, and he quickly dismissed them as completely worthless. He wasn't wrong. They wouldn't get me a thing on the table. Most of them were twisted wire badly soldered together.

"Right," I agreed.

A single silver coin that I had found on the street flashed in my hand as I tipped it onto the table. It spun, and the symbol of pride landed face up. It was my only coin, all I had left now, but saving them had never been my forte.

I jerked my chin to get his attention and asked, "Can I use my dice?"

The game was simple. He had six lucky numbers on display, and four dice lay in front of me. If I rolled the number he displayed, I won. If I rolled anything else, he would take the coin. It wasn't my best game, but also not my worst. If given the choice, I preferred a game with stacking cards, where the numbers added up and I could keep track of the deck. If I concentrated, I could add them up before they came out.

"Sure," he grunted. His dirty fingers scooped up his four red dice before he jerked his head in a nod at the table. "Hurry up, I don't have all day to take your money."

At the smug tone of his voice, I scoffed. I reached inside my jacket for the two green lucky dice and then unlaced my boot. In a harsh movement, I pulled off my shoe and extracted two more dice out of the loose lining in the heel. Even lucky totems needed spares, after all.

"Get a move on," the guy bit out, the words muffled in his mouth.

"Alright, alright," I muttered back and weighed up the feel of all four dice in my hand. Each one was familiar, subtly worn down at certain edges to roll the way I wanted.

"Lucky dice," I told him and laughed as I flashed him the green and blue.

He grunted dismissively.

Almost instantly, I felt my muscles relax as I indulged in the game, and the corner of my mouth twisted in the ghost of a smile. With my lucky dice in hand and one coin to my name, I had been in and survived worse positions. At that table, with the chance of lady fortune smiling down on me, I finally felt at home. I was more comfortable here than in any other place in Ilrea.

Besides, I could have sworn I felt the guarantee of a win in this roll of the dice. With a soft exhale, I loosened the tension in my wrist. Just as I flicked my fingers and sent the dice flying, a loud and wailing alarm screeched through the back alley. It echoed through the entire town—no soul would be left undisturbed. Everyone would rise to this call.

The dice skittered wildly off course as I flinched at the noise. One of them fell right off the table and no longer counted in my total. My dark eyes latched onto the dice that were left.

Frantically, I started adding up the numbers in my head and leant over the table in eager anticipation.

Four and three was seven, and… the dealer was faster than me. With a low chuckle, his fingers snagged at my only remaining coin. As it slipped out of view, my pulse raced, and acidic dismay flooded through my veins. My very last coin, gone in a few precious seconds.

"House wins," he announced, sounding spectacularly smug. "Now piss off."

"No!" I breathed the soft protest, and my voice rang with pure desperation.

"Piss. Off. Unless you've got more to bet," he grunted. "Rules are rules."

My heart thundered against my broken ribs and then dropped in resignation. It felt like a stone had lodged in my stomach, harsh and erratic in the way it beat. It hurt. I was left with a rolling queasiness that overrode the anguished hunger from earlier. I couldn't stomach the thought of eating, not when I had worked myself into such a dire predicament.

Without another word of protest, I collected my die and pushed myself to my feet. I felt foolish as I staggered backwards from his table. A sense of overwhelming hopelessness threatened to pull a rough sob from my lips.

"I'm fucked," I whispered as I backed away from the table. I wrapped my arms around my middle for some semblance of comfort, my ribs aching with the movement. "Completely and utterly fucked."

He said nothing. In the dealer's mind, I was already long gone. Upset, I turned and followed the source of the alarm, the call to attention. There was nothing else left for me to do.

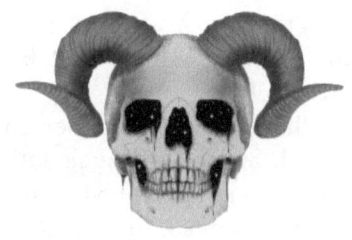

Chapter Three

I lrea was a small place, a speck on the earth in the grand scheme of it all. It was bigger than the post-fall settlements that had risen outside the eight major cities, but too small and too forgotten to be considered of any worth.

It was a place that would never quite be enough—it would never evolve. Ilrea had been ravaged on the day when the Angels of Sin arrived on Earth and had never quite found its footing in the world that came since.

As the bedtime stories were told—a recurring theme in my childhood—the naughty devil was not, in fact, pushed out of his world alone. Instead, as he tumbled from the last world and into this one, he pulled seven other angels with him. Each of them was doomed to complete his sentence, too, and instead of falling from his world and into the fable that was hell, the devil landed in our world. Or perhaps it just meant that this place was and always had been hell, and now it had been reshaped in the depravity of his design.

After his fall, the devil rose, unrepentant, and turned Kaida into his perfect world. Seven lost angels fell with him, and each rose to stand on the earth as the embodiment of human sin.

Pride, Envy, Wrath, Greed, Lust, Sloth, and Gluttony.

Together with the devil, they ravaged the earth. They took their time as they ventured from one side to the other and annihilated us all. The stories recount that technology fell first, unable to handle the magic these beings released into the world.

It worsened quickly after that, as the angels released their influence and flexed their will. Just as they wanted it, the men and women of this simple world turned on each other. Cities were decimated and livelihood became a myth of the past. The world was firmly reminded that, compared to these symbols of immortality, they were nothing at all. These immortal gods settled among us, and they made Kaida their own.

The devil created Eternis, his kingdom rebuilt within our world. Eternis was said to cater to every want, whim and need imaginable, and it is there that souls find their immortality. The eternal paradise on in our world. Each of his angels settled in their cities, where their influence encouraged sin, and they delighted in punishing it at the same time. Those who settled in the cities, those who could survive the sheer amount of magic there, had a better quality of life. Albeit, often a shortened one.

Those who were left behind struggled through the ruins of what had been left in the wake of destruction—they just barely rebuilt and settled into small towns. Ilrea was one of these settlements.

Ever one to maintain control of the pitiful race he had overtaken, the devil sent wardens to manage each small uprising of human beings. They were his chancellors, but beneath these men, these towns did not thrive. In fact, they barely survived. The fallen eight had brought magic into a world that did not want it. Everything changed in their presence—the landscape, the food, and when proximity was maintained, also the people.

Under their influence, humanity was never quite the same. The angels conjured their demons and set them loose in the world, just another predator for the people, just another way to die.

The immortal and the mortal couldn't thrive together, but as the humans remained both stubborn and alive, they were all damned to try.

Those who lived in Ilrea were hungry and ravished by poverty that had now expanded generations. The people who survived it appeared only in the weak light of day and avoided the darkness of night, and wealth was funnelled through the few chosen families who were blessed by the angels in positions of power, and who couldn't help but spend it. The only other grand source of income came from a black market that expanded across most towns, under the very noses of those in power.

At least this was the fanciful history we were taught in early education—twisted stories to make our poverty seem a little more explainable, maybe even a little more palatable. I was a child of Ilrea, and I had spent my entire life in the twisted streets and shadowed alleys. I had climbed through historically ruined buildings and listened to lectures on the danger of upsetting the devil, but I took it all as fantasy and myth.

There was no devil. I had never seen him, and angels were just a story designed to keep me from growing too big for my boots. There was nothing except misfortune, bad circumstance, and misery in the winding streets of Ilrea.

A few moments later, I emerged from the alley and joined the gentle shuffle of townsfolk pulled from their beds and headed towards the town square. It was all adults as the children were left in their beds for the night. It was some semblance of a small mercy on all of us, since wild and tired children only created tension in the entire town.

Self-consciously, I pushed my fingers behind my ears and loosened my dark hair to fall across my face. It was just long enough to cover the scrapes and bruises that decorated my skin. To avoid drawing attention, I ducked my chin and hid my fingers in my pockets. I weaved through the streets with the rest of the crowd, just another sheep in the herd. It wasn't often we were called to attend in the dead of the night. It must be something urgent, I realised, for we had only been awoken once like this before that I could remember. That time, I had been one of the fortunate few to be safe in bed.

We all spilled out into the main square of our town. It was grey and forged of broken bricks, which gave the appearance that the ground had been shattered.

The centrepiece of the square was not in the concrete offices that housed those given the honour of running the town. Not even in the gleaming windows, and stark worn-out yellow and blue of the chancellor's headquarters.

Instead, it was in the garish structure that lined the central canal—a twisting river of grey water. The structure was a large wall, built of brick and rendered smooth, and the wall was painted black, graced with seven colourful animal symbols representative of the seven sins.

Greed's golden toad, Envy's green python, Wrath's red lion, Gluttony's purple pig, Sloth's blue snail, Lust's pink goat, and Pride's white peacock.

The garish wall was lined with several large metal spikes that protruded outwards. They looked sharp and dangerous. I had no idea why it even existed. Ever since I was a child, I had been told to avoid playing in this area and warned of the dangers of touching the wall. Most people tried to ignore and avoid it at all costs.

My stomach turned violently as I stumbled further into the square with everyone else, and realised that, for the first time, those deadly spikes were not empty. Sharp, bitter bile rose in my throat and burned against my tongue.

"Oh, shit," I murmured, with no small amount of horror. Whispers and cries began to pour out of the people of Ilrea. We all seemed to pack in a little tighter, and I gasped as a man slammed into my side.

"Watch it!" I cried as pain flared at my ribs, and I pressed my hand against them, which did nothing to help.

"What the ever-loving hell is this?" a man whispered in horror to my left, before everyone began to talk over each other.

"Is that—"

"No, that can't be? It's not—"

"Ryan. Ryan?! Where's my son? *Where is my son?*" a woman was shrieking at the top of her lungs as she pushed her way through the crowd in search of him.

The townspeople moved in alarm. Some tried to scramble away from the sight and others pushed forward for a better look. Despite the growing desire to stay far, far away, I was shoved forward, too. The sight was morbid enough that I couldn't help but look up at the monstrosity we had all been called to see. Four bodies had been pinned to the metal spikes like butterflies displayed in a glass-covered frame. The spikes protruded proudly from their hearts. Rich, red blood had spilled down the front of their chests and hazarded at the fact that they had been alive when they were mounted on the wall. They were macabre and there to relay an important message.

"This is bad," I whispered. "So, so bad."

In that instant, I couldn't stop myself from imagining their pain. I wrapped my arms firmly around my body to keep the shivers at bay. Their heads were covered with dark black bags. Their identities stripped away like they were undeserving of them. Like their families were undeserving of closure. Across

19

their faces, written in bright red paint, was the name of their sins:

LUST. ENVY. LUST. GLUTTONY.

I squinted at the words on their faces, but when they weren't instantly familiar, I stopped trying to read them. The only thing I could think of to explain this away was a story about the devil's court, where he could render judgement on men. It was said he could decide the fate of their souls, and if they were deemed depraved enough, he would declare them unsalvageable, and their lives would end in punishment. The story had never said that they would be turned into a vile example of death.

I had always thought the concept of souls and immortal judgement were fanciful tales, the sort that would keep children and teenagers on the right path. The only person I had ever seen pass judgement was the chancellor himself, and he had never been quite so brutal. He denied rations or had men beaten... but he never had them killed. I couldn't remember a time when someone had been pinned to the wall.

As I backed away through the crowd, I wished I had never answered the call of the sirens, and that I had not been drawn in by my curiosity. My eyes raked over their clothes as I took in the size and shape of their hands and their shoes in a careful study. My face crumpled with focus as I looked for anything familiar. Alongside the desperation to flee, I felt an intense desperation to make sure that it wasn't one of my very few nearest and dearest on that wall. Even if we weren't as near as we once had been, all I could do was hope that my older brothers hadn't become one of those human butterflies. I couldn't think of a single thing they could do to have deserved this fate.

My gaze flickered around the milling crowd to seek out their familiar faces. It would be better to see them living than to have identified them as dead. Just by the wall, a family climbed onto a large solid stone dais, and we all turned to face the four people who stood tall in front of the desecrated bodies.

The chancellor of Ilrea was said to be blessed by the devil himself. He was in his early fifties, and he was one of the few who did not look like the world had taken its toll on his body. His hair and beard were a shock of white under the bright lights; his eyes were such a dark brown that they were almost black beneath the depth of the night.

To his left stood his wife. Some called her the most beautiful woman in the town, untouched by poverty or struggle. There were whispers that she had been born immortal in the City of Eternis and that was why she never seemed to grow old.

Even in the middle of the night, she looked perfect. Her long, dark hair fell over her shoulder in a thick braid. Her lips were a soft pink and pressed into a severe and disapproving line.

Behind them stood their twin boys, both tall and overbearing grown men, each one dressed in a suit that always seemed slightly out of place in Ilrea. A little too put together amongst the dirt, the grime, and the hunger. The twins had sharp, angular features. They had been born as identical copies of each other and had matched all throughout their childhood. Now they only stood apart because of the bright swirling ink that marked most of the available skin on one brother. That one stood with a scowl, while his brother looked impassively out at us.

Individually and together, the Heira family emitted an air of intimidation, emboldened by their status and power in the community. They commanded attention. Rumour had it they were a family of soul-sucking demons. That rumour was a particular favourite of mine, mostly since my older brother, Mason, was the one who started it.

"Citizens of Ilrea," Chancellor Heira's voice carried across the square.

It was met with an eerie quiet, like we were all holding our breaths at once.

"Thank you for abandoning your beds tonight." He didn't sound particularly thankful at all. "Some of our own from Ilrea have faced the ultimate judgement. They have challenged the sins themselves and failed."

He let this announcement fall on the crowd. Whispers sparked and rippled across the square like a wildfire. I could hear familiar names thrown into the mix as the town named and shamed their most troubled neighbours in soft accusation. There had always been stories of the repercussions of challenging one of the seven angels of sin. There had also been wild tales of the repercussions that came with those challenges.

Yet another thing I had previously dismissed as pure fantasy.

My gut churned unpleasantly as I idly wondered how many of those silly stories were true. The chancellor cleared his throat again, and the whispers cut short. The entire crowd rippled with a sense of uneasiness, and we waited with bated breath for him to call the name of the next person to be pinned to the wall. Why else would we be here? I shuffled back a step just in case it was me.

"As you can see—" The white-haired Chancellor gestured towards the wall. Our new and horrifying town feature.

"They have paid the ultimate price. They will remain here, on the Penance Wall, as a display of our sins, of our disgrace, until their bodies rot to nothing." His voice was grave. "This is a warning that if you give in to these humanistic urges, you will not survive in this world."

A beat of silence passed amongst us all.

"If you touch them in any way. Or, devil forbid, if you attempt to remove them, then you will join them," the chancellor threatened. His voice was hard, sharp, and unforgiving. His gaze swept across his townspeople. More than ever, it felt like he was the representative of the fallen angel deemed fit to judge us all. I shrank back from his gaze and couldn't help but wonder again if he hadn't picked out those people himself. If he hadn't been their judge and their executioner in one. My gaze dropped to his hands and I decided that they were far too clean for such things.

"Goodnight." In a curt tone, he dismissed us all.

The entire Heira family turned and walked away. It was like the display and the threats were part of their day-to-day business. After a second of stunned processing, the crowd followed their lead. Most of the townspeople were more than ready to forget the display and head back to bed. That was the way of small towns such as ours, and in the world we lived in. You closed your eyes and tried to forget the worst of it. If you could ignore the horror, you could survive it.

Bodies shoved against me as people passed, but instead of moving out of the square, I slipped through the crowd and moved to the base of the wall. It took a few moments, but I waited for everyone to shuffle out. I found a moment to study the wall properly after everyone else had left. My pointed chin stuck out and my teeth sank into my lower lip as I turned my gaze back to the wall and took one last long look at the bodies.

My eyes narrowed as I studied them as closely as I could. Nothing seemed recognisable, and I could only know if it was either of my older brothers once I returned home. My mouth twisted into an unimpressed line. I felt impatient for answers, but also reluctant to face my family. The toe of my boot nudged against the wall, and I glanced down at my feet.

"Better you than me," I said finally and turned my back on them. "I sure hope the next world is better than this place."

Right then, it felt that very little could be worse than Ilrea.

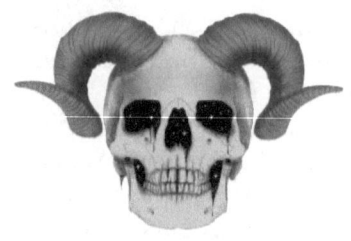

Chapter Four

With my head ducked, I moved quickly out of the west side of the square, not unlike a rat fleeing a sinking ship. My shoulders hunched as I huddled into my jacket and slowed once outside the main square. My eyes roamed over the different market stalls as I soaked in the lack of life that came with the night. They were dark and empty, with no food nor coin inside of them to lift.

Tomorrow was a Thursday, which was not a market day, so my chance of making the money I needed dimmed even further.

As I passed by the trading post, something caught my eye and I paused mid-step. It was the shining surface of fresh posters that sparked my interest. They were layered one atop of the other, and, unbeknownst to me, they formed a countdown.

The Devil's Trials were coming.

I pulled at the edges and the first poster ripped as it came free of the wall. I let it hang limp and reached for a second one instead. This one peeled off nicely, and I looked stupid as I stood in the low light and squinted at it. My lips moved slowly as I began to mouth the numbers at the base and worked out what they meant in this order. I jolted as I realised that the date lining the base of each poster was the next day. As I turned the golden poster in my hand and looked over all the unfamiliar words, my lip curled, and I sneered at the picture on the paper. Very little of it held any meaning to me.

The trials were my mother's favourite bedtime story, so I knew of it—she was enamoured with the promise of immortality. When I was fourteen, she took us to watch three people sign up. All of whom never came back to town again. They had all been forgotten days after they left. The nights of my childhood had been filled with stories of ageless, strong beings who had won the trials. The competition apparently enticed entries with the chance to become one of the devil's favoured few. The stories usually ended with death, and I doubted that the poster preached the risks to those of us with mortal souls. That would ruin their fun.

I folded the poster twice and jammed it into my pocket. It would be something to laugh about later. In the dead of night, six months from now, I would find it as stories of fallen competitors came back to us and mock the poor fools who chose to participate in a game with terrible odds, and false rewards. Not even I was foolish enough to gamble with the odds of winning a fairy-tale.

I twisted my way out of the inner streets and slipped past the makeshift structures there as I continued to venture away from stalls that appeared and disappeared as often as the seasons did. I turned out of the centre of town and onto dustier open roads, into the residential area where the inhabitable buildings were stretched a little further apart. Not because we had yards of space, but because every second building couldn't be resurrected without falling again. Too many lives had been lost to crumbling buildings. In the long years since the fall of the devil, we had expanded from a few sturdy structures to extensions and second levels. Each one was made from a mismatch of materials found in the rubble, and often, they looked like patchwork structures on the brink of falling.

Of course, it was the only way to try to contain the excess of people in the streets with nowhere to live. They were all rented out at exorbitant prices from the few families strong enough to hold on to them, and usually only exchanged hands because of death. Deaths that were not always an accident when people became desperate enough. Inside, the homes were overcrowded and uncomfortable, with people pushed in so close together and living on each other's last nerve. There were never enough homes though, which left too many people out in the cold.

I bypassed my home—a single room shared with my parents and siblings. It lay buried in the basement of an overfull house that smelled like roasted toad and ashes. Roasted toad never ceased to make my stomach turn, but our landlord and upstairs neighbour was particularly fond of it. The room was too small and too cramped. Even though it was only one room, they charged us per occupant. There were too many hungry members of the Nox family to truly afford it. My family was being robbed blind just for a roof over our heads, but we had little other choice as to where to live. My grandmother was the first to secure this room with her two sons, and as the oldest, my dad had held onto it long after she died.

If he abandoned it, there would be nowhere else to go. It was because of this that I didn't like spending any more time at home than necessary.

With the moon still high in the night sky, I shuffled around the next bend and approached a house with a broken front door. It was dark green with flaking paint and sat slightly crooked where the top hinge had come loose. Since it was completely useless, I moved around the side of the house and tapped my knuckles on the windowpane. After a beat, the curtains peeled back and the window slid open a fraction.

"Come on in, Octavia," a voice rasped in a tired tone. Even though I knew she wouldn't have been asleep, I felt a pang of guilt at the fatigue I heard. I hooked my fingers in the small gap provided and grunted as I forced the window up higher. I was thin from constant hunger, but not as thin as the space she had left me. A second later, I wriggled my way through the window. The wood dug into my hips.

"You're lucky I'm skinny, Hel," it came out as a low mutter, beneath my breath.

"Huh?" Helina Archer barely glanced up from where her nose was buried in a book. When she did, her eyes flickered over me dismissively.

"No, you're lucky you're skinny. You're the one crawling through windows in the middle of the night, little rat."

I scoffed and then sank down onto the single bed. The old springs groaned beneath my weight, but I relished how much comfier it was than my bed. Helina had always been incredibly fortunate, which was something I had envied her for a long time.

"It's not my fault you lot never open the front door… if you did, I wouldn't have to climb through the window." I sniffed.

Helina stared at me. "The door is broken."

"So?" I shrugged and glanced around the room. It looked just as it always did, filled with piles and piles of books. Very few of them belonged to Helina; mostly, they had been relocated from the town archives where she worked. I didn't know how she relaxed with them towering around the room and suffocating her space. We had argued many times over my thoughts that bringing the books home was theft, and that meant she was no better than me when I lifted a coin or two from someone's purse. Helina firmly disagreed, of course. She didn't feel a lick of guilt about it, so they continued to pile up in her room. Evidence of her constant quest to know more. They made the already tiny room feel even smaller, with barely enough room to breathe. I knew if I mentioned that again, she would toss me back out the window.

With a huffed sigh, I moved to lie back and realised there was a pot plant in the middle of the bed. I moved it into my lap to inspect it better. The leaves were withered and wilted in a strange hue of yellow-green. When I brushed my fingers across them, they were brittle. Much like all the rest of the plants Helina had brought home, in sure determination that she could make them live and become self-sustainable. It was well on the way to plant hell.

"That's supposed to be edible," Helina answered the unspoken question. I placed it on the floor, just out of the way. Kicking it over seemed like it might be a small mercy to the plant though, rather than letting it wither beneath Helina's neglect.

"It looks miserable," I commented lightly. All I got in return was a shrug.

"Been busy," she told me. Helina was always busy. She considered herself a scholar—one of few in Ilrea, and she knew more than I thought any person should. Helina Archer was a strange, walking encyclopaedia. A source of constant, unexpected, and mundane information. Most of what she knew was from the old world, before the devil had arrived in Kaida, and oftentimes, the pieces of information she fed me made it seem like the before time had been just as bad as now. It was no wonder I was her only friend, although that didn't explain why she was mine.

"You're always busy," I voiced my thoughts, my nose crinkling before I continued. "You know that if you don't return some of these tomes soon, they're going to axe you at the archive. Surely, they've noticed their records are getting smaller."

I couldn't help but poke at Helina slightly. Especially when she wasn't giving me the full focus of her attention. It gained the reaction I wanted. Helina finally turned in her chair in acknowledgement and lifted her head out of the book. Her shoulders drew back, and her chin lifted slightly as she peered through her bent wire spectacles at me. With the way her eyes narrowed, I began to regret drawing her attention at all. Helina sighed as she took in the abrasions and bruises that decorated my skin. My tokens of this long and rough night so far must not have been pretty, if her expression was anything to go by.

"Maybe if you applied yourself a little more," she snapped. "You wouldn't look like complete shit."

It wasn't an uncommon sentiment from my friend. Helina's eyes narrowed, and she tossed one of her long dreadlocks over her shoulder. They were long enough to reach the curve of her butt now but were always styled well. "A job and some self-respect would do you good, Octavia."

I sighed and bit back the argument that I did have self-respect. Nothing good ever came from arguing with Helina, who would push her point until she was blue in the lips and I had run out of words. She called these pointed remarks her sharp truths and felt that everyone needed to hear them to grow. Predictably, Helina had a very high penchant for delivering these truths, and a very low tolerance for hearing them about herself. Hot shame burned through me as she stared, and my eyes darted to my boots. I had never really been one for confrontation.

"Yeah... well..." Helina had never understood the draw of the bet, the high of the win, and the way I couldn't do anything else once the temptation hit. "Whatever. I'm fine, it is what it is.

I just…" My head snapped up as I reluctantly met my friend's eye. "I need a bit of coin."

"No." Rejection was another sharp truth, and she gave it without remorse.

"Please, Hel, just enough to tide me over, or anything you've got spare? It's not a big ask. I just need to pay someone back, get some food, and get on my feet."

"Yeah, is that person me, Octavia?" Helina interrupted, her tone curt. She had never been one to shy away from conflict. We were opposites in that way, and I could have killed a man for an ounce of her confidence. "You owe me. Over forty coins," Helina stated.

"No, I don't." I frowned.

"Yes, forty-three, actually." She had that matter of fact, I know more than you do, tone of voice. I rolled my eyes.

"There's no way that's right. I owe you maybe three coins, I—" My mouth snapped shut when Helina picked up and threw a small notebook at my head. I barely managed to catch it before it hit me in the face. It was leather-bound and worn in the front cover. I had seen her carrying it around before.

"Third page from the end," Helina stated as she watched.

My bitten nails scratched against the pages as I prized the book open and flicked through to the back. My heart sank a touch when I located Helina's scratchy handwriting.

The book contained my name at the top, a tally of numbers loaned and paid back in black and red, respectively. The numbers blurred together as my brain slowly processed them. It took a moment, but numbers had always been my skill over words as I needed to understand numbers to be good at the table. As I slowly counted, I could see that I had managed to take, and take, and take. There was much more black ink than red on the page.

"Oh." The book snapped shut between my hands, and it was quickly handed back.

"*Oh*, is damn right, Octavia. No more." Helina's gaze was sharp and unrelenting.

I looked at my shoes again and wiggled my toes inside of them.

I was not entirely sure what to say. Every other time, Helina had relented and given me a few coins to get me to stop asking.

"Not until you get your shit together," Helina declared. "Get a job, grow up, and I'll wipe the debt completely."

Heat rose high in my cheeks. "I didn't realise you were counting it up."

Helina raised a single brow, it was a smooth and haughty move. "Octavia Nox, I am the most well-organised person in this shithole town. I keep track of everything, and you know it."

Silence stretched between us for a second, and I picked at the edge of the thin blanket draped over the bed. It was neatly made and in its right place, just like everything else. I had the urge to mess it up in a petty punishment.

Finally, I sighed and changed the subject. We could circle back to money later, or once Helina fell asleep, I could see if there was any left in the tin she kept at the back corner of her closet. I had known about her little stash for a couple of years, but only lifted from it when I was desperate. Boyd's threat had made me desperate.

"Did you go tonight?" I asked quietly, even though I already knew the answer. Helina attended every dull meeting that the chancellor's office announced. Even the ones to vote on extending hours of market trade. She said it was so she was well informed and wanted to know all she could about how the town was being run.

"Of course, I did. I was to the left of the platform." Helina had already picked a book back up and flicked absently to the next page.

"I thought it was all a myth," I admitted out loud. It sounded even more foolish now that I had given the thought a

31

voice. "Big, scary stories to make the world outside Ilrea seem scarier than it is. You know, so we'd stick around and give the chancellor someone to kick when they're down."

"Of course, it's all real, you idiot." She shook her head. "The cities exist, the Angels of Sin exist. There are records of it everywhere if you just look. The downfall of Kaida, and birth of the devil's oasis. The end of the world came, and our forsaken great-grandparents survived it all. Devil knows how they managed that."

Suddenly, I felt uncomfortable. I rocked on the bed and folded my legs beneath my body as I thought about the display by the canal—the dehumanised butterflies.

"Real enough that four people are dead, I suppose," I muttered.

Helina's gaze was sharp as she responded, "People die here every damn day."

I argued sharply, "They're not all hung up like a celebratory ornament."

My fingers curled into my palms for a moment, and my nails bit into my palms. It grounded me so I could calm down a little. "Just seems a bit… much," I added.

"It is what it is."

This was how Helina was… she accepted the world for what it was at face value so that she could work out how to fix it. She was determined to know and become all that she could. "The sooner you accept that, the sooner—"

"Yeah, yeah," I cut her off and quickly pulled myself onto my feet. I didn't want another lecture about bettering myself, getting a job, or becoming someone. There wasn't as much work out there as Helina wanted to believe, and she was the only one in the room with dreams of becoming chancellor one day. I didn't have any ambitions to change the world. I just wanted to survive each day as best I could.

"I gotta go home," I announced and shrugged back into my jacket. I offered up a platitude to repair whatever fissures my argumentative attitude and abrupt departure caused in our friendship. "I'll get your coin tomorrow, 'kay?"

"Sure, Octavia," the edge to Helina's tone proved that she didn't believe it. "Goodnight."

"Night," I replied.

With practiced ease, I climbed back out of the window feet first and landed upright in the dirt. I had an unsettling feeling in my gut as I walked home.

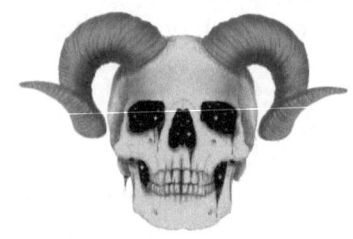

Chapter Five

As I shuffled down the empty road, a huffed sigh fell from my lips. I felt irritated by Helina's attitude and the pompous way she spoke to me; it left a lump in my throat that was hard to swallow down, and it made me want to scream and shout that just because I didn't know as much as Helina did, it didn't mean I was stupid. Foolish, maybe, but not stupid.

For one thing, I had more experience in the streets than Helina. Even though I had never fallen into proper employment and the security it provided. I didn't have literate parents, let alone someone to nurture me into being of use to the chancellor. Or any use to anyone at all. Unlike Helina, I was just another body on the streets and another hungry mouth for my family to feed. The grand total of my skills was limited to thievery and counting cards, and the latter didn't equate to being good at mathematics.

Once, I had a single day trial in the town treasury, which lasted two hours at most. I had been tossed out when it became apparent that I couldn't find the strength of will to leave the coins alone. Still, I'd made it out with four gold pieces stowed in my socks. Although, I had lost all four in a bet by the time the sun had set.

Lost in my thoughts, it felt like it took less than a minute to get home, and when I looked up, I was in front of the house. My stomach swirled with dread, but I couldn't delay going in and checking on my brothers any longer. This time, I entered through an actual door. It was around the side of the house and half-buried in the ground. The door creaked as I threw it open, and stairs led below the main structure. I clattered down the passageway with little thought for anyone else within the room.

"Selfish brat!" one of my brothers hissed into the darkness of the room as I almost tripped over his lanky legs in the low light. I didn't bother to apologise and instead flipped him off.

My body ached in the reminder that I was hurt as I leaned on the lone bench top and waited for my eyes to adjust to the dark. I could have fallen asleep leaning there as fatigue pulled heavily at my limbs.

Our home was pitiful. It was a single room with no windows, little light, and paint that peeled off the walls. Thin mattresses stretched across most of the floor and were pushed together to house the sleepy bodies of my parents, two sisters, and three brothers. Each of them looked peaceful in their sleep, and far nicer than they were in the waking hours. In the light of the day, we were all at each other's throats.

My father was an aged and worn-out man; his body had curled over from working in a constantly stooped position. He worked on the potato farm just outside of town for a mere pittance. Most of what he earned was lost in the charge to get a ride in the cart out to the farm and back each day. His back was wrecked from the constant manual labour and his mood was always dark by the time he came home. I would be a bleak soul too, I supposed, if I were in pain and struggling to provide for my family.

My mother was once a soft woman who had grown calloused by circumstance. She cleaned at Heira House, which was the chancellor's primary residence. Within those walls, she was invisible. A servant and nothing more. My mother had birthed six children and lost two more. A woman who seemed to wither further into despair with every day that her youngest children couldn't get enough to eat and cried out of hunger.

Both of my older brothers were lanky and too tall for their own good. They took up most of the room with their long limbs and penchant for shuffling around in their sleep. Mason, the eldest, snored loudly, and Byron, the one who had spoken to me, settled back into sleep with an ease that I envied. They worked on the town rebuild project—a long and tedious plan to restore Ilrea as a place of glory and prominence. It was a project that never seemed to improve or end.

My younger siblings ranged from ages five to twelve. Scarlett, Logan, and Keira. There was a twelve-year gap between Scarlett and me. It was a chasm that left me unable to relate to any of them, nor willing to look after them for even a moment. I was not their mother, and I was terrified of doing anything that might leave me in that position if something happened to our mother. They were better off with Mason.

I vaguely remembered the day Scarlett had come screaming into the world. She was tiny, fragile, and wailed each time I went close. Soon enough, I was screaming wildly back. All I knew was that when they had come along, there had been less of everything for me. It created a resentment that burned in my soul. I knew nothing about them and cared little for what they did each day. I harboured a silent anger for all they had taken from me. In my mind, they were just a further burden on the family and our livelihood. I couldn't help but think that the world had been a better place when I was the youngest Nox child.

After I pulled off my boots, I twisted on the spot and opened the only cabinet in the room. There was very little inside—containers of murky water, empty tin cups, and some loose potatoes. I gulped down half a bottle of water quickly and tried to ignore the stale taste. After I checked over my shoulder, I reached for one of my brother's brown work bags and pulled it free. As quietly as I could manage, I opened the drawstrings and pulled out the first item. It was an empty cup, one that I quickly discarded on the counter. Next, I found a tin, and with my breath held, I worked the lid open. I couldn't help the excitement that shivered through my entire body at the thought that there could be coins inside. I just needed enough to flip them at the table for a little more. Just enough to get me out of trouble for now.

Instead, I found the cold remains of a fire-blackened potato. My nose wrinkled in a pickiness I couldn't afford, at the very same time that my stomach cramped in hungry demand. We always ate potatoes. Dad smuggled them home, one tucked in each pocket as he finished work in the evening. Two potatoes for eight people didn't stretch far though, and we had limited funds for anything more. I stuffed the bland potato in my mouth and chewed slowly. I closed my eyes and tried to pretend that it was anything else. In the depths of my imagination, it became a sweet piece of juicy fruit. Fresh fruit was a rarity these days in Ilrea, my last piece had been dried and was a treat for my eighteenth birthday.

Which felt like it was like an age ago.

It took an effort to peel myself out of my clothes. I bit down on my lip to stifle my gasps as I tried to inspect the cuts and grazes on my body as best that I could. The blood had dried, and

I scrubbed it off my skin with the rest of the bottled water and a dirty rag. My teeth pinched my lip harder to stop my whimpers and winced in pain with each pass over the injuries. There were darkened bruises on my ribs, and they ached when I moved wrong or breathed too deeply. Slowly, I pulled myself into a pair of soft sweatpants that my brothers had outgrown, and a thin singlet, to get ready for bed.

With slow steps, I picked my way to a free spot amongst the tangled bodies and lowered myself down onto the mattress. Compared to Helina's bed, it was thin and mostly compressed foam instead of springs and padding. The ground was hard beneath my hip as I curled onto my side. Once there, I couldn't sleep. The next hour ticked by as I stared dully at the ceiling and pictured patterns in the damp mould that grew in the corner. These nights came too often now, nights when I spent more time awake than asleep, and felt the heavy pull of fatigue in every part of my body the next day.

My mind replayed the night, and all I could think about was Boyd and his threat. My hand drifted over my body as I imagined losing my stomach, my lungs, and the heart that beat too fast beneath the solid palm of my hand. A sheen of sweat broke out across my skin. It was ignited by pure fear as I imagined what he might do to me and how I might die.

With a painful cramp, my stomach revolted and rejected the meagre amount of food within. My mind raced and my breath came in short bursts before I sat upright. There was no use in staring at the ceiling. I sighed and pushed my hair out of my face. In an anxious movement, I twisted the thin bands of metal around my fingers until the race of my heart slowed. It was a nervous habit I had never stopped, much like biting at the edges of my nails when life became too stressful.

As the night wore on, I began to feel like I was choking on the weight of the world, even though I only existed in the tiniest fraction of it. Everything was too heavy, and it all settled in the centre of my chest. I was an immovable weight that kept me awake, aware, and trapped. The best option to survive the panic, I had found, was to get out of the house and inhale fresh air for an hour. The open night sky helped ease the claustrophobia a little. Once the idea settled in my head, I reached for my jacket and shouldered my way into it. It was difficult to move slowly and not wake up everyone else.

I almost fell as I pulled myself to my feet. My gaze flickered over my family, and resentment bubbled up inside of me. If only I could sleep so soundly. Envy burned a hole in my heart as I wondered how they could forget about their constant struggles for long enough to sleep and dream.

It was a short path to my discarded boots and the door, but I hesitated. My gaze lingered on the peaceful sight of my slumbering parents, and in three quick steps, I crouched beside my father. He was a quiet and heavy sleeper. He had strong features, and I inherited his dark hair, sloped nose, and too-large ears, which had always seemed too big against my other, smaller features. I hated my ears. As a child, other kids had poked fun at them until I'd learned to wear my hair in a way to keep them out of their sight.

My slender fingers snagged on his discarded pants, and I rummaged through the pockets. A relieved sigh flowed from my lips as my fingers brushed against the smooth and familiar octagon shape of a pride stamped coin. The coins jingled slightly as I shifted them around to get an idea of how many there were. Under my breath, I counted four of them.

"Yes!" I cheered softly and pulled them free from his pocket.

As I straightened, a hand clamped tight around my wrist. My head jerked sharply, and my gaze bounced from my wrist to the alert and furious eyes of my father.

"Dad," I breathed, my voice soft and placating. Panic was a hot liquid that ran through my body, and I felt like I was burning alive, incinerated beneath his gaze.

"What do you think you're doing, Octavia?" he growled, and it sent a shiver down the length of my spine. Suddenly, I felt six years old again and in trouble because I'd knocked over and wasted an entire pot of food.

"Nothing! I... *nothing*, I swear. Your pants were in the way. I'm folding them up." I could bluff, and I had a decent enough poker face, but I wasn't skilled at bold-faced lying. Anxiety saw to that as I bit my lip and my face turned hot. My father saw straight through the tremor in my tone and the fear in my eyes.

"Are you stealing from your family, Octavia?" he asked, his voice thundered through the room. My brothers rustled into consciousness behind us, and my dad continued, "*Again*."

A light turned on to my right and illuminated my mother's face. Her olive skin looked sickly beneath the yellow light. Her lips pinched with disappointment. Although I couldn't see my brothers properly in the darkness, I heard Mason ask what the hell was going on.

"Dad—" I began.

"You think this can keep happening, Octavia?" he roared at me. I tensed beneath the gazes of my family who witnessed my shame. "You're twenty-four bloody years old and you contribute nothing to this family. Nothing at all. You sleep under our roof, eat our food, and have the gall to steal from our pockets."

Silence echoed, before Scarlett had the audacity to add, "Yeah!"

I turned and glared like this was all her fault and not the consequences of my own actions. Quickly, Mason clamped a hand over her mouth. "Shut up!" I snapped.

Dad squeezed my wrist tightly and drew my attention back to him. It was a tight shackle, which kept me anchored in front of him. His anger burned bright in front of me. I opened my mouth to defend myself, but nothing came out. A hot and burning shame flushed through my body, and deep down, I knew he was right. I was self-aware enough to acknowledge that truth.

"Let go of the coins, Octavia," he demanded roughly, and we both glanced down at my hand. Dad's gaze narrowed, and I blinked with surprise. I hadn't even realised I was still holding them. Despite the hot fear I felt at getting caught, my fingers curled tightly around each coin. My palm ached where the edges pushed into my skin. Everything in my body rebelled at the thought of giving them up—a feeling so violent that I felt acutely ill, and my head spun dangerously. My fingers shook, but I couldn't bring myself to let go. I needed the coins, I needed something to bet, and he didn't understand how badly that mattered. I started to tell him about the threat from Boyd, but shame burned in my belly, I just couldn't find the words to explain the position I was in. The position I had put us all in.

My family couldn't find five coins for a decent meal. The four in my hand were Dad's fare to work tomorrow. There was no way they could find a hundred to make sure I lived to see another day. I didn't want to see their horror and disappointment if I told them what was at risk. Dad's fingers covered my own, and then he roughly pulled my grip open. I just stared. His hands were so different to my own, thick instead of slender, work-worn and calloused instead of bruised and tender.

The starkest similarity was that we were both still dirty from grime that wouldn't scrub free. A strange and terrible thing to have in common. The coins hit the mattress with a dull thud, and my father grasped my scraped chin. An unwanted gasp of pain rolled from my lips as he forced me to look at him. We also shared our dull, brown eyes, and I considered this and missed the first part of his warning.

"Get out of this house, Octavia!" he hissed. "You're no longer welcome in my home."

This I caught, and I flinched. "What?" He refused to repeat himself. "Dad?" I whispered. He remained stone-faced, so I turned my pleading eyes on my mother instead. My eyes shined with tears. I had always been good at tears on demand. It had helped me more times than I could count. This time, the tears were real.

"Mama?" I croaked.

In response, her brows rose, and her face twisted in pure unhappiness. She didn't tell him to back down. Neither my mother nor any of my siblings spoke in my defence. Instead, they all sat in silence and waited for someone to move. The weight of their judgement prickled at the back of my neck, and my bottom lip trembled. It shouldn't have been unexpected. Everyone had a limit to their patience, but I had always thought that my parent's forgiveness would stretch just a little further. At least for the eldest daughter.

"Out! Now!" my father barked at me when I didn't move. This time, I reeled backwards with surprise. In my haste, I almost tripped over Byron's feet again. I glanced between them all, my dark eyes were wide, and they glittered with pure desperation.

"Where am I supposed to go?" My lower lip trembled and dropped into a pout. "I have nowhere else to go."

A deafening silence met my question. They didn't care because my addiction and my desperation had pushed my father to the end of his patience.

"Go, Octavia," Mason advised, and his voice cracked. He looked tired and defeated. "We need to go back to sleep. I have work…" His words hurt the most since I had always considered him my closest brother.

I straightened and turned my back on them all. Despite the lump lodged in my throat and my worsened anxiety, I swallowed down tears. I jammed my feet into my boots, snatched a box of half-empty matches from the bench top, and fled for the stairs.

I needed to get out.

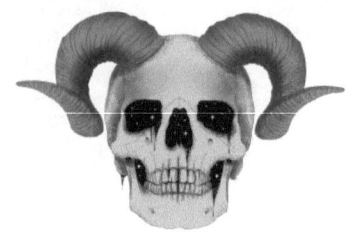

Chapter Six

The glass of the windowpane rattled in place as my fist slammed against it, the metal bands on my fingers digging into my skin with the impact. The bite of pain was refreshing and was just enough to pull me from the anxiety that threatened to overwhelm me completely.

I had wandered the darkened street for the best part of an hour trying to sort out my thoughts and feelings before the path took me back to Helina's home.

As my only friend, it was really the only place I could think to go.

"Hel! Helina! Wake up! Come on!" I yelled loudly enough to wake half of the street. I pulled my fist back to knock on the window again.

There was a shuffling from inside the room, and the window slid up and out of the way. Helina's head appeared in the window frame and she blinked away the remnants of a dazed sleep. Her dreadlocks swung over her shoulders as she peered out at me.

Her eyes narrowed as she glanced suspiciously past me to see what was happening on the street. Anyone would have thought I had led a riot to her door, but the street behind me was cold and quiet.

"What's happening, Octavia?" Helina yawned.

A frown pulled at my lips as I settled my fingers on the windowsill and forced myself to offer her a grin. I meant for it to be casual, but it felt too forced and pulled uncomfortably at the edges of my mouth. My mouth was stiff and awkward, and in the distorted reflection of the window, I could see that I was grimacing at her instead.

"Can I stay here tonight?" I asked in a rush.

Helina blinked. She was silent like it was taking her brain a moment to process the words.

"Or you know, for a while? Maybe a week? I just need somewhere to stay for a bit," I continued. I looked at my hands, filling the space between us with words. My knuckles were blanching on the windowsill. While begging was second nature, I could never hold the eye contact that came with the direct confrontation of pleading for a place to stay.

Helina bit her lip and was silent for a beat before she asked, "Why?"

"Dad threw me out."

"Yeah, but why?"

"I don't know, he just…" I glanced up again. A quick peek to see how the words landed and watched how Helina's brow raised with disbelief.

Beneath her stare, I shifted uncomfortably. I sighed.

"So, I took a couple of coins, and he got a bit mad." As I elaborated the story, I could hear the defensiveness in my tone. "So, what? It was nothing."

Even though I didn't look up again, I knew the expression my friend wore—the grim disapproval that had appeared on her face. It was the exact reason we never really discussed my thievery and gambling. Helina refused to acknowledge that her only friend was nothing more than a petty criminal. Scum of the streets, as she called those who begged for what they needed. The first time she had referred to me like that, we hadn't spoken for two weeks.

The heavy sigh that slipped from Helina's lips said more than words could. "Not tonight, Octavia." Helina swung her head back into the room.

"But... where am I supposed to go?" I whispered softly and my grip on the windowsill tightened. I considered that I could just refuse to leave. It crossed my mind that if I was quick enough, I could slip inside the room before Helina could shut the window. It was a foolish and desperate thought—nobody was that quick.

"Try the bus yard," she told me. The window closed quickly, and I barely managed to get my fingers out of the way before it slammed shut.

I struggled to pull a full breath of air into my lungs as invisible bands tightened around them. I rocked back onto my heels and my teeth scraped against my lower lip. It stung. Slowly, I sighed and took Helina's advice.

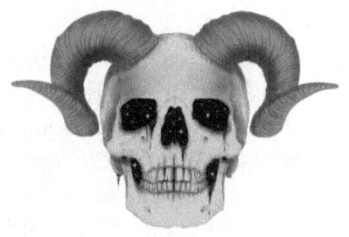

Chapter Seven

The bus yard didn't only house buses, but a mismatch of metal shells that were supposedly once used for transport. Nobody had used a car in generations. I had never seen one run on the streets of Ilrea, although my grandfather had once told stories about them. The remnants of vehicles from decades ago lived in a big yard on the outside of town, piled up and discarded like junk. It was one of the few places where those without a roof over their head could find shelter in the dark.

Nobody spent too much time out in the dark, not when demons had come with the angels, and our world crawled with creatures we couldn't even begin to understand.

Not that I had seen one. Desperate men were a bigger threat on the streets of Ilrea, but the stories were scary enough for most people to stay inside, regardless.

The yard was a strange and gloomy place. The inside of the cars occasionally glowed with the flicker of candles, or small fires which threw light in all directions and gave shadowy outlines to the occupants within. There were more cars here than I had expected. Smaller, rounded shells were scattered around the front of the yard, and bigger trucks and so-called buses sat near the back. I stepped carefully into the yard.

Too many of Ilrea's lost souls slept through the night here, and I couldn't help but wonder if I would have what it takes to remain among them. If I was honest with myself, I knew that I had been tired, hungry, and left wanting for much of my life, but I had never been forced to sleep in the cold.

When faced with having to sleep in one of these metal contraptions, I realised that maybe I didn't always have it so hard. The thin foam mattress stretched across the floor at home was a luxury compared to the look of these things, which seemed cold and uninviting. A lot of the metal was dented and damaged, and I couldn't help but wonder if it was from before or after the fall. Some cars were painted with symbols and words. Amongst them, I recognised each of the symbols of sin. They were bright coloured copies of the ones displayed on the Penance Wall. There was more of a presence of those marks here than anywhere else in Ilrea, and it marked it as a place where sinners slept.

Idly, I wondered if that made me a sinner, too.

As I shuffled through the yard, I avoided the small cars. A sense of foreboding left me skirting around the metal structures. I attempted to stay quiet and go unnoticed, I crept around another rusty shell and peered in the window. I reached for the cold metal handle on the door and tugged on it. Before I could get it open, a face appeared in the shadows within. They pressed up against the glass and I jammed my knuckles against my mouth to suppress my scream from echoing in the air. I scrambled backwards and almost fell in my haste to put space between us.

I wasn't looking to repeat that experience, so I turned my attention instead to the larger buses up the back. They were far more intimidating. Helina had once told me that school buses before the fall were bright yellow, but these were the colour of tarnished silver and orange, brown rust. They didn't look as happy as the picture my friend had conjured up in my mind so many years ago. The cheerful and vivid concept that I had held onto so tightly as I walked to the bus yard, in hopes that it would be a happier place than the rumours foretold, abruptly disappeared at the sight of them. Now I had the feeling that the bus yard could never be considered a happy place.

My fingers grazed against the front of the bus as I approached it. The metal beneath my fingertips was cold, and it felt unfamiliar, like a great, demon beast. I couldn't quite find any other way to describe it, and my stomach twisted with apprehension. My head tipped back, and my chin stuck out as I glanced up into the darkened windows. I wasn't foolish enough to think that there would be nobody in there, but the metal beast looked big enough that I could hope for just a little spare room.

The strange door left me fumbling in a panic, and it took a moment before I managed to force it open. My steps were quick and clumsy as I clambered my way onto the bus. Halfway down the aisle, a soft lantern flickered, it threw ghastly shadows across the bus and gave off the impression that the bus was longer than it looked from the outside.

A gasp rolled off my lips as I took in the sight of the bus's interior. Every inch had been brightly painted with graffiti. There was more colour here than I had seen anywhere else in town. Tiny symbols of sin were woven into bigger patterns, and the name *HEIRA* repetitively appeared on the walls. The bus reeked of mildew and sweat. The smell was so strong that my stomach cramped in warning that my pathetic dinner might come back up.

I shuffled past the first few rows.

Bodies curled into each of the seats—men and women fast asleep—and I couldn't shake the idea that they weren't fully unconscious. Their eyes seemed to follow my every step, and I had the feeling I was walking straight into a trap. By the time I stepped carefully over the lantern, I still hadn't found an empty seat to hide in. I passed two more rows before I suddenly became aware of the group of people who were lounging at the back of the bus. I counted five people sprawled across the back seat. They spoke to each other in low tones. My body prickled uncomfortably with warning. I was possessed with the idea that I needed to get off the bus as quickly as possible.

I slowly stepped backwards.

The moment one of them stood up, I froze in place and watched him warily. My breath caught in my throat. He was tall, and he took his time as he stretched languidly. He turned slowly to face me and there was something innately dangerous about the way he moved, in the way his shadow danced behind him on the colourful walls. My subconscious whispered to get going and get out as quickly as possible. I could find another place to sleep, or I could force my way through Helina's window.

There was a loud crash as I stepped back into the lantern. I had forgotten about it, and it tipped over. I barely had time to groan before it rolled beneath one of the occupied seats. The light dimmed and everything seemed even more dangerous. While I debated attempting to right the lantern, I was too distracted to realise the danger had approached well before I could run to safety. Danger in the shape of a man.

"Hello, love," his voice sent a shiver right down my spine. His tone held the strange curl of an accent that came with privilege in these parts, distinct to two or three people alone. It is said to have been inherited from their mother, and stronger in one man than the other. My head whipped up to look towards the end of the bus, but the man already stood firmly in front of me, the bulk of his body pressed into my personal space.

It was then that I realised just how badly I had fucked up. Between one breath and the next, his strong fingers wrapped firmly around my throat. He secured me in place with his firm hold. A soft squeal pulled from me as he squeezed; gently at first, but then he started to apply enough pressure that spots began to dance in front of my eyes. He was going to kill me. It felt like a certainty, and I wondered if this wouldn't be a better, quicker death than the one promised to me at Boyd's hand.

Out of pure self-preservation, my fingers lifted to wrap around his wrist in a futile attempt to pull his hand free of my windpipe. His skin was mostly smooth under my grip, but I could feel the puckered, rough edges of badly healed scars. There was no time to dwell on how he felt though, or where the scars had come from, as he softened his fingers on my throat. I gulped down a quick breath.

"I don't remember you paying the toll," he stated casually. I hadn't even known there was one. The man pushed forward, and I stepped backward with the force of his movement. The lantern was kicked back out from beneath a seat, and suddenly, light washed over the man. Even though I'd already known who he was from the sound of his voice, my mind flared with instant recognition.

Niklaus Heira was a force to be reckoned with. Right now, he was standing with his hand around my throat and violence in his eyes. He was tall and lithe, and I could feel the powerful muscle in his forearm where I gripped it. I pushed at his arm in a futile attempt to get free.

"Let me go," I breathed the demand.

Niklaus was strong enough that my movement didn't seem to bother him. The sharp line of his jaw and cheekbones are accentuated in the low light. He had an angular face that seemed like it belonged at the end of a sculptor's chisel, instead of on a living, breathing person. Bright lines of ink ran from his fingertips up his forearms until they disappeared beneath the rolled sleeves of his crisp white shirt. The images reappeared at his collar, curled up his skin, and stopped just below his jaw. My throat bobbed beneath his palm. His fingers flexed at the movement. He wasn't squeezing hard enough to choke me, but it was a precarious position to be in all the same.

He was a far cry from the small child who had chased me around the warehouse during early education, and who had laughed when he'd managed to grasp a rough fistful of my pigtails. He was no longer the little boy who had cried when I shoved him to the ground, at six years old, for pulling on my hair too hard. We had once been strange friends, at least until my parents had decided education was not in my best interests. I didn't show any interest in learning, and it never seemed to stick. The fee to the chancellor was too steep to pay for a lazy child. While he had grown into a man, I felt much as I had on the cusp of my teenage years. Moody, unrepentant, and constantly in trouble. As teenagers, and without daily access to one another, we had mostly parted ways and the friendship completely dissolved.

There had been a night of fumbled fingers and tongues, at seventeen, behind a shed while everyone else celebrated at the Samhain markets. Our bodies struggled to find rhythm, and it was over before it truly began. We collided again at twenty, drunk on home brew and celebrating the turn of a new year in a stranger's house. His skin had been untainted by ink then, and our bodies found a little more synchronicity as we fucked feverishly in one of the back rooms. Then I left him there. I let him sleep as I tucked every coin I could find into my boots and fled. I had no desire to sleep beside him and deal with an awkward situation the next morning.

I had avoided him for four years. Until now.

I couldn't bring myself to look away from Niklaus, and I couldn't stop the invasive thought about how much of his body those images might cover. At least not until he smirked, and my brain went blank as I realised that Niklaus Heira was still exactly as dangerous as he had always seemed from a distance. No amount of history or moments of lust could change that. His fingers moved, they tightened a fraction, and I whimpered in response. His eyes lit up at the sound, and I got the feeling that he liked it.

"Stop," I pleaded and gasped for a mouthful of precious air. The need to get away increased, I struck out at him with my fists and feet. Niklaus moved easily to the side and dodged my flailing limbs.

"It costs three wrath coins to stay the night in my yard," he told me solemnly.

In the seconds of silence afterwards, the implication was clear. I couldn't pay, and he expected it. Niklaus tilted his head and narrowed his eyes, his full mouth pressed into an unforgiving line. There was something in the movement that reminded me suddenly of one of the feral street cats.

I sucked in a breath as he tightened and then relaxed his hand. He gave me a brief chance to breathe. It didn't last long enough before his fingers squeezed tight again. "I…" I spluttered. I didn't have the fee. Not even the more common lion printed coppers. The truth of the matter was that, even if I had them, I wouldn't spend them sleeping on this bus.

"Pay up and we'll find you a nice bed in the back," he suggested.

I might have been suffering a panic-induced hallucination, but I thought something flickered in his eyes. Niklaus Heira wanted something else from me, and I thought he wanted me to say something specific back to him, but I couldn't quite work out what it was. If he thought I had a magic word, or that he was getting a repeat experience of four years ago, he was dead wrong. I wasn't that desperate… or at least I hoped I wasn't.

My eyes skittered from side to side as I glanced around frantically. My lungs burned with the strain of not getting a full breath of air and darkness pulled me towards unconsciousness.

"I don't have anything," I wheezed out. The words sounded garbled.

For a moment, Niklaus' grip loosened enough for me to breathe, and I gulped down air while he considered his leverage. His green eyes narrowed on my face, and I trembled beneath his scrutiny.

"What's your name?" he asked.

The question lingered between us, and I blinked stupidly. Niklaus waited for an answer, and I tried to process what exactly he wanted. He knew exactly who I was… you didn't forget the kids you were raised with. I certainly hadn't forgotten the first boy I slept with, or the way he had bragged crudely after he had tumbled me. That was half the reason I robbed him the second time. He had repaid me, in turn, with a nasty rumour that I was a lady of the night, and anyone could buy me for a single copper. There was no way in this world or the next that he had forgotten who I was.

"Your name?" he repeated, and his fingers tightened with his insistence.

"Octavia Nox…" I whispered as realisation dawned that this was nothing more than a power play. He wanted to make me feel small, and it worked.

Niklaus was silent for so long that I wondered if I had been wrong, and he didn't recognise me at all. In the tense silence, I wondered if he could hear my heart as it thrashed against my ribs to break free. Or if, with his penetrating green gaze, he could see right into the depths of my mind to bear witness to that primal part that screamed to get free and flee to safety. In a fight-or-flight situation, I was firmly in team flight. His softly feral smirk widened, and my heart rate doubled for all the wrong reasons. I shouldn't have liked that smirk, but I did.

"Tell you what, Octavia Nox." He dragged me closer by his tight grip on my throat. My shoes scraped uselessly on the floor as the space between us disappeared. He lifted me from the ground. All my focus zeroed in on him as I struggled. My rough nails bit into his skin and I scratched at him as I tried to get free. His hold on my throat was one thing, but I panicked once my feet were off the floor.

"I'll give you a seat for the night. You'll get full Heira protection from all the nasties that get violent in the night, but you'll owe me a favour. Any favour of my choosing, and when I call it in, you won't refuse me. In fact, you will express your utmost gratitude."

"What?" I whispered.

"You heard me."

I could feel the way I was trembling, too distracted because my feet were not on the ground to argue further. Simultaneously, I felt overwhelmed by the smoky scent of his nicotine that spoke of his indescribable wealth, and I was flustered by the danger of his sheer proximity to comprehend the bargain properly. I was far too focused on my own imminent peril at his hands. The silence stretched too far, and he shook me by the neck—a sharp movement that caused my head to spin. After my panic spiked, I lifted my eyes to meet his narrowed green gaze. All my instincts told me to run. As far away as I possibly could, but I knew that I had never survived a night out in Ilrea alone before. That was the essence of my entire being, the imprint on my soul which foretold that I was nothing more than a greedy rat who would save my own skin first and foremost. No matter the cost. Niklaus Heira was the danger I knew... Ilrea at night was the danger that I didn't.

"Deal," I rasped with a blatant ring of defeat in my voice. "You have a deal."

Niklaus let go of my throat and I staggered backwards. My fingers moved to my neck, and I massaged what would become more bruises to add to the ever-growing collection of tonight's insults and injuries. Warily, I watched as he calmly straightened the rolled sleeves of his shirt.

"Come this way then, love." He gestured further down the bus.

"Right." I recoiled at the nickname. Ultimately, with nowhere else to go, I moved a few steps closer and avoided looking at the other inhabitants of the bus. "Okay," I affirmed again and nodded to myself.

Niklaus led me three more rows down. He gestured to an empty seat with a flick of his fingers and a jerk of his strong chin. He didn't move out of the way, and that forced me to brush past him as I squeezed into the seat. As I shuffled past him, my nose filled with the cloying scent of nicotine once more.

"Remember, love," Niklaus whispered into my ear. The hair on the back of my neck stood on end. "Whenever and whatever I want, and you'll oblige. No questions asked. No hesitation."

I swallowed roughly. My mouth had gone completely dry, so I didn't answer him. I had no idea what sort of favour Niklaus would ask for, but I knew it was unlikely to be anything good. His comment went unacknowledged, and I simply dropped down into the bus seat and pulled my knees up to my chest.

My face pressed against the cold glass window, and I stubbornly ignored him. His footsteps were heavy as he moved away, back down to the rear of the bus. I could hear them as they whispered, and a faint laugh tainted me. The group of men walked past my spot again to exit. I huddled in the seat and tucked my chin against my chest to avoid their notice. Niklaus stopped at the front of the bus and glanced back. My heart pounded as it seemed like he was staring right at me. He nodded and disappeared.

I wondered why Niklaus Heira spent his late hours in a bus yard, and how I had ended up here, too. Mostly, I just worried about what tomorrow would bring. I expended the rest of today's energy on as many 'what-if' scenarios my brain could conjure up.

Exhaustion pulled at my limbs and, eventually, the heaviness of the evening won out. Anxiety turned into vivid nightmares as I succumbed to sleep.

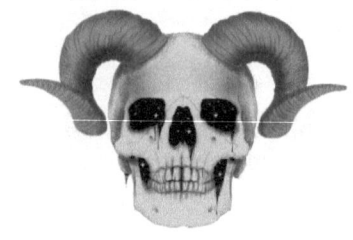

Chapter Eight

The first rays of sun appeared far too early. They trickled through the dusty windows and a groan slipped from my lips. I rolled into a tighter ball and drew my knees further into my chest. The pain from the night before came alive. I threw an arm over my head and huffed with annoyance.

The last thing I wanted was to be awake and facing the new day. Not when it seemed so bleak. There was no padding left on the seat, and the stiff metal had left me cold and broken. It was better than nothing though, or so I told myself. For a single, fleeting second, I could forget where I had slept, and I imagined that, in a moment, my brothers would stretch out and get up for a new day. Their voices would fill the room in a soft grumble, and I would roll to pull the thin pillow over my head and stubbornly ignore them. Just like every other morning, I would block out all signs of life as I chased a few extra moments of sleep.

The fantasy disappeared quickly once the other inhabitants of the bus rose for the day. They stamped their boots against the metal floor. The entire vehicle rattled and shook with their movements. The bus yard was not a quiet place in the cold light of the day. I stuffed my fist into my mouth and suppressed a sob. I was overwhelmed by a sense of hopelessness and dread. Men and women shuffled around me, and I tried to keep as still and invisible as possible. I wondered if I stayed here long enough, would anyone come looking? Would anyone remember that I even existed at all? Most likely not, I supposed. My family was too busy attempting to survive, and Helina often struggled to think of anyone that existed past the end of her own nose.

The noise level softened, and my body relaxed into the peace of the moment. Minutes ticked into hours as I laid on the cold metal seat and tried to work out what to do next. There were approximately seventeen hours left to clear my debt to Boyd.

I rolled onto my back and stared at the roof as I calculated the need to steal over five coins an hour with no break to meet his ridiculous deadline. When that realisation dawned, the world felt too big, and everything appeared impossible. In denial, I closed my eyes and hoped that the world, and Boyd especially, would just forget about me. I wished that I would sink through the seat and disappear completely.

Fate and fortune were less forgiving than I liked, however, as the bus door slid open and heavy footsteps stomped down the aisle. The intruder spoke roughly, "Get out, all of you lot. Town meeting in the square! Everyone's gotsa go!"

An object clanged against the metal bar at the top of the seat. It commanded my attention immediately, and I flinched away from the source of the violence. "Up!" The voice was so close that I could have sworn he was in the seat with me. I bolted upright at that thought and both of my hands raised defensively. "Or I'll throw youse out myself!"

He came close and I cringed away.

"Alright, alright, I'm up," I muttered. "I'm going." I moved cautiously and edged past him to get into the aisle. He was a solid bulk of muscle with eyes that seemed a touch too wild to be safe. He gave me the distinct impression that if I lingered too close, he would try and take a bite from my flesh. My tongue curled and my nose wrinkled with horror at the thought.

"Get yous'self down to the square. Heira's orders." The man sneered and I blinked.

"Is that his favour, then? Attend a meeting?" I asked. There was a thread of hope in my voice and the man scoffed.

"Not a chance." He laughed. "When he calls in his favour, you'll know it. Just my order. Git everyone off the bus. Git everyone at the meeting. So, you need to giddout." He reached out and forcibly shoved me further down the aisle. I stumbled, but when he reached for me again, I sped up and scurried off the bus. My eyes flickered over my shoulder as I exited the yard, just to make sure he wasn't following. I practically jogged to the centre of town so that he couldn't catch up.

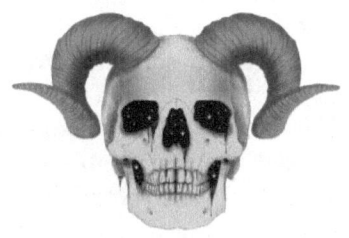

Chapter Nine

The square was jam-packed with more bodies than the night before. Adults and children shuffled into all the free space until we were so tightly pressed together, we could have been vegetables in a ration tin. The dais was littered with flowers woven into wreaths of white, gold, silver, and bronze. A long table sat amid it all, covered with a cream cloth that looked more luxurious than anything I had ever seen in my life.

When I squinted and turned my head to just the right place, I could see a stack of papers on the table with a fountain pen resting beside it. There were other objects, including strange bands of pearlescent metal, but I had no idea what they were, and I was not courageous enough to push forward for a better look. I found a place where I could stand diagonally from the dais, and I tucked myself away into the corner, next to an old woman who sniffled constantly.

It was close enough to see what was happening, but far enough away that I could hide if it was another meeting that glorified death. The mere thought of more unexplainable horror left me exhausted, and the idea of this second meeting in less than twelve hours didn't seem promising. What if they were about to make us witness the mounting of more men onto the Penance Wall?

The chancellor stepped onto the dais. He stood before us in a pristine suit of pale pink, his long white beard knotted in a tight bun beneath his chin, and his hair was combed back. His devil's ring glinted on his left hand as the light caught it. Chancellor Heira stood in expectant wait until all the whispers had died away. He wouldn't speak until he had our complete and undivided attention. At his side stood a robed figure. The robe swirled like the moonlight off the top of the greyed canal water, glittering with even the slightest movement. The hood dipped low over the person's face, so even as I leaned forward and craned my neck, I couldn't tell who was beneath it.

The person stood eerily still. I found that my gaze flickered between both them and the chancellor. Mostly, I watched to see if I could pinpoint whether they were breathing. I was beginning to think the answer was no. After a few moments of silence, Chancellor Heira cleared his throat. The noise boomed across the square, amplified somehow. Surely, he could be heard halfway across the town... but maybe that was the point.

"Welcome, welcome!" He smiled grandly at us and flashed his too-white teeth. His arms spread wide like he was embracing us. It reminded me of the night before, and my eyes lifted to the four bodies pinned to the wall. They provided an ominous backdrop to this whole affair.

"Another ten years have passed us by, and the time has come again for The Devil's Trial," Chancellor Heira announced. Scattered whispers rose from the crowd. My fingers dropped to my pocket and I pulled out the folded poster from the night before. I stared down at words that meant nothing and the macabre image of the horned skull in the middle. Dread pooled in my veins. I didn't know why, but I had a bad feeling about these trials.

Chancellor Heira took a step forward on the stone dais, which drew my attention back to him. With a wave of his hand, he gestured to the robed figure. "This is Cyn. They are an envoy hand-selected by the devil," he told us. "They are here to explain the trials. The rules, the risk, and the reward." He paused in an unnecessary dramatic effect. "They will open sign-ups for any who think they can bring glory to Ilrea by winning the devil's favour."

He smiled magnanimously. "You will be our favoured child."

Cyn stepped forward as the chancellor inclined his head. I found myself holding my breath as the robed figure moved around the table and settled at the very front of the dais. They moved like they were gliding on the air—their steps didn't seem to make any sound. As my lips parted in wonder, I couldn't take my eyes off them. They were what created the sense of foreboding that swirled deep in my gut. Cyn removed their hood in a smooth movement. A gasp rippled across the crowd. Cyn barely looked human at all. They were the palest person I had ever seen, with unblemished, snowy skin. I noticed that they had no eyebrows, eyelashes, or hair, and wondered what happened to it. With a round chin and strong nose, Cyn's head was a smooth dome, and they were a portrait of curvature.

Even from the distance I stood at, I could see that their eyes swirled with a strange light. They held themselves tense and strained, like they had seen all that the world had to offer and scoffed in the face of it. Like they didn't trust it, or us. I wouldn't blame Cyn if they didn't trust us... we barely trusted each other. Their body was covered in thin black swirls, lines, and whorls in a pattern that glowed beneath the early morning light. The pattern extended from the tips of their long, thin fingers, and ran up their neck and over their scalp. I had no idea if they were a man or a woman, but in the grand scheme of things, I supposed that hardly mattered at all. The more important problem was that I still couldn't tell for sure if they were breathing. Cyn's voice was a soft growl. I wondered if they, like the fallen angels of fable, had come from an entirely different dimension. There was something heavy and entrancing within their tone.

"The devil is a benevolent being," Cyn began. "He sees the world around him. He sees the cities and the towns, the people within them and their potential for greatness. He sees *you*, Ilrea, and once a decade, he offers you the chance to reach your full potential." Cyn clasped their hands together in a sharp clap. "However, you can't just walk to the devil's door and ask for his forgiveness and favour," they said, and I scoffed.

Of course, you couldn't. Because the devil didn't exist.

It occurred to me that this could be the world's way of managing overpopulation. The chancellor could free up homes by giving us the chance to compete, all while slaughtering those who were stupid enough to enter. Cyn was still speaking, unaware of the thoughts that distracted me.

"Where he sees your potential, he also sees the depravity of humanity. The sins that drive you into debasement, corruption, and perversion. The core motivations amongst you all. He does not want this to sully his kingdom, but he offers you a chance to prove that you can rise above it all and face his judgement." Cyn smiled. It was a vision of nightmares—their teeth were filed into thin points, sharper than a blade. I found myself cringing back into the wall. My gaze darted left to right as I mentally mapped out the closest exits and the best way to flee.

"For this he offers you a series of trials to prove yourself," Cyn told us as I checked back into the speech. "It is not impossible. Many humans have passed through the seven sins to face his judgement and found his favour. It is relatively simple. Visit the seven cities of sin, complete the tasks you are given, and proceed to Eternis and he will bestow favour on your soul."

"Why the hell would we do that?" someone screeched loudly from the crowd. My chin dipped in a silent nod of agreement at the question. What sort of idiot signed up for a fairytale quest? Chancellor Heira stepped forward, and a frown creased at the edge of his mouth. His brow furrowed deeply at the disruption. He looked uncomfortable at the idea that we could render Cyn with a bad impression of his rule.

"Well, you see," Cyn was nonplussed by the interruption. "For some, it's a better life. For others, it's the riches, and for most, it's the glory. Ilrea is such a small, small place, don't you think?" There was a beat as the town considered this, and soft whispers of agreement fluttered through the square. I nodded to myself again. Ilrea *was* painfully small. "Are you not hungry? Are you not left yearning for more? If you earn a place in Eternis, you will want for *nothing*. Your families will want for nothing. It is a place untouched by famine and hardship. Are you not tired of working so hard only to gain so little? He offers you more. You will be untouched by fear and satiated by your desires. Does that not sound like pure perfection?"

Cyn looked at us all again. There was a flickering second where they appeared to catch my eye and looked right at me. I wondered if it was not Cyn that rendered judgement, as they seemed to see straight through me. I tore my eyes away just in case their focus was not imagined, and instead, I stared down at my boots.

"You would be immortal," Cyn added. "You would thrive in luxury forever."

There was a heartbeat of silence before men started scrambling forward. Men who were old enough to have heard this same spiel in decades past, but who had previously been too cowardly to enter. Tired men, who now just wanted the world and the ease of life that Cyn promised. They shoved their way towards the dais roughly and knocked over anyone in their path. The first of them made it three steps up the stone platform before Cyn's voice froze them in place.

"*Stop*!"

Cyn's tone was sharp, and the single word was like the lash of a whip. "I have not yet told you the rules. I have not invited you to sign up." Their sharp teeth flashed at the closest man, and the look in their eye marked them as predator and him as prey. Wisely, the man stumbled back down the steps. The echo of voices in the crowd fell silent again as we waited to see if he would be punished for his haste.

"Now," Cyn spoke softly, pleasantly, like the threat had never been issued at all. "There are only five rules in these trials, but you must heed them all:

One, participants must be between the age of twenty and thirty years old.

Two, each *deadly* sin must be challenged.

Three, you must pass every trial, and receive the marks of completion.

Four, deadlines will not be extended.

Finally, you may not refuse a direct order from an Angel of Sin." Cyn's slim fingers plucked at their wrist, and they rolled the sleeve of their robe upward. Marked amongst the dark ink on their skin were seven small-coloured etchings—the symbols of each sin. Cyn dipped their chin, a smooth inclination of their head.

"That is all. Those are your only rules."

They waved their hand towards the table. Diamonds on their fingernails glittered in the light, and the sight of them sparked my interest in this rigmarole for the first time. Diamonds were worth a lot of coins in any market. I leaned forward and then deflated as I realised how difficult it would be to steal literally from the end of their fingertips.

"Who will be first to approach your Chancellor and sign up?" Cyn asked.

This time, fewer people moved in the crowd. The eager men and women from before were too old to meet the conditions. They no longer qualified for the glory we had been offered. I remembered scoffing at the idea the night before, at the game of slim chance of survival, and I wondered if anyone at all would sign up. They seemed like crazy odds and fanciful rewards.

"Me!"

The voice of the first participant came from behind the dais. Everyone in the crowd craned their necks to watch, and Chancellor Heira gaped as his eldest son took the stairs two at a time to settle in front of the table. His fingers smoothed out invisible creases from his crimson suit. He was a near copy of the man who had his fingers around my throat last night. Only, Mikhael was a little sleeker, a touch more polished, and didn't have any mark on his skin. He stood, unfazed by the crowd or by the eyes that burned against his shoulder blades and raised a single brow at his father in silent expectation.

The chancellor stared at his son, and the younger man met his gaze without flinching. They looked so alike in that moment, with their broad shoulders and postures that spoke of entitlement. I felt a pang of pity for the chancellor as his son signed himself up for death. No wonder he was hesitating. It was only as Cyn re-joined his side that he managed to find his voice.

"What's your name?" the chancellor asked. Laughter rippled through the crowd. The young man ignored them, and he rolled his shoulders back. He stood tall.

"Mikhael Heira," he answered.

"Why are you joining The Devil's Trial, Mikhael?" Cyn asked in that silky smooth tone. Mikhael smirked. His green eyes were bright with mirth and challenge. He reached for the fountain pen and studied the contract in front of him. In a quick and sharp movement, he signed his name across the base.

"Now…" He grinned. "That would be telling."

Cyn's laugh carried across the crowd, and the crowd echoed it back. Like Mikhael's words were hilarious instead of frustrating and evasive. Cyn took his left hand and secured one of the iridescent cuffs firmly around his wrist. Their dark eyes snapped up and over his shoulder as they sought out the next challenger, studying those in the crowd for a hint of anyone who dared approach.

"Next," Cyn called.

"You aren't going anywhere without me, brother." Niklaus Heira strode up the steps as confidently as his brother had, and they stood shoulder to shoulder. Chancellor Heira looked shaken as he lost his heir and his spare within a few brief minutes. I felt a grim satisfaction at seeing him so put out.

"Name?"

"Niklaus Heira."

"Why are you choosing to participate, Niklaus?"

"Where he goes, I go," he said firmly and jerked his head at his twin. Niklaus left no room for argument in his statement. Cyn secured the cuff around his wrist after he signed, and both brothers moved to stand to the side. They were an intimidating sight, and I supposed I shouldn't have been surprised that if anyone had decided to participate, it was them. I barely had time to breathe between when they cleared the front of the dais, and when the next voice carried from the crowd. It was loud and all too familiar. My stomach flipped, and my lips parted gently in a plea of protest that never came out. All while I turned my head to seek her out.

"Helina Archer."

The crowd parted and offered her a wide berth as Helina strode from where she had been settled in the thick of the crowd. She approached the dais like it was her birthright. Helina looked just as she always did. She wore dark tights, shined leather shoes, and one of the three pinafore dresses she owned. Her oversized jacket was slung around her shoulders and her dreadlocks had been left loose and hung to the curve of her butt. They swung with each step she took. Helina moved with confidence and answered the question before she had reached the top step. Well before Cyn had even asked it.

"I'm entering because I know I can win," she remarked.

Cyn looked less than impressed that Helina had not waited to be asked. It didn't seem to matter too much, though, and Helina's long dreadlocks fell forward as she leaned over the table and signed her name on the next contract. She proudly offered up her wrist for the cuff without a word and moved to the side. It seemed for a moment like she glanced into the crowd and found my face, like the subtle tip to her chin was her way of bidding me goodbye.

I had always known that Helina aspired for more. I knew that she wanted to be all-knowing, she wanted to be right, and I thought she wanted to be the next Chancellor of Ilrea. I had never realised that on her list of wants was the option to leave me behind and become immortal. A devil's consort, or just a dead woman walking, depending on how you looked at it. The crowd hummed with idle gossip as the townsfolk discussed the three on the dais and who had the most potential to win.

The next voice drifted from the back of the crowd. He spoke in a slow and unhurried tone. "I'm next."

Again, the crowd parted. A young, blonde man disentangled himself from a dark-haired man who tried to keep him from moving forward. They whispered to each other in a short and heated conversation, but I couldn't hear what they said from my place in the crowd. I leaned towards them to try and get a better gist of it all the same.

When the dark-haired man visibly deflated and sighed, he let go. The blonde loped towards the dais. He was gangly and looked strangely too tall, like his body had not received the message to stop growing, and it left him towering over other people. His shirt and pants didn't quite fit and flashed inches of skin at the cuff of each.

"Name?" Chancellor Heira asked quickly, even though the young man had not yet made it to the base of the stairs. Instead, he moved forward at a leisurely pace, like we could all wait on him, and time was the thing he had most of in the world.

"Nash Aaron Wickham."

My attention was drawn away from the rest of his enrolment into the trials. A heavy hand landed on my shoulder and squeezed firmly. I was startled and turned. I half expected one of my brothers to stand at my shoulder with apologies on their lips, but I came face to face with Boyd. He grinned widely and his rotten breath assaulted my senses. Instinctively, I bit down on a gag and took a step to the side. The old woman hissed as I bumped into her. In the thick crowd, there wasn't far I could go.

"Just a reminder, missy, youse got 'til eleven. Hundred silvers, or I'll be carvin' it out of youse heart," Boyd said cheerfully.

To demonstrate his seriousness, the sharp blade of his knife pressed against my side. I sucked in a sharp breath, my eyes widened, and I tried in vain to swallow down the immediate fear that crested through my body. Dimly, I realised I was shaking.

"E-eleven," I stammered a repeat of the time he had given. "G-Got it."

The knife pressed harder, and a sharp pain bit into the curve of my hip. I couldn't help the whimper on my lips as I battled to stay calm and still, so he didn't do anything worse. He didn't move, and so I forced myself to nod another acknowledgement.

"Don't be late," Boyd hissed in my ear.

"Of course not," I squeaked.

One minute he was there, and the next he was gone as he melted into the crowd. I grit my teeth to stop myself from crying out. My breath spilled out in short pants. My body pressed back against the storefront. My heart ricocheted in my chest, and panic swirled through my entire being like poison in my veins. Distantly, I could hear Chancellor Heira as he wrapped the event up. He congratulated the four participants and announced that he will host them all for dinner. Then, more out of obligation than expectation, he called for any last volunteers beyond those who stand beside him. My eyes strayed to the four people on the dais.

My best friend, who looked bored. Niklaus, who would take my favour-debt with him to his death. His twin, whose jaw was tight, and eyes were flat. Nash only stared at the dark-haired man who had held him back, like he hurt to be apart from him. They all seemed like idiots.

I glanced back at Boyd's disappearing body in the crowd. One hundred and fourteen silver pieces, all pride stamped, that was what I owed him. There was no way I could get them in time. They were foolish on the dais as they signed their own death warrants, but I was the fool who signed mine a year ago. The first time I had borrowed coins to play cards. That was the first day of the end of my life.

It was strange how I could only see it now that the last day had arrived. It felt hard to breathe as I realised that I was truly going to die tonight. Die and get carved into pieces for sale, no better than an animal at the monthly meat market. Boyd would make a fortune on my organs. I was apparently worth so much more to him dead than alive.

"Wait!" my voice was thready. I sounded unsure.

"Wait!" I repeated, louder this time. I pushed off the wall and forced my way through the crowd. Once they realised what was happening, people shuffled aside, and the path cleared.

"Take me, too."

"Oi!" Boyd sounded livid in the distance.

His voice turned my gut and I picked up my pace to get to the dais as quickly as possible. Panic flooded through me. I stumbled and weaved through the crowd to avoid him. Those stone stairs were only a few steps away. His fingers brushed against my jacket. It was a fast movement and my heart lodged in my throat. If Boyd found a grip on me, I knew he would exact his revenge immediately. I surged forward, then Cyn was right in front of me, standing halfway down the stairs. Their tattooed hand extended, and I reached for it desperately. The moment Cyn looked over my shoulder, their eyes darkened, and their teeth flashed in warning. Boyd fell back. His wisest move in years.

"Octavia?"

The sound of my name startled me. I turned my head to find the source. Mason pushed his way to the edge of the crowd. He looked confused and nervous as he took in Cyn. I sucked in a harsh breath and searched for something to say. Dad appeared just by his shoulder, and my heart squeezed painfully. The devastation on his lined face created an unexpected scar on my soul. Suddenly, none of the explanations on the edge of my tongue felt like they could never be enough.

"I'm sorry," I whispered to them. I saw my mother, and her face collapsed like she had lost another child. I couldn't bear to look, so I turned away and followed Cyn up the stairs. It was better to say nothing.

Once I was safely out of harm's reach, I slowed down, and my gaze flickered nervously at the chancellor. He looked so much older up close as his lips pressed into a thin and disapproving line at the interruption of his tidy closure.

My eyes moved to Cyn. Their swirling gaze left me swallowing against a sudden dryness in my throat. It was at that moment I realised how thirsty I felt, and a headache pounded at my temple in reminder of it. Not only was I thirsty but my stomach roiled in demand for more than the meagre half a potato I ate last night. Cyn had been right in their speech. I wanted so desperately for everything. I needed so much more than I had to thrive. We all did.

Out of the corner of my eye, I studied the other participants closely. Helina's brow was raised in disbelief and question, she looked unhappy. No doubt she couldn't believe that I would have had the gall to participate in the trial. Niklaus' lips twisted in wry amusement, like he knew a secret I didn't. Mikhael paid me no attention at all, which was unsurprising because, despite his brother's preoccupation with me in our childhood, I was certain the older twin didn't even know I existed. Nash didn't even look away from that man in the crowd. Not one of them spoke. I was completely alone at this moment.

I turned my focus to the table and shuffled towards it. Out of pure habit, my right hand dipped into my pocket, and I sought out the familiar feel of my worn lucky dice for comfort. They turned between my fingers and clinked together softly.

"What is your name?" Chancellor Heira demanded. Impatience rang in his tone.

I hesitated. "Octavia Emilia Nox."

"Why do you want to participate in the trial, Octavia?" Cyn asked. The full force of their otherworldly focus suddenly settled on my face. Beneath the scrutiny of their gaze and the intensity of their presence, I couldn't hold eye contact for longer than a second. I fought the urge to shrink beneath their attention. It was easier to be invisible in this world, and suddenly, there were too many eyes burning a curious hole right through me.

When I answered, my voice was small and soft. My shoulders rolled forward in a self-conscious shrug. "Because I have nowhere else to go," I whispered. There was no need to add the other reasons. That I wanted to survive the night, at least one more of them. That I desperately needed the coin at the end. Anxiety was a living being inside of me, I didn't want to spend the next and last of my living hours afraid and imagining the ways the butcher would come for me.

Cyn gestured to the contract, and I glanced down. I could tell there were words on it, but the symbols known as letters bled into each other. A few common words stood out, but not enough for me to make much sense of it. I didn't know what any of the longer ones meant.

"Uh." I breathed my unease at being unable to tell what it said. Suddenly, I wished I had a little more discipline and desire and knew how to read anything put in front of me. As I stared down at the paper and trailed my fingertips along the ink, I could only make out the most basic of words. Cyn stepped closer, too close, and I realised there was no heat rolling from their body.

"It only reiterates the rules and some consequences," they informed me. "You need only to sign at the bottom."

I nodded sharply. My face flushed hot as their words announced my shortcomings to everyone on the dais. My movements were jerky as I picked up the pen, and before it could be commented on again, or worse, before the crowd realised what was happening, I signed my name. It was messy, scratchy, and sloped right through the line that I had meant to write above.

"Good." Cyn gently plucked the pen from my fingers and grasped my hand again. Their grip was firm, despite having such delicate hands, and they held me firmly. Pain coursed through my arm, that same wrist was the one Boyd had stepped on. My gaze dropped to where our hands met. Cyn was pale but practically glowed from the ink on their skin. In comparison, my skin was an odd colour, and I was decorated with bruises. The cuff snapped into place around my wrist. It was a fraction too tight and pinched at my skin.

Then, I was released, and I stepped backwards. My hand was cradled against my chest as I inspected the cuff. It was an inch thick and created of strange metal that shined with colours like the pearl buttons on Chancellor Heira's best suit. It felt lighter than I had anticipated.

"That will be all," Chancellor Heira announced in his magically projected voice. He easily dismissed the crowd and they milled towards the exits of the square. They all had somewhere else to be. I turned and stared out at my family again. I wavered at the idea of moving towards them, but still had no idea what I would say to make this better.

"You lot." The chancellor's eyes pinned his sons first and then drifted to the rest of us as an afterthought. For a second, I thought I caught a glimmer of hopelessness in his eyes, but I couldn't bring myself to call him out on it or question it. He was, after all, still the chancellor of Ilrea. A devil-blessed man.

"Follow me to Heira House."

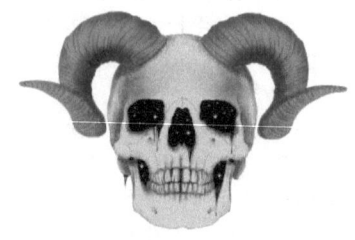

Chapter Ten

Heira House was exactly as I had always imagined it, and that was to say completely pretentious. Once, at seventeen, while spending time with Niklaus, I had thought I would see the inside of this house, but it never quite happened. My daydreams of a romance and marrying into this house realistically ended in a quick, rough three minutes against a cold wall. Niklaus Heira had been looking to get laid, not married.

I stepped into the pristine foyer and blinked at the artwork that lined the walls. The faces of unknown people stared back at me. They shared high cheekbones and similar frowns showed that they all had Heira blood. The floor shined; it had been polished to perfection, and I couldn't help but wonder if my mother had been here in the hours earlier and scrubbed at the tiles until she could see her worn out reflection.

The other participants filed in behind me, and the door slammed closed. I couldn't help but brush my fingers against the place where the cuff bit into the skin of my wrist. The colour captivated me. I remembered the last time the chancellor had worn the jacket with the buttons in this sheen, at an announcement where he told the community that grain rations from Eternis had been stolen in transport, and we would not be receiving them that year.

It had been a hungry and violent winter.

"Any questions so far?" Cyn interrupted my thoughts.

A thousand questions spun through my mind and I had no idea where to start with them. I didn't want to be the first to speak and draw even more attention to myself, but I also burned to know the answers to the thousand what-if scenarios that haunted me.

"What do these do?" I lifted my hand and tapped my finger against the slim cuff in question. So far, everything made sense, except these. I didn't understand the need for the shackles.

Cyn smiled like they had been expecting the question.

"They're tracking devices, so we know where you are throughout your trials. After all, we wouldn't want you getting lost in the big city."

It seemed like an innocuous answer, but as I considered the cuff, I couldn't shake the feeling that there was more to it than that. Cyn didn't seem like they wanted to offer up any further information, though, and I couldn't work out what it was about them that made me uncomfortable, so I refused to press for a more detailed answer.

"Alright," I finally agreed. I moved on to my next question. "And... what happens if we don't pass a task in the trial? Or if we run out of time?"

This was a question I should have asked prior to signing up, and maybe it had been in the small print that I couldn't read, but I couldn't change the fact that I hadn't asked before, only ask questions and seek answers now. Besides, it never did anyone well to dwell in the past.

Suddenly, everyone else's attention turned to Cyn with keen interest. It seemed like I was not the only one who hadn't given that risk consideration prior to signing up. Cyn's demeanour didn't change. Their fingers laced in front of their waist, and they nodded gently. "If you fail to complete a task, you forfeit yourself to that Angel of Sin."

My mouth, which was already bone dry with thirst, became drier with this information. "What does that mean?" I whispered.

Cyn's infinite gaze latched onto mine. "They will own your soul."

"And what will they do with my soul?"

"Anything they like." Cyn laughed. "You will be in service to them for the rest of your mortal life."

The words blurred together, and not for the first time, I cursed the fact that I couldn't read, and more so the shame that had stopped me from asking for the contract to be read out loud.

It was unlikely that knowing this beforehand would have stopped me from signing up, though, or portrayed the trial as a bigger threat than Boyd and his sharp knife.

The fact remained—I had no idea what I was involved in, or how I would survive it.

"If that's all." Cyn gestured to someone in the corner, and the chancellor's wife approached us. "We invite you to dine with us tonight before the trial officially begins at dawn tomorrow. In the meantime, Prudence will show you to your rooms."

Prudence Heira didn't look at all put out at being ordered around in her own home. Again, I wondered if she was soulless and not alive. The twins disappeared, and Cyn followed just as fast.

"Come now," Prudence instructed. I pushed my fingers into my pockets to hide the trembling of my fingers before I followed her down the hall. Helina caught up to me, and her shoulder bumped into mine as a bid for attention. I shrugged in flippant acknowledgement that she was there but didn't speak.

"You okay?" she asked, her voice a little too high-pitched. "What were you thinking, Octavia, honestly?"

I shrugged again. I didn't have an answer. I hadn't been thinking, just panicking.

"You know that saying my dad used to always come out with?" I asked as I caught her eye.

She scoffed lightly. "Which one?"

"Better the devil you know, than the one you don't?" I whispered and we stopped as Prudence showed Nash into his room.

Helina made a sound of agreement and knocked into my shoulder again. It forced me to catch my balance. My teeth grazed against my lip and I shifted uncomfortably before I drew in a breath to continue.

"Did you do this to show me up?" Helina interrupted before I could get the words out.

"What?" I asked, stunned.

"You heard me," Helina shook her head. "You've never shown any interest. Yesterday you said it was all a myth, and once I was up there, you suddenly decided that you needed a piece of it too? Come on, Octavia, you're always hanging onto me. You couldn't let me have this one thing?"

Discomfort was a living entity that breathed down the back of my neck at that moment. I didn't answer her tirade until we reached Helina's room, and she was on the verge of disappearing inside.

"Me entering this has nothing to do with you, Hel," I admitted. "Barely any of my life choices have anything to do with you. It's just this is the devil I don't know, and I'd rather it than the one I do." It explained nothing but felt fitting. I didn't need to explain my demons to her right now, not when Helina had never been interested in listening before.

Helina's chin tipped down and her eyes took on a familiar condescending glimmer. "That's because what you know, Octavia, barely fills a teaspoon."

My lips parted in surprise, my next breath a gasp. What a bitch! Before I could say anything in my defence, Prudence Heira placed a firm hand on my arm and pulled me further down the hall. I was tempted to hesitate and turn back, but eventually, I nodded and followed Prudence. I found some semblance of resolve as I refused to look back at Helina. Nothing could change what she had said, or the hollow pit which now swirled in my stomach.

"This is your room," Prudence offered as we stopped by a door, and it forced me to stop thinking of my friend. She didn't wait for me to enter or to make sure it was okay. Instead, she disappeared down the hall within seconds.

The room was spectacular. There would never have been any question of it being enough. It was technically two rooms—one main room with a bed and a smaller room to bathe in. The bathing room was as big as the room I lived in with my entire family. The main room was painted a soft cream and looked so clean that I felt grimy and out of place.

It was this that made the bathroom my first stop. The water ran cold from a faucet. I stuck my mouth right under it and drank until my belly felt uncomfortably full. I filled the tub with hot water and lay in it for what could have been an eternity. The fresh bar of soap lost half its weight by the time I felt clean. My skin was pink with irritation and slightly sore, but I was cleaner than I had ever been.

It was tempting to collapse into the big bed, but I pulled my dirty clothes back on and slipped out into the hall instead. A brief investigation to satiate my curiosity couldn't hurt.

Heira House, as it turned out, was impossibly big and hard to navigate. Whenever familiarity struck, the path turned into another unknown hallway. The only common factor within the house was that it all looked too clean and too still, like nobody lived there at all. I was lost before I could even consider where my room had been, and every door looked the same. I turned left and then left again before, suddenly, I was no longer alone.

Nash Wickham stood halfway down the long hall; his head lifted as he studied the painting. I considered turning back, but the object in his hand gave me pause.

I moved closer, and when I was only three paces away, I realised that he was holding a thick black marker. He twirled it around in his long fingers. I had no idea where he found it.

"They look a touch too perfect; don't you think?" Nash said in his slow drawl. I was fascinated by his voice as he pulled and stretched at all the vowels before they left his lips.

"Maybe." I hedged and sidled a step closer to take in the portrait too.

It depicted a surprisingly life-like rendition of the Heira family. Mother, father, and identical sons. The twins had been painted as children of roughly twelve, on the cusp of becoming men, long before Niklaus' skin had been marked.

"Easy enough to fix," Nash turned, and he flashed me a smile that spelled nothing but trouble. His brow crumpled in concentration as his focus turned back to the painting. Nash reached up, and the thick black marker squeaked as he added features to the portrait. A thick black and bristly moustache appeared right beneath Prudence's petite nose. The marker squeaked against the canvas again as he etched in crude dresses and oversized pigtails for the twins. They looked like the stick figures I'd drawn at four years old.

"Better make them match." He chuckled like we shared a secret. His laughter felt like it lifted something in my soul for the first time in days. Suddenly, the day didn't seem quite as dire as it had before. When he stepped back, I swallowed nervously and studied the new devil's horns and tail that decorated the chancellor himself.

"Fitting." I laughed, despite myself. Nash flashed another crooked grin. I decided I liked him.

"Perfection," he corrected me brightly. His laugh, like everything else, sounded like slow-dripping honey from the end of his tongue, and I was stunned by the sound of it.

"Catch you around, Octavia."

He threw the marker into the air, and I fumbled to catch it against my chest to stop it from hitting the floor. Then he moved faster than I had ever seen and left me alone again. It took far too long to realise how I looked as I held the marker while the vandalised painting sat proudly before me. Loudly and colourfully, I cursed Nash to the devil himself and dropped the marker. It bounced off the floor, and I ran for the other end of the hall to put as much distance between myself and the evidence of his vandalism as possible.

I sped around the corner and slammed right into another body. I crashed ungracefully on the hard floor.

"Ugh!" I groaned.

"Well, well, well..." The pretentious Heira tone was unmistakable.

Please be Mikhael, please be Mikhael, I prayed. When I glared up at him, I groaned again. Niklaus Heira towered above me, a smirk twisted onto his full lips.

"On my bus one night, and in my house the next, love," he sang cockily. "Anyone would think you were desperate for a third round. I guess I am just that good."

In that moment, he proved he had always known who I was. My face flushed. His cockiness knew no bounds. I swallowed roughly and he offered me his hand. Dumbfounded, all I could do was blink at it and wonder what exactly he was offering up.

My teeth caught on my lower lip, and I bit down until I tasted blood. I attempted to bring myself back to my senses.

"You're not going to make it far in these trials if you're too slow to recognise a helping hand, love." Niklaus pushed his hand further into my face. I couldn't shake the feeling that this helping hand would toss me right off the edge of a cliff if I took it. Not my best choice, but I reached out and clasped his hand. His tattoos started at his wrist, and I stared at the black and white rendition of the map of Kaida that stretched across his forearm and evolved into brightly coloured flowers. I hadn't seen flowers like those anywhere around Ilrea. There was more colour on his right arm than in the entire town.

Each of the eight great cities marked his skin—Glorae, Cupitidas, Gula, Invidia, Desidia, Ira, Avarita, and Eternis. I noted each dot and the jumble of letters beneath that I could slowly sort into city names. The muscles in his forearm bunched, and Niklaus pulled me to my feet like I weighed nothing at all. The space between us disappeared again. My gaze dropped to my shoes to avoid looking at him properly, again. He seemed to be waiting for something and didn't let go of my hand.

"Thanks," I muttered as I realised what he wanted a fraction too late.

"That's better, love," he mused, in that all too condescending manner.

His grip felt too tight, and he still held me firmly. I wiggled my fingers and pulled my hand backwards. My jaw clenched tightly as I forced some space between us.

"That's twice now I've helped you," he informed me. His eyes burned a hole in the side of my face. "You're racking up quite the debt."

My gaze snapped up to his face with a furious glare and my hands fisted by my sides.

"I don't owe you for that! That's complete bullshit!"

He stepped forward and closed the space between us again. He was too close, and my heart rate picked up as my body tensed for danger. I needed out. I wanted nothing more than to flee.

"No, love. That one's a freebie." A laugh rumbled deep in his chest. "But you do owe me for last night, Octavia Nox, and I'm going to collect in the trials."

I scoffed, but confidence abandoned me. He smirked right back.

"Just remember, you can't say no to the angels." Niklaus' hand shot out; his strong fingers held my chin so tightly that I gasped. He leaned into my space. "Consider me your own personal angel, love."

Niklaus tipped my chin up and inspected the bruises where he had held me by the throat the night before. His lips thinned with displeasure, but he let go and turned to stroll away without commenting on them. Luckily, the bruises weren't too dark. I hated that he had noticed them though, and that we both knew exactly what caused them. My eyes lingered on his broad shoulders as he walked away. I wasn't a threat to him, I realised then. After years with my back to the wall, I knew the fact that he could turn his back so easily on me meant that I was nothing at all.

"Wait," the plea escaped my lips before I could stop it. Niklaus paused but didn't turn. He waited.

"How... how do I find my room?" I asked. He's the last person I wanted to engage further, and I had to force the words over my lips. He smirked, and I was reminded that he was an asshole.

"End of this hall. Take a right, then another, and you're the third door down," he answered. Even though I couldn't see his face, I could tell he was laughing at me.

"That one you do owe me for," Niklaus added. He disappeared before I could protest. His directions were accurate, though, and five minutes later, I collapsed onto my soft bed. The exhaustion of everything weighed heavily on me, and I pulled the blanket over my head to block out the world. Sleep came too easily this time, and even my nightmares were too tired to make an appearance.

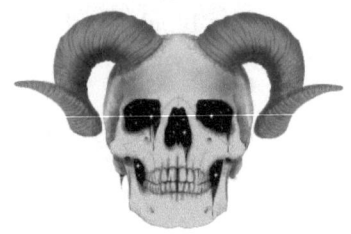

Chapter Eleven

A sharp knock on the door startled me into consciousness. It was so abrupt that I shot upright, and the world tilted for a moment. I struggled to work out where I was and if I was in danger. The knock rang out again, stronger this time. I brushed away the cobwebs of sleep as I kicked off the sheet and staggered to the door. The person behind it was unfamiliar and wore a maid's uniform just like the one my mother donned each morning. They smiled blandly at me. I caught myself in the wish that it was my mother who stood there instead.

"Dinner is in half an hour," they said softly, like speaking too loudly would gain unwanted attention. "You're reminded to wear something clean."

My eyes dropped to my dirty clothes, and by the time I looked up, they had left.

"Right." I huffed and surveyed the room again. Finally, I noted the polished wardrobe in the corner. When I opened the door, I realised it was filled with clothes in varying shapes and sizes. My throat constricted as I reached out and rubbed the material of a dress between my fingers. It felt luxurious, and it was far too much. I was overwhelmed but also struck with a sudden fear that I would arrive to dinner as the only person who didn't change. This thought had me peeling off my jacket and pants quickly.

Piles of clothes grew around me as I pulled clothes from the hangers and inspected them closely. I wondered who they belonged to before I discarded them completely.

The world seemed to move along without me, but eventually, I managed to rouse myself into a state of action. The dresses seemed impractical. I hadn't worn a dress in over a decade, and as I looked down at my bare legs, I decided the scrapes on my knees needed to be covered. I shoved all the dresses back into the base of the wardrobe.

After some searching, I found a loose plum coloured top with sleeves that reached my wrists. I then picked up a pair of soft and strange harem pants, which hung tight around my waist and ankles but billowed out to hide my legs. They had deep pockets—the most important factor. I exchanged my ratty jacket for a new one, and the material felt stiff between my fingers. Fresh socks were the ultimate luxury, so I pulled on two thick pairs atop of each other. I couldn't bring myself to give up my boots, so after I checked that my spare dice were safe in the heel, I laced them tightly. I rifled through the pockets of my old jacket and found my emerald dice before I flicked the playing card dismissively onto the bed. I transferred everything else into my new jacket.

It wasn't hard to find the dining room, because the maid reappeared as I opened the door and escorted me through the halls.

The dining room was as luxurious as the rest of the house, and as I walked inside, I realised I was the last person to arrive. My face heated at the attention my arrival drew. The chancellor and his wife sat at opposite ends of the table. Mikhael sat on his father's left, and Cyn to his right. Niklaus lounged next to his brother, Nash next to Cyn, and Helina next to them. There was a space left for me between Prudence and Niklaus. Not exactly where I wanted to be, but I didn't have any other choice.

Without comment, I slipped into the seat beside Niklaus, and his knee nudged against mine gently. I ignored it. He reached over the table for my glass, and his entire shoulder knocked into me. He filled the glass, put it back, and bumped into me for a third time. Again, I refused to acknowledge him. I didn't know what sort of game he was playing, but no game of his would bode well for me.

"Come on, love," Niklaus whispered.

"Fuck off," I hissed back. His mother made a sharp noise from the back of her throat. It didn't bother me; I was not a stranger to disapproval.

"I like that dirty mouth," Niklaus told me a beat later.

"Of course, you do." I rolled my eyes. "You freak."

He huffed out a laugh. From beneath my lowered gaze, I turned my attention to Helina instead. She kept her own patchwork jacket but was now wearing new linen overalls over a bright mustard coloured shirt. It suited her strangely, but after her earlier words, I couldn't bring myself to tell her as much. Maybe we had only been friends of convenience before now, and our friendship would not survive the devil's trials. Instead of acknowledging Helina, I glanced at Nash. He looked much as he had before, except that he wore a navy sweater. The absurdness of it all—that we were sitting at the Heira dining table—hit me hard, and I laughed.

"What's so funny?" Niklaus demanded quickly. He leaned intrusively into my space. I wasn't going to tell him, and thankfully, the doors at the end of the room opened so I didn't have to outright reject him. Servants carried in tray after tray of rich, hot food. A roast pig and more vegetables than I had ever seen. It was the smell that did me in, and my stomach growled in angry demand. I gasped and pressed my fist against my belly to muffle the sound.

Helina laughed at me, but Nash cut her off.

"I'm starving too." When I looked up, he caught my eye and flashed a smile. I nodded right back, not wanting to seem outwardly grateful. I was desperate not to owe anyone else.

The food piled up in front of us, but before anyone moved to eat, the chancellor began to murmur thanks to the devil for his meal. I barely paid attention to the words though, the entirety of my attention was focused on the meat-laden tray that sat directly in front of me. As soon as he allowed us to eat, I piled my plate high and shovelled it into my mouth with such haste that my chest burned with a searing pain. It was only when I slowed my pace and forced myself to chew and swallow properly that I realised Cyn wasn't eating at all.

There were three main archetypes at the table. Nash, Helina, and I, who were eating like we might never see food again. The Heira's with their refined pace and small bites. Then, Cyn with only their goblet. Dinner gave way to dessert, which was sweet and tart in all different ways. I couldn't get enough of the thick, red grapes they served, and they piled high on my plate. As they burst with juice on my tongue, I decided that this, above all else, was pure luxury.

Servants cleared away the food, and a heavy silence descended on us. Within a moment, I began to fidget with my sleeves. "It's time for the more exciting part of the evening,"

Cyn announced after they picked up their glass and drained it dry. "Your trial begins at dawn. The first sin you will face is…" My breath held for a second, and I wondered if there was such a thing as an easy sin to start off with.

"Gluttony."

My thoughts flashed to the full table of food we had just consumed. How apt. Admittedly, I didn't know too much about each of the sins, but I knew the basics of what they meant. My eyes flickered to Helina, but I dared not ask what she knew. Not here, not now.

When nobody commented, Cyn continued, "In every city, you will receive a trial. They will be delivered to you in gold envelopes like these." The doors at the end of the room opened again, but instead of food or sweets, the staff delivered a gold envelope to each participant.

It sat squarely in the place of my plate and shone beneath the chandelier light. I didn't touch it, even though Mikhael had already opened his envelope. Both of his brows rose as he read the contents within. I kept my head down and waited for instruction or dismissal.

"He is generous, and so you will start off with some of his blessed coins," Cyn continued. The maids moved forward again and dropped a small pouch on the table with a thud. This time, I moved quickly to snag the bag and loosen the strings. With my breath held in my chest, I tipped the bag upside down.

Fat, gold coins spilled across the table. My fingers pressed down on one to stop it before it rolled away. My eyes widened as I wondered if our food had been dosed, and my fingers began to tremble. I turned that errant coin slowly between my fingers. The mark of the devil flashed with each rotation. I had never seen so much money before—it was more than I had ever had to my name. I found myself longing to flash the coin at a card table. A grin pulled at my lips as I imagined the look on Boyd's face when I doubled it in a smooth stroke of luck. I started to quickly count out the coins, but Mikhael beat me to a total.

"Only ten?" he asked, his tone silky smooth but incredulous. A scoff followed the chancellor's nod, and the pouches of coins disappeared from around the table. Ten devil's coins would feed my family for a year or pay off my debts across town. I stacked mine into a towering pile and then pocketed them.

"Dismissed." The chancellor's voice cut through my coin-induced haze. His chair scraped against the floor as he moved backwards, and his eyes brushed over his sons in turn before he beckoned his wife and took his leave. One by one, we all followed suit.

My room provided a haven, and I turned the lock on the door once inside. I smoothed a hand over the blanket on the bed and dropped each of the gold coins on top of it, one by one. My eyes flickered to the window. I could climb out, find Boyd, and pay off my debt and run with the rest of the coins. My eyes dropped as I became conscious of the tracker around my wrist and cringed. Some sense of intuition told me this would be a very bad idea. So, I tried to ignore the call of the table and the coins that were begging for a game.

Instead, I turned the gold envelope over in my hand. My thumbnail slid beneath the devil's black seal, and I flicked it open. The words had no meaning, but I stared at them all the same. After five minutes, I became frustrated and flicked it onto the other pillow before I collapsed into the bed.

The bold, incomprehensible instructions haunted me, the script on the plain cream card offering no insight at all as I struggled to sound out the words.

STEPHANIE GLUCK

ENTER THE BELLY OF THE BEAST
ENJOY THE FEAST OF SAMAEL
CONQUER THE BATTLE OF ONE BITE
YOU HAVE ONE HALF CYCLE
OF THE MOON

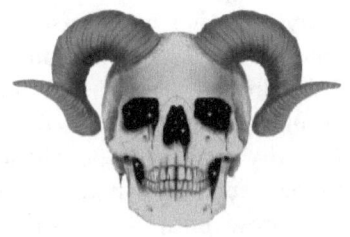

Chapter Twelve

I was awake well before dawn, since I never really went to sleep. Before the sun was shining, I was rifling through the wardrobes again, searching for a bag, a weapon, or anything they had left for me on this fool's quest. I had been plagued all night by images of monsters, and what I imagined the devil would look like. Violent images flashed behind my closed eyes until they had chased me from sleep. I died at the mercy of them, time and time again, so I stayed awake to avoid them. There was little of use hidden in the room, so I curled up on the floor with my knees pulled towards my chest until dawn crept closer. Then I slowly stood and looked around the room. I wondered if I would ever see such luxury again. Probably not, something told me that my life was about to get much worse. I turned away from the room and heaved a sigh. In three quick steps, I was at the door, and I pulled it open forcefully. The sight of the passive maid from yesterday, with her hand raised to knock, scared the living shit out of me. I yelped, but she didn't seem to mind.

"This way," she droned, then turned to lead me through the twisting hallways until I stood in the foyer again, where the others were awkwardly waiting. The chancellor and his wife were nowhere to be seen. Cyn hadn't made an appearance, either. The silence grew until it became apparent that there would be no fanfare and no farewell. The trials had begun, and now we were left to our own devices. Mikhael and Niklaus were, of course, the first to exit the house. As the rest of us followed them, I fell into step with Helina.

I bundled my hands into my pockets and fiddled with a devil's coin. I had spread the gold coins between my boots and my pockets—a distribution of wealth. As we followed them through the quiet town, I stared intently at the mouth of a nearby alley and wondered if I could turn these ten coins into twenty with one simple game.

The biggest double or nothing I had ever played. We left it behind far too quickly for me to act on the thought, but the adrenaline spike I felt still burned in my veins. It was Nash who broke the silence, twenty minutes after we had left the residential area. He waited until we walked along roads that were made of dirt, where the grass grew a little greener. "Where are we headed? I ain't been this far out before."

Mikhael glanced over his shoulder, and sharp surprise flashed across his face like he hadn't expected us to follow. "Glorae," he answered simply.

Nash scrunched up his nose and Helina scoffed. "But the task is in Gula!"

"Obviously," Mikhael sounded bored. There was little doubt in my mind that he thought we were beneath him. *Pretentious prick.* He turned on his heel though and set the full intensity of his gaze on Helina after her protest. She met it without flinching and leaned forward into his challenge. I began to wonder if her confidence was plain stupidity. Mikhael Heira was not a man you openly challenged.

"Do you know *how* to get to Gula?" he asked Helina. "Have you ever been before, locks?" His eyes fluttered over the long dreadlocks that she had piled high atop her head, and his nostrils flared. I expected her to say yes, even though I knew she hadn't been to the city before, and surprise registered on my face as Helina shrugged, all too nonchalant.

"Of course, I don't, but I know enough to know it's not to the east of Ilrea," Helina's voice held a grated edge that told everyone she didn't like not knowing.

"Well," Mikhael turned his back on us and continued walking. "It's a three-day walk to Glorae, and then each of the cities are connected by Charon's rail. Trains are the fastest way, but they only run city to city. That's how we're getting to Gula."

It was very apparent by his tone that his version of 'we' didn't extend to all of us. Nonetheless, we all kept walking. I didn't have a better plan and I was happy to follow him if it meant I stayed alive. Hours later, my feet ached sharply in protest of our journey. I had never walked so far in my life. As the twins powered on ahead, the rest of us fell behind. I was stubbornly unwilling to stop until they did, even though I was struggling to keep up.

"Hel," I whispered when Nash had fallen so far behind that we had some privacy. "About last night?" I broached, and she nodded.

"Don't worry," Helina responded. "You're forgiven."

Confusion ebbed through me. I hadn't thought I was the one who needed forgiveness. I was still considering it when Helina's hand dove into my pocket. I caught her wrist before she could withdraw it, the edge of my nails biting into her skin.

"What are you doing?!" I asked. She wriggled her hand, testing my hold.

"You owe me," Helina stated. I hated that phrase… I owed everybody far too much. I was drowning in debts that came from nowhere and extended beyond anything I could imagine. At the sharp edge of Helina's tone, I loosened my grip.

"You're a shit pickpocket," I told her and pulled a face. She just smiled smugly in return, all crooked teeth, and glittering eyes. She thought she had won as she showed me the single gold coin she stole from my pocket.

"There," Helina sounded as smug as she looked. "All squared away." It took everything in me not to remark that one devil coin was worth far more than what I supposedly owed her, but I needed Helina's help, so it was wiser not to argue.

"I'll take you along for my win," Helina hummed, all too proud of herself.

"You think you'll win?"

"I know I will."

If only her confidence could be poured into a bottle for everyone to share, Helina Archer would fuel an entire city. I pulled in a deep breath and decided to try platitudes and butter her up before I asked for help. "You'll be the first of us to win, Hel, how could my best friend not be?" A grin pulled lopsided at the edge of my mouth. It felt forced and fake, but Helina bought it. She smiled right back.

"So," I didn't wait any longer. "Do me a favour, Hel?"

The scepticism that twisted onto her features would have been laughable if I didn't need her help so badly… if I didn't already know that Helina would agree to help once she knew what I wanted. I reached into my pocket and extracted the gold envelope. It had crumpled, and I took a moment to try and smooth it back out, then I waved it in front of Helina's face. It took a second to force the plea from my lips, but I needed this more than I needed to avoid the sting to my pride.

"Read it to me?" I asked her softly.

As expected, Helina's eyes lit up. They flickered with a condescending glimmer even as a smug smile stretched across her face. She liked to be the one with skills that others didn't possess, and reading was the one she flaunted most often. Especially over me. Helina snatched at the envelope and turned it over. The wax seal had fallen away, so she pulled out the card with ease. Her face scrunched in a frown and her lips moved as she read each line.

"I thought yours would be different to mine," Helina commented.

"Oh?" I asked and blinked. "Why?"

Helina shrugged. "No reason."

It was a hasty answer and not the truth, but I didn't know how to call her out on it. I couldn't risk offending her before she told me what it said. I chewed on my lower lip.

"Okay," I relented finally and leaned over to stare at the crisp piece of card. I was already at a disadvantage. It was the first task, and I couldn't even tell what I was supposed to do. I would need to move forward in blind faith that Helina was going to tell me the truth. "But what does it say?" I pressed. "What is the task?" A huffy sigh rolled from my lips and I reached for the card on instinct. If she wasn't going to tell me, I might as well try my luck with Nash instead. Helina laughed and jerked the card out of my reach.

"Okay, okay," she agreed. Her breath was hot and ticklish against the inside of my ear as Helina whispered the contents of the card to me. I nodded after each line and tried to commit them to memory. As soon as she had finished talking, I snatched the card back and hastily shoved it into my pocket. I would have asked her what she thought it meant, had Nash not let out a long laugh from behind us.

"What secrets are you two whispering about, hmm?" He chuckled and tapped the side of his nose with his finger.

"Rumour has it that it's not a good idea to share strategy…" He pushed past us to catch up with the twins and I had to wonder if he was right.

We finally stopped at the mouth of a forest. The trees ahead were thick and dark. Once we set foot inside of the thicket of trees, it would be the furthest I had ever been from Ilrea. I dropped dramatically to the ground and stared up at the near cloudless sky.

"Finally," I grumbled. My body ached with exhaustion and my belly let out a loud rumble. I pressed my hand to my stomach in admonishment and then forced myself to sit back up. Nash was chewing on a long piece of green grass. Helina looked completely fine, and the twins held a large plastic bottle of water and a roll. I stared hungrily as Mikhael ripped the roll in half and tossed it to Niklaus. His brother caught it with ease and bit into it savagely. The bigger draw was the bottle of water, and I couldn't believe I spent so many hours awake, staring at the ceiling instead of stealing food and water from the house. I should have stolen a week's worth of food from these wealthy bastards. My eyes were glued to the bottle as Niklaus lifted it to his lips and drank deeply. The next minute, I realised he was staring back at me.

"Want some?" he asked so loudly that everyone else glanced at us. I wanted the ground to open up and swallow me whole. My throat constricted as I became intensely aware of how thirsty I was after walking for hours. I leaned towards him and it was on the edge of my lips to agree.

"It'll cost you," he added. A dimple appeared on his cheek as he smirked widely. I recoiled back from him. I couldn't stand the thought of owing him anything more. Not when it was begging, borrowing, and stealing that had ultimately got me into this mess.

My eyes darkened and I tried for a dismissive sneer. "I'd rather die of thirst."

He laughed, a low and throaty sound. "Have it your way." Niklaus settled back into the grass and devoured the rest of his roll without bothering me again.

We didn't talk—we weren't exactly a group of friends on a grand adventure. There was no awkwardness to the silence either. Instead, we all waited each other out to see who would move first. I pulled my knees to my chest and decided that I wouldn't be the first one to stand. Of course, it was Nash who broke the silence again.

"If the tales of the devil and his trial are true, then how about the Erlkangs?" The question hung grimly in the air. My head snapped up and I leaned forward to hear the answer. The Erlkangs were another of my childhood bedtime stories, but I hadn't heard of them in years. It took a moment to place the story, and when I did, my throat tightened. They were said to be demons of pure shadow, who hunted stray humans and stole their souls. They only hunted in the brightest part of the day, when the sun set high, and shadows scattered across the earth. The story had always said they were what happened to children who skipped out on early education to make Mason and I go to school.

I bit down on my lip, hard. "Of course, they're not real," I whispered, but my protest was mostly because I didn't want them to be real. Mikhael and Helina scoffed in tandem and then stared at one another.

"Octavia, when are you going to open your eyes?" Helina asked sharply and shook her head dismissively. "All of the stories are true. Just because the monsters don't show up in Ilrea, doesn't mean they don't exist."

I flushed, mortified, and realised that I should start considering every story to be true. The world was a lot bigger and scarier than my little piece of Ilrea.

"Actually," Mikhael interrupted. His voice was silky smooth. "The only reason they don't get into Ilrea is because the chancellor sends out hunting groups." He shrugged as if this should be common knowledge. "He's more than a pretty face or figurehead, you know. He's been keeping you ungrateful brats safe his entire life."

"I didn't know that," Helina's tone was sharp and argumentative. It held the implication that his words were a lie.

Mikhael rolled his eyes. "You don't know everything."

"I know more than you!"

"Do you want to test that ridiculous theory?"

Helina just glared, and I cleared my throat to break the tension. "Have you ever seen one, then?" I asked Mikhael. I was curious, despite the way my stomach turned in fear. "An Erlkang?"

"They're exactly what you'd expect," Mikhael answered after a beat. "Demons. They come out of nowhere, melt in and out of the shadows. One moment they're there, and the next they're not. They make this sound. It's the worst thing I've ever heard in my life. It's enough to make grown men cry."

"What do they look like?" I asked.

He hesitated. "Like a scribble?" I was beginning to think they weren't real and Mikhael was just pulling my leg. There was a hardness to his gaze that said otherwise.

"Like..." Mikhael continued, glancing at Niklaus for confirmation. "If a little kid picks up charcoal and draws a body by scribbling it side to side in fast movements." He moved his own hand in explanation.

"They're like that... harsh lines of flickering shadow, sharp edges..." he trailed off. "They have these eyes... deep yellow like a cat and they sort of shine in the dark. If they manage to bite you deep enough, they can take you." For a second, his face looked haunted.

"Take us?" Nash interrupted, and there was a hint of disbelief in his tone. "Take us where?"

Mikhael didn't answer straight away. He pulled himself to his feet. Niklaus followed suit and shoved the half-drunk bottle of water into his backpack.

"Into the shadows. They take your soul to the shadows... that's how new Erlkangs are created. Now hurry up, or we're leaving you behind." Both men turned and entered the forest without looking back.

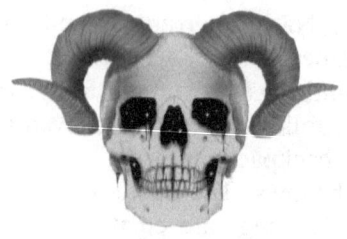

Chapter Thirteen

I jumped to my feet to scuttle after them and left the other two behind without a second thought. They could catch up, and Niklaus Heira was scarier than anything in the forest, so it was better to stay close. The devil I knew, after all.

"How do you kill them?" I blurted out once I caught up to them. The path was rough, and I stumbled through it. "How do you escape an Erlkang?"

How the hell was I going to survive if the silent, stalking demons of the shadows slipped from between the trees and came for my throat? The thought terrified me enough that I walked so close to them that I could feel Mikhael's body heat. Neither twin bothered to respond for a moment, they just shared a look. I had the feeling they were holding an entire conversation without me.

"Come on?" I tried again, the other two were gaining behind us. Niklaus was the first to turn, and both twins stopped dead in their tracks to face me. They were still as statues for a moment, and my throat bobbed with sudden nerves. I shuffled a step away from them, conscious of how close I had managed to get.

"How do you kill anything?" Mikhael asked me. His tone was too pleasant for such a horrible topic. His green eyes glimmered with a malicious edge in the low light. My lips parted and I shrugged.

"Can't say I've killed anything before." My voice was an octave too high. "Except maybe a roach."

"Somehow, I'm not surprised."

Helina bumped into my shoulder and sent me sliding forward. It closed the gap between me and the twins again. Niklaus' grin turned positively feral, and he withdrew a knife from his belt. It was double the size of the blade Boyd had wielded two nights ago. My breath caught in my throat as he leaned forward and twirled it between his fingers, but I held onto the idea that he wouldn't kill me until he claimed what he owed.

The end of the knife was cold against my skin as he suddenly pressed it below my chin. "You stab it in the heart, love," he whispered and trailed the knife down along the hollow of my throat. The grin pulled wider at the edge of his lips when I whimpered. The point of his knife pressed right above my thundering heart.

"Niklaus," I whispered—a warning and a whine.

"What are you doing?" Helina demanded shrilly, but she didn't make a move to stop it from happening. Nobody moved an inch.

Until Mikhael finally sighed. "Enough, Nik."

"What?"

"I said enough!"

Tensions relaxed as the point of the knife was removed, and Niklaus turned back to the journey ahead. He uttered under his breath to his brother.

"Just keep walking, everyone," Mikhael commanded the rest of us. He easily stepped into the position of leader and moved to the front of the group. We traipsed our way through the forest, and the further we ventured, the more I found myself huddling closer to the other participants. I couldn't help but think that a shadow demon was going to lurch from every twist and bend in the path. It left me jittery. At one point, I was so close to Mikhael's back that he let out a low growl.

"Chill out, Nox," he spat. "There's no light getting through to cast shadows this deep, and the sun is about down, anyway."

I craned my neck to look at the trees and take in the darkness he meant. He wasn't wrong. I forced myself to slow down and get out of his space. I fell into step beside Nash instead. We walked for another couple of hours before the twins slowed down again. Mikhael pulled us all off to the side. "We'll sleep here tonight."

I grimaced. "Sleep in the forest?"

He arched his brow. "Do you think you can keep walking all night?"

"No worse than a bus," Niklaus added.

I snapped my mouth closed and said no more. Mikhael smirked and looked startlingly like his brother at that moment before he started giving out tasks. "Nik, find something to eat. Nash, you're on firewood, I'll get the flames going."

Helina glanced between us. "What about us?"

Mikhael's gaze flickered; the corner of his mouth turned down. "You two just don't worry your pretty little heads about it," he murmured dismissively.

If Helina glared any harder, he would have burst into flames on the spot. She didn't like that answer, and I wondered if she might lurch forward and slap him.

"I'll help Nash," she stated.

Mikhael and Niklaus both laughed loudly.

"Want to come with me then?" Niklaus called to me. I scrunched my nose, my arms wrapped tight around my stomach.

"I'm sure you're fine on your own," I muttered, not meeting his eye.

"Suit yourself."

He disappeared into the trees, and I found myself a place to sit. I was less concerned about the equality of tasks than Helina had been. My arms wrapped around my knees, and I watched Mikhael as he started clearing space for a fire. After stories of demons and shadow monsters, I wasn't going to wander the forest alone just to prove that I measured up. The silence stretched out, and I watched him from beneath my lashes until I felt compelled to fill the silence between us.

"Does it suck?" I asked.

"Does what suck, exactly?" Mikhael didn't stop what he was doing.

"Being a twin?" I asked. "Being so identical to someone else? I just can't imagine it... the only thing I share with my brothers is our ears."

At this, he did look up, and my ears burned under his scrutiny. I unhooked a lock of hair from behind my left ear to hide it. He smirked when he realised why I had moved.

"We're not identical, you know," Mikhael mused as he took the nearby twigs and bundled them into a pile and brushed dried leaves into it too.

"Of course not," I scoffed, the corner of my lips curled upwards despite myself. "He's painted in colour, and you're as pale as a ghost. Beneath that, you look nothing alike." The sarcasm rang clear in my tone.

Mikhael's eyes narrowed and darkened. It took me a heartbeat to realise he was offended. It showed in the clench of his jaw, which made the lines of his face sharper. He didn't like it, I realised, when people looked at Niklaus instead of him.

"It's not that," Mikhael insisted as he reached for the brown backpack and started to pull out the contents. A bottle of water hit the ground and rolled away. Another roll and a handful of some sort of bars wrapped in thin plastic film were discarded beside him. "We're mirror twins."

The bottle of water came to a stop at my toe, and I took advantage of his preoccupation to slowly pick it up and twist off the lid. "What does that mean? Mirror twins?" I murmured before tipping the bottle upwards and drinking greedily. Water sloshed down my front at the desperate action, but I kept going until I was fully satiated. When I lowered the bottle, Mikhael was watching with nothing short of amusement.

"It means we're as opposite as we are identical. I'm left-handed to his right. My birthmark is on one side and his is on the other." I was on the verge of asking where their birthmarks were located, but he changed the subject before I could get it out.

"Of course! He doesn't pack devil-damned matches." Mikhael's nose flared with no small amount of indignation; his lips pressed into a tight line. "Can't trust Nik to plan his way out of a wet paper bag."

His abrupt bad mood was surprising, the first big flash of emotion I had ever seen from Mikhael Heira. I realised he was a far cry from the stoic statue that stood by his father's side through every unpleasant and harsh announcement.

"Here," I dug my fingers through my pockets and produced the single pack of matches I had taken from my home on the night I was kicked out. My fingers flicked the box of matches in his direction, and he caught them with one hand.

"Will you look at that," Mikhael chuckled. The match scraped down the side of the box, and fire flashed bright in his palm. "You are actually useful."

A strangled noise rose in the back of my throat, half a laugh and half indignation. Nash and Helina stamped back into view as that single flame smoked and grew. A fire crackled and I relished in the small amount of heat it provided. It took longer for Niklaus to return, and when he did, his fingers ran crimson with blood, but he held a freshly skinned rabbit for us to see. The mere sight of it made my stomach turn but I said nothing, not as he lodged it forcefully on a stick and threw it on top of the fire. We watched in tense silence as it roasted away.

After some time, it started to smell enough that my stomach roared a demand. I leaned back in wait and watched on as the two brothers muttered to each other in low voices. A smile stretched at the corner of Niklaus' lips and Mikhael grinned back. I wished I knew what they were saying. The bright laughter in their eyes led me to wonder if it was a joke. If I hadn't seen it with my own two eyes earlier, I would have never believed that there was a trace of envy between the two of them. Even now, I wondered if I had imagined it all.

"Sounds like it's done," Niklaus commented louder now as fat hissed and crackled from the open flames. He stood and stretched, his shirt rode up his stomach and gave up the first glimpse of the artwork painted around his hips. When he noticed me looking, he smirked, and my gaze darted away. The rabbit was pulled from the fire, and his knife loosened from his belt. Everyone watched closely as he carved the rabbit into sections.

"Ladies first." He brandished the hind legs at Helina and I. They disappeared from his grip quickly before the rest of the rabbit was divided between the men. I devoured my piece as quickly as possible, the heat of the crisped skin burning my fingertips while I sucked the juices off the ends of my fingers. It was only once I stopped and reached for the plastic bottle of water that Niklaus turned his attention back in my direction.

"Where did you get that?" His voice was low and threaded with danger. It didn't matter, I had already drained it dry. He was across the fire a moment later, that knife pressed back against my skin in idle threat.

"Aren't you a little thief?" His hot breath spilled against my cheek. I turned my head to the side, and my breath hitched in my throat.

"Well…" I stammered. Once again, nobody moved to stop him. Not even his brother attempted to deescalate the vengeful brightness in his gaze. It took a moment for me to find my voice. "More of an opportunist. Can't blame me if it just fell into my lap."

I hated the breathlessness that rang clear in my voice. The next few seconds passed tensely as I feared breathing too deeply. The edge of the knife was sharp against my skin, the edge of my life balanced in the movement of his wrist. It seemed like he would never back off, but his laugh flushed hot against my lips. For a second, I wasn't sure if he would kill me or kiss me. He pulled away and snatched up the bottle; the group seemed to let out a collective sigh of relief.

"Get some sleep," Mikhael bossed. "I'll take the first watch; we'll leave before dawn."

As much as I would have liked to protest, the length of the day and journey we had undertaken left me exhausted. I moved away from the rest of them and checked my pockets for my dice and coins. Once I knew they were safe, I curled up in a ball and passed out.

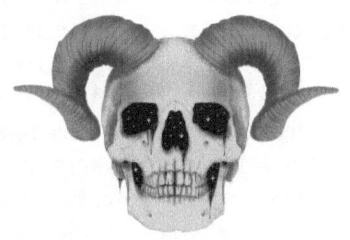

Chapter Fourteen

The screaming began in the early hours of the morning. It jolted me back into consciousness and I bolted upright. My heart hammered in my chest as the next scream echoed through the forest. Surprisingly, Helina was sleeping through it. Nash groaned, and when I searched for the twins, I found them both upright. Their green eyes were bright in the darkness, and I could see the shadowy edge of Niklaus' knife in his hand.

"What is that?" I asked them both, my chin jutting out as I peered up at the canopy of trees. It sounded like someone was wailing in grief, and it poured so solidly from their chests that it rattled my bones. It caused the hair along my arms to stand up on end. Intuition, which had never quite set me wrong before, whispered in my ear to get up and run, and get as far away from the forest and the screams as possible. It took every scrap of my will to remain in place and repeat the question.

"Harpies," Niklaus spoke softly, so as not to disturb the others, and then he craned to look above the treetops. "Winged creatures from the last world. They look like rotted bodies who can fly and have claws. You don't want to let one get near you."

I sucked in a deep breath. "Sure, that's not going to give me nightmares at all." It was Mikhael who chuckled in response. "What's the story with the Harpies? Erlkangs are the demons of shadow and these…" I questioned.

Mikhael hummed. "Harpies are said to be the representation of the devil's rage at us. Each time he loses it, a new Harpy manifests to spread his rage across the world. Load of bullshit if you ask me, though, they're just twisted souls rejected by the devil."

"Is there anything in this forest that won't kill us?" I groaned a moment later, then I crossed my legs beneath myself and struggled to get comfortable on the ground while we waited for morning.

"Besides the rabbits?" Niklaus asked, his green eyes secured on me with too much intensity. He seemed to be considering the question. "Probably just Nash."

It was a joke, but it didn't fall right. My eyes flickered to the sleeping man. His hands were fisted into his sweater, and his legs sprawled out in a way that took up too much room.

"I wouldn't put a coin on that," I told them. Sometimes it was the ones that seemed least hostile that were most dangerous of all. "He's probably deadly, too."

Neither of the twins answered. The screaming continued, and I dozed in and out of a fitful sleep, awoken by every new scream. It continued until Mikhael began to wake the others. I stretched, pretending I had been sleeping as well as everyone else, and then joined the back of the queue.

The further we trekked into the forest, the thicker the underbrush became, until I tripped through it and felt like every step took twice as long as it should have. In front of me, Nash was whistling a jaunty tune.

"Nash, that's a street walker song," I laughed, and he glanced over his shoulder at me.

"Is it?" He frowned and tested out the tune again. "No, it's not! It's a love song, right?" He whistled through the tune three more times. It got louder and louder until something flew at our heads.

"Quiet!" Nash barely managed to duck in time, and I lurched to the side.

"What is wrong with you, Mikhael? Are you always this grumpy?" Nash called out, his voice loud enough to send birds shifting out of the trees in disapproval. Mikhael turned on his heel and came stamping back towards us. He shoved past Helina on the way, and she barely managed to keep her balance.

"Shut up," he hissed.

He didn't have to raise his voice like Nash, nor did he have to lean in like Helina, or snarl like Niklaus. No, he projected a dangerous threat in the slippery tone of his voice and the inherent power that seemed inbuilt in him.

"It's daylight now. You'll call the—"

I screamed, a shrill noise, as I was launched backwards by my jacket. My feet left the ground and my back slammed hard into a tree. The breath rushed from my lungs, they spasmed painfully, and I crumpled to the base of it. I was completely winded and struggled to inhale as tears prickled harshly at my eyes. I had already felt damaged, but now I felt crushed. It took far too long for my lungs to start cooperating again, so I lay in the aged roots of the tree and could only watch on in complete and utter terror.

They slithered out of nowhere, like they didn't quite exist between this dimension and the next. Once, just the shadow of the leaves that blocked out the sun, and next, they transformed into horrible knights of darkness. When they opened their mouths, they flashed rows of sharp teeth and inhaled. The sound of it echoed through the forest as a death rattle. The perfect imitation of a human's final breath. Every hair on my body stood on end in primal fear.

I couldn't move, but even if my body had been cooperating, I didn't think that I could have forced it to go where I wanted. Instead, I watched in abject horror as they slunk through the trees towards the path. They disappeared and reappeared every few steps, growing larger with the new shadows that flickered from beneath the sun. The Erlkangs carved a path away from me and towards the rest of the group. It felt like they took an age to get there, but it had only been a few moments. After my heart rate slowed a fraction and my lungs seemed capable of drawing a full breath, I groaned and pulled myself shakily to my feet.

Then, I wet my lips, opened my mouth, and let out another shrill scream. I tried to emulate the Harpies of the night before. "Look out," I screeched through the trees. "Erlkang! Erlkang! Erlkang!"

The creature turned rapidly, those gleaming yellow eyes pinned straight on me, and latched right to my heart. My stomach dropped. It was coming. The death rattle that echoed out, as it leapt towards me, shook my very bones.

"Oh, fuck the devil and his mother!" I turned and fled. My feet caught on every stick and tree root as I stumbled through the thick and knotted undergrowth, with the singular aim of getting as far from the Erlkang as I possibly could. The next chilling breath proved that it was gaining on me, and I choked down on a sob. My cheeks were wet with tears, and all the pain seemed to have fled from my body as I ran for my life. I veered sharply to the left, and my foot caught on a gnarled tree root. My palms hit the ground first. The foliage rustled as I collided hard against it, and the air was ripped from my entire body for the second time in mere minutes.

"No," I groaned pitifully. The rattle felt like it was inside my soul, and if I survived, I knew that it would haunt every moment of my sleep until the end of my miserable life. I curled into a tight ball.

"Devil, make it quick," I sobbed to myself. A prayer I'd heard once before. "Devil, make it painless. Devil, lead me into the third world." It wouldn't be painless or quick, I realised, when my body lit up with trepidation. The rattle was so close that it nearly scrambled my brain. I realised that this end—my end—would be the most painful moment of my life. Out of sheer desperation, I rolled onto my stomach and tried to crawl forward.

Long, black claws raked down my back in a smooth swipe, and I wailed with pain. The cold morning chilled my back where my jacket and shirt shredded through. Hot pain seared down my spine where the skin shredded like thin paper.

"Just hurry up. Kill me," I wheezed; a sob caught right behind it. I cradled my head against my arms. "Just hurry up and *kill me* already!"

The Erlkang was so close. Its weight pressed against me, and I couldn't stop wondering how shadows could have weight at all. How these things had a presence, and mind enough to come for me. The claws scraped down my arm and pain flared brightly through me. I was roughly rolled in the roots of the tree until I was lying on my torn back. I wanted to block out the world, but I couldn't stay that way.

Morbid curiosity called my name as I peeked up and stared death in the face. Its eyes were voids, reminiscent of Cyn's, but they weren't the yellow of a cat like Mikhael had said. No, they looked like the moon during sunrise, luminous and burning. At the exact moment the dawn reflected off it. I thought they were the last thing I would see.

The Erlkang loomed above me and opened its mouth wide. I found myself searching for teeth in that void of shadowed darkness, but I couldn't find any. The rattle seared through me as it lunged for my neck. I braced for the end, but it didn't come. A knife slipped right through the creature, it slid through its back and pierced into its shadowy heart. It pressed so deep that it sliced against the skin of my breast.

I sobbed as the creature slipped into the shadows around us and real, human weight settled over my body instead. Powerful muscles caged around me, and I forced the words out again, *"Fuck you!"*

"As much as I want to take you up on that offer," Niklaus' now-familiar tone made me cry harder. "Thanking me might be a better start." His fingers brushed dark locks of hair out of my face and pressed against the pool of blood that welled on the front of my shirt. Belatedly, I realised what it was from.

"You stabbed me!" I knew I was being irrational.

"I saved you," Niklaus pointed out.

Carefully, he lifted his weight back off my body, grasped my hand in his firmly, and wrenched me back up onto my feet. I screamed with the movement, and it felt like every place the Erlkang's claws had been split back open.

"Forget favours," he whispered as the world swam with dark spots. "Now you owe me your life."

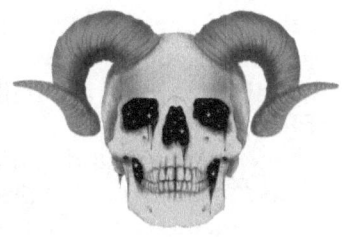

Chapter Fifteen

We were a bedraggled group. I could feel the blood dripping down my back from the Erlkang's claws. Mikhael's arm was bleeding and wrapped in a shirt, and Helina had a cut on her head. The most telling thing was that Nash had nothing to say.

"We can't stop moving," Mikhael announced, and there was a collective groan. I felt like I could sink to my knees and pass out for a third time. The darkness had claimed me twice while Niklaus had carried me back. I kept my eyes firmly on the back of Helina's head, and vaguely counted out the dreadlocks that had fallen free of her bun, to avoid looking at Niklaus.

"He's right," Niklaus added, just to back Mikhael up. "We may as well sit and scream out that we're prey if we stick around here. If the Erlkangs don't come back, the Harpies will want to pick the meat from our bones."

Mikhael jumped back down onto the path and pointed in the direction we had been heading. "If we keep going this way, we should reach the next town by nightfall. Better there than with the demons of Kaida on our heels."

That image left me feeling faint. I shifted my weight from one foot to the other and glanced down at the red smear of blood that stained my shirt. It lasted all of one day before I'd ruined it.

"Let's just go," I croaked out. "I feel like shit. I almost died."

Nobody commented on the fact that if I got any paler, I still could. I turned my gaze on Helina for a second and she stared right back at me. I could only imagine what my friend made of me, with my tear-stained face, shredded clothes, and the crimson blood that seemed to coat me from head to toe.

Helina's face twisted with sympathy, and she shuffled back to where I stood propped against Niklaus' side. A moment later, I flinched in pain as Helina wrapped an arm around my back to help brace me, and it pressed firmly against the open gouges in my skin.

"She's right," Helina agreed. "Let's get to the town and get some help."

The path through the forest was conquered at a much slower pace as we started again. We didn't talk about the competition, and we didn't talk about the Erlkangs. Instead, Nash took up a place as he braced my other side and filled the space in conversation by describing the best pictures he had ever drawn. He was a self-described artist, and after an hour, he revealed pockets filled with pieces of brightly coloured chalk. They were utterly useless for the competition, at least in my uninformed opinion, but it seemed to make him happy, and his prattling helped stop me from falling into the darkness again.

Every time spots danced in front of my eyes, I felt a bone-deep terror that more Erlkangs would form from them, and I would finally meet my end. As the night and the town came closer, the conversation turned to the inevitable.

"Enter the belly of the beast," Helina hummed aloud. "The beast could be any manner of things, don't you think?" Nobody answered, and so she continued, "It could be a Harpy, or an Erlkang, or a beast of old. It could even be the devil himself," she announced and squeezed my ribs for acknowledgement. I whimpered in pain; it had been a cruel move.

"It's not the damned devil." Mikhael scoffed from ahead.

With her free hand, Helina flipped him off. "You don't know that!" she argued back. Helina would argue her point until she was blue in the face, even if she realised that she was wrong.

"Oh, come on, the devil won't be showing his face at the first trial. It's a reward to meet him at the end," Mikhael stated pointedly. Now that he said it aloud, it made a lot of sense.

"How creepy would that be, though?" Nash jumped into the conversation. "How would you know if he was interjecting himself into the trials? Watching us the entire time?"

"Exactly my point!" Helina sounded all too smug. "He'd want to get to know us properly and form a basis for his judgement. After all, how's he truly going to know us when we get to the end?"

"I highly doubt it," Mikhael was quick to rebut.

"Yeah, well," Helina was undeterred. "You don't know everything either, Heira. I—"

"What do you think he looks like, hmm?" Nash posed the first question that caused me to stir. I lifted my head slightly. It looked for a moment like I was about to reveal the deepest secrets of the world's forgotten, like I had met the devil before Niklaus saved me from the Erlkang. Instead, I let out a whimper.

"Can we rest?" I whispered. Pain and exhaustion left me feeling heavy, and all I wanted to do was go to sleep. My body was falling apart—I was beyond battered and bruised. Both twins glanced over their shoulders, and Niklaus' brow furrowed. He murmured in low tones to his brother. Mikhael glanced ahead of us, down the path that twisted to the right, and said something back.

"One more hour and I think we'll be there," Mikhael said firmly, a tough rejection. One of Helina's sharp truths, even.

"Oh, come on!" Helina hissed, and I was beginning to think she just liked to argue with him. She said no more when he offered her one of those signature Heira looks. The subtle raise of his brow said that Helina wouldn't like the result of challenging him right then.

"Nik will take Octavia—" he stated firmly. "And we'll all keep walking until we're safe."

Niklaus stomped back through the undergrowth and lifted me out of Helina's grasp. He pushed me forward to inspect my back. "Not too deep, they've stopped bleeding at least. Will still need a healer, though."

I got the feeling he was telling Mikhael, not me. He lifted me like I weighed nothing, and he wasn't gentle. He held me tight and secured me against his chest. I jostled as he marched back up into place beside his brother, and I groaned at the movements. I didn't voice a protest, though, not when the alternative was dragging myself along for the next few miles or falling over completely.

The sun had disappeared behind the mountain peaks by the time the little town came into view, and the stars were out in full force once our weary group found the way to the centre of the town. The town looked worn out, forgotten in a way not dissimilar to Ilrea, but mostly in much better shape. The buildings appeared strong and freshly repaired, with a few notable businesses standing proudly in place. Mikhael assured us that this town would have somewhere to spend the night away from the beasts of the forests. The townsfolk seemed wary of our group, their eyes focused on the twins before they flitted away to avoid both confrontation and the hassle of having to help. It took a frustrating fifteen minutes before anyone would point us towards an inn.

Silence fell across the main tavern when we entered. I lifted my head from Niklaus' chest to gaze around, and I watched on as Mikhael approached the bar. The man behind it was cleaning a glass with a dirty rag, and he didn't bother looking up.

"We require," Mikhael turned his head to look at the bedraggled group of Ilrean's that stood behind him. "Five rooms for a single night."

The man behind the bar studied us intently. His eyes secured on the iridescent cuffs on each of our wrists before the corner of his lips twisted up into a mirthful grin. "That 'ull be two of th' devils coins, eh," he announced after what felt to be the world's longest pause. Mikhael nodded firmly, and the man leered back. "*Each.*"

"What?!" Mikhael spluttered. "Ten gold for the rooms?! Last time I ventured out here, it only cost me four pride-silver for two nights!" His voice was sharp with disgust, his green eyes narrowed on the man.

That grin turned vile, his dirty teeth flashing as the barkeep leaned forward in absolute challenge. "If ye don't like it, ye can carry on through, can't ye?" He knew we had very little other choice, though, especially as his beady gaze flickered over me. "Spend anotha night out in th' forest, can't ye?"

Mikhael's jaw clenched with irritation. Niklaus moved to stand beside him, although he was considerably less intimidating with me cradled against his chest. Still, he stood in solidarity with his brother as Mikhael slammed a hand down on the bar and put himself in the barkeep's face. Through the haze of pain and fatigue, I wondered if Mikhael would wrench him right across the wooden bar top.

"It will include a hot meal tonight and for the morning, baths, and fresh clothes." It wasn't put forth as a question, it was pure demand. Mikhael's eyes flickered to Niklaus and dropped down to me. "And a healer's visit, too."

The barkeep's expression didn't change, but his throat bobbed slowly before his jaw hardened and his teeth ground together. "Millie!" he hollered a moment later, and a woman scurried in from a door to the left. "This trial trash will be needun' rooms, some water, an' some grub. Get a move on, girlie."

She squeaked in acknowledgement before she fled from view. The barkeep set the glass down. It thumped against the wooden surface, and he nodded his head, teeth still gritted unpleasantly. "Ye be payin' up now, won't ye?"

Mikhael glanced over his shoulder, his eyes dark and unimpressed. "Two each, you heard him."

Coins were passed forward, and even Helina was too tired to argue. I struggled to try and reach into my pockets and found them empty. Panic flared hot in my veins—my chest tightening like iron bands had secured around my lungs. "Let me down," I wheezed at Niklaus. "Let me down! Now!"

Niklaus gently dropped my feet down to the floor without complaint, and I swayed on the spot as I struggled to get my bearings. Once upright, I searched through my jacket a little more thoroughly.

"Where are my coins?" I hissed. My eyes were wide with panic before I turned them accusingly on the tattooed man. "What have you done with them?!" I had lost one to Helina, but with two stashed in my boot, I should have had five in my jacket and two in the deep pockets of my pants. All the coins from my jacket were missing completely, which should have been unsurprising given it was falling off my body. I must have lost them when the Erlkang knocked me down.

"Give them back, Heira!" I hissed at him, wild and irrational, and his lips twisted into a grim line. His eyes flickered to his brother—another silent conversation.

"I didn't steal your damn coins, Octavia," he hissed; his face darkened like an oncoming thundercloud. "I was too busy saving your bloody life."

I scoffed and held out a hand in demand. Niklaus' nose flared. "Oh, how easily you've forgotten that, and after I carried you half the bloody way here."

Mikhael cleared his throat pointedly. His hand was outstretched. I frantically patted down the side of my thighs. The iron bands on my lungs loosened just slightly as I realised those two coins were there. *Thank the devil.*

"Here." I pulled them free and thrust them hard at Mikhael before my legs gave way and I leaned heavily on the bar for support. I couldn't quite conquer the rising anxiety that I had lost most of my lifeline in this foolish game. The ten coins seemed to bring life back into the bar. The barkeep swept them up before anyone could comment, and Millie returned with five long skeleton keys in her hand.

"This way," she stammered. Millie led us to a rickety set of stairs that rose to the next level of the building. Niklaus moved to help me as I tackled the stairs, and I shrank away from him. I brushed dark hair from my face and glared at him in warning.

"Don't touch me," I hissed and he raised his hands in the air submissively.

"Suit yourself."

My progress up the stairs was slow, and I could have wept when the first key was pressed into my hand. A big number three graced the front of the door, and I blinked at it before pushing my way through. Finally, I had somewhere to rest.

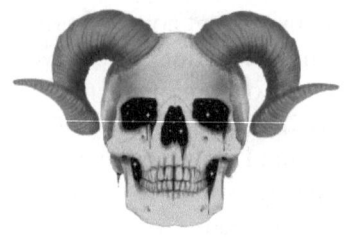

Chapter Sixteen

I t was nothing like the room at Heira House, which had been the world of luxury, but it was so far above huddling in the forest that I thought I could have happily stayed here a week.

My feet were heavy as I staggered further into the room and collapsed to sit on the side of the bed, exhausted and in pain. I barely noticed when the door swung open again. Two women lugged in a big, round metal basin before systemically appearing and disappearing with kettles of boiling water.

They filled the tub almost to the brim, and steam drifted lazily to fog up the mirror. I couldn't bring myself to move over and look. I knew I should bathe, but it felt like such a hassle, so I focused only on breathing in deeply and shucking off the remains of my jacket. Once it had been pulled into my lap, I could see that it had been shredded to pieces by the Erlkang's claws. I rubbed the coarse fabric between my fingers repeatedly as tears began to fall from my eyes and drip from my chin. I had always been an ugly crier, but exhaustion made my crying even worse.

I should have faced Boyd instead of entering this competition. With a little luck, I might have still been alive now, but it seemed unlikely. Today seemed to have proved that death had laid claim to my soul, and he was coming to collect. One way or another.

The door creaked open. Once again, I didn't bother to raise my head and note who entered. I kept my gaze firmly on the jacket, even as the floorboards squeaked under the visitor's weight.

"Chin up, Octavia." Niklaus' rough fingers gripped my chin and tipped it until our gaze met. For a moment, I felt like I was drowning in the green of his eyes. "Good. Now get up," he demanded in a firm tone that left nothing open for negotiation. His other hand cradled my elbow, and a moment later, I was swaying on my heels again, fighting for balance. A hiss of pain rolled from my lips. The jacket in my lap slid to the floor.

The sound jolted through the fogginess in my head, and my dark eyes dropped to the floor to study the tattered cloth.

"Why are you even here?" I whispered.

"Well," Niklaus' hands wrapped into the collar of my shirt, the muscles in his forearms bunched. A moment later, he tore it straight in half and pulled it off my back. "Family is everything, and if he wants to do this, then I'm here with him. Mikhael likes to win, and he likes to lead. If you let him, he'll take you all to victory. I'm here because I'll eviscerate anyone who comes for Mikhael." His voice had turned icy at the proclamation, stoked by an undercurrent of rage that seemed too big for the room.

His grip ripped easily through my singlet next, and I shivered in the cool air. I should have been more self-conscious,

I supposed, but the pain stole that from me too. He dropped to his knees and began unlacing my boots.

"I meant in my room," I clarified, my voice still sharp with pain.

Tears pooled at the corner of my eyes and spilled when Niklaus looked up. For the first time, instead of looking like he wanted to put me ten feet below the hard earth, there was a touch of concern in the twist of his brow.

"You're not very good at taking care of yourself, are you?" he commented, and forced me to lift my feet, removing one boot and then the other. The socks followed.

"What?" I asked, stunned. His fingers hitched into the waistband of my bloodstained pants.

"You heard me." He kept his green gaze firmly on my face as the fabric pooled at my ankles. Goosebumps prickled along my legs and I shivered.

"Your sense of self-preservation is high, but actually taking care of yourself... thriving? You're a bit shit at that," Niklaus continued. It wasn't a question this time. I stiffened, discomforted and offended. Suddenly, I was all too aware of how naked I was—every inch of myself bared in front of him. Even if he hadn't looked at me yet. My arms raised to cover my breasts. He laughed softly beneath his breath.

"Why are you here?" I repeated the question as he divested me of the material around my ankles. His grin pulled slowly at the edge of his lips, and that touch of feral reappeared in the gleam of his olive eyes.

"Just protecting my investment." One muscular arm banded around the back of my thighs. The next moment, I was hoisted off my feet, and the air rushed from my lungs in a squeak of protest.

"What are you doing, Nik?" I screeched, my fists flying to slam against his shoulders. It was wild and ineffectual, and he seemed completely unfazed by the blows. One bounced off the side of his head, and he unceremoniously dropped me straight into the water. I screeched again. This time, from the pain of the still-warm water against each of the gouges in my skin. When I surfaced, my hair stuck to the side of my face, and I glared at him with the inherent wish that the devil would appear and consume him whole. Spots appeared in my vision.

"You're an asshole!" I gasped.

"I know." He smirked and lobbed the bar of ivory soap at my head. It slipped precariously through my fingers and skidded to the floor. Both of us turned to look at it like it was the most offending thing to have crossed us all day. Niklaus let out a long-suffering sigh and moved to reach for the bar of soap.

"Like I said, when it comes to taking care of yourself, you're a bit sh—" As soon as his attention was diverted, I swept my arm across the surface of the warm water, a wide movement that splashed it all over him. Everything went still. It crossed my mind that he could try and drown me, and I was too tired to fight it. Then he laughed, startled but amused. Niklaus glanced down at his saturated shirt and shook his head. A slow grin tugged my lips despite my pain and how much I wanted to remain upset at him. He dropped the soap back into the tub and it sank to the bottom.

"Clean yourself up," Niklaus directed as he pulled himself back to his feet. He stretched slowly, his wet shirt sticking to his body. The white material turned transparent, and I could see the swirl of colours etched into his skin. My eyes trailed the now visible outline of his muscles. My lips parted as I followed the swirls and whorls of his ink towards the waistband of his pants. As he turned, Niklaus flicked the wet edge of his sleeve at me. I could see the stark outline of a skull imprinted onto his left shoulder. I shivered, tore my gaze away, and went searching for that soap.

"Healer is on their way," Niklaus commented from the doorway. "So, clean up and get ready for them." My nose scrunched up. I didn't want to see a healer, but the ache in my back and pink tinge to the bathwater told me it was necessary.

His head turned as he lingered in the doorway; his eyes seared right through me for a moment before he issued the final demand. "I'll see you at dinner."

By the time I felt clean again, the water was dark and dirty with blood, and it had cooled until it became tepid. It took effort to climb back out of the tub, each of my muscles screaming in protest, only exacerbated when the rough towel scraped against my back. There was a knock on the door, and it opened before I could speak up. The healer was a surprisingly young woman, who set herself up on the bed without speaking. She gestured for me to sit down, and I perched on the edge of the bed and let her wrestle the towel from my body. The healer didn't speak much, but she made disapproving clicking sounds as she inspected the bruises and gashes all over my body. When she finally met my gaze, her eyes seemed a century older than her body.

"Drink this now." She held up a vial of a pale orange liquid. I grimaced at the sight of it but nodded and tossed it back. It wasn't a magical and instant cure, but as she turned me roughly to the side and began to prepare a paste from various smelly weeds, the pain slowly ebbed away. By the time she had slathered it across my back and covered my wounds with soft pieces of cotton, I could barely feel anything at all. The healer washed her hands in the basin and spoke about the bandages falling off and the skin knitting back together. I didn't listen, at least not until she was standing in front of me again.

Her dark eyes were assessing me, and they saw too much. "Here," she said and took out a small glass jar from her bag. It was filled with a cream the colour of the underbelly of a toad. "It'll help with the bruising and you... I am beginning to think you're not olive-toned, just a walking bruise."

I flinched and unscrewed the top of the jar and sniffed at the contents within. By the time she left, I was still staring down into it. It took me a further ten minutes to start slathering it on each bruise I could find. She hadn't been wrong. They were everywhere.

I stared into the dirty mirror half an hour later and scrutinised my reflection. I could see my ribs where they pressed against my skin in an ugly attempt at escapism, and as I turned just slightly, I could see the edges of the bandages she had applied. The skin around them was pink and irritated, but I couldn't see blood anymore. Much like everything else, they'd close over and heal with time, but there would forever be a mark left behind. I wondered if I would have more scars than skin. With a soft sigh, I turned my back on my reflection and rifled through the clothes that had been left behind. Dark pants in a flexible material clung tight to my thighs and calves. Disappointingly, there were no pockets. Next, I found a men's shirt in blue—it was a button-down and two sizes too big. I pulled everything on and searched for my socks and boots by the bed. Armour was armour, no matter what it looked like, and I needed layers between myself and the world.

After I checked that my remaining two coins were in place, I crept out of the room and paced down the hallway. For a moment, I dwelled on the loss of my lucky green dice and the coin that had been with them. Luck hadn't been with me so far unless you counted surviving the Erlkang attack. At the end of the hall, I paused and peered over the rail at the room below. The main tavern bustled with activity, the ruckus of noise was loud and overwhelming. A fire crackled in the corner, and I wondered if the open flame could even touch the chill that settled in my bones since my life had flashed before my eyes.

At the back of the room, I could see my fellow Ilrean's, and they all seemed fine. It caused my stomach to twist. When I was falling so far to the back of the pack, was it worth staying with them at all? Suddenly seized by an overwhelming feeling of helplessness, I turned and pushed my way through the first unlocked door I could find so that I could buy myself a few more moments before dinner. Thankfully, it was empty, but it didn't take a genius to realise it belonged to Nash.

He had taken his piece of pink chalk and etched a rendition of the Penance Wall from Ilrea. Only he had penned names beneath each man. The sight of it gave me the shivers as I worked out the letters of my name beneath one in the middle and realised he had named each of us.

My boots smudged the corner of his artwork as I started rifling through the room, eager to find anything that could give me an advantage. The room contained no weapons and Nash had not been so foolish as to leave coins lying around. The only item of use that I found was a thin leather belt, which I secured around my hips, just below the base of the bandages. It was enough to secure the oversized shirt without exacerbating my wounds.

I slipped back out of his room and crept to the railing to peer down into the room below again. Nerves twisted in the pit of my stomach. I rubbed at the edges of the iridescent cuff around my wrist and wondered idly if it would have informed the devil had I died, an alert to come and lay claim on my soul. Since my only other option was hiding in my room, and the medicine had left me hungry, I descended the stairs.

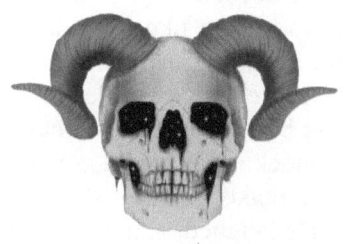

Chapter Seventeen

It felt like every man within a five-mile radius was shouting at the top of their lungs, like half the patrons of the tavern were fighting to be heard above all else. I found the place we had been tucked into at the back of the room. Our ragtag group were stretched across a long table, with a few visitors thrown in. Helina was deep in conversation with a dark-haired man who sat backwards on his chair from the next table over; and Niklaus had a russet-haired woman perched in his lap, her lips lazily tracing a path along his collarbone. My stomach twisted unpleasantly. With great effort, I managed to avoid looking at either of them. I pushed my way into a seat beside Mikhael instead.

"Are you feeling a little more human now?" he asked politely. One of his hands raised into the air to indicate that we needed another plate of food.

"As opposed to feeling like…?" I inspected the contents of his bowl out of the corner of my eye. It looked like some sort of stew, with chunky pieces of vegetables in it.

"Like Erlkang bait?" Mikhael's mouth curved into a smile. My lips parted in shock, and I stared at him.

"Did you just make a joke, Mikhael Heira?" I asked, a fraction too loud. He laughed, and it drew attention from the rest of the table. I flushed bright red when Niklaus caught my eye and arched his brow in a fluid movement.

"What's the joke?" Niklaus asked, and the woman on his lap pressed a kiss on the edge of his jaw.

"Nothing," I muttered, dropping my eyes to the stew as a bowl was set roughly in front of me and a spoon tossed down against the wooden table. I didn't like being seen, and after his comments from before, it was beginning to seem like Niklaus Heira easily saw right through my defences and straight into my soul. To avoid him pushing further, I picked up the spoon and shovelled stew into my mouth with gusto. The conversation picked back up, and I found myself watching Mikhael as he looked at the rest of us, his eyes moving between each person. I wondered if he needed reassurance that we were all there.

As I twisted the cool metal spoon between my fingers, I considered whether Mikhael and I had one thing in common in the soft thread of anxiety that tinged everything within our lives, and which oozed from the constant, alert tension of his body.

"Have you been to Gula before?" I asked him and took a cup from the table with both hands, drinking deeply. The liquid was sour and caused me to splutter.

Mikhael nodded slowly. "Once. That's where Nik got all his tattoos. We were there for days on end as they worked on him. It's a place of complete excess, you know?" His eyes slid to me and then he shrugged. "Think Heira House amplified by a thousand inside their woodland homes. It has absolutely anything you could dream of and more of it than you could ever need. They indulge in everything, they eat all night, and sleep and fuck away the day."

I couldn't fathom it, so I said nothing and drained the cup dry as quickly as I could. It didn't take long before I had another question though. "What about the Feast of Samael?"

Mikhael was silent for a moment as the edge of his jaw clenched and unclenched in a repetitive motion. "I don't have a clue," he said finally.

I stared at him for a moment as I debated whether to call him out on the lie, but eventually, I decided that I would have to trust that he was telling the truth. Nobody would want to give up their secrets and advantages in a game of life and death. With my back against the wall, I watched the rest of the tavern. As the minutes drifted into hours, our group thinned out. Nash disappeared first, followed by Helina. The twins only moved after Mikhael caught his brother's eye and jerked his chin.

"Right, bedtime for us." Niklaus drawled. As he stood, he lifted the woman with him. His hands clasped beneath the soft curve of her arse, and as he pressed her to his chest, she giggled loudly. When he stood, her perfume washed all over me, and I became conscious of how I smelled only of ivory soap and sadness. He was on his way out, one step behind Mikhael, before he twisted to catch my eye. I didn't want to look at him, not as the woman's hand snaked between them and the telltale sound of his belt unbuckling echoed between them, but I couldn't look away.

"Get some sleep." For a moment, with his bossiness, Niklaus sounded like his brother. "And lock your devil damned door."

My eyes flashed at his audacity and my nose flared with indignation. I wasn't the one inviting strangers into my room, although if the woman kept moving the way she was, I doubted they would make it to his room.

"I'm not stupid," I countered, and he smirked lazily.

"Aren't you?" he murmured before turning his attention back to the woman in his arms and carrying her up the stairs and out of sight.

"*Aren't you?*" I mimicked snottily beneath my breath. The empty bowl clattered as I shoved it backwards and scowled. I hated that he had left before I could get the last word in. I hated that, with those two simple words, I did feel stupid. I hated women with red hair most of all, right then. All my best judgement said that he was right, and it was better to sleep soundly to prepare for the night ahead, but something else had caught my eye. At the back of the room, behind the three bards and their fiddles, was a small round table occupied with men playing cards. The moment I spotted it, my heart raced because, finally, I had a solution to all my problems. I could turn two coins into twenty, and the trial would become considerably easier. In my experience, money was the one thing that smoothed the path of life, and the high of the win left life a lot more bearable.

I kicked back in my chair, unlaced my left boot, and pulled out one of the last coins. I held it like a lifeline and scooped up Nash's abandoned mug with my free hand. Once up from the table, I turned my back on staircases and proper sleep, and instead, ventured closer to the game of cards. It didn't take long to assess each of the men at the table. One appeared drunk with a hazy film across his gaze. The next was too confident and his tell was the soft turn on the edge of his lips as he thought he was winning. I couldn't make a thing of the third man, who was too quiet and kept his eyes down. The barkeep sat in place of the house, his thick hands dealing out the cards at a measured pace.

"Can I join you?" I asked and lifted the half-drunk mug of ale in what I hoped was a smooth salute. Suddenly, four pairs of eyes travelled up the length of my body and back down again. Each of the men took in the cuff on my wrist and smiled a little wider.

"Ye know how to play?" the barkeep grunted.

As I scanned the cards and the layout of the table, I had little idea of the game they played, but I was also a firm believer in a beginner's natural luck. Beyond that, desperation was what drove me to nod firmly.

"I'll catch on."

He seemed to consider it for a moment, and then nodded in a gesture at a nearby chair. I sat my mug down and dragged it over, the legs scraping loudly against the stone floor. Two of the men shuffled over to make room as I settled into place. They both smelled like ale with an undercurrent of sweat and dirt. I breathed slowly and deliberately through my mouth so I wouldn't have to smell them.

"Give me a quick rundown?" I asked the barkeep, and his black eyes glittered like beetles beneath the low light. Something seemed to amuse him, and I couldn't pinpoint it.

"Tavern Wars," he grunted. "One card dealt to each of ye, 'cludin' me. Ye win if you get a higher card than me."

I considered this for a moment. "What if it's a draw?"

"Ye can surrender and win half, or ye can go to war," the barkeep announced. When he grinned, I noticed he was missing a few blackened teeth. "But if ye go to war, ye got ta double up on ye bet."

Double up were my magic words. My chin rested in my hand for a second, and I attempted to calculate the odds. Fortune favoured the bold, and after the day I'd had, I was due a blessing from Lady Luck. A better blessing than a Heira twin stabbing me in the chest, at least. My grip loosened and I flashed him the single devil's coin. In response, his beetle eyes only seemed to grow brighter.

"This is all I have," I admitted, and my teeth scraped over my lower lip. Little lies hurt no soul, after all.

"Betting it all or breaking it down?" the barkeep asked casually, and the man to his left shuffled with impatience. A hissed demand to hurry up echoed from beneath his bristly moustache.

"Break her down," I demanded then, and tossed the singular piece of gold onto the table. It spun and was snatched up almost immediately. The barkeep turned to his box of coins, and within a few seconds, there were twenty-one coins sitting in front of me. A devil's coin broke down into three from each sin district in a mix of shaped silver and copper. They sat in seven little piles of three, and I studied them for a moment. Added together, especially with the value of the Envy and Greed coins, they came to the value of fifty-odd Pride coins, which was the currency we used in Ilrea. Two of those gold devil blessed pieces and I would have been squared right away with Boyd.

The barkeep leaned forward and tapped his fingers on the table in demand.

"Place ye bet."

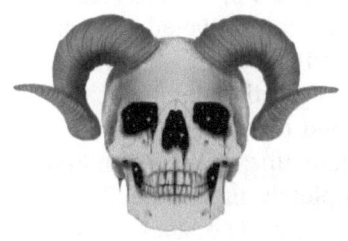

Chapter Eighteen

E
ach of the men shuffled coins forward. I considered what I had available and decided to work with Gluttony. It was our first task, and therefore, surely that alone would bring me a touch of good luck. I pushed three silver coins bearing the piglet insignia into place.

The barkeep moved with surprising speed and splayed four cards across the table before he flipped one for himself. My gaze bounced between my card and that of the barkeep. My pulse thundered and my mouth burned as I tried to work it out.

"Queen beats eight," I whispered, and then repeated it in a crowing voice as I realised, I'd won. The barkeep grunted and doubled my bet so that my stack of three sat six high. A grin had settled across my face, wide and smug, as I sat back in my chair and watched him steal the cards and coins from the other men.

None of them looked impressed. Next, I pushed forward three Envy silvers. The cards played out, and for the second time, Lady Luck smiled down on me. Her favour, I believed, was grander than that of the devil. As my bet doubled again, I laughed and turned the coin between my fingers. There was no better feeling than this; with adrenaline flooding through my veins, I felt completely invincible. There was nothing at all that could bring me down. The stack of Wrath coins went forward next, and once more, I found myself on the winning side of the cards. This, I decided, was a straightforward game and my best one. Confidence flooded my body as I leaned forward for the next bet. I needed to make money on the more valuable coins to really come out on top.

"Three snakes, all six lions, six pigs, and the goat coppers." With a grin, I pushed it all into the betting space, utterly certain that this would be the perfect win. This would be the absolute moment, and I would throw six wrath coins at Niklaus' chest in the morning and tell him to shove his favour where the sun didn't shine. Debt paid.

The cards flicked across the table, and realisation took a moment to dawn as it settled in front of me. I had received only the two of diamonds, and short of the barkeep drawing a two himself, everything beat that card.

"Fuck. Wait!" I breathed, but it was too late. He had already turned over his king and swept my bet away. My heartbeat in a solid and resounding thump, but it felt like it was lodged in my stomach at the loss. The feeling of my hair against my skin irritated me, and I blamed it for the loss. With a huff, I shook my head and tucked it behind my ears to keep it out of the way.

"Alright," I whispered to myself. "I can make it back." I knew I could make more than I had lost and walk away with a tidy little profit.

Easy peasy in the devil's speakeasy.

I pushed forward another bet, and another, and another as two passed us by. I regained a few coppers and lost many more. Adrenaline burned in my mouth like the tang of a Wrath-coin beneath my tongue, until the startling moment came. When I glanced at my stockpile, I realised I had nothing left.

"Looks like yer done," the barkeep crowed.

He sounded smug. My eyes flashed up to him. Anxiety had the rings on my fingers twisting around, again and again. I couldn't breathe properly. All my coins padded his pockets, and we both knew it. My gaze flickered desperately to that chest of coins. I needed it back, and I needed it back now. There was only one way to do it.

"Not yet." I breathed and reached to unlace my boot again. I fumbled with my remaining coin and then dropped it down onto the table with a light thug. "The whole thing!"

One of the other gamblers chuckled beneath his breath, and I heard the sentiment that I was a silly little girl. My knuckles turned white as I held my empty mug and watched the table over its rim. Cards skimmed across the wooden tabletop. My breath held in anticipation. The king of spades stared up at the space in front of me. Instant elation flowed through my body, and I relaxed. It was one of the highest cards and ever so difficult to beat. My chin lifted as a smug smirk rolled onto my lips. I looked down my nose at all of them.

"Thank you, Lady Luck—" I lifted my gaze to the barkeep, but he was smirking too, and his fat fingers stole away my coin as his other hand tapped at his card proudly. The ace of hearts. I swore beneath my breath.

"What a good night for us, boys!" the barkeep laughed.

Suddenly, all four of them were laughing, and my skin turned hot in response. I was ever the sore loser. Somewhere deep in my chest, my heart was shrivelling up in my chest as I stared at the red and white card. My body felt hot and cold all at once.

"You cheated!" I accused instantly and jumped to my feet. The chair tipped over backwards, and almost instantly, all four of the men were on their feet and turning in my direction.

"Dirty cheats!" I screamed in panic and outrage. Before I could think about it properly, I swung my arm and slammed the metal mug against the head of the man on my right. He swayed, grunted in sharp pain, but didn't fall like I expected, so I launched myself at him.

"Give my coins back!" I shrieked. My nails dragged down the side of his cheek, and the man with the moustache twisted. His clenched fist flew towards my face.

My cheek felt like it cracked on impact and snapped my head to the side. With a screech, I launched myself at him again, but before I managed to get close enough, I was wrenched backwards and landed hard on the stone ground. My entire body screamed on impact, and I struggled to get back on my feet.

Niklaus Heira stepped right over my legs and his fist slammed hard into the face of the moustached man. The man's nose shattered beneath Niklaus' patterned knuckles, and he dropped like stone to the floor. With rage burning deep in his gaze, and his jaw set in a hard line, Niklaus planted himself between me and the remaining three men. His fists bunched at his side, and the muscles along his back tensed. Dazed, I realised he was shirtless, and the front of his pants were still undone. He didn't seem to care, though. His muscles rippled with every movement, and my mouth went dry at the sight of him. Niklaus was prepared for a fight, and he was prepared to win.

"What are you—" I breathed in deep and scrambled to my feet. Almost automatically, I scowled at him. "I don't need you fighting my battles, Nik," I protested and tried to shove past him towards the barkeep instead.

With one hand and little effort, Niklaus pushed me back again. I staggered to the left—a move which roused one man out of their stupor. The man pulled a knife from the table and launched himself in my direction. Fear licked at the core of my soul, and I stumbled backwards to keep myself safe, but ended up tripping over my shoelace and hit the floor again.

Niklaus intercepted a second time. He growled and launched himself forward, his shoulder driving into the man's gut before he wrestled the knife from his hands. I watched on, wide-eyed and quaking, as the Heira twin stabbed the blade deep into the man's chest three times. Blood spilled forward, coating the attacker and Niklaus as the light went out in the man's eyes. He was dead before I could draw my next breath. Despite my better judgement, I pulled myself back on my feet, intent on searching the dead man's pockets.

It was Niklaus' fist curling into the front of my shirt that stopped me short, and the black look that he turned on me that stopped me in my tracks completely. I whimpered as the material pulled tight against my back, but he ignored my discomfort. The message was obvious—do not move. When his attention turned back to the barkeep, the fat man cowered beneath his fury.

"Tell me—" Niklaus spat from between clenched teeth, and hot fury laced his every word. "Why you shouldn't join your bastard friend."

The barkeep shook his head, his hands lifted in a placating manner, and they trembled in the air. The scent of hot urine wafted between them all, but the man finally found his tongue. "She attacked us first, I tell ye," he spoke. Niklaus looked less than impressed by this answer. "Gambled it all away, I'm tellin' ye. It's not up to me to pay out 'cause yer bitch got regrets or she gone an' made a bad bet. Tha' bitch lost her all fair and square, eh. Now she just be causing trouble because she lost."

Silence was a deadly thing, and it helped me realise that this was no longer going in my favour. I tried to edge out of Niklaus' grip, and his black gaze turned in my direction. I looked everywhere but his face as I attempted to struggle free of his bloodied grip.

"Is that true?" Niklaus asked in a furious whisper, and when I didn't answer, he turned to grab my shoulders. He shook me so hard that I saw stars.

"No! They just—" I still wouldn't look at him, and abrupt movement cut me off mid-sentence. Niklaus pushed me against the wall. Cold stone pressed sharply against my back and drew a panicked whimper from my lips. The sharp edge of his blade pressed beneath the curve of my chin again.

"Don't lie to me!" Niklaus hissed. "I just killed a man for you."

The world seemed to narrow into a pinpoint. I went to shake my head, but the blade pricked against my skin in a soft sting as he drew blood. I lifted my trembling hands and placed them against his chest to push out. The skin was smooth beneath my fingers, and slippery with fresh blood. My mind whirled as I tried to think of any lie, or any gentle half-truth that would get me out of this mess. My brain was working overtime and he could tell.

"Octavia!" Niklaus roared in my face, his breath rolling over my lips, and I squeaked in fear. Finally, I looked up from his chest and met his eye.

"Yes, okay, yes!" Tears spilled over, and the pitch of my voice rose shrilly with panicked consternation. "I lost all of it! He cheated though! He *cheated* and stole my coin!"

The knife, and subsequently, all the pressure of Niklaus' body fell away. I sagged on the spot and watched him wearily as he turned back to the barkeep. One of his hands dropped to his pocket, and my throat bobbed, wondering if he had a second knife there.

"My apologies," Niklaus ground out. It sounded like the words pained him. I gaped at him and brushed at the tears on my cheeks with the back of my hands. I found the nerve to stand up straighter.

"What?" I hissed at the back of his head. "Why are you apologising to him? I'm the one who got—" He offered me a glare so dark, it indicated that it was in my best interests to stay silent. I watched on in furious silence as he pulled a gold coin from his pocket and tossed it to the barkeep. The man caught it with ease.

"We'll be out of here at dawn," Niklaus assured him. The barkeep nodded, his beetle eyes flat as he picked up his chest of coins and backed away with his remaining conscious friend. As soon as he disappeared, Niklaus turned the full force of his attention back on me. I shrank beneath it.

"Nik," I began.

"Not a word, Octavia, I swear," he growled. In a swift and unexpected movement, he took hold of my waist and swung me over his shoulder. I slammed against his back and proved that I was completely unable to follow his command when I shrieked, "Let me down, you are brute. I didn't need you t—"

His palm slapped hard against the curve of my arse in reprimand, and I squealed and squirmed against the shock and the spark of pain. He'd spanked me, and I felt both angry and ashamed.

"I said not a fucking word!" Niklaus growled. His shoulder dug in against my stomach and jolted the breath out of my body with every step he took. He climbed the staircase and stomped down the hall—an angry man on a mission. At the entrance of my room, he kicked open the door and it bounced off the wall to come back to us. Niklaus dropped me unceremoniously onto my feet, and I barely caught the door before it slammed into the side of my body. He towered above me, his mouth a thin line of disapproval and his eyes glittering with a hardly contained blood lust. I wondered if he wished he hadn't stopped the fight.

"Lock your fucking door!" He hissed and I cringed.

"Nik—" I whispered.

"We leave in two hours," he continued like I hadn't commented at all. "I suggest you get some fucking sleep like I told you to hours ago." Niklaus turned to leave. My face scrunched up with anger.

"Like you were?" I couldn't help but snap at him.

"What?" Niklaus hissed as he turned back to face me. The scoff on my lips was as derisive as I could manage when my butt still stung with the pain of his slap.

"That harlot was half in your pants and wrapped around your hips before you left the table, so you don't get to preach the benefits of *sleeping*, Heira!" I spat. He braced himself in the door frame. His cigarette-laced scent was covered by the distinct aroma of drying blood. My jaw clenched as I tried to hold my ground.

"Jealous, love?" he asked.

"Of her low standards?" My nose flared and I stared resolutely at the flecks of crimson marring his tattoos. Dead men bled a lot. "Hardly." I stuck my nose in the air.

Niklaus' eyes travelled over my body like a gentle caress, and he shook his head. "You're more fucking trouble than you're worth, Nox."

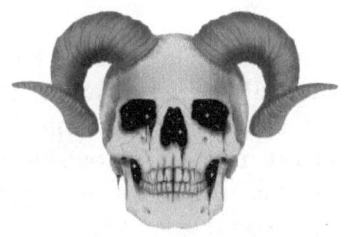

Chapter Nineteen

Regret was a pitiful feeling, and I was filled to the brim. The sun shined too brightly the next day, and lack of sleep left my head pounding to the beat of every step we took. I hadn't said a word to Niklaus all day, nor to anyone else when we had been ushered out of the inn before receiving our promised breakfast... before the sun had even come up.

Mikhael had protested until Niklaus mildly commented that they should all thank me for their lack of food. Beneath Mikhael and Helina's stares, I merely studied the hole in the toe of my left boot.

It was Helina who commented first, with a loud scoff, "Trust you to screw up a good thing!" She had shouldered past me, her body slammed hard against mine, and she stomped away from the inn.

Hot shame burned through me, so I kept my eyes on my feet until everyone had filed ahead and started to walk through town. The townsfolk watched us with suspicion and their accusation followed us right to the outskirts of the town. There would be a funeral here and it was all my fault, even if it had been Niklaus who killed the man. I had never been so relieved to see the gnarled forest in my life, never so keen to leave the comforts of a town behind us. I'd take the Erlkangs again over this feeling. We walked in the uncomfortable silence through the early morning hours and continued until the sun rose too high and too hot for the birds to keep singing. It was only then that Mikhael granted us a break.

With a sigh, I settled at the side of the path and re-knotted the strings on my boots. The others talked in low voices—a conversation that passed right over my head. From the corner of my eye, I watched the twins speak, and their eyes slid to me twice. The vein in Mikhael's neck stood out as he clenched his jaw hard. When both of their eyes flickered to me for a third time, I looked away. My throat burned with a needy thirst, but I refused to ask them for any of their water, and I lacked the foresight to pinch some before we left the inn.

"How much longer until Glorae?" Nash piped up from the other side of the road. In our three days on the road, he had lost some of his inherent good humour to fatigue. He no longer filled the space with whistled tunes, and the dark circles beneath his eyes had deepened.

It was Mikhael who answered. "We should only be a few hours off, if we can keep this pace up." He stopped in front of me and blocked my view of anyone else. I was forced to look up and acknowledge him.

"What?" I asked, and I knew I sounded petulant.

He held out the bottle of water. "Drink."

"Why?" I spat bitterly. "I don't deserve it."

"You need it if we're going to make the necessary pace." His tone was insistent, although the flicker of his eyes indicated that he agreed—it wasn't deserved. Reluctantly, I cradled the plastic bottle in my hands and took his offer. I drank until my body stopped cramping in demand for food. Until my voice didn't sound quite as raspy. All too soon, we were back on the road.

Glorae appeared first as shadows looming in the distance. Ilrea felt minuscule in comparison to the big city, and the closer we moved, the bigger it seemed to become. Until the five of us stood on the cusp of the city and gathered ourselves before we walked through a door in the glass outer wall. The wall was a large circular structure that was tinted darker than any glass I had seen before. Mikhael explained that the shade kept the Erlkangs out on the days that the mere presence of Pride himself did not. As I glanced down the wall, I realised it was just a sleeker version of our Penance Wall. Bodies hung on this outer limit of the city, suspended by white rope that circled their necks, and the sins of each man were etched beneath their bodies. My stomach turned and I focused on the city ahead to avoid thinking about it.

Glorae was a city of glass skyscrapers and mirrored surfaces. They stretched high above the earth, and on nearly every surface, I could see myself reflected. Not distorted like the polished back side of a spoon, but with startling clarity and such detail that I couldn't bring myself to look for longer than a moment. The last thing I wanted was to notice all my shortcomings. Helina, on the other hand, was enthralled. She stopped at almost every new building and adjusted her bun or her spectacles. She inspected her outfit, tweaked it, and smirked at her reflection. Nash and the twins couldn't seem to care less.

The second most obvious difference between our small hometown and the City of Glorae was the amount of people. The city was packed to the limit. People scuttled through the streets in groups, and each looked wilder than the next. It seemed like every citizen of this city wanted everyone to look at them, and I couldn't help but give in to their desire. They were brightly coloured peacocks, and I couldn't look away. As we crossed into one of the busy intersections, I found myself trapped within the mill of people. They bumped me from side to side like they all moved, firm in the knowledge that everyone else would notice them and move out of their way. I felt like I was dancing as I dodged out of the way of one person, and then the next, until it left me dizzy. When the traffic slowed and I had moved out of their paths long enough to look at them for more than a moment, I realised that each of these citizens wore a covering to obscure their faces.

Netted veils, gauzy cloths, and masks of intricately woven gold and silver obscured their eyes. Their mouths were no less of a feature, though, with bright and rich painted lips, plump and inviting. They were designed to be tempting, and to be seen. Even with their gaze hidden, I didn't think I could stop looking. The flow of foot traffic thinned further as people hurried this way and that, until I realised, I was now standing alone in the street again. My head turned as I looked for the familiar faces of my travelling companions.

"Helina?" I called. "Hel? Helina?!"

I spun a full circle and glanced back around the corner of the building I had just passed. My teeth sunk into my lip, and when I couldn't find the unmistakable stride and towering height of the twins either, my anxiety only intensified. To try and retrace my steps, I paced my way down the long road, but I had been too entranced by the people of Glorae, and now it was hard to work out where exactly I had come from.

The day was disappearing, and I was yet to find any of my odds and ends group. The idea that I was lost in this strange city left me unsettled, and so I skirted around the edges of buildings and tried to ignore my reflection as it followed me through the streets. Every time I thought someone was standing in the corner of my eye, it was my reflection that stared sullenly back. I was haunting myself. I turned another corner, and a familiar face caused my heart to leap.

"Nash!" I cried and lurched forward to grab a hold of him. The lanky young man crushed me into a hug that caused me to hiss in pain. Nash gasped in horror and let me go.

"Thought I'd lost the whole lot of you. There are so many people here!" Nash grinned. I grinned right back, flooded with pure relief.

"Where do you think the others went?" I asked him.

Nash rolled his shoulders in a shrug.

"I've got no idea in the world, but we'll find them," he sounded so optimistic about it that I couldn't help but nod. "Let's just take a look around first?" Nash suggested and laced his long fingers with mine. He moved with enthusiasm and tugged me down the streets until we found a splash of bright green amid the cool-coloured glass. A park sprawled out in front of us, an expanse of green with twisting brick-lined pathways, and large ponds throughout. The grass was as vibrant as the people who sat within the park. Both of us gazed at the space in awe. The path through the middle was lined with bright purple jacaranda trees which dropped soft petals everywhere.

"I could paint this," Nash sighed, his tone laced with unadulterated awe. "I ain't never seen so much colour in one place before." He tugged on my hand and led me forward as he strolled down the path to take it all in. Other people strode past us, their shoulders back and head held high. After a third person passed, I leaned into him to whisper softly.

"Why do you think they wear those masks?" I asked.

Nash shrugged. "I don't know."

"Me either."

"Why don't we ask them?" A grin—crooked and cheeky—split his face in half. He bounded towards the nearest person, and I had no idea where he found the energy. The question flowed off his lips before he had even said hello, and the stranger went still for a second. Her full bronze painted lips pulled into a mesmerising smile.

"Isn't it just amazing?" she asked us. Her voice was clear and regal. She turned her head again to give us a view of her cheekbones, which were illuminated with a strange glittering dust. The grand metallic headpiece she wore crossed over her eyes and sat like a crown atop of her head. Long golden spikes fanned out across the crown. Beneath it, her long vibrant blue hair tumbled down to the curve of her waist.

"Yes, it is," I found myself agreeing in earnest. I leaned forward onto the balls of my feet and realised I wanted to reach out and touch the pointed tip of those spikes. The woman hummed a throaty laugh, and it sounded almost like she was purring like a cat, basking in the face of praise. I couldn't help the grin that curled at the edge of my lips

"It is fashioned after the morning sunrise," she told us. "Am I not the most beautiful you have seen today?" Those full lips pouted, and Nash nodded his head in quick agreement.

"As beautiful as the sun and the sea," he told her quickly, and was rewarded with a proper, preening smile, her pearly white teeth flashed. Once the woman drank her fill of adoration, she leaned in close to us like she was about to share the power of a secret that only she knew. Nash and I both moved close to receive it and solve the mystery of the masks.

"Lord Pride demands we wear them," she whispered. I sucked in a sharp breath, startled to hear someone speak of an Angel of Sin so casually. I'd barely believed they existed, and this woman spoke of one with reverence.

"But why?"

The woman laughed, her voice slightly breathy, and her laugh inexplicably perfect. "Pride is the essence of loving oneself, adoring oneself, knowing that your worth extends above all others. Lord Pride decrees that for us to fully master our self-confidence and be truly prideful, we must be able to project and stand apart from all others, even when our faces are closed off to the world. Our pride must carry us through."

I blinked slowly, trying to reconcile what the woman said but also processing the adoring, near-infatuated way that she had spoken of one of the seven angels. "So," I frowned as she picked through my thoughts. "You've worn a mask your entire life? That must be a lonely existence." I couldn't imagine having never looked another person in the eyes properly... having never truly seen another person's face.

"Oh no! Devil above, no!" The woman laughed and I flushed at her mirth. "Lord Pride changes his mind every so many years on what best tests the pride of his people. For four years straight, we had to master our confidence and vanity without a shred of clothing at all."

Nash's eyes slid to me, he looked like he was about to burst out in laughter. The giggles rose in my throat as well. "Well..." Humour glittered in his eyes. "Thank you for your time, we best let you return to showing your beauty to the world."

He tugged me to the side and out of the woman's way, even though I was burning with a thousand more questions for the woman about the rules that the Angel of Pride set for them all. I wanted to know why anyone would subject themselves to such antics, and why she spoke of the Angel of Sin with such fervour.

Most of all, I wanted to know what he looked like—Lord Pride of Glorae.

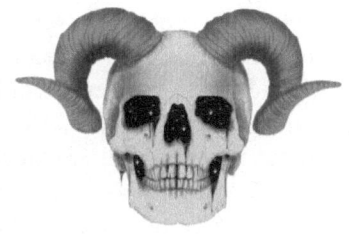

Chapter Twenty

Time slipped by so easily in the company of Nash Wickham. Every time I turned to speak to him, he had fallen behind and stopped to look at another passing fancy. He was easily distracted and captivated by everything. He wanted to see all the wonders and colours in the city, having spent over an hour by the pond in the park, determined to memorise each of the colours that flashed upon the scales of the luminescent fish in the water. As I glanced over my shoulder and realised, for the eighth time since entering the city, that Nash had disappeared, I let out a groan. My boots scuffed on the pavement as I turned and once more started retracing my steps through the city.

With Nash, we moved in a slow dance of one step forward, two steps backwards and one to the left. If we kept going at this rate, I would be back in the forest by nightfall and completely turned around. It took two blocks of exploring before I spotted him. On the opposite side of the street, Nash had joined a couple at a café with an outdoor dining patio. He sat backwards on a chair; his entire face lit up with fascination as he chatted animatedly with both. They basked under his attention. By the time I reached them, he turned his joyful attention in my direction. When he smiled so widely, it was hard to remember why exactly I had been mad at him. It was hard to focus on negative feelings when Nash radiated pure exuberance.

"Octavia Nox!" he cried out. "There you are!"

Like I had been the one who was lost all along.

"These are my new friends, Peridot, and Aliyah!" he introduced them both. Two masks turned in my direction. The man's mask was formed from a set of his namesake peridot stones, which were scattered across his eyes and glittered on his lips. The woman was wearing roses wrought of iron, which covered half of her face. I offered them a tentative smile.

"I need to put you on a leash, Nash," I told him by chastising him for running off again.

Peridot laughed and lifted his coffee to his lips. He smiled behind the rim of the cup before he commented, "How very naughty."

I flushed and protested, "Not like that!" This time, Nash joined in with their laughter and rocked his chair until the back legs came off the ground.

"Come on, Nash," I groaned, desperate for a change of subject. "We're supposed to be finding the others."

For a moment, Nash looked confused. "Says who?" he asked like the idea had never occurred to him. Maybe it hadn't, since he had been so busy experiencing the city instead of worrying about what came next like I had.

"Uh, me?" I was aware of how unsure I sounded in that statement. "Do you not want to find the others?"

"Why do you?" Nash asked and leaned back in his chair. Peridot and Aliyah watched the conversation bounce back and forth as they sipped at their coffee, but they contributed very little. I glanced down for a second as I considered the question. For lack of a good answer, I shrugged.

"I don't care if we never see the twins again, but I want to find Hel. She's my best friend."

Nash was quiet for a long moment, and I began to think he had fallen asleep with his eyes open. "She's a bad best friend," his words were gentle, like he was afraid that I would shatter when he delivered this news. It was not a revelation, though, not anything that I didn't already know. My chin stuck out as I drew my thick, dark brows together and locked my gaze firmly on him.

"I know, but she's the only one I have."

"Really?" Nash asked quietly.

"Well... yeah."

"Not the only friend that you have though, huh?" Nash added, his voice high. I thought about it, my eyes locked on him.

"No," I shook my head. "She's not."

He had become my friend over the past few days, despite us having little to do with one another. We were headed to a shared trauma. There was something in the way he stared back at me and in the slight tightness at the corner of his mouth that told me Nash was unhappy. I didn't have the gall to ask why in case I was the reason, but I wondered what he knew about Helina, and what had been said when I was out of earshot.

"Even if we don't find them," I switched tactics then, "we still need to find our way to Gula for the Feast of Samael, and we don't even know when that is! What if it's tomorrow? We can't be late, Nash."

This time, his new friends did interrupt, and they cooed like pigeons as they flapped their hands at me. "Oh! You're going to the Samael celebrations in Gula?" Peridot asked brightly "That's in five nights time. Practically forever away, darling! You have plenty of time to stay here and enjoy the sights of Glorae! We could take you to do something fun tonight instead."

I was shaking my head at the exact same time that Nash leaned forward and vehemently agreed. "We'd love to!" Nash's eyes shot up to mine. They were big and pleading, like a child who wanted sweets. "Wouldn't we, Octavia?"

The sigh that tumbled from my lips sealed the deal.

"That settles it!" Peridot slammed a hand on the table. He grinned broadly like we had made all his biggest dreams come true. "Tonight, we dance!" The man stood and offered a hand for Aliyah to rise from her chair. His eyes flickered over us quickly and lingered on a bruise on my cheek that I had missed with the paste before he clicked his tongue in disapproval.

"Don't worry, my dear." Aliyah smiled, and it took a moment for me to realise she was consoling Peridot not myself over the bruise. "It's nothing a mask cannot fix."

"Yes, yes!" Peridot found his exuberance again. He took one of my hands and reached for Nash to link us all together. "We cannot make you as beautiful as us. Nobody could manage it, but we will turn you into nothing short of your own perfection for a night dancing with Lord Pride."

The man tossed three silver pride pieces onto the table and gestured to us. It was time to leave.

Soon enough, we had stepped into a strange metal box which seemed to tremble and then lifted from the ground into the air. A strangled gasp escaped me as I clung to the sides the entire time it moved, certain that my stomach was to drop out at the movement. Similar terror tinkled in Nash's eyes. We were moving into the sky, and I just knew in a moment we had to fall through the earth, too. What went up must come down, and we were rising too high. The two of them lived on the thirty-fifth floor. I hadn't known that buildings could stack so high into the atmosphere. We swept into an apartment three times the size of any house in Ilrea, and it became apparent that while the buildings were mirrored on the outside, you could see through them from the inside.

Both Nash and I stood for a moment at the edge of the family room, with our noses pressed against the glass and breath caught in our throats as we stared down at the city below. From that great height, the people looked even more like ants in the way they scurried about. Once we could be peeled away from our horror and awe, Peridot disappeared in one direction with Nash and Aliyah took my hand in her warm grip and led me the opposite way.

"We'll start with your mask and dress you around it," Aliyah advised, never raising her voice too loud as she showed me to a large walk-in wardrobe. It was a large space with walls painted in a deep grey. The left wall held a large mirror with bright lights, with a silver vanity beneath it. A plush couch stretched through the right side of the room. In the centre sat a large glass case, the shelves within filled with velvet-covered spheres, and on each one, a mask was displayed. My eyes widened and a gasp left my lips as I looked them over, they were amazing.

"One for every occasion and one for every mood," Aliyah crowed proudly as she unlocked the glass door at the front of the case with a petite silver key. "I'm certain I have the biggest selection in all of Kaida, so please, pick whichever one strikes you." Indeed, she had masks in every fashion that I could have dreamed of, and some in styles I couldn't even comprehend. From the simple plain geometric shapes to veils and chains, and then an entire range of intricate headpieces. After five minutes of staring into the displays, I started fidgeting with a loose thread at the hem of my shirt. Everything in the case seemed too grand and too much for me.

"Well?" Aliyah prompted.

"I don't know," I confessed. "I've never dressed up before."

"*Never?*" Aliyah sounded horrified. Dark locks of hair fell from behind my ears as I shook my head. There had never been an occasion to dress up in Ilrea—most people only wore their very best to get married and then never dressed so finely again.

"I don't know what would look good," I admitted. I dared not voice the fear that nothing would look good at all. My reflection mocked me in one of the floor-length mirrors as a plain young woman with badly cut hair, ears that were too big, and a sloping nose that could hardly be called delicate or refined. The light scoff from Aliyah caused me to blush, and the woman steered me to investigate the mirror properly. I flinched when I managed a good look at my face—the healer's paste hadn't managed to get rid of all the bruises and I still looked battered.

"We have a bit of work to do." Instead of looking at my reflection, I stared at Aliyah on the surface of the mirror. If only I could look and be as confident as her. "But with my help, you won't even be able to recognise yourself!" I didn't know if that concept scared me more than anything else.

"When you look at them—" Aliyah prompted and gestured at the masks again. "Which one stands out the most?"

Each mask was considered again before I lifted a finger to point. "Actually, it's that thing…" Aliyah blinked but she didn't immediately laugh, which was a relief, and instead, she swiftly moved to the glass case in question and opened it.

"It's made of real humans, you know," Aliyah boasted and lifted the accessory from the cabinet. It was a corset piece constructed entirely of gold bone. It began with a tight circlet around the throat—a choker necklace. Long bones extended down and settled in the valley between breasts to emulate the sternum before they branched out and lengths of gold bone arched out in a copy of human ribs, circling the breast and torso before settling at either side of the spine. I didn't quite know what I liked about the piece, only that I couldn't stop looking at it, and Aliyah simply beamed. She uttered soft praise as she set the bone corset on the vanity and glanced back at the cabinet of masks.

"I know just the piece to go with this!" she cried suddenly and began to pluck at my clothes in a demand that I remove them so that she could get started. True to her word, by the time Aliyah was finished with me, I didn't recognise the woman in the mirror. I wore a black dress with a print on it. It featured a sharp square neckline, and the bodice sat so tight against my ribs that it was an effort to breathe. The boned material sat snugly against my ribs and pushed my breasts up to give the illusion that there was more there than I truly had to offer. The sleeves fell to my elbows, soft and fluttering with the hint of body, and the skirts flared out from my hips and tumbled right to the floor. The golden corset of bones had been fitted over the top of the dress. The metallic ribs curved over my breasts and tucked in at my waist until I could almost be mistaken for curvaceous. If I was anyone else, I would have called myself beautiful. The mask was another strange beauty. It was the front portion of a human skull, once again wrought from a real woman, and gleaming gold. It sat light against my face, and it took a while to get over the discomfort of literally having another person's face on top of my own. My stomach churned unpleasantly. It left my lips and chin bare but curved over the top of my head. From the top of the skull, two large onyx horns curled upwards and into the air.

They reminded me of the caricature horns Nash had drawn back in Heira House of the devil's features.

I studied myself through the eyes of the mask, which had been filled in with a glass that appeared mirrored from the outside but let me see out, not unlike the exterior of the building we stood in. My lips were full and stained with gold dust. My dark hair had been curled and brushed loose so that it no longer sat blunt at the hollow of my collarbone, but curled softly against the sides of my face and grazed the edges of my jaw. My chest ached as I stared at the stranger I had become.

"I look…"

Aliyah appeared by my shoulder in the reflection. Her mask was clever in that it was made of stained glass, and therefore, met all the requirements of wearing a mask at all, but every gorgeous piece of her face could be seen through the litany of colours. She was stunning with a mask, and even more so without it.

"Darling…" Aliyah all but purred. "You look like the devil's concubine!"

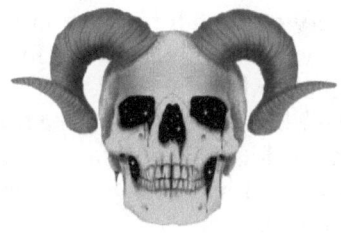

Chapter Twenty-One

We approached Pride Palace in a carriage drawn by black horses, on the whispered promise from our hosts that everyone who was anyone would make such a grand entrance. If they were to be believed, Peridot and Aliyah were certainly someone in the social scenes of Glorae.

I studied Nash from the corner of my eye as we neared the ball. His blonde hair swept to the side, and it changed his look completely—features which had once seemed gangly now appeared distinguished when his clothes fit, and his hair shone. He wore a suit that made him seem impossibly taller, with a button undone at the top and his tie conveniently missing. His

STEPHANIE GLUCK

mask was a triangle with points at each temple and the top of his upper lip. It was too big to read his expression behind it, but on top of the triangle, there was an image, a shifting roll of thunder clouds and the story of the fall from the last world. It showed an angel with failing wings. I turned all my focus back to Aliyah to avoid being caught staring.

"How did you know there would be a ball for us to attend tonight?" I questioned as I fought the urge to lick at my golden lips. They felt dry, but I had been assured that it was just a side effect of the metallic dusting.

"Oh, well," Aliyah tossed her long hair over her shoulder and giggled brightly. "Lord Pride holds a ball every night."

There was a beat of silence. "Every single night?" I repeated in disbelief. There was no way that this was normal life for the people here. I couldn't comprehend that they existed without the exhaustion from a hard day at work or grumbling temperaments from not having time to relax or have fun. It seemed it could be a lie that there was a ball to attend every night, and their enjoyment was encouraged.

"Of course!" Peridot nearly squealed. "It's not mandatory to attend, of course, but if Lord Pride has a good night, he often bestows his favour. New jewels, money, any sort of finery, and we wouldn't want to be the ones to miss out on these things," he spoke like it was all perfectly reasonable.

"Of course, being who we are, we often receive favour. Things that others don't, and that means we stand out more." Peridot and Aliyah spoke together, "That means we win!"

I blinked behind my mask and tried to control the lower half of my face so that my disbelief and the creeping edge of horror I felt wouldn't show. The carriage slowed to a halt, and where I might have questioned it further, the door was already thrown open. Peridot and Aliyah exited first, their hands offered back to help Nash and I out of the carriage. Nash was the first to accept. He took Aliyah's gloved fingers, unfolded himself from the seat, and stepped down. A heartbeat later, I followed suit, too scared that I would be left behind in the carriage. Peridot quickly swept me against his side, and somewhere in front of them, lights flashed in a manner that left me dazed and blinking. They flashed again, and again, and I couldn't quite focus from behind my mask.

"Smile for the photos," Peridot instructed as the flashing intensified. At Aliyah's whispered instruction, I closed my eyes behind the mask to shut it out and forced my lips into a smile. "We'll be all over the Daily Glory columns tomorrow, I'm certain of it!"

Then, he took Aliyah's hand and tucked it in the crook of his elbow. Nash moved to follow his lead and reached for my hand. Together, we walked the grand steps up to the sprawling palace and entered the residence of the Angel of Pride.

"Do you ever feel you've been thrown into an entirely new world and it can't possibly be real?" I whispered in Nash's ear as I twisted in my gold shoes to try and get a better view of the foyer we had entered.

"Definitely," he replied. "It seems so mighty strange that they have so very much, and my Ma is at home with barely anything at all." He sounded so sad that I found myself wanting to give him a hug but settled with a squeeze of his arm. His words had me wondering what my family was doing right now. Eating burnt potatoes and swapping stories of their day, most likely.

"It's one night," I said, unsure if I was reassuring myself or Nash. "Think of the stories we'll be able to tell when we get back to Ilrea."

Nash nodded, and neither of us voiced the thought that we may not make it back to Ilrea at all. It was better not to acknowledge that reality. As we followed our escorts through the foyer, we spilled into a grand ballroom, which pulled a gasp of astonishment from me.

The room was bigger than an entire house at home, and the roof was so far above us that I had to squint to make it out. The walls and the ceiling were all created from stained glass windows, and the light glinted against them. It threw colour in every direction and left each reveller looking like they were a glittering jewel in Pride's collection. A grand bronze staircase spiralled up from the centre of the room. I couldn't help but wonder where it led, and if anyone had managed to make their way to the top of it. The lighting by the ground floor was moodier and provided by flickering candles, which danced and threw shadows across the room. What appeared to be sculptures of men and women in gold, silver, and bronze occasionally shifted and twisted into a new position. They were living mannequins, and vainly exploited the best of their features to the adoration of the crowd.

The best of the best of Glorae were here, or so Peridot insisted, his twisted rabbit mask moving slightly with each overeager nod of his head. They would dance and dance until Pride noticed them... until they had earned the Angel's favour. When I asked how long that might take, I received a tight smile, and the reluctant confession that they had once danced and paraded through the room for forty-two hours on end before Lord Pride even looked up from his preoccupation, and his only comment had been that they needed to try harder to impress him. Apparently, many people died that night, and even more had been lost to the thrall of pride and ended up on the outer wall of the city. Aliyah stated that she had not attended a dance for a month thereafter because of the pain in her legs.

"Why impress him at all?" I asked Aliyah, and the woman offered a knowing smile.

"You'll see. Pride's smile lights up the entire world. Who wouldn't want to be touched by an angel?" It took all my willpower not to scoff aloud, and to hide my disbelief. I turned to face Nash and lifted my chin to look up at him. His mouth twisted into a wry smile as he took me in.

"That mask is awful, Octavia," he murmured the words as he took my hand in his again. "When we win this trial, I would like to paint it." His hand gestured to the length of my body as if to illustrate his point, and I flushed beneath the cool surface of my mask.

"I have no idea why you would want that," I muttered, uncomfortable with his praise.

Nash offered me a tilt of his head, and I would have given anything to see his full expression in that moment. "Octavia." He shook his head and tucked my hand into his elbow to advance on one of the living statues. "There is so much beauty in horrible things," Nash drawled. "You just have to pay a little bit of attention to what seems normal." I bit my lip, assuming the sentiment had been said about me, but then Nash smiled widely and continued. "My partner in Ilrea, Alby—" he added. "He's the most stunning person I have ever met in my life, but I bet you couldn't pick him in a crowd. Your eyes would just drift past him. But his beauty on the inside, Octavia, paints my whole world with colour."

I was left in stunned silence. "You left someone behind in Ilrea? Nash! But, what if the trial ends in…"

Nash's mouth twisted down, and I realised he had already thought this possibility through. His bony shoulders rolled in a shrug. "He's sick. Got the slow cough…"

I could only shudder, lost for words at that comment. The slow cough ran through our town every chilled season and took lives as it passed through. The people deteriorated slowly, over the length of the next year, but they always died. Too many of them died. "Nash, I'm so sorry." It didn't seem like enough.

His chin tucked into his chest and Nash shrugged a second time. "You know what Eternis has though?" he asked me but didn't wait before he answered. "No sickness at all. So, it must have a cure," Nash pointed out. "I'll win him a cure. Why not enter and try, and if I die along the way, at least I'll be seeing him in the next world. He's not long off seeing it."

With that said, he turned his attention away and studied the woman on the podium. Her entire body was painted bronze and covered in strange black spots. She smiled down at us and twisted into a new position to give Nash a better view of her full breasts.

"Aren't I beautiful?" the woman hummed, and he nodded sharply. A wide and placating grin pulled at the corner of his lips before he drew me away again.

"Not enjoying the entertainment?" I teased to break the tension, and Nash snorted gently. "Exhibitionism should be for beauty to shine through. But she's begging to be validated." He glanced around the room and then gestured towards the swirling mass of people who circulated the staircase.

"We could dance?" Nash suggested. There were already many people in the middle of the floor, swirling in wide circles to a tune that seemed to appear from nowhere at all.

"Ha." I shuffled uncomfortably. "I don't know how to dance."

This time, his grin seemed a touch more genuine. "Neither do I," Nash admitted. "But how hard could it be?"

Those, it quickly became apparent, could have been his famous last words. The two of us stumbled into the middle of the floor and instantly disrupted the general flow. People shuffled around us or staggered to the side when we didn't move as they expected. They fell out of step and had to find the rhythm again. Stubbornly, I ignored them all, and instead, turned nervously towards Nash. Since Aliyah had deemed it a 'walking hazard' to place me in heels, the thin, flat shoes moulded to the soles of my feet left me standing more than a few inches shorter than my dance partner. I had to crane my neck to look at him properly. The masks felt like more of an annoyance now that I couldn't see his face.

"So…" Nash surveyed the other couples to work out how we should dance. "You give me that hand and put your other one on my shoulder." I slid my hand up his arm and settled it on the very top of his shoulder, all while Nash placed a hand rigidly at the lowest rib of my bone corset. It felt stiff and strange to stand this way. We stood there for what felt like an age; Nash took his time to attempt to work out how our joined hands should sit, and then stared at me from behind his mask once we were in place. Neither of us moved, both unsure of how to enter the music or how to move within it at all. The twirling couples that brushed around us made it seem perfectly and deceptively simple.

"Alright," Nash pulled at the word like taffy, and I nodded. We both moved at once, and both sailed forward a step. My chest slammed into his, and then we jumped backwards, untangling from each other in an instant.

"Oof," Nash pressed a hand to his chest. The collision did more damage to him because of the bones that encapsulated me.

"Shit, sorry," I muttered, my chin tucked against my chest as I flushed red and attempted to find an excuse to flee. Dancing had now entered the list of my most undesired activities.

"Come on," Nash insisted. "Try again." Instead of touching my waist this time, he scooped up both of my hands and laced our fingers together. Then, as we stood an awkward distance apart—not quite close, but not far enough apart either—he began to shuffle in a small circle. Our joined hands forced me to follow him around.

It was awkward, and I wanted the ground to swallow us up, but he persisted and with time, I relaxed into our strange version of a dance. For every few shuffled steps he took, I straggled along after him, and while everyone else swirled in graceful arcs, our circle awkwardly became a square of sharp corners and squashed toes. I stepped on Nash too many times to count, but he didn't protest after his own shoes crushed my toes as well. Eventually, the embarrassment faded to exasperation, and then I was left with no other choice. I tipped my head back and laughed.

It was only when my voice bounced too clear and too loud around them that I realised the music had ceased. The skirts of other party-goers didn't brush against my sides as they moved too far into our space. Everything had gone deadly still, and the room pulsed with an inherent power that caused the hair on my skin to stand up on end. It was far too late before I realised the space to my left was filled with a dominating presence. My throat tightened. Nash glanced over, and a sharp inhale on his lips caused us both to come to a dead halt. I couldn't bring myself to look up and acknowledge what he had seen. My dark gaze latched onto my shoes, and I stared at them like they were the most fascinating items in the world.

A strange power flowed through the room, and despite myself, my head raised as my spine straightened notch by notch. My chin lifted and I caught myself looking at the curve of Nash's jaw instead of at the gold flats that connected me to the floor. I hadn't meant to look up, but the power had slipped beneath my skin, pulsed in my bones, and forced me to stand straight and proud. It was so strange and so otherworldly that I felt like I was going to vomit. Never had I wanted to run and flee off sheer human instinct so badly.

"Sir." Nash's drawl bordered on haughty now, and I wished I could see his eyes to know whether this strange power affected him too. I could only assume it did, even as he smirked lazily and lifted his chin in challenge, drawn up to his full height. I tried to steady my breathing. I stared at Nash's chin and refused to acknowledge the being by my side. If I did, I would have to admit that my night had surely ended, and we had been marked as intruders. My fingers trembled in Nash's grip, even as he seemed to understand what I didn't, and started to pull his hand away. He stepped back to put space between us.

"Leave." The single word echoed with such power that it left my heart trembling. I was once again reminded firmly of my mortality. A muscle twitched in Nash's cheek. He bowed in a low and sweeping movement and disappeared before I could protest. The presence beside me was overwhelming, but I determined that if I didn't look at him, it wouldn't become real. I already knew who stood by my side, and it made me want to crawl right back to the gutters of Ilrea.

"Dance with me, mortal." His voice was firm. It was not a question but a demand, and irritation sizzled under my skin at yet another man deciding they could tell me what to do. The same power that forced my spine to straighten encouraged the indignation I felt at the idea of being ordered around. I was worth more than that. My teeth grit together and the line of my jaw sharpened with tension as I drew on all my courage, and lifted my head to meet the gaze of the Angel of Pride.

Pride smirked back at me.

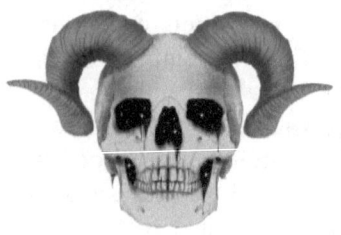

Chapter Twenty-Two

The mere sight of him took my breath away. I had once thought that Nash was the tallest man I knew, but Pride towered several inches taller. He was built of solid muscle and exuded sheer and unimaginable power. I looked him over, and the ability to speak was stolen right from my vocal cords. He stood tall, and perfectly tailored suit pants hugged his muscular thighs. The sleeves of the crisp dress shirt he wore were rolled to his elbows to display the tattoo of a peacock in a metallic bronze on his right forearm. The peacock seemed to shift and preen against his skin, and more writhing symbols of power shifted beneath his shirt, glowing in the light.

It was power contained in symbolism. The same way that he was raw catalytic power, the end of a human world contained in the appearance of a man. For the most part, he did, in fact, resemble a man, with broad muscled shoulders, a strong chin, and a slightly off-centre nose. His mouth was full, and it looked soft, designed to draw the world in. His blonde hair curled a fraction too long and fell over his eyes.

Even though he was given the title of Lord by his people, there was the unmistakable and otherworldly feature that proved Pride was not a man. Pride was not human at all. He was an angel, and he had dragged his wings with him to Earth. They arched high from his strong back, and Pride had flexed them out so that they swept and curled around the two of us. It offered the strangest illusion of privacy, if not for the whispers of the crowd from behind him. His wings were huge, with silky dark grey feathers that his power encouraged me to reach out and touch. Just to see if they would be as soft as they appeared.

He watched me stare at them, and they flexed just a touch, almost like this god amongst men was preening beneath my gaze. I swallowed roughly and forced myself to look at him, careful not to get lost in those luminous, endless eyes. It was his eyes that foretold the endless well of his power. They swirled with a depth and intensity of a world that did not belong to us. Those eyes had seen the last world, had been rejected, and that gaze had ravaged and rebuilt. This, I thought, was exactly how the Angels could claim souls. They wrapped them up in a single moment, when time and problems felt suspended and unimportant, and then fed them a look at the power beneath those luxurious faces.

It would be easy, I thought, to forget that these angels had come and ravaged Kaida to build their world. It would be so simple to take his proffered hand and step into his arms. My chin lifted stubbornly, and I prepared to reject the angel, when his hand shot out and grasped at my wrist. He lifted my arm and tapped a finger against the cuff I wore—the evidence of the contract that had me bound to the devil, and by extension to Pride himself.

"Uh, uh, uh," he admonished.

"Oh." I breathed, my eyes widening as I realised the rules of the game meant that I couldn't refuse a direct order from an angel, and Pride had not asked me to dance. He had commanded it. His grip loosened on my wrist, and he offered his hand for me to take, full of arrogant expectation. I wondered if it was a sting to his pride that I had to agree, instead of wanting to agree. I hesitated and inspected the tattooed bands on his fingers and the script against his skin, which flashed in that same bronzed metallic ink from his tattoo. Pride was truly something else. Nerves coiled deep in my belly as my sense of self-preservation screamed a demand to deny him, yet my fingers curled into his in a display of reluctant acceptance. Pride pulled me forward. His wings ruffled and tucked tight against his back as he let the rest of the world back in. Whispers and giggles flowed louder now, and I felt grateful for the mask as eyes burned holes into the back of my head.

"I can't dance."

His luminous eyes rolled haughtily. "Everyone can dance," Pride purred dismissively. "Especially with me."

"Liar."

His grip on my hand tightened—a warning. He used that gripped hand to pull me forward until I stood flush against him. I fought to breathe evenly as his power pushed in on me from all angles. It forced the curve of my spine to straighten again and lifted my jaw. Liquid confidence heated my veins until my eyes practically glowed behind the skull mask. In that moment, I truly believed that I belonged there and that I was deserving of every man and woman in the crowd who watched on. I was Pride's favoured… I was the very best. A rational part of my brain knew this to be false, and it whispered against my skin, but when the angel moved and his power pressed in against me, those doubts were silenced. His artificial hubris took over.

Pride would not let me cower away.

"Stand on my feet," he instructed. In blind faith that this would work, I did just that.

I worried as my weight balanced on his feet before a sense of foolishness swept hot through my body, and I remembered that he was not human. My weight was nothing to him.

"What now?" I whispered as his arm anchored tight around my waist and trapped me in place against him. The only way to freedom was to bow to his request and dance. I prayed that, in the end, it would be a singular dance and not days on end of attempting to impress him. Instinct warned me that impressing Pride might be the worst mistake I had ever made, and my life was riddled with mistakes and regrets in equal measure.

The angel started to move in graceful circles that sent us both spinning across the room. After a beat, his revellers joined back in, and twirls of bright colour flashed in my peripheral vision. They all danced a fraction too close in a bid for a moment of his attention, until it felt claustrophobic, and I realised how impossibly trapped I had become.

"It's rude to not look at your dance partner," Pride interjected. He sounded almost offended.

"Dancing," he breathed against my ear, "is supposed to be intimate."

I shivered, and Pride grinned broadly. I forced my gaze from the fixed point on his chest that had held my attention and deigned to meet his eye. Again, I felt like I was drowning, but I did not dare to look away. We spun and spun and spun. Through one song and into the next, until I lost track of time. Everything disappeared from my mind except the worlds that seemed to flicker in his gaze.

"Too scared to speak?" Pride enquired a moment later. I knew this was a question, but I could sense the oncoming demand that came with it. I bristled at the idea of losing my free will again and huffed out a sigh. The angels, I decided, were demanding bastards.

"I just don't think I have anything to say that you would find interesting," I told him, channelling Helina's signature matter-of-fact tone. Pride laughed. The sound was rich, and I could feel it vibrating through his chest with the way he held me tight.

"Why don't you allow me to be the judge of that?"

Behind my mask, I frowned. I hadn't expected him to push it, and since I had hoped to get through the entire trial without having to directly face one of the seven sins, I still had little idea of what to say. They were treated like royalty, born of unbridled power, and I was nothing in comparison. As his power pushed against me as a way of forcing an answer from my tongue, I blurted out the first thing that came to mind.

"I thought your wings would be white." Said wings rustled. Pride's mouth turned down at the corners.

"They were once, the purest of white you had ever seen," he commented.

"What happened to them?" I asked. The look I received in return was haughty and condescending

"The devil took me by the throat and launched me from the last world to this pitiful place." It should have been obvious, I realised, but I never claimed to be smart. My teeth caught my gold dusted lip for a second as I searched for something else to say.

Finally, I whispered, "He launched you. As in… he threw you all the way here?"

If nothing else, Pride may condemn me for my curiosity alone. There were a few moments of stillness, in which I realised that aside from their lazy and practiced rotations of the room, Pride was completely still. His chest did not move, and his gaze did not leave my face. It occurred to me that he didn't need to breathe air, eat food, or get sleep. He was no mortal, and he would exist long after my bones turned to ash.

"I'll indulge you," he said finally. His wings flexed and swept out. His grip kept me pressed against his chest as our rotations took the air. My entire body trembled with fear as we rose high and higher towards the stained-glass ceiling. I might get my wish to know what stood at the top of that staircase as we neared the top of the ballroom. He kept everyone else dancing, even from the skies. His desire and demand were to be heeded, and beneath us, his people were glittering in the light for his amusement. We hovered there, his wings shifting to keep us aloft, his arm banded around my hips to keep me close. His people had completed three rotations of the room before he spoke again.

"The devil passes judgement on your soul. He is but the judge, jury, and executioner of the last world, this one, and the next," Pride stated. "That much has not changed between the first world and each that came after it. We have long since moved from earth to earth." The idea that they had decimated worlds before us sat uncomfortably but Pride continued before I could comment on it.

"We, the seven angels, were something much different in the last world. We have not always been the image of depravity and desire." My throat felt too tight to force out my question, so I scrutinised the silver inked inscription along his collarbone. Words I didn't understand.

"What were you before?" I asked finally. Even as I feared that he would reveal that he had been something much, much worse in the last world.

"We were the seven virtues," he announced. Pride flashed across his features.

"What?"

Pride frowned. "The seven virtues," he repeated, and I shook my head.

"I don't know what they are…"

He did not look surprised, and his lips pulled to the side in patronising humour. "The people of this world are so finite, in everything, especially their knowledge of all things."

I huffed a foolish sigh and waited for my explanation.

"Patience, Humility, Kindness, Temperance, Charity, Chastity, and Diligence." He listed them all with an unexpected fervour. Where the humans prayed to these sins, he seemed to pray to these names instead, like they were everything. His eyes were hard, and his gaze pointed like he was trying to pass a message on to me, one that I couldn't understand.

"Which one were you?" I asked him, emboldened as his power pulsed through the room. He tightened his grip on me and we floated in a wide circle around the staircase until he pointed at an image in the stained glass. His breath was hot against the shell of my pierced ear.

"Humility."

I laughed. Almost instantly, Pride's face shut down. His lips curved into a thin line, and his eyes darkened with his stark disappointment at my reaction. I snapped my jaw closed as my humour died in my throat.

"That's enough for tonight." His wings folded in and we dropped from the air like stones to the bottom of a well. I clung to him and screamed, but there was no harsh impact against the ground.

The rest of the party still spun around us as Pride let go and I staggered back out of his embrace. His face darkened further and further, the ominous roll of an incoming storm. I stepped back again, suddenly nervous. "I said *enough*!" he roared a moment later, and the glass in the windows rattled within their fixings.

My stomach turned in place, leaving me breathless and queasy. My heart raced at his tone, and my body trembled. Still, he did not remove his gaze from mine, and still, I could not bring myself to look away. The music cut off abruptly, and the dancers gave us a wide berth.

"You should come and dance again tomorrow," Pride said suddenly. I shook my head and attempted to loosen the tension that coiled through each of my muscles in preparation to flee.

"Is that a command?" I whispered, cautious to find the loophole because he could keep me dancing, night after night, if he so wanted. Just as he did with the people of Glorae. No more than pretty marionettes to pass his time in this world.

"A suggestion," he clarified, and I relaxed fractionally.

I tried to stand tall and channel this god himself in the arrogant smirk I offered the Angel of Pride a moment later. I collected fistfuls of my skirt in my hands to hide their shaking and dropped into a curtsy that was vaguely mocking.

"Then I will regretfully decline, Lord Pride." I watched the shock splay across his face. He was a being not used to rejection. I hurried on before he could issue an order. "I have to meet one of your brothers. I have a task to complete."

I took three measured steps back as he watched on. Balanced in a precarious place and unsure if he would let me go. The attention of this angel could be all-consuming, and he could keep me if he so desired. He would tire of me quickly. I knew that, without Aliyah's magic touch, pretty dresses, and golden decor, I was much too plain to be of any worth to the Angel of Pride. Still, my heart hammered with fear that he would steal me away, right then and there.

Much to my surprise, he simply slid his hands into his pockets and inclined his head. Strands of soft blonde hair fell across his face before Pride nodded.

"You'll be back."

I grinned. It was a wide and sinful smile that felt so utterly my own. "Of course, I will," I promised in my next breath. "I still need to pass my trial of Pride."

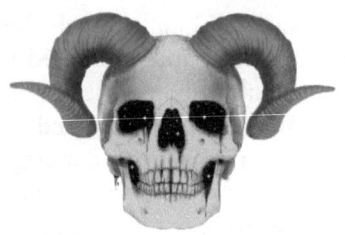

Chapter Twenty-Three

Peridot and Aliyah didn't let us leave their home until the midday sun had passed through the city. The two of them basked in the fact that I had been received with such favour, and the implications they believed that would have for them as the ones who introduced me to Pride.

"Are you sure you won't come again? Just stay one more night. You have plenty of time until Samael," Aliyah pleaded as I tried to push Nash towards the door.

"We don't have the time," I groaned and tugged on his arm as forcefully as I could. "We'll see you when we come back. *I promise.*" Both looked so crestfallen that I had to look away. I lifted an elbow and jammed it hard against Nash's ribs when he said nothing to help the situation. He blinked, and for a moment,

I thought he was about to agree with their new friends and make me a liar. Once a liar, always a liar.

Much to my surprise, he nodded. "We've got a train to catch. Half-past three you said it goes?" he drawled, and his eyes flickered up to their giant timepiece on the wall. Peridot let out a long-suffering sigh. We were the bane of his existence.

"Yes, yes. I suppose we will see you downstairs then. But you *must* visit us when you return," he instructed. "I don't want to hear that you were in the city without us, okay? There is so much more me and Aliyah need to show you!"

Twin smiles flashed across our faces. "Of course," Nash drawled, that slow pull of his words and half-sleepy tone instantly placating, and even I couldn't help but let the tension in my shoulders fall away.

Before we knew it, we were back out in the street. I huddled into my oversized blue shirt, which did nothing to protect me from the chilling wind and glanced down the street.

"Three blocks to the left, and then four to the right." I turned to Nash with a frown. "That was what they said?" He frowned right back.

"Four then three," he insisted, and I huffed.

I was more than sure that I was right, and he was wrong, but I bit back my desire to argue. It felt like Pride's power still settled in my bones this morning, and it left me wanting to argue and win every point.

"Okay, okay, let's just go..." We had to traipse halfway across the city to find the store of antiques, which housed stairs to the underworld of Glorae. Peridot had assured us that it was an inside joke since nobody in this city wore an outfit a second time, or kept their decor for longer than a season, so antiquities were the last thing that the people of Pride wanted. The store sold nothing and led to a network where you could buy every enhancement for your person you needed. It helped them transform into the most astonishing, eye-catching people they could be. It was from there that the train network ran. We walked four blocks to their left, and my feet ached. We traipsed three more blocks along. I could have cried when the store that had been described to us was nowhere in sight, even if I was simply relying on Nash to read the words above each of the mirrored storefronts.

"Seems you might have been right then," Nash admitted as he frowned at all the stores. "It was three and then four."

I straightened and smirked at him. Pride flowed through me, the aftereffect of the angel's presence all too real. "What was that?" I taunted softly as I revelled at having won a disagreement that he hadn't realised was occurring.

Nash frowned back at me. "This city is rubbing off on you. On both of us." That shut me up almost instantly, and I said nothing more as we retraced our path along streets without names. They all looked the same—grey and glass—which hindered our progress as we set a new path in a better direction.

"There it is," Nash cried after what felt like long, cold hours.

"Ann-tee-quee-tisss," he sounded out the word and I wondered what it meant. There really was nobody to ask with Helina missing, and as I peered into the mirrored windows, I realised there was barely anything inside the store at all.

"Let's go," I said to Nash and glanced over my shoulder to ensure that he was paying attention and hadn't wandered off again. He offered me a nod and strode ahead into the store. The presumptuousness that he went first irritated me, and I could barely squeeze through before it swung closed again. There were more items within the store than I thought. It was filled with tables, dressers, and other luxurious pieces of furniture, and all of them had been carved of wood and polished to perfection.

"They're gorgeous," I whispered, my ire at Nash forgotten as I ran my fingers across the smooth surface of a dark oak dresser.

"Yeah," Nash agreed with a hum. "A bit out of place though, don't you think? In this city where everything is built of metal and glass." He glanced at a nearby wardrobe as we passed it. "You can't see yourselves in these pieces, now, so there's not a soul in this big old city that would want them."

He pushed open a door to the back room, and I considered this for a moment. Antiquities, I decided, must mean a place for the lost. Lost beauty, and the entry to a place where people lost themselves. Lost, because that's what we were, Nash and me.

The staircase stretched down three stories, but when we emerged, I realised we were back in a place that seemed fitting for Pride and his people. The underground was a world of glass and mirrors, but here you could see through to see exactly what was being offered. Which was every form of body modification possible. I could not read a word of it, so I squinted instead at the images of the people instead—most of them naked, with certain features pulled to the centre of attention. A woman in a half face veil of ivory cloth approached us both.

"My dears!" she cried like we were long lost friends. I stared at her in complete lack of recognition and jolted in shock as the woman's cold fingers pressed against my cheeks. "Have you come all this way for some modification?"

"Uhh," I stammered, unsure of what to say.

"I could fix you right up now!" the woman assured me. Her hands dropped to my shoulders as she looked me up and down.

"We'll add a touch of curve to your hips, and of course to those breasts! My, you've got barely anything there. Perhaps, you'll need more than a touch." I raised my arms to cross them across my chest self-consciously.

"We could give you a few extra inches of height as well," the woman continued. "We'll have to do something about that nose, of course, although highlighting your cheekbones may just do the trick."

Somewhere behind us, Nash snickered. Mercifully, he wrapped his arms around my shoulders to pull me firmly out of her clutches. I stumbled backwards into his chest.

"Sorry, but we're just looking about, gathering some ideas..." Nash interjected, and I flashed him a grateful smile. "Unless," he paused, and my eyes narrowed. "I mean, you could really do with those few extra inches in height, you know..." he was teasing, I knew, but humiliation burned all the way up to the very tips of my ears. I jammed my elbow back at his ribs and let out an exasperated huff.

"No!" The word was so abrupt that the woman from the store stepped back and raised her hands placatingly. She smiled softly, her pink lips twitching.

"There's no shame in seeking perfection, nor for moving in the way which our Lord Pride desires," the woman said delicately, like it was merely the red in my cheeks and not the entirety of the shock I felt that kept me from agreeing.

"No," I repeated firmly before I remembered my manners. "Thank you. I... not today." I didn't bother to clarify that the real answer was not ever, especially when I didn't know exactly how this woman thought she might add a bit more here and there. I had never been curvy or well filled out—that required the luxury of food.

"Thank you," I repeated awkwardly and pulled away. My steps were quick and sharp as I avoided looking into any more of the stores. I didn't want to tempt anyone into another sales pitch.

As I hurried from the predicament, I raised my hand and traced the tip of my finger down the broad slope of my nose. Now that the woman had pointed it out, all I could think was that my nose was a little big and unsightly. I bit down on my lip and tried not to think about it. Instead, I focused on slowing my hurried steps until Nash could catch back up.

"Octavia—" He beat me by commenting first, so I cut him off.

"I am not that short!"

He laughed and glanced away; my nose scrunched.

"I wasn't about to say that you were, shortie," Nash drawled and lifted a hand to point to our left. "Trains that way though, if we don't want to be missing it." He declared that like he wouldn't mind spending another day in this city, lost to the things he had found here. Not for the first time I wondered how he didn't feel as uncomfortable and out of place as I did. I didn't want to stay, so I twisted on my heel and headed towards the train. If Nash didn't follow, I decided that was his own problem, and I wasn't going to spend more of my own precious time chasing him around the city. I had a feast to attend.

The inside of the train platform was cold. It was built of grey stone and utterly unimpressive considering the extravagance of the city. I peered up at the flashing sign above us and then dismissed it instantly. Even if I could work out the individual letters, I had no hope of turning them into anything of sense.

"City circle," Nash read slowly from behind me, and he pulled the words apart syllable by syllable. "Three, three, zero." It told us when the train left and nothing more.

"What do you think a train is exactly?" I asked Nash. He just shrugged.

I imagined it was something like the bus. Suddenly, Ilrea and my night spent on that uncomfortable metal seat felt so long ago. The last hour stretched between us as I waited, until finally, a great metal beast roared and thundered through the tunnel. It screeched loudly in violent metal pain and came to a halt in front of us. In my eyes, it did, in fact, look like many of Niklaus' buses, just pinned together like a giant metal snake. Each one was destined to help us find our way. The doors of one box opened and slid to each side at an incredible pace.

A bland-looking man stepped out first and hurried past us both like he was incredibly late for something. Two more women exited after him, their long fingers fixed their veils into place as they went. I wondered if they were returning home, or just visitors who met the cultural expectations of the city in a way that we had failed. A last man stepped just outside of the door and watched us expectantly. He had burnished skin and bored, dark eyes, a hunk of diamond glittering in his right ear. I caught myself staring at him for a moment, more specifically, his diamond, and I wondered if I could pick it straight from his ear.

Nash approached him first. "We need to go to Gula," he commented, and the man inclined his chin in a quick nod. He wasn't surprised, and I rubbed at the edge of the cuff on my wrist. It seemed like they made us identifiable and predictable.

"Five Pride silvers. Long journey ahead, but it'll be your fourth stop," the man sounded like he was bored of us, and of ferrying people out to Gula.

That was the exact moment that panic lit back through my veins. Train travel was for the rich, and that did not include me. All the confidence this city had injected into me disappeared with the drop of my stomach. I had never felt more myself than when I was faced with one more impossible situation and a high rate of failure, but this one I couldn't see a way to get through. Nash paid the man and ambled onto the train. He didn't look back at me and didn't notice the panic that flickered across my face.

I stepped up to the man and twisted the metal rings on my fingers around in circles. "We have to pay?" I asked him, a breathy thread of anxiousness in my tone. The man nodded and his eyes narrowed like I was thick. One of his dark brows raised as he waited for his payment, and I realised that too was threaded with a glittering gem. My heart squeezed in response, and my fingers skimmed across my pockets even though I knew I had nothing left. It was no small wonder that I had survived the last forty-eight hours without a single form of payment.

"But..." Shame burned hot through my body. "I've got nothing."

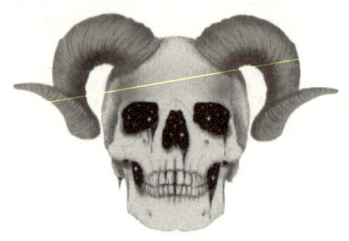

Chapter Twenty-Four

My saviour arrived in a flurry of gossamer pink, and a dress that looked like the translucent wings of a butterfly.

"I'll pay for you!" The girl screeched at the top of her lungs. "Hold the train, hold the train!" She ran forward as fast as she could, and the backs of her shoes slapped against the stone floor with each step. The girl had shopping bags piled into her arms, and her blonde hair flowed loose as she bounced up to where we stood. Her face was bright, and I had never seen someone who appeared to be so very alive. She was nothing more than radiant.

"Gula, right?" she asked and turned to offer me a blinding smile. "Two tickets, I'll just..." After fumbling awkwardly through her many bags, while I hesitated around how to help her, the girl managed to find a shiny silver purse and extract a handful of coins. She thrust them at the man, and he took them like they were poisonous. Then, she rearranged her hold on all her shopping and grasped at my wrist. The girl moved like a whirlwind and dragged me right onto the train before descending into the carriage.

Nash was already sprawled across one seat, and the girl piled all her bags onto the one opposite him. It was a loud process that had the blonde man staring at her like she was mad. Then she turned and it was my first opportunity to look at her properly, without her mountain of shopping in the way. She had pale skin with dark circles beneath her eyes, a button nose, and a very full, pink-painted mouth that held a glossy shine. There was something shiny about her in general, and I couldn't help but feel comfortable in her presence. Her smile lulled me into a strange sense of relaxation.

"I'm Phee!" she announced and launched herself forward. Her arms wrapped around me and drew me into an impossibly tight hug. "It's so, so lovely to meet you! Oh! I wondered if I'd run into anyone else doing the trial while I was out." Phee drew back and beamed, and it was then that I noticed the identical cuff around her wrist. She had painted her name across it in pink glitter.

"Oh." I breathed a sigh of relief. "That's how you knew where I was going?"

"No! Well… yes! But no!" Phee rambled happily as she dropped into one chair and kicked her feet up onto the cushion of the seat across the way. "I'm a participant too! But I'd have known anyway because I live in Gula, and we've known for weeks we'd be hosting the first trial." I nodded, wide-eyed and not quite following as I took my seat. "That's why I'm here, in Glorae, after all!" Phee bounced back onto her feet for a moment, she seemed to be a pint-sized ball of boundless energy.

"I had to get my lips done! Every eye will be on me during the Feast of Samael. I'm the only participant from Gula, so my lips have to be puuuuuuuurfect."

Phee leaned forward and pouted her plump lips for inspection. They just looked like unusually large lips to me, but she grinned in a manner so infectious that I caught myself grinning back. I glanced towards Nash and then back to Phee before I asked why her lips needed changing at all. It was at that moment the train moved. A great rumbling and screeching echoed as the beast awoke, and fear ran hot from my scalp right down to my toes.

"Oh, devil above." I breathed in panic, my eyes fluttering to Nash and spying a not dissimilar horror painted across his features. I gripped the sides of the chair and held on so tightly that my knuckles turned white.

"What's happening?" I gasped.

Phee, in response, let out a bubbly laugh. "Haven't you ever been on the train before?!" She giggled and then flicked manicured nails in our direction. "Oh, relax, relax! It's as safe as anything and the quickest way to get from city to city. Everyone uses it!"

While I supposed Phee might mean to sound reassuring with her boundless enthusiasm and flippant comments, it came across as condescending. It took a long time for me to relax back into the seat, long after we had pulled out of the station. I only truly relaxed once we exited the dark and claustrophobic tunnel and the world seemed to open in front of us again.

The train raced across the earth at speeds I couldn't really comprehend and seemed to hum beneath our bodies as the metal vibrated with power. Before long, Nash had his face pressed up to the glass window as he peered out at the world in awe. I couldn't quite bring myself to look away from Phee yet to truly appreciate the view. Once the blonde girl noticed me looking, she propped her long legs on the seat and patted the cushion next to her instead.

"Come sit over here, we have so much time to get to know each other." Phee laughed, and I slipped into the seat. She offered me a slice of candied lemon, and after placing it on my tongue, I cringed. It made the girl laugh again.

"It's much, much faster than walking, but it'll still be hours," Phee groaned, and I felt my lips twitch in amusement. Hours of sitting on a cushioned seat was far better than the hours of walking we had managed before. Phee started rummaging in a nearby bag, and then pulled out a few items. A moment later, she was pulling my hands in her lap and inspecting my cuticles with furrowed concentration. She lined up three bottles of colour by my wrist for inspection and then discarded one.

"I'm Phee, by the way. Did I tell you that already? My name is Ophelia, but nobody has ever called me that in the history of ever. I'm twenty! On the dot! My birthday was the fifteenth. That's why I joined; you know? I'm going to be famous, and I thought it's absolute kismet! I became eligible on the very day the trial opened... what could be a bigger sign from fate that I am destined to win?"

Phee rambled so exuberantly that I didn't need to get a word in edge-wise, and instead, watched on in fascination as the girl massaged my hands and then took a small metal bar to start scraping away at the sharp edges of my rough fingernails. It was only when the silence lingered that I realised I had needed to say something in Phee's pause for breath. I drew a blank, but Phee filled the space with an enviable ease.

"What's your name?" Phee prompted cheerfully a moment later.

"Uhh, Octavia Nox, and erm, that's Nash Wickham over there." Phee bounced her head like she had already known our names, like we had been best friends for a long time. It was a strange sort of validation considering that there was no way she would have heard of us. I swallowed and felt compelled to add something more. "We're from Ilrea... it's a small town," I admitted, and then persevered with a question to follow up. "What's it like living in Gula?"

Phee's head bounced up and her clear blue eyes glittered with unhindered enthusiasm. "It's the absolute best. I've lived there my whole entire life, and so have my sisters and my brother, even the ones that are all grown up. I'm the youngest, you know, and the first to do the trials, but really Gula is the food capital of the entire country." Phee beamed and switched hands, tackling the nails on my left as she continued to prattle on. "We have so, so much good food, and you really have to try all of it, there's always an occasion. We go out to celebrate, or just to try a new degustation menu. Then there's breakfast and brunch, and we must always have lunch. It's a horrid day if I can't have a small sweet for afternoon tea, too. Or, you know, I'd be ravenous by dinner. Then supper, and a touch of dessert before bed."

I wondered how Phee managed to remain so thin when she talked of eating so much. Her hips flared into supple curves that seemed disproportionate to the utter indulgence she spoke about. My curiosity must have shown, too, as my eyes dropped to the blonde's waist and Phee let out a bright giggle. She leaned forward and hid her lips behind her hand, like sharing a secret that Nash wasn't to know before she whispered, "We got it all sculpted right off. The plumpness? That's why we come to the Glorae underground. Mama's been taking us girls since we turned eleven."

Phee sat back and grinned then, her smile only faltering as she looked me over and realised that it was not a problem that we shared. For the second time in less than an hour, I felt self-conscious of my complete lack of a figure.

"That's... I didn't even know before I left Ilrea that you could even do things like that," I admitted to Phee, and suddenly, my entire world felt so very small again. There was no need for body modification in forgotten towns. Helina had been right when she said all the things that I knew could fit into a teaspoon, or half of one.

Phee pushed a long lock of blonde hair out of her face and nodded sagely before she picked up a small pink cube and started buffing out my nails. "It must all seem super-duper strange, but you'll get the hang of it, I swear! Especially because we're both in this competition. Trial besties, and I'll show you all of the best things to do in Gula and we'll explore the rest of the cities together." Phee lifted her face and it shone with open earnest. "You'll love it as much as I do, Octavia, I swear Gula is the best city on Earth. Except Eternis, you know, but that's... different."

We lapsed in calm silence as the train moved onwards. I occasionally added a few words to one of Phee's anecdotes, and when I looked up again, I realised Nash had fallen asleep. He was stretched across his seat with his feet hanging right off the edge and into the aisle. Phee followed my gaze.

"He's the most beautiful man I've ever seen," she admitted, and I blinked because we had just come from Glorae where the standard seemed to be for everyone to be astonishingly beautiful. Nash Wickham was strange and lanky, and the Adam's apple in the front of his throat seemed too pronounced. Beautiful wasn't a word I would have thought to use for him. He had said that beauty came from the inside, not the outside, and so I supposed in that way, it could apply to him, too.

I wet my lips with the tip of my tongue and snagged one of Phee's candied apricots next. "He has a partner." The words came out a little sharper than I had intended, and Phee sighed heavily like the fates were conspiring against her with this news.

"The good ones always do." She giggled. "He's much handsomer than the men in Gula; none of them ever get any work done."

I was rendered speechless for a second, unsure of how to tell her that Nash had had no modifications, he was just hungry. So, instead, I lifted my free hand and inspected my fingers closely before changing the subject.

"That man said Gula is the fourth stop, so where are we passing first?" I asked.

Phee bit down on her glossed lip in thought for a second and then raised her fingers to tick them off as she listed out the cities. "Glorae gives way to the wastelands, then we pass right beneath Desidia before we make it to the forests of Gula."

"Forests?" I whispered, thinking of the Erlkangs. My stomach twisted and the candied fruits no longer sat right.

"Yes," Phee enthused, and she missed my discomfort. "We're a woodland city. We live in enchanted oaks our entire city was wrought in the Acheron Forest."

I couldn't help the shiver that ran down my spine. "Maybe I should have stayed with Pride."

The tools in Phee's hands dropped to the floor, her blue eyes went wide. "You've seen the Angel of Pride? Ohmidevil!" She was nearly jumping out of her seat in excitement and snagged both of my hands in a death grip as she leaned forwards. I nodded, and Phee squealed again. *"Ohmidevil!"*

Before I knew it, I was faced with a pout similar to my youngest brother's and I laughed at the sight. "Please, please, please, Octavia, tell me all about it! I'll paint your nails while you do, I have a colour in here that would be so, so perfect for you! It's the best shade of cerulean blue." Phee fished it out of the bag and waved it around.

Laughter bubbled from my lips. It was a long journey and I had nothing else to do beyond telling stories. As Phee worked, I recounted the entire story, starting with how I had lost Nash at least six times that day. I was so engrossed in the story, and so flattered to have found someone who wanted to listen to what I had to say, that I barely noticed when we rolled to stop and departed again. The view was a speck in the distance by the time I remembered to look out the window and take it all in.

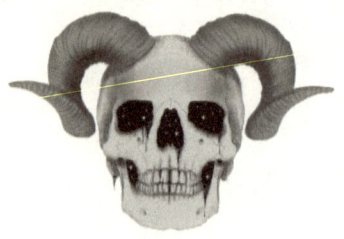

Chapter Twenty-Five

The sights of Desidia were lost to the dull, black brick of the tunnel that sheltered the passage of the train beneath the city. I fell into the seat beside Nash with a sigh. I had been hoping to find some sort of clue in the sights of the city as to how I could survive each round of the trial, but so far, I had no idea how to do that.

"We have to get ourselves through this one first," Nash said like he shared in my disappointment and understood exactly why my nose had been pressed against the cool glass.

"It's the first one," I forced false optimism into my voice and stretched out in my seat. My body felt tired, and the wounds down my back itched uncontrollably as they healed. "They would want us to pass this one, surely?"

My eyes flickered to Nash for confirmation, but he just frowned out the window. "Phee?" I called a moment later, and a mass of blonde hair flew up as the girl bolted upright.

"Sorry." I grimaced as Phee wiped drool off the side of her lips.

"Don't be! Don't be!" Phee reassured me, and her slender fingers rubbed at the dark rings that had smudged beneath her eyes. "What's going on? Are we there?" She stood and pushed herself onto her toes to peer out the window, only for her face to fall when she took in the empty plains on the other side of the city.

"Another few hours!" Phee dropped unceremoniously back into her seat and rummaged through her bag for a little mirror to check the state of her lips.

"Phee?" I repeated and sat forward as I pulled each of the silver bands off my fingers and massaged my knuckles slowly. My hands looked strange without them, with bands of slightly paler skin denoting their absence.

"Mmhmn?" the blonde hummed right back.

"What's the Feast of Samael?" The compact mirror in Phee's hand snapped shut with a resounding click. It clattered back into one of her bags a moment later, and the girl picked herself up to move into a closer seat. The fluttering edges of her dress caught the light in the window, and for a moment, she looked ethereal. It was an illusion quickly broken when she reached forward and picked up one of my rings to spin it on its edge.

"It's a grand festival we have every year. It's never been as special as this before, though!" Phee admitted, her rounded face was bright and her blue eyes wide. "Usually, we all go into the deep forest, and we feast for a week, and on each day, and at each course, we pay a tithe to Samael. We thank him for the world and privilege he has given us." She sighed. "Mummy says it's one of our most important rituals and it's what fuels Samael to give us the best of the crops and the creativity to make magic out of our meals." There was a reverence in her voice that spoke volumes of Phee's adoration of Samael, of her traditions, and her belief in fortune for the year to come.

I sat back and couldn't help but wonder if I had ever believed in anything with such complete conviction. A moment later, I realised I did, but it was usually mid-gamble when my blood pumped wildly and adrenaline drove me to bet again, make more, and stretch out my luck. My chest ached as I realised how badly I missed it. It had only been two days since my last bet, too.

"Who is Samael?" I asked to change the subject.

Phee blinked, and Nash snorted a soft laugh. Embarrassment flushed across my face when I realised everyone else knew. Once again, I was left behind. My fingers curled into my fists, jagged nails biting hard into the palm of my hand.

"Octavia." Phee pressed her soft hand over mine. With concentrated effort, I relaxed my fist. "Samael is what they call *him*."

"Him?" I was confused.

"Yes. *His* true name." The silence that followed was deafening. Phee laughed until she realised it wasn't a joke, and pressed her lips together tightly.

"The devil, silly," she whispered a moment later, and then grinned. "In Gula, we honour him by name, and his name is Samael."

"Oh."

"Yes, and just you wait until you see the feast we put on for him! It is no wonder he favours us above all others out of Eternis!"

I thought for a moment of the reverence I had seen in Glorae for the Angel of Pride, the desperate desire to win his favour, and frowned. "What about Gluttony?" I asked, and Phee stilled. For the first time since we had clambered aboard the train, she seemed discomforted.

"Samael's angel?" the girl asked, confused. Phee tapped a pink fingernail against the back of my hand as she considered the question, then she nodded. "What about him?" It failed to sound as nonchalant as she meant it to be.

"Why don't you honour him at the feast? Isn't he... sort of... the king of your city?" I asked as I attempted to piece the hierarchy together, compared to the city we had left behind. Phee's nose wrinkled, and her lips twisted into a pout. I exchanged a look with Nash, who was suddenly paying attention.

"Of course, we do, don't get me wrong," Phee said hastily. "The Angel of Gluttony rules all of Gula, and he is our most generous benefactor, but..." Her pearly white teeth scraped against her glossed lower lip; a shiver seemed to track down her spine. "He is often busy. Mummy says he is consumed with his place in the world, and it is Samael who favours us more. Gluttony is... well, I suppose you'll both see!" Phee said this all in a rush, and then smiled blindingly in her attempt to move on. "Can't go spoiling the surprise now, can I?"

"Of course not," I muttered and slumped back into my chair. I slid each of my rings back into place and flexed my fingers. Somehow, I felt more confused now than I had before. Phee's stories hadn't helped at all. The sun sank between the mountains, and the journey was a quiet one. Nash was snoring softly within minutes, and I watched below lowered lashes until Phee's breathing evened out too. I watched her as the time ticked by and the darkness settled outside the window until temptation called my name.

With a soft groan, I shifted in my seat and stretched my arms above my head. I watched the other two carefully and picked my way out of the seat to step over Nash's long legs. He murmured in his sleep when I knocked his knee, and I winced.

"Bathroom," I lied and edged my way out of the seats and into the aisle. Phee's belongings spread from one side of the carriage to the other. I glanced wearily back at my new friends and began rifling through the bags. I pushed aside brightly coloured dresses, and a pair of shoes, and then moved on. By the fifth bag, I found the shiny silver purse that Phee had flashed before paying for the train fare. My eyes flickered nervously over to Phee to check that she was still asleep. Trepidation curled down my spine as I pushed my fingernail beneath the clasp and pulled it open. It snicked as it let go and jangled softly as coins shuffled around. My heart squeezed and began to race. Her purse was littered with coins of all denominations, and I scooped out a handful. When I opened my fist, it was a mix of silver, bronze, and gold. Carefully, I glanced back over the Phee, sure I was about to get caught. It was so tempting to take the entire fistful, but I recalled Phee's reverence for the devil. She would notice, I realised, if the devil-branded gold disappeared. So, instead, I picked out a fistful of the plentiful silver and gently returned the rest to her purse. The train shuddered, and I gasped in alarm. I quickly closed the little silver purse and put it back where I had found it before splitting the fistful of silver into two parts and dropping the coins into my boots.

When I stood, my feet ached in protest as the coins slipped and I had to walk on top of them, but I swallowed my discomfort. I took slow and measured steps to make sure they didn't jingle as I moved before I returned to my chair and laid my head against the window. It took a long time for my heart to settle.

I pretended to be asleep as the train shuddered to a halt during a giant forest. I kept my breathing even, although I was too on edge to get any rest. My mind played out a thousand scenarios of Phee calling me a thief, or Nash quietly murmuring that he had seen me and demanding I give the coins back. So, I closed my eyes and reassured myself that it was a victimless crime because Phee already had so many coins, and I had none. I told myself that she wouldn't miss them, anyway.

I didn't move, not until Phee placed a hand on my shoulder and shook gently. I blinked up at her, and she beamed back. It was the sight of her smile that relaxed me.

"Wakey, wakey, rise and shine, sleepyhead," Phee crowed and started gathering up all her bits and pieces. "We're here!"

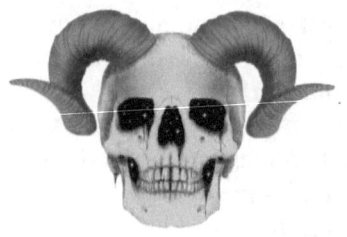

Chapter Twenty-Six

The sight of the forest lodged my heart firmly in my throat as the memory of the Erlkangs flooded the forefront of my mind. It froze me in place on the long, polished wooden platform that served as a train station. I bit down hard on my lip at the sight of the darkened trees and scanned them for any sign of the shadowy creatures.

Suddenly, the coins stabbing into my heel felt like the least of my problems. The gouges along my back itched worse in warning that they could be split back open again.

The trees rose tall above us, and as Phee clutched my hand tightly and pulled me from the platform, I could see that they were older trees than the ones from the forest beyond Ilrea. Some of these trees appeared to be as thick as a house, with big, gnarled roots that tangled across the ground. The branches above stretched wide and blocked out the moon.

Not that it mattered. Tiny twinkling lights had been draped along the canopy of the trees, and walkways cut through the ancient roots. The people of Gula had carved their way into the forest. Phee led us through the pathway. She never let go of my hand, but I pulled back and walked at Nash's normal slow pace. I wanted to take it all in and see everything.

Gula was, simply put, an enchanted forest.

If I looked hard enough, I thought I might find little winged faeries from my mother's bedtime stories. Phee climbed onto the next tree root and the lights flashed up from the city below. Low light and shadows danced against her pale skin and illuminated her soft nose, the curl of her hair and her figure in the gossamer dress.

Ophelia could have been a faerie. Especially when the girl turned on her heel and giggled brightly, gesturing for us to follow her up the roughly carved steps. We scrambled up behind her, and I received my first good look at the city.

It was nothing short of incredible. There were houses built into the thick trunks and extended high up into the trees. Children swung from branches and giggled brightly from high above us. As we stumbled further into the city, I could see a glimpse inside some houses through open front doors.

"You live inside of the trees?" I asked the obvious, surprised at how differently they existed, and how it felt a world and a half away from home.

"Yessss!" Phee beamed. "You must come and see *my* house! We might even catch Mama before they all go to dinner. Or... Or... You could come with us to dinner and truly experience Gula!"

Phee had grasped one of our hands in each of her own, and somehow, Nash and I had both ended up holding her shopping. I glanced over the blonde's head to Nash, and he shrugged slowly.

"We've got nothing else to do tonight," he pointed out. He wasn't wrong, I had no idea what came next. With Mikhael missing, I had nobody leading my way.

Every step towards the middle of the city became more and more painful as I stepped on the coins in my shoes, and by the time we reached a great big oak tree, I was hobbling.

"Oh dear!" Phee gasped as she noticed. "I'm sorry, I forgot you must be so, so, *so* tired, and here I was taking you the long way to my house so that you could see absolutely everything." Phee sighed and pouted, her lower lip wobbling for a moment. "Never mind though because we're here now!"

She didn't knock, and simply waltzed into the tree with the two of us left standing outside dumbfounded. I offered Nash another long, doubtful look.

"They live inside trees," I stated again. "Right inside of them."

"Imagine getting a splinter in bed." Nash made a face.

It sounded so strange, that we stared at each other for a heartbeat and burst out laughing. Full, proper laughter for the first time since I had left Ilrea. We laughed and laughed and didn't stop until Phee's head poked back out the door.

"Are you coming or not?" she asked in a tone that said it wasn't truly a question. I wiped a tear from my eye, and with a nod, I followed her in.

It looked much like I had expected or would have expected had I ever considered the possibility that they would have lived here. The inside was polished brightly, not unlike the furniture in the antiquities store, and nearly all the furniture was built of the same rich wood.

"You can put those down," Phee suggested, and I glanced at the bags in my arms. I'd forgotten they didn't belong to me. They crashed against the floor after I let go without hesitation. Nash did the same; his snicker made me grin.

"Now, come on, you must meet my mama!" Phee cried and led us both to a twisting staircase in the centre of the tree. The hollowed trunk seemed to be mostly a receiving area. It was decorated with rich velvet couches and a tea set. The round biscuits on the plate were set out like a work of art.

Nash snagged one as we climbed the staircase, and it snapped loudly under his teeth.

"Stale," he muttered.

"Sucker," I teased.

The staircase opened to the main canopy of the tree. Floors had been constructed between each of the thicker, more supportive branches, and then rooms had been constructed on top of them. The tree was so big, and the branches so wide that they had more space than I expected. The soft twinkle of little lights glowed from within the rooms, and I could see shadows as people moved within. Some trees were even connected to others with arching wooden bridges.

They put the one treehouse of Ilrea to shame. It had been an old door wedged between branches for stability.

"That's Mummy's room." Phee pointed out one room with a sweep of her manicured hand, and as she moved through them, it became apparent that her family occupied interconnecting space across five grand oaks. The idea of owning five houses astounded me. "Then mine, then my sister, Claudia, and then Lydia, and then Celina, but she's moved out to be with her husband, so now that's a closet. My brother, Benji, is usually in that one there, but he won't be here because he works down at *The Lost Herring*. He's a chef there," Phee babbled, and a bright-eyed, older version of Phee stepped out of the room a moment later.

The woman looked startled to see us. An unsettled expression twisted onto her face, but then she caught herself and beamed widely. "Phee-Phee, darling, what are you doing here?" the woman asked and swept her daughter into a hug. Her eyes trailed over Nash and I, and her gaze lingered on the cuffs around our wrists. It was something I was beginning to expect from strangers.

"Mummy!" Phee laughed, although she had winced at the question. I couldn't help but wonder why she wouldn't be here, in her own home, but that question was answered when Phee's mother stepped back and clasped her daughter's cheeks between long fingers.

"You know you're supposed to be staying at the Lord's house with the other competitors." She clucked with disapproval, but her expression was so loving that I had to look away. I wondered how my parents were faring. Probably better without having to feed and house me, too. I wondered if they missed me.

"I missed you, Mummy!" Phee pouted grandly. "We thought we would come and see you for supper with my new friends. This is Nash and Octavia. Guys, this is Mummy... I mean, Fiona." The woman smiled over her daughter's shoulder, and the stiff tension melted from her body at the exact moment she decided to relent.

"Okay, my darling. I will change and we'll go and see Benji. He'll cook you up a delight." Indulgence rang in every syllable of Fiona's tone as the woman caressed her daughter's face again. She then disappeared into one of the nearby rooms. She looked like she could refuse her children nothing, and I found myself burning with envy at the idea of a mother who could indulge every whim.

I took the chance to beg for a bathroom, and after I had taken care of business, I untied my shoes and slid them carefully off my feet. Coins spilled out onto the floor, and I made quick work of piling them into the hole in the heels of my boots. It would be a little more comfortable. I placed the final few in the front pocket of my shirt. When I righted myself and stood again, I almost groaned with relief at the lack of sharp pain in my feet. By the time I appeared in the downstairs foyer, everyone else was waiting.

"Sorry," I apologised sheepishly.

"Don't be!" Phee grasped me by the arm and dragged me out into the centre of the street again. Our arms linked together, and she spun us to the right and traipsed right through the centre of the path. Other people moved out of her way as she dragged us forward.

"Supper first," Phee announced. "My brother's creations are to die for, and then we'll take you up to be introduced at the palace."

"The palace?" I echoed, confused, and Phee giggled.

"Of course, all competitors live with the Angels in their cities." She turned her bright face towards me without judgement and shrugged. "Didn't you know?"

"No." The word was sharp.

"Oh." Phee shrugged, unfazed and still smiling. "Well, now you do." As she dragged me to supper, I couldn't help but fret over the fact that not knowing was probably going to be the death of me.

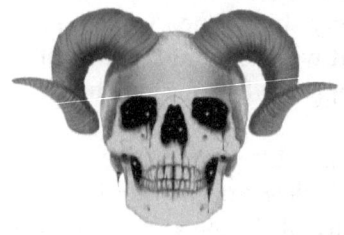

Chapter Twenty-Seven

The Lost Herring was located at the base of a large tree with red flowers that splayed out above the outdoor dining. The kitchen was carved into the trunk, and I could smell the scent of roasting meat around us. Little candles had been scattered around the area to give us light. Every so often, it sounded as though the tree itself sighed and one of the flaming blooms on its branches floated down to earth. We had been placed at a table with an assortment of mismatched and brightly coloured chairs. The back of mine rose higher than my head while Nash's seat looked too small for him. His long legs kicked out under the table and kept nudging into me. I kicked him for the third time in as many minutes. He grinned right back.

"What do they serve here?" I asked as I leaned forward to look first at Phee, then her mother, and then at the other two women who had joined us. They looked startlingly like Phee once she would grow older, but I had decided it was probably best not to comment on that.

"Oh, who knows!" One of Phee's sisters said with a wave of her hand.

"Right? He comes up with the most beautiful things every day. You don't order at The Lost Herring." The middle sister laughed like I should have known that. When I flushed in response, Phee elbowed her sister in the ribs.

"See, the thing is," Phee spoke over her sister as she tried to make amends, "Benji heads out at dawn and moon-break to pick fresh ingredients and then he cooks off inspiration alone. You can't order in advance here because he doesn't know what he's making until it's all set in front of him."

Fiona was nodding, a wide smile stretched across her face, incredibly proud of her son. A woman paused by our rectangular table and dropped two corked bottles atop of it, even though we already had glasses of the clearest water I had ever seen. Elegant looking glasses were placed in front of each of us, and after swirling the bottle three times, Phee's mother uncorked it and started pouring it in each of the glasses. It was pale lavender in colour and fizzed with tiny bubbles. I reached for it and lifted it to my nose, sniffing deeply. Strangely, it didn't have a scent.

As I lifted the glass for a taste, someone grasped my wrist. "Not yet!" one of Phee's sisters cried. "Wait until the food is here."

I narrowed my eyes at her, suspicious. "Why?"

"It's just better if you wait."

"But why? It's just a drink, isn't it?" My teeth scraped my lips and I glanced at Phee for confirmation, but she was in deep conversation with the server and didn't answer.

Fiona stepped in. "It's called Ithlium. It's a drink that expands your stomach and suppresses the feeling of satiation." She spoke like this drink was normal, but I struggled to wrap my head around it. "It's best sipped in between courses."

My mouth dropped open, and I nodded even though I didn't really understand. When the first course arrived, I stared down at the plate in awe. It was a small meal and all the women assured me that it would be one of many. It looked as beautiful as everything else in this forest city.

"It's like art on a plate," Nash exclaimed. He sounded so pleased that I couldn't help but grin. I watched him for a moment as he turned his head to the side and studied his plate to commit it to memory. He beamed at it as he picked up his fork. I tried to figure out where to start. There were twirls of an orange vegetable and a small piece of meat that was brown on the outside and still red in the middle. Beneath it, a sauce was dotted across the plate in a strange pattern.

Someone yelped as Phee jabbed her sister in the ribs again, whispering to her in a low tone. After a moment of shuffling, they switched places so that the bouncing blonde was sitting next to me and across from Nash instead. Phee turned her head and whispered in my ear, a secret reassurance, "It's a carrot and roasted hare." She told me gently. Nash had already started eating, but I was caught in the hesitancy between my burning hunger and the fear of the unknown.

"Is it any good?"

"Try it and tell me." Phee giggled, and she turned back to her own food.

I twirled my fork between my fingers, and then reached for the knife. I attempted to emulate the refined movements of Phee's family as I cut through the thin and crispy slices of vegetable and placed a piece on my tongue.

"Oh, it's sweet!" I gasped, and everyone laughed. I was uncomfortable but said nothing as I moved on to the meat. A tiny bit was placed on my tongue to try, and it melted away. Before I knew it, I had wiped the plate clean. The gilded plate was taken away quickly, and I settled back as the sisters laughed and bickered in equal measure. I couldn't really keep track of what they said, but the hum of their voices lured me into relaxing. We weren't kept waiting long before a second plate appeared.

Phee leaned into Nash and I. "Forest turtle ceviche cured in demonberry spirits."

This time, my nose wrinkled because the white meat looked raw. I poked at it with my fork and bit down on my lip. I watched on as Nash tried it first and decided that if he died on the spot, then I would know not to eat. Nash Wickham, unknowing poison taster.

Instead, he grinned widely and waved his fork in my direction. "I dare you."

A shiver rolled down my spine because I had never been good at turning down a dare. I held my fork firmly and cut a tiny piece of the turtle off. I was already cringing before I had even tasted it. I had no idea what a turtle was, let alone how it was supposed to taste. To my surprise, though, the flavours amounted to what might have been the best thing I had ever eaten. It was strangely zesty and refreshing on the end of my tongue. The texture, however, left me pulling faces with every bite as I worked my way through the dish. Next, we were served a strange medley of bright vegetables, which burst sweet and sour on my tongue. Even though the plates were small, by the end of the third course, I slumped back against my chair and rubbed my palm against my belly.

"I'm stuffed," I groaned.

Phee nudged me in the ribs. "Drink the Ithlium."

I stared at the bubbling drink and then looked at my new friend out of the corner of my eye, suspicious.

"Have I told you a lie yet?" Phee smiled. "Just trust me."

"If I die," I told her dramatically, "I'm coming back to haunt you."

With the glass raised to my lips, I hesitated, but ultimately took her advice. I knew Ithlium didn't have a smell, but I had expected the liquid to have a strange taste from the colour. It just tasted like water, with a clear, refreshing feeling that fizzed slightly against my tongue. The over-full feeling that pushed against my belly disappeared between one breath and the next. Both of my brows rose in surprise as my belly ached slightly, and as the pain smoothed away, it grumbled with hungry demand. It was like I hadn't even eaten at all.

My chin jerked up, and I felt rising panic as I looked at Nash for a moment. His eyes revealed a similar conflict—there was a storm behind them that he didn't voice aloud. Both of us laid down our cutlery and stared at the next course. It was a sweet broth, and tiny live fish swam within it. Perfectly safe to eat, Phee's mother assured us.

"Hunger on demand," I muttered in a low voice, and I felt sick in a way that had nothing to do with the loss of my satiation. "Suddenly, I'm not very hungry after all."

Five minutes later, when the others had finished eating, Phee's mother looked up and a tense silence fell over the table. The sisters whispered and glanced between each other with nearly identical frowns. The older woman cleared her throat delicately when she realised, we hadn't continued with the course. "It, ah… it's considered the height of rudeness to decline to eat a meal in Gula."

Nash rocked in his chair, and I stared at the little fish. "Sorry, we don't mean to offend you, it's just…" Nash floundered for the words. I wondered how we could ever describe how knowing what it felt like to starve made it unappealing to force down more and more food through a concoction that created hunger. Like hunger pains were fashionable instead of debilitating.

"It's just—" I couldn't find the words to help Nash finish his sentence.

"We're just raised differently in Ilrea. It would be bad manners to eat more than our fill," Nash lied so fluently that it left me blinking in his wake.

"Oh!" Fiona Bell laughed loudly. "Well, you wouldn't be rude to eat more in either of our cultures then." The woman flashed her pearly white smile. "I mean, you don't feel full, do you?"

My head jerked quickly to look up at the woman, who was smiling sharply that said she thought she had won. It couldn't be denied... after a single sip of the Ithlium, I was ravenous again. "How many courses will there be?" I asked, my voice strained as I wondered if I could do this to keep the peace.

"The Lost Herring normally serves a course of fifteen."

My breath caught uneasily in my throat, and I nodded slowly. The hair on the back of my neck seemed to rise uncomfortably under the gaze of the older woman. I had the distinct impression that it would be a very bad idea to refuse right now.

"Four down," I said to Nash and picked up the spoon. Something akin to pain flickered in his eyes. "Eight to survive."

"Eight to survive," he echoed.

We ate, we drank, and we sipped at their liquid hunger. The conversation fell short where Nash and I were concerned, unable to relate to the indulgences that the Bell girls raved about. The courses became richer and more extravagant, and we drank when we were told, but we did not participate in the laughter and the bubbling fun that arose between the women with each bite they consumed. It was like more food and Ithlium threw them into a frenzied state of revelry, their eyes alight and their faces animated. By the time dessert and the last course came—a pudding with a chocolate bark and flash fried wood ants—I felt fatigued just from pretending. I swallowed the last mouthful and dropped my spoon to the table with a clatter. I felt queasy and unsettled, but the meal was over, every bite consumed.

"I'm sorry," I apologised and pushed back at my chair. I self-consciously untucked my hair from behind my ears to hide from the scrutiny of the women. My eyes darted around the forest for an idea of where to go next, but I couldn't sit at the table for a minute longer.

"I think I'm late to introduce myself to your... Lord?" I gave Nash a pointed look.

His chair clattered backwards into the dirt in his haste to get up. His eyes flashed in warning that I better not leave him there alone. "Thank you for the most generous meal I have had in a lifetime..." Nash flashed one of his ever so placating grins. He pressed a gold coin to the table, and then reached for my hand as we fled. It took only four minutes to get lost amongst the trees, and then four more for Phee to appear like a woodland sprite between us. Her blue eyes were narrowed with a childlike unhappiness.

"You know!" She huffed, her hands planted on her hips, her full lips twisted into an exaggerated pout. "You're going entirely the wrong way."

"Oh." We turned around on the spot and asked, "Which way?"

"I can't believe you didn't even stay to meet Benji."

"Sorry."

"No, you're not!" Phee huffed. "What about after-dinner toffees and coffees?" Her loud chastisements carried us all the way to the palace.

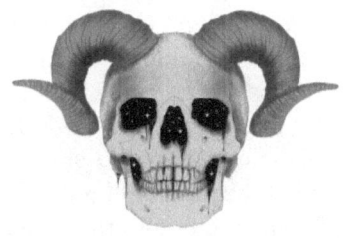

Chapter Twenty-Eight

The Palace of Gluttony lay sprawled within a darker part of the woods. It was a mansion not unlike the one we had entered the night that I had danced with Pride. The roof was dark ochre tiles, the outer walls were whitewashed and covered with ivy that curled upwards, like it was desperately trying to reach the sun.

The ivy had little hope of success as the thick trees seemed to bend and bow towards the house, crowding it in. A tree on the left side of the house seemed to have grown right through it. I let out an exasperated sigh at the sight.

"Why," I swayed, and my shoulder bumped into Nash, "do they always look so intimidating?"

Nash chuckled. "This place looks like it swallowed Heira House for breakfast."

The imagery was bright in my mind after the shared struggles of suppertime. I couldn't stop the wry smile that curled at the edges of my lips. In contrast, however, Phee had grown quieter with every step we took towards the mansion. She walked slower and held the fragile skirts of her dress in two hands as she rubbed at the material bunched between her fingers.

"It's okay," Nash swung an arm around her shoulders and pulled Phee into an awkward hug. "It's just someone's house. Just our house. At least 'til after the feast."

Phee offered him a sad look but nodded.

"So, we'll live here for eleven nights?" I asked. Four more until the feast, and the seven days of the feast itself… at least that was by my count. Which meant that the last day of the Feast of Samael would also coincide with the two-week deadline to complete the task. The timing of it all left me feeling strange.

"Just for four nights," Phee corrected softly.

"Not for the feast?" I was surprised and looped my arm through Phee's, pulling her along as her ever slowing pace meant we were getting nowhere at all.

"No," Phee muttered. "You don't leave the deep forest for the entire seven days. Leaving would be the worst disrespect to the Lord and to Samael," she whispered with a frown. "The last of the competitors should be here in four days though, I think."

There was nothing to say except to agree, so I stood at the base of the stairs with Phee and looked up. The ivy, as it turned out, was not just climbing the mansion in search of the sun, but it was crawling through the cracks in the walls to tunnel inside to any light it could find. Up close, the illusion of grandeur from a distance was shattered, and I realised the building was in a state of complete disrepair. Confusion furrowed between my brows as I took it all in.

"I thought it would be…" My voice trailed off.

"A little more?" Nash supplied, and to his left, Phee heaved a heavy sigh. I could understand her growing sadness a little more now when this supposed palace looked more befitting of Ilrea compared to the rich and comforting luxury of Phee's treetop home.

"Lord Gluttony, sometimes he just forgets..." the girl muttered.

"Forgets?" Nash echoed. "Forgets his house is falling down around him?" He started laughing, and I fought not to giggle too.

"Shhh." Phee's fingers slapped over his mouth quickly, and my laughter escaped at the sight of this pint-sized girl taking on Nash, when he nearly doubled her in height.

"You don't want to offend him," Phee hissed.

Her words seemed to resonate, and we all fell silent. We stood at the steps and looked up as we considered how bad it could be to offend the embodiment of Sin. If he exuded even a fraction of the power that Pride had, I thought it would be an absolute disaster. Ahead of us, the two large doors at the front of the mansion opened, and a deep voice boomed from within.

"Come in!"

There was no mistaking the otherworldly inflection that seemed to curdle the blood in my veins. Gluttony had spoken, and we were not allowed to refuse him. I nodded, bouncing my chin so hard that hair fell in front of my face. Somehow, I found the courage to be the first to climb the stairs.

The entryway was dark as I crept through the large doors. The carpet beneath my feet was a dulled red and caked with dirt and dust. It was not just the outside of the mansion that had rotted away, but the inside too. Beneath my weight, the floorboards creaked. I heard when Nash and Phee arrived as it groaned at their intrusion too.

"In here!" Gluttony boomed, and I shivered.

I glanced over my shoulder then for Phee, who lived here and knew her Lord. Phee, who should have been fine to enter

213

first. The girl was paler than normal, the dark circles beneath her eyes were more pronounced, and her clear blue eyes widened with an obvious fear. She gripped one of Nash's hands tightly, and her entire body seemed to tremble. It was the sight of her actual fear that set me on edge. I didn't know what it was that Phee knew... what it was that had her so terrified. Her fear left me wanting to flee instead of walking into the next room to find out. I had never been anyone's hero, and certainly not anyone's shield. Never had I stood between someone else and a monster, but when I glanced helplessly towards Nash, who was anchored in place by the blonde, I realised that nobody was going to step in front of *this* monster first. There was no hero coming to save me.

I felt violently sick for a second. My knees trembled as I considered the run from my current position to the door. I swayed towards it before I realised that I couldn't disobey the direct order from this Lord—he who didn't hesitate to command. Pride seemed preferable now; at least he had given me a choice. Pure instinct told me the punishment for disobeying would be worse than the trouble of escaping. Three deep breaths later, to loosen the invisible iron bands that had settled around my lungs, I thought I was ready to enter. My fingers shook with growing panic, so I hid them behind my back. Emulating the confidence of Pride himself, I marched into the room.

The Angel of Gluttony formed a stark contrast to the first angel I'd had the misfortune to meet. He sat sprawled in an oversized throne with two tables pulled up on either side of him, both piled high with food and wine. His feathered grey wings did not look sleek or soft. Instead, they hung limp from his back, and I wondered if he could fly on such frailty. Gluttony was, without a doubt, the largest being that I had seen in my life. He reminded me of newborn babies who could have their fill of milk at their mothers' breast but not yet walk it off. In the way that their skin rolled out in chunks that left them padded and warm. Gluttony was like one of these babies, but bigger than a man. He spilled over the waistband of his purple shorts.

When he clambered to his feet, it seemed to take an enormous effort, and he shuffled in my direction. I felt my throat tighten as the Angel looked me over. There was no denying the raw power he held. His dark hair fell straight and had been secured at the nape of his neck with a leather band. As he stepped forward, his wings rustled like they were trying to stretch out but had forgotten exactly how.

"Who are you?" his voice, like the rest of him, was excessive.

"Octavia." I breathed. "Octavia Nox of Ilrea."

As he shuffled closer, I trembled with fear. Up close, he was so much bigger, and I could see that beneath the rolls of softness, he had strong muscles. Gluttony was dangerous beneath an appearance that many would crinkle their nose at. His eyes too were something else. Just like Pride's, they were a void that seemed to connect from this world to the next, and burning hunger flickered in his gaze. An insatiable and uncontrollable beast. A quick glance into his eyes left me struggling to breathe.

"And them?" he roared. His hand flew out in a sweeping movement, which almost hit me in the shoulder. The power of it would have knocked me to the floor. I craned my neck to glance back. Nash and Phee hovered in the doorway. The girl trembled and looked like she was about to faint.

"Nash Wickham of Ilrea and…" I said loudly to draw the attention of the thundering angel back to me. "Ophelia Bell of Gula."

The angel considered it. His curiosity had been indulged, so he moved back to his throne. I watched as he threw himself into it. From his left, he picked up plump red grapes and swallowed a handful in one swift movement.

"Competitors or patrons?" Gluttony asked, still unnecessarily loud.

I nodded. "Competitors." My voice had lost any shred of the false confidence I had brought into the room. "We're here to honour you at the Feast of Samael."

Phee squeaked indignantly from her place in the doorway, and I knew why. The feast was not for this angel, but flattery had helped me out of many unfortunate situations in the past. It seemed to work this time too. Gluttony stood up a little higher. As he moved around, I caught sight of the shining tattoo on his forearm. The sigil of a plump pig, etched in purple ink, crawled against his skin.

"Hmm." Gluttony considered my words. He picked up another ripe, red grape and held it between his thick fingers. It rolled around before he settled it between finger and thumb and squeezed. The grape bulged and exploded. I was treated to the unpleasant thought that he could remove my eyes similarly if he didn't like the way I was looking at him.

This angel was a beast to be appeased, but I didn't know exactly how I was supposed to do so. With no other options, I stayed quiet, my head bowed slightly as I waited slowly for him to decide on his next question or command. It was acquiescence that would help me survive this moment, much like it had helped me survive supper with the Bell family. Life was full of doing things you didn't want to do, being an adult meant making the best of it.

"You may stay," he thundered finally. He flicked his fingers in my direction as dismissal. I felt a wet, juicy piece of grape land against my cheek, but didn't hesitate to turn and flee.

I had Nash and Phee's hands in my own and dragged them out of the room before Gluttony could change his mind and make us do anything else. At the base of the stairs, we ran into another person who wore the same cuff on their wrist, and I hesitated. He had sun-kissed skin and curly hair. The guy shrugged before I could speak and pointed up the stairs.

"Just find a room that isn't occupied and it's yours. Gluttony doesn't even seem to realise we're here during the day." He disappeared before I could ask anything else, his hands stuffed in his pockets as he loped out the front door and out of sight.

With a firm grip on both of my friends' wrists, I had them almost halfway up the stairs before I realised the impact of my own thoughts. Despite our limited time together, I truly felt these two were my friends. Friend enough to try and coax a smile from Nash when he frowned, or to walk before Gluttony so that Phee could hide behind my back. It was a strange concept, and an even stranger feeling to have.

At the first empty, undisrupted room we found, I pushed Nash inside of it. He wrinkled his nose and looked around. "It's so bland," he complained, and I shrugged back at him.

"So?" I pulled a face at him. "You've got chalk, right? Brighten it up."

There was a ghost of a smile on his lips by the time he closed the door, the piece of dusty pink chalk and a marker already in his hand. It took four attempts to find the next empty room, and I wavered in front of it as I glanced down at Phee. She still looked like she wouldn't be able to stand up without help.

"You take this one," I insisted. Phee looked upset by the idea and glanced down the corridor, lips parted to protest. "I, uh… I hate staying in west wings, they give me the shivers," I added. The lie came easy, and I watched as relief crested like a wave across the blonde's face.

"Are you sure?" Phee whispered. "I could take another room. I don't have any of my stuff anyway so maybe I could go home, just for one more night, and maybe—"

I silenced her by pressing a finger to her bold lips.

"You can't go home," I whispered the truth that we both knew. "You can't leave until Gluttony says so." It wasn't something I had realised right away, not with Pride, or not even until the second angel had flicked the piece of grape in my direction. There was some strange magic that came with being invited into the sanctuary of an angel, and once in, we were theirs until they let us go. That was how Pride kept his patrons dancing for hours and hours on end, and why Gluttony lived in disrepair with so few visitors from the inner city. The Gulans were too scared to visit in case he trapped them. They celebrated Samael and disregarded Gluttony because, while they basked in his sin, they feared his control. Phee nodded slowly.

"Get some sleep," I told her, and Phee pouted.

"But I haven't had dessert!" I would have passed it off as an impulsive request, except that Phee seemed properly panicked that she was going to miss out on a meal. There was no way for me to solve this problem on her behalf.

"Well…" I had no idea how to get food, and after the supper adventures, I had very little desire to find out. "Dream of cake."

Without giving Phee the chance to respond, I turned on my heel and traced my way back down the hall. It was harder this time to find a room that was unoccupied. Some screamed out to leave them alone before I had the door halfway open. Bypassing the first few doors, I sighed and then picked out the next to try because it truly felt like a game of chance—something I should have been used to really! The doorknob rattled beneath my fingers but remained tightly locked.

"Well, well, well," a hauntingly familiar voice caused me to jolt. I twisted on the spot and came face to face with Niklaus Heira.

"I leave you alone for two whole days, and then find you here trying to get in my bedroom." He smirked. "Miss me, love?"

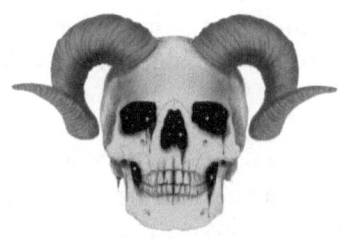

Chapter Twenty-Nine

M y face scrunched in distaste. "You wish!"

"I know you did."

"I was *not* trying to get in there to wait in your bed." I felt my face heating up and I refused to look at his face. "I was trying to find somewhere to sleep."

His lips twitched. "So, you're telling me you wanted to climb into my bed and sleep?" Niklaus advanced on me then, and the closer he got, the more the air between us seemed to thin out. "Nothing else?" he whispered.

My nose flared with indignation, and I lifted my flaming face to glare at him. "I wouldn't fuck you again, even if you were the last man in the world and we needed to birth the next Devil."

One of Niklaus' brows rose with sleek surprise. He shifted his weight back onto his heels and folded his arms across his chest. He said nothing and simply stared at me for a moment until his gaze frayed the last edges of my temper.

"What?" I spat.

"Nothing."

"Bullshit!" My jaw clenched. "You're staring for a reason."

Niklaus didn't budge, but he did grin down at me. "Not particularly. I was just thinking that I like you like this, a spitting drowning cat instead of a cowardly little rat."

I rolled my eyes. "I'd prefer it if you didn't think of me at all." I lurched forward and shoved past him to continue down the hall in search of a room. Much to my frustration, Niklaus followed a single step behind.

"Leave me alone." I turned a sharp left down the next corridor.

"Where's the fun in that?" Niklaus called out, and I came to a dead stop in the hall and turned to face him again. I studied his face and the twisted smirk on his full lips.

"Look," I snapped. He tilted his chin up, an indication that he was listening. "You have no idea what I've been through these last few days! No idea at all! I wish I'd never left Ilrea, I wish I'd let Boyd gut me like cattle for the meat market." Niklaus blinked and I advanced on him with my hands fisted by my sides.

"So, go away, please," I spat the words, but it sounded like I was begging. "I don't want to see you. I don't want to look at your stupid face and think of home. Or of how I struggled while you had an amazing life. I don't want to be reminded that I've left my whole family behind to die at the hands of an angel who will crush my soul like a rotten red grape."

My breath was coming in heavy pants, my chest heaving with each word. I glared daggers right through Niklaus Heira. The smirk had fallen off his lips, and his brow furrowed with thought. I wondered if my words had hurt him, and viciously hoped that they had. I was sick of being the one that hurt, sick of being the one person that everyone walked over for their own gain. I hurt for more reasons than one and didn't need another to add to the list.

"Fine!" The word sliced between us. I hadn't expected him to agree. Niklaus was a very disagreeable person, in my limited experience. "On one condition…"

I groaned aloud.

"Why are there always strings attached with you, Heira? Can't you just be a decent person and piss off? Seeing your face makes me want to punch it."

He ignored my rant. "Do something with me tomorrow?"

"No."

"You don't even know what it is."

"The answer is still no."

"Fine," he said again, as harshly as the first time. Niklaus gritted his teeth, tension tight in his neck. It caused the images of flowers that had been etched there to shift as he forced himself to relax. "Then I'm calling in my favour. You owe me."

"*What?*" I swept my hands through my hair and pulled it out of my face. Single strands knotted and caught in my rings. I winced.

"You heard me!"

"No! No, no. *NO!*"

"You owe me, Octavia. No complaints, remember?" Niklaus stated, his smirk securely back in place now that he had backed me into a corner, both literally and figuratively. I realised this a moment too late as he advanced forward, and I instinctively stepped back.

The dusty wooden wall panels dug into my shoulder blades, and I stared accusingly up at his face. I had forgotten about the favour owed. My nose flared as I tried to figure a way out of it. He crowded me in, his body so close I could feel the subtle heat that rolled from him. The smell of cigarettes clung to him so heavily that I realised he must have just had one between his lips. A heartbeat later, I realised I was staring at said lips and dropped my eyes pointedly to his collarbone. I scowled at the deep chuckle that rumbled through his inked chest.

"One condition."

Niklaus scoffed. "You don't get conditions on debt."

"Just one." There must have been something in my voice because he paused and nodded slowly, curiosity burning bright in his eyes. "It can't involve food." I stared up at him. If I could stand tall against Gluttony, I could look Niklaus Heira in the eye and make my demands.

He didn't even pause to consider it. "Done." Niklaus pushed above my head and shoved the door behind me open, the hinges screamed at the movement. "I'll pick you up from here in the morning."

I flipped him a vulgar gesture and he laughed.

"Dream of cake," he whispered mockingly in my ear before he sauntered off, proving he had been watching me for much longer than I had thought. I shivered at the thought and locked the door tight.

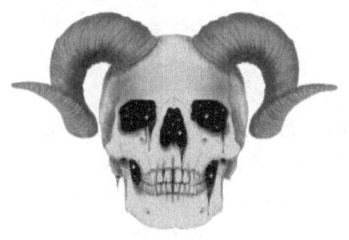

Chapter Thirty

A knock at the door pulled me from nightmares of shadowy beings and unfathomable pain. The person knocked again, louder and harder to ignore now. I shook my head and squeezed my eyes closed. I ignored the knock as I waited for the shudders to disappear. The next knock sounded like they were trying to punch straight through the aged wood.

"One minute!" My throat was tight, my voice high pitched. The knocking stopped abruptly.

"Only one. Then I'm coming in." His voice caused me to groan and scrub my hand down my face. I had forgotten, in those first waking minutes, that I had agreed to fulfil that ridiculous favour. "Ready or not!" he sang a moment later.

I jolted and kicked off the sheets that were knotted around my legs and found my feet right as the door handle turned. I could have sworn I had locked it. "No!" I screeched and staggered over to where it was opening. All my weight slammed into the door, and I shoved it closed.

Niklaus laughed, a deep and silky sound that echoed through the wood. A shudder worked down my spine again, we both knew I had only managed to close the door because he let it happen. Niklaus Heira had appeared in both my dreams and my nightmares last night.

"I locked this," I told him, still pressing all my weight against the door.

There was a silent pause, long enough that I dared to hope he had left before he commented lightly, "You and I both know that locks can't keep everyone out." He was right, but I couldn't help but wonder how he knew I could pick a lock.

My forehead pressed against the wood. "Give me five minutes, I need to get dressed."

"I could help with that…"

"Piss off!"

I turned and tried to find my clothes. I dressed quickly, and then flung the door wide open. Niklaus grinned lazily as he looked me up and down.

"What now?" I sighed at him.

"You're drowning in that shirt, and your laces are undone," he commented, and then leaned in and sniffed in an over-exaggerated way. "And you smell. That's all."

My eyes could have burned a hole through his head, and I realised that, for the first time, he didn't smell of smoke. Instead, he smelled strangely clean and a little like the fresh juice of a clementine and worn leather. I only knew what the fruit smelled like because of the long supper of the night before.

"Right." I crouched down and tightened the laces on my boots. After giving it a second thought, I knotted them twice. As

I rose, I sniffed at my shirt as discreetly as I could. He was right; I did smell a little, but there wasn't much I could do about it. Niklaus was already striding down the corridor on the assumption I would keep up.

I nearly had to jog to catch him as he strode along the hall with purpose.

"Where are we going?" I asked as he rolled a cigarette between his fingers. He said nothing and moved down the stairs. I glanced over my shoulder and bit my lip. I hesitated for only a moment before I followed. When Niklaus strode right out the door, however, I stopped dead in my tracks.

"I thought…" I called, and he glanced back.

"Hmm?" Something dark flickered in his eyes for a second, and I wondered if he had a cruel remark that he held back. Helina, I knew, would have said that thinking too hard was too risky and might cause my death.

"I thought we couldn't leave." My eyes flickered to the great throne room, and I could hear movement from within. "Not without…?"

Niklaus scoffed. "Don't worry." He strode back to the house and grasped my hand. A breath later, he roughly pulled me over the threshold and towards the stairs that led back into the twisting forest. "I already got permission from the big bastard." He took me through the forest and made it to the first big bend before I was tugging my hand back out of his grasp.

"You don't need to lead me around like a mangy mutt," I told him, and he laughed out loud.

"Are you a mutt?" he asked innocently.

I huffed and stomped through the forest behind him to keep pace. As we moved further from the old mansion and deeper into the city again, I slowed to look around. Gula seemed so different in the daytime, when tiny cracks of sunlight peeked through the leafy canopy of the trees. Everything was a little less glamorous in the harsher light, and I could see the cracks in a world that otherwise may have seemed perfect.

"Everything is so quiet," I commented, and when my gaze drifted to Niklaus, he was nodding in agreement.

"Gula is more of a nocturnal city. Most of the cities are, I guess. Except for Ira and Invidia." Niklaus shot me a look, his green gaze dark and cheeky. "Sinning is so much more fun in the dark."

I tore my gaze from him and kicked at a nearby branch. "Why are we out here during the day then?" I asked him. "If the city sleeps."

Niklaus turned to face me and grinned. For a moment, he seemed younger than me, bright and boyish instead of his usual serious and domineering self. "Well, that would be telling," he repeated his brother's words from the trial sign-ups. I rolled my eyes at him. "You'll see," he added.

We turned a corner, and I could see the sprawled seating area for The Lost Herring in the distance. My stomach turned slightly with the idea that he could be taking me to breakfast, even though my stomach grumbled softly in demand of more food now that I had slept. My rational mind wasn't over the excess with which I had eaten the night before.

"You said this wouldn't involve food," I accused hotly. I stopped walking and folded my arms across my chest. When Niklaus turned, he didn't look amused. He met my glare head-on.

"Come on," he prompted, and I shook my head.

"I'm not going," I insisted. "I don't want to do this!"

His eyes narrowed, and he sucked in a breath. "It's really not about what you want right now, is it?"

I scrunched my nose at him. "It should be!"

"Why?" The question threw me for a loop, and I took a step backwards. Niklaus tilted his head in challenge, his eyes flickering darkly.

"Well?" he prompted. "Why should what you want matter now? It hasn't mattered for any other lonely minute of your life, has it?"

I flinched and realised that what he said wasn't untrue. My life had so rarely gone in the way I wanted it, and I didn't have a good reason for it to start going that way now, other than that I so desperately wanted it. Above us, birds woke and started to chirp. Somewhere to our left, a man started setting tables for the few early risers who wanted their breakfast.

I exhaled slowly. "I don't have to explain myself to you."

Niklaus seemed strangely pleased by this answer. He ran his hand over his jaw, and I realised it was rough with a shadow of beard. "No, you don't, love," he admitted. "But you still owe me."

It was the only warning he gave before he swept forward and hooked his arm around my thighs. He tipped me over his shoulder and settled me there, with my face pressed to his lower back and my arse in the air. All too reminiscent of the night spent gambling in the bar.

"Put me down!" I screeched, in hope of gaining the attention of the man at the nearby cafe. The man looked up, but he just chuckled and moved on to his next task.

"Nik! I mean it! Put me down!"

He started walking away and I swatted at his back.

"I like that, you know," he commented, and I froze.

"Me hitting you?" I asked. "That doesn't surprise me, you freak."

"Well, that too," I could hear the touch of amusement that laced his tongue. "But I meant you calling me Nik."

My teeth ground together so hard that my jaw ached, and he carried me through the carved entryway in the gnarled roots of a tree. "Good to know," I ground out. "I'll be sure to never say it again."

The scoff at the back of his throat told me that he didn't believe a word I was saying. Admittedly, I didn't know if I believed it either. From my current position—suspended upside down—it was hard to tell where we were going. The blood rushed to my head, and so when he placed me back on my feet, I was dizzy. The world slid sideways. I grasped hold of his arm for support, and Niklaus gestured to a sign above a door with a bright grin.

"This is what we're doing!" he announced. I squinted at the letters above the door and then stayed silent. My face turned a soft shade of pink.

"What?" Niklaus frowned. "Nothing to say. No swearing? No vehement protests?"

"Protests?" I asked him. Confusion twisted across my face.

His frown deepened and my eyes widened. I squinted at the sign again. "None?" he sounded completely and utterly shocked. He had been expecting a bigger reaction and some sort of fight, and somehow, I had disappointed him.

"I can't read," I admitted softly. "I don't have a fucking clue what it says or what we're doing." I meant to sound harsh, and threw in the curse word for effect, but I could hear the thread of vulnerability in my voice. I just sounded pitiful.

"Oh," Niklaus said and cleared his throat.

"Oh," I mocked back.

"It says: *Crone's Curse Tattoo Parlour.*"

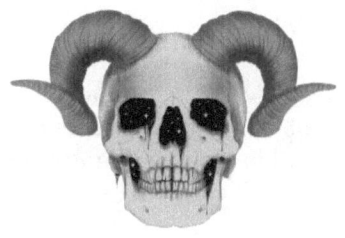

Chapter Thirty-One

I blinked at Niklaus in shock. "The favour you're calling in… is for me to get a tattoo?" I gasped at him and planted my hands on my hips as my expressions transitioned from shock to confusion and then rage. "What the actual fuck, Heira?"

His tense expression relaxed. "There it is!"

"What are you talking about? This is serious!" I threw back at him as my gaze flickered to the sign.

"This is the reaction." He grinned. "The protests I thought I'd get because Octavia Nox can't just go with the flow and do something for fun."

"What?"

"You heard me."

I scoffed at him, first because getting images seared onto my skin didn't seem like fun, and secondly because I *did* know how to have fun. Mostly as cards were flipped and dice were rolled, but it was still fun in the moment. "I had fun dancing," I countered in a desperate attempt to pick a different fun memory, because bringing up the card tables only reminded me of the image of him covered in blood with rage in his eyes.

"Do you dance in your dreams?" His tone was slightly mocking.

"With Pride," I insisted. "When I was in Glorae, I danced with Pride."

It was Niklaus Heira's turn to look shocked. His lips parted and he gaped at me for a moment while his brain connected words with his tongue. When they did, he exploded into action and shoved forward. He pinned me against the rough wooden bark of the tree, his hands planted on either side of my head. His eyes were dark with fury.

"Are you fucking kidding me?" he growled, and I shoved against his chest. My determined lack of a response indicated that it wasn't a joke. "You went and put yourself in the sights of the fucking Angel of Pride?" His gaze flashed darkly. "What if he decides he wants to keep you and hunts us all down?"

I shoved at him again, but he didn't budge. His face was an inch from my own and there was nowhere to look except into his violent green eyes. "Do you have a fucking death wish?" Niklaus glared at me, and I glared back, unwilling to open my pursed lips and grace him with a response.

It was the soft clearing of a throat that had him backing away. As soon as his body and the overwhelming scent of him backed off, I felt myself slump against the tree. Niklaus turned to the person behind us, and I tried to settle the tremble in my fingers and the race of my heart while the adrenaline fell away.

"My time is money," a strangely familiar voice growled, and I pulled myself upright to peer over his shoulder to receive the second shock of the morning.

"Cyn?" I gasped. "You're his tattoo artist?" It made sense, of course, with all the swirling tattoos on their own skin. Cyn turned and offered me a grin that flashed all their pointed teeth. "I thought you lived in Eternis?" I asked, confused, as Cyn opened the door in the tree and ushered us through to the staircase and up into the branches.

"I don't qualify to live in Eternis," Cyn answered as they climbed the stairs behind Niklaus.

"Why not?" I couldn't keep the curiosity out of my voice. "I thought you won the trials."

Cyn said nothing until we had ascended into a large, cool room covered in sketched illustrations, with a long purple velvet couch stretched out in the centre. "That is a lie," Cyn admitted, but they didn't answer the rest of the question, leaving me with burning curiosity at how one could not qualify for Eternis. Cyn gestured for us to sit down and then moved to the corner of the room to extract a file from the intricately carved desk there. "I don't qualify…" they continued in their soft, growly tone. "Because I was born a demon." Cyn smiled with feline amusement.

"Demons are real?" I didn't know why I was whispering, only that admitting it to the room any louder might make it a little truer. Niklaus laughed.

"You've been attacked by an Erlkang, what did you think they were? Or the Harpies?" He draped himself across the velvet lounge and then patted the empty space on his right. I ignored his invitation, and instead, mulled over this new information.

"What are you made of?" I asked Cyn.

They blinked at me, and confusion pulled at the edges of the ink on their skin.

"What do you mean?"

231

"Didn't the Harpies start as something else? And aren't the Erlkangs born of shadows?" My arms crossed over my chest defensively while my gaze flickered to Niklaus for validation.

"I was *born* a demon," Cyn repeated their earlier sentence and stressed the word as they handed the pages over to Niklaus for him to inspect. "To human parents. Here in Gula."

I chewed on my lower lip, and my eyes danced over Cyn again. Their complete lack of hair, endless eyes, and sharp teeth should have been some sort of indicator. Even the fact that they hadn't eaten in Heira House, which now seemed even more bizarre considering they lived in Gula.

"It's okay." Cyn waved a hand to indicate that I should sit. "Humans are delightfully good at ignoring what is right in front of their faces."

It felt like a backhanded compliment, even if I didn't quite understand it. I dropped onto the surprisingly soft couch. With nothing else to see, I glanced over Niklaus' shoulder at the thin piece of paper in his hand. It contained the image of a lion, or more to the point, an artful half face of a lion.

His head turned as he caught me watching. "If you look carefully," Niklaus' voice rumbled, "each of the signs of sin are incorporated into it somewhere. Peacock, pig, toad, snake, goat, snail." I squinted at his skin to try and make each of them out. "Then the lion is the overall image."

"Why the lion?" I asked.

"Isn't it obvious?"

Devil above, I hated when people answered a question with a question of their own. I pressed my lips together and shook my head.

"It's my sin to bear," Niklaus said simply and gripped his shirt at the collar.

Any other question fled my mind as he pulled his simple black shirt over his head and dropped it onto the floor. Niklaus had strong muscles and tan skin, interrupted by bursts of grey and colour. The tattoos lined the column of his throat and spread across his chest. They spanned his strong abs and decorated a raised, badly healed scar on his left side, before disappearing below his waistband.

"Finished staring yet?" he practically purred.

I startled, realising my gaze had been caught on the soft hair that started below his navel and led lower. "I wasn't staring!" I gasped and secured my gaze firmly on his face.

"Sure, you weren't," Niklaus teased, and behind us, Cyn laughed.

"What do they mean?" I bounded to my feet and moved a little closer to Niklaus as I inspected the images and flowers that started at his throat.

"It's the story of the ravagement." Cyn came to stand next to me, there was pride in their tone. "Haven't I depicted it perfectly?"

My eyes skated over his body as I tried to determine what exactly that meant, but the images all seemed to melt into each other in smooth transition. I was distracted by the thought that the powerful muscle beneath his skin and the feral smirk that often graced his lips likened Niklaus Heira to a lion more than even he might have realised.

"Here." Cyn pressed the pad of their finger to the florals decorating Niklaus' throat. "This is the untouched purity of the world before the devil came." They then pointed to the space above Nik's heart. "That is the devil, thrown from the last world, and the spanning galaxies he fell through to arrive here. Down one arm is the war that raged as the angels stood and took the earth in his name. Up the other arm is a true likeness map of Kaida for where the cities rose in their success."

Niklaus interrupted, "I want Ilrea added."

Cyn nodded and turned my attention to Niklaus' lower stomach. "This bit is a work in progress… I haven't finished drawing it yet. A depiction of the devil's many faces. Then, not that you can see, demons grace his legs." Cyn lifted a finger and twirled it. Without complaint, Niklaus turned around and flashed his surprisingly bare skin to us both.

"Oh." I breathed and watched as Cyn lifted the drawing and they lined up the midpoint of that half-lion face with the length of his spine. The great creature would span to the left.

"If he survives these trials, I'll begin work on a depiction of Eternis itself to surround the sins." My throat felt tight, and I wasn't entirely sure why, as I tried to picture what that might look like on his skin. Eternis was the ultimate myth, a world of perfection. It was where we would end up if we won. How could Cyn etch perfection into his skin properly?

"Why?" I asked, and Niklaus' shrugged.

"I always like the stories and making them my own removes the fear." He glanced over his shoulder and grinned widely. "Like the lion, I'm going to be the apex predator, afraid of nothing."

I bit my lip and glanced at Cyn, who pushed Niklaus towards the velvet lounge. He draped himself across it, lying on his stomach. "Octavia's here to hold my hand," he told Cyn a moment later. "Then, she's going to get one."

"No!" I rejected the idea quickly.

"We'll see." He sounded so assured that I wanted to slap him.

Cyn said nothing, and just watched us with unhindered amusement. Then they disappeared to a nearby cupboard and started preparing for the tattoo. I settled on the ground beside the couch, level with Niklaus' head. He murmured something beneath his breath, and I ignored him. Instead, I focused on watching Cyn as they pulled over a chair, arranged their table, and a soft buzzing filled the air. Ink went into his skin, and blood drops pooled out. After ten minutes, I was watching with intense fascination. Half an hour later, I realised we were going to be here for a long time, and I fell back into place beside

Niklaus. I glanced up and realised he had his eyes closed, and his jaw clenched. I knew he had wasted his favour in asking me to sit here for the day. It was easier to think of it as a waste than acknowledge that maybe the most popular, well-off man I knew was as lonely as I felt all the time.

Morning gave way to midday, and outside of the treehouse, I could hear the stirrings of the city around us as the citizens decided to rise from their beds and greet the day. This roused Cyn, as they wiped blood from Niklaus' skin and glanced at me with genuine surprise. They had forgotten I was even there, but I wasn't offended—it happened more often than I would care to admit.

"It is mid-meal from the sounds, but I don't have any human food," Cyn apologised. My stomach knotted at the idea of having to sit through another round of food so soon. It twisted and turned until the feeling of nausea was all-consuming.

"I'll be fine," I told them quickly.

"Are you sure?"

"I don't have any Gluttony coins anyway," I lied. Phee's coins were still stacked in my boots, but Niklaus would ask questions if he saw them. I settled against the couch and thought of the silver pieces etched with a fat pig indulging in a meal. I wouldn't spend these coins on food, anyway.

"Suit yourself." Cyn didn't really seem to care for my human needs. They turned back to their task, and that was that. The rest of the afternoon passed with ink and pain.

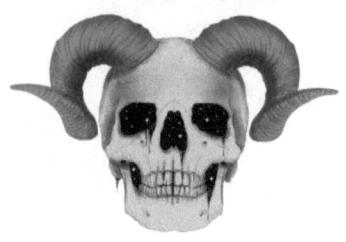

Chapter Thirty-Two

By the time we walked back to Gluttony's mansion, the city was in full swing, and the citizens of Gula swathed out in their best dresses to enjoy the feasts of the night. The skin on my ribs burned slightly. Just beneath the swell of my right breast, a tattoo marked my skin. A set of electric blue dice, a homage to the lucky dice lost in the Erlkang attack. I only hoped that the luck had been symbolic, and not literally attached. I would need some luck throughout the oncoming celebrations. I twisted my neck to peer behind us as I heard a cry in the distance, demanding the placement of bets. I couldn't work out where it had come from exactly.

"You ever think you have a problem, love?" Niklaus broke the silence between us.

"What?"

"Your little performance at the tavern. And now getting dice marked on your skin. It's a bit telling, don't you think?"

"I don't have a problem."

"Yeah?" He twisted mid-step then and turned to face me. "How would you feel if I told you I knew where there was a game of cards happening right now?"

He crowded me in as he spoke, until I stepped back. My gaze snapped to his face, all the same, and I couldn't help the reaction that shivered through my body. A cold whisper and a sharp hot flush as my heart stumbled into a too-quick pace in my chest. The ends of my fingers felt like they were tingling, and my dark eyes dilated as Niklaus stared into them.

"Do you?" I breathed hopefully. The question hung in the space between us. His full mouth didn't twist into a smirk, his brows didn't sink into a frown; instead, he stared back with the best poker face I had ever seen. Desperation curled through my body and licked at my nerves until I shuffled around, a restless agitation settling amongst my bones.

"Do you know?" I repeated as I stepped forward, and for the first time, I was the one squeezing the space from between us. He was citrus and leather, danger, and power, and I was a woman who hadn't showered in two days, jimmying with unadulterated need—not for him, but for the game, and for the win. He was steadfast and I was desperate. My lungs seemed to squeeze tight, and it left me breathless when he still refused to answer.

"Nik." I pressed forward until my chest pressed to his, and I had to tilt my head up to continue looking into his impassive face. I leaned my weight into him, and his pupils dilated slightly. My tongue swiped across my lips as I realised what that meant. "Do you want to play?"

Those words seemed to snap the rubber band of tension between us. Niklaus' throat bobbed and he jerked back in a hard step. "Not in the way you're thinking." His voice was rough, and he stepped back again.

I chased after him, the flicker of desperation turned into a full-fledged fire that heated my blood. "Niklaus!" My fingers curled around his wrist, and my nails bit roughly into his skin. He turned back to face me again, his expression hard.

"The table?" I asked, and I could feel that I was sweating. I felt wild and frantic.

He scoffed. "There isn't one. They go to Avarita to gamble."

Disappointment was a crushing tidal wave that sent my body from heated to instantly chilled. It was only the flickers of shame that kept me warm enough to live.

"Like I said." Nik pulled his wrist from my grasp and started to stomp back through the undergrowth towards the mansion. "You have a problem."

Objections died on my lips because he was quickly too far away to listen. I trailed him all the way back to the decrepit building, and he didn't offer me another word. That blank, impassive look settled back over his features as Niklaus Heira cut himself off. As we passed through the threshold, he turned and disappeared through a door beside the staircase. I was left standing inside the ruins, with my heartbeat still trying to find a normal rhythm. I frowned after him, and my teeth scraped on my lower lip until anger seeped through in place of my shame.

"Well, fuck you, too!" I snarled at the door.

"I hope you don't mean me," a voice called from halfway up the stairs. "Because I've been looking for you all day, and what a waste that would be if you decided you hated me between yesterday and today."

Phee came tumbling down the stairs and slammed right into me, forcing me backwards. "Where did you go?" Phee asked. "We're not supposed to leave."

It was pure whiplash to go from Niklaus' moody silence to her bright questions, and it took me a moment to adjust. "We went to Crone's Curse," I told her, then added, "we had permission."

Phee's pale brows pulled together, and her full mouth puckered in thought for a second. "You got a tattoo?" She sounded so shocked that it gave me pause. Was I so boring that it would be a surprise?

"Yeah." Suspicion laced my tone. "Why?"

Phee shrugged, ever so flippantly. "Nothing, nothing really! It's just… you can't get those removed, not the ones from Cyn," she explained in an earnest attempt to make sure I wasn't offended. "There's something in their ink. Not even sculpting can get it back off."

I said nothing, unsure of how to tell Phee I would have never had the means to get anything sculpted from my body, and even if I could, I would have fixed my ears, not my hypothetical tattoo regret.

"Can I see it?" The glory of Phee Bell was that there was no need to add too much to the conversation since she felt the compulsive need to fill the empty space with words. "You can show me when we get changed for dinner!" At the word dinner, I realised that I truly was hungry now. My belly let out a grumble that caused Phee to giggle brightly.

Before I knew it, I was shut inside of Phee's room, which had been filled with all her belongings at some point. There were dresses, jewellery, and shoes everywhere, piled up in a strange state of disarray that seemed to suit the girl.

"Show me! Show me!" Phee demanded, and I pulled my shirt up to flash the small pair of dice. Phee pressed so close to look that I could feel her hot breath tickling against my skin. "It's cute! I like the colour blue!"

Her inspection left me feeling off-kilter, so I stepped back and let the material fall back over my skin. I swallowed and glanced around the room at the dresses Phee had laid out. "Where are we going to dinner?"

Phee blinked. "Right here."

"What do you mean?"

"We dine with Gluttony until the feast. In his throne room. One boy told me today," Phee explained, and then unhooked a dress from the bed frame and held it against her body for a second. She looked down in frank inspection, and then glanced up at me in want of an opinion.

"Uhh…" I breathed. "It's nice."

Phee nodded as if she had expected my agreement. "They're all so nice, but I want to stand out," the blonde explained. "I want *everyone* to notice me." I couldn't help but wonder if that came from being the spitting image of her sisters and mother. I wondered if Phee had never quite felt like she stood out.

"Wear that one," I supplied and pointed out a dress at random. I knew nothing about dressing well. It looked rather like one of the bulbous flowers that sprouted amongst the tree roots in the inner city. "That's your colour."

Phee discarded the dress she held by dumping it to the floor, and then scooped up the dress. "It truly is," she agreed quickly. "Isn't it?"

A smile slipped across my lips and I backed towards the door. "Definitely," I agreed softly and opened it behind me. "I need to go get ready." Truthfully, I also needed a shower and to rinse away the still lingering scent of clementine.

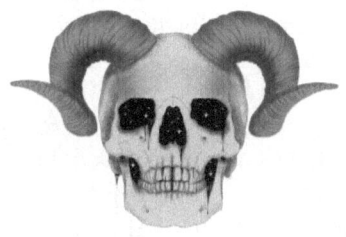

Chapter Thirty-Three

Gluttony held court in his throne room, and it seemed as if he had not left his spot since I last saw him. Instead, tables had been built and decorated around him. They stretched down either side of him and across the back of the room. Each of the chairs were mismatched, from single-seat couches to grimy white plastic and everything in between. A mockery of the bright and elegant settings within the city.

I hesitated in the doorway and wiped my hands down the front of my shirt nervously. I had showered, but I hadn't dressed up for dinner. There were more people competing in the trials than I had realised, and they shuffled around the room, taking seats before I could consider the consequences or the politics regarding the seating arrangements.

In a moment of paralysing fear of not having a place at all, I threw myself into motion and ended up sitting on a moth-eaten armchair of bottle green. Not the worst chair available, but not the best, I realised, as the springs dug uncomfortably into my butt and thighs. As my eyes drifted around the room, I noted familiar faces. Niklaus and Mikhael were together, with the boy from the stairwell last night crowded in next to them. Helina rested three seats to their right, deep in discussion with two other people. They looked like they belonged, and I had never felt so out of place.

In a flickering moment, my best friend glanced up from the discussion and caught my eye. I lifted a hand in greeting, but Helina's lips pressed into a thin line, and she turned back to her conversation. Something hard lodged in my throat at the rejection.

"Why do you think everyone is crowded right over in that one corner?" Nash dragged back a chair and dropped into place beside me.

I followed his gaze, confused, and realised he was right. In my haste at thinking I would miss out altogether, I had not realised that everyone was seating themselves as far from Gluttony as possible, and I had inadvertently left myself in the open space to his right. As other competitors drifted in, slightly late, they seemed to groan or gasp, and slowly, the chairs around me began to fill. They appeared glum, and I inspected the angel from the corner of my eye to see if I could work out why.

He seemed half asleep, draped across his throne, and once again, it occurred to me that maybe he was not as dangerous as the stories told. He did not seem fast, or particularly motivated to move from the rich chair. If anything, he looked like he was bigger and slower than yesterday. It was only when the last chair was occupied that he moved. His entire body rippled as he woke up, and I was reminded of the tinned food that Ilrea had received from Eternis when times were particularly hard. When it was dumped onto a tin plate, it held its form precariously, jellied and wobbling in place. I couldn't take my eyes off the angel. Not even as the throne groaned beneath his weight, and his eyes opened to survey us all.

"Welcome," he boomed and flicked his fingers. A long table appeared directly in front of his throne; it pressed into the expanse of his gut, but the angel didn't seem discomforted, even though I imagined there would be an angry red welt in its place soon. Gluttony inspected us all again like we were the items on his menu, and his jowls wobbled as he picked up a tart from his side table and waved it imperiously towards all the competitors.

Then, in a quick movement, he crushed it within his fist. Jam and dough scrunched together as it squelched between his fat fingers. He slammed his fist down on the table hard, and I cringed back as pastry flew in our direction. Food appeared in front of us, although out of thin air, and the hunger in Gluttony's eyes burned like the well-fuelled flames of a wildfire. His power expanded through the room and pressed against my body.

"EAT! EAT! EAT!" the angel screamed, and the power of the words shivered right through the room. It felt hard to breathe beneath the weight of his power.

"No cutlery?" Phee piped up from where she had settled in beside Nash. She stared down at the plate in front of her and the piles of food beyond like she didn't know what to do without a silver spoon.

"Use your hands." Someone laughed.

Phee didn't hesitate and reached for the roasted bird just in front of her plate. Her painted nails sunk right into its succulent flesh as she ripped the leg right off the carcass and dumped it on her plate. I shared a look with Nash, and all around us, competitors started claiming their food. The hunger in Gluttony's eyes dimmed slightly, even as his gaze glowed with otherworldly power at the sight of us all. His power pressed against me, and I reached forward to jerk a platter in my direction without meaning to do it.

"Move." On my other side, a girl pushed forward and reached over me for a wing of the roasted bird. When the girl dropped back into her seat, she spoke, "You better eat. You heard him... it was a command."

A direct order, I realised, too late. Not that he needed it. His power was already compelling me to move. I inhaled sharply and glanced at Nash again. He looked queasy but reached forward in slow and deliberate movements to pick up a fistful of green beans.

"For Alby," he whispered, his voice full of a sad longing, and then he said no more as he started to shovel food past his lips. Gluttony drew my attention again as he shuffled forward and peered down at the loaded table in front of him in contemplation. Then he inspected us, and my sense of self-preservation kicked in right before he reached me. I had dunked my fingers into the nearest bowl and was pushing the contents into my mouth. It was potato, and it left me longing for home as I scooped up a second handful.

When Gluttony was satisfied that we were all eating, he turned and tucked into his own food. Within seconds, he proved exactly why it was a bad idea to sit close. He ate with such abandon that food flicked everywhere. I was flecked with gravy and the juices of some form of animal as he savaged its carcass. A piece of bone bounced off my cheek a second later. I hesitated, my stomach twisting again. His power pushed against me, and I reached for the beans. Nash nudged me, a hard jab to get my attention.

"Eat to survive." I watched as he slowly piled vegetables on his plate and broke them all into small bite-sized pieces. "Eat until you're full, Octavia." I saw it then, how he chewed each piece like he was savouring it and moved in contrast to Gluttony's abandon. All while he met the direct command to eat.

"Eat until I'm full," I repeated the advice, and it became a mumbled prayer as I reached for sliced meat on a platter. "Eat until I'm full."

The boy on my left snickered loudly but didn't comment. A glob of mint jelly landed down both our fronts. "Ugh!" I tried to ignore it and chewed my way through pieces of meat. "It's so…"

I didn't really have a word for the indulgent abandon of the room, and nobody was listening to me anyway, so I fell silent and worked my way through the meat, which I recognised as rabbit. Once I started eating, it became easier. I fisted a roll, tore it apart, and slathered it with a herb-filled butter. Bit by bit, the bread disappeared, and I scooped out a spoonful of mashed potato. I worked my way through some of the roast birds, and then dragged an entire tray of honey glazed carrots in my direction, picking each of them up and biting into them savagely. The more I ate, the more my stomach burned and groaned with hunger. Gluttony's power caressed my skin in encouragement. The more I ate, the more I felt like I was going to die of starvation if I didn't eat something *more*.

When the carrots didn't stop the hunger pains, I groaned deeply and reached towards the sweeter items that started appearing on the table. Cream squished between my fingers and decorated my entire body, courtesy of Gluttony, and chocolate smeared at the corners of my mouth. Sticky honey smeared over the curve of my skin and against my neck. I reached for fruit and pulled some bananas out of their skin. I was barely chewing by the time I swallowed them down, and my chest ached with indigestion, all while my stomach roared for more. I felt like a woman possessed. I was sin itself as I indulged in every sweet I could find. It was only as I reached forward, and my fingers slid into a fistful of ice cream, that I snapped out of my own frenzy.

The armchair was uncomfortable as I shoved myself backwards from the table. My hunger morphed to horror, and my breath came in short pants as I pressed my fist to my stomach. Gluttony's power ebbed as he moved to a new meal and then slammed against me. My stomach roared in a desperate cry for more, more, more. A need so great, I couldn't ignore it, and I reached for one of the cherry-red glazed tarts despite my own disgust. I pushed it past my lips.

"Just until you're full, Octavia." I breathed. "Just until you're full." I felt like I would never be full again. I was starving, withering away to nothing, and the only way to save myself was through food. Caramel slipped through my fingers as I scooped at the innards of a different tart and forced it past my lips. It all tasted amazing, and I wanted more. I needed more. On one side of me, Nash grunted, his mouth full of food, and on the other came another snicker, which turned into a loud and incredulous laugh.

"Don't you get it?" the boy asked, and when he turned to face me, his eyes were wild, and he bit half through an eclair. I could see the flickering hungry flames of Gluttony's power in his eyes. "You will never be full."

Something twisted deep within my soul, the knowledge that this didn't sound right, and felt even worse, but the waves of hunger I felt did not relent. Senseless and frenzied, I reached for another sweet.

Honeycomb fizzed and melted against my tongue.

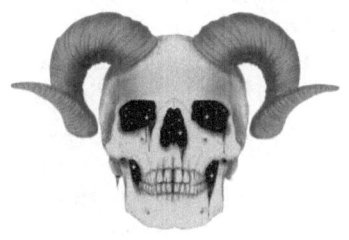

Chapter Thirty-Four

The feeling of intense over-indulgence returned with the rise of the sun. After dinner, I had stumbled back to my room with a belly aching for more. Tears had streamed down my face at being denied another course, but Gluttony's deep bellied command of '*Enough!*' had not been one I could ignore. I had trudged away with the crowd, covered in food, and sticky beyond reason, but I sobbed for fear of my death if someone didn't give me food. Once I found my room, I rubbed at my over-extended belly, curled into a ball on the floor, and sobbed.

An hour after the sun rose, my stomach became acutely aware of what I had filled it with. Hunger turned into a sharp pain from how it had stretched to accommodate too much food.

The feeling of being bloated was entirely new and discomforting for me. As my body adjusted, my stomach cramped.

I couldn't pull myself to my feet but managed to crawl from the bedroom to the adjoining bathroom. The tiles were slick from a leak in the roof and late-night rain. Each movement felt painful. I didn't make it all the way to the toilet before my body convulsed and rejected the food. I vomited all over the floor twice, and then sat back with a groan. A shudder wracked through my body again, and I could not find the energy to move. This time, I vomited down the front of my food-splattered shirt. I was too far gone to mind the smell, and after the third round of expelling the contents of my stomach, I wrapped my arms around my midsection and curled into a ball. Sobs wracked through my body again, and the feeling of hopelessness hit me in waves. I fell asleep there, in the pool of my vomit and the evidence of my overindulgence. I slept soundly through the midst of the day.

When I woke up, the vomit had dried around me and I felt like I had survived another demon attack. I slipped in the puddle as I attempted to pull myself upright. For a moment, I thought that I would have rather faced another Erlkang than my own appearance in the mirror. The reflection within it told me that I looked as bad as I felt. Food and vomit had dried on my skin and in my hair, and it was matted against the side of my head. My clothes were soaked through, and I couldn't look any more. I unbuttoned my shirt with shaking fingers and let it fall to the floor. I forced my way out of my boots and tossed them into the sink with a resounding thud. My pants squelched with squished food as I peeled them down past my thighs and tugged them right off.

The day prior, I had realised that the bathroom was completely overgrown. It had been invaded with a snaking green vine that occupied most of the far wall and curled around the clawed feet of the dirty tub. It had taken me half an hour before bathing to pull all the pale pink flowers from inside the tub. Now, when I edged my way to the tub, I could see that they had bloomed within it again, undeterred. The faucet groaned as I turned the handle and decided I couldn't bring myself to care. Not even as the water ran dirty and cold, or as the flowers floated to the top. There were threadbare towels beneath the sink, and a small bar of soap on the floor that smelled of strange spices. I had abandoned it all so carelessly to make it to dinner the night before, and now it was covered in splatters of my shame.

I picked the soap up and threw it quickly into the tub. I braced for the cold and slid in after it. The vines tangled around my legs and the cool water left me shivering. My breath held as I dunked my head beneath the water, my fingers scrambling against the porcelain base of the tub for the soap. Then I scrubbed and scrubbed until my skin felt raw, until my dark hair smelled only of the soap bubbles, and until food floated in chunks in the water instead of clinging to my body. When I couldn't tolerate sitting in my own filth a moment longer, I crawled back out of the tub, stood on my shirt, and wrapped the thin towel around my body.

Shivering, I fled the bathroom. Not that the bedroom provided any more solace. It was only in the empty room that I realised I didn't have any clothes. Nothing except the soiled ones in the bathroom. I could not help but retch at the idea of sliding those back onto my body. With half a sob, I sunk onto the mattress and sat with my head buried in my hands. I didn't understand how I had become so possessed last night. I stayed in place until my hair had dried, wild and fluffy, and tickled against my skin. Until I realised I couldn't stay in the room any longer, trapped with the permeating scent of vomit.

The answer, I realised, came in the form of a blonde girl and her piles of discarded clothes. She had so many that, surely, she wouldn't hesitate to share. At least this time it wouldn't be stealing, I reassured myself. I would just be checking in on my new friend, and if I borrowed clothes along the way, all the better. I opened the bedroom door and peered out into the hallway. It was quiet and eerily still. I felt safe in the certainty that I was, for the most part, alone and ducked out into the hall.

One hand kept a tight hold of the towel wrapped firmly around my body, and the other fought to keep my balance when I stumbled down the hallway on weak legs. It seemed stuffing myself full and then purging it all did nothing for my energy levels. After a hard left turn, I was in Phee's hallway, and only three doors away from relative safety when a groan echoed down the hallway behind me.

"For fuck's sake!" the cry echoed. I went dead still like a rabbit caught in a trap, and the towel clenched hard in my fist. My legs wobbled for an entirely different reason now. I knew that voice.

"It's not this bloody trial that's going to kill me," he stated in a breathy growl, and I could feel it as he stalked closer and closer to my back. "That's for certain."

Niklaus Heira's breath tickled the back of my neck, and my new tattoo felt itchy. I closed my eyes, cursing the devil in my head that I couldn't have had this moment to myself, not after so many people had seen me lost to the feeding frenzy the night before.

"Go away," I found my voice. "I don't have time for you, Heira."

"Nik," he corrected.

My flimsily erected spine collapsed when the pad of his finger traced the marks at the back of my shoulder blades, and he drew a shudder from me that took all the fight from my body. "Go away, Nik," I mumbled. He said nothing, and I wobbled forward a step, my eyes fixed on the exact door that led to Phee, and to safety.

"Where do you think you're going, love?" His tone had dropped and was silkier—a touch more dangerous. I couldn't stop the shiver that trickled down from my scalp to my toes. "I'm talking to you," he added when I didn't stop and staggered further forward.

"Visiting a friend," I muttered, and soon, I would be there, safe from the lion prowling at my back. The noise that echoed from his throat was strangled. I had my fingers outstretched, three steps from the door when he burst into movement.

"Oh, fuck the devil and his wife," Niklaus Heira growled and scooped me into his arms. I shrieked loudly in his ear and thrashed against him.

"Put me down!" I shrieked and kicked out until I realised it was pushing the towel higher up my thighs. I was sick of him lugging me around like he owned me. I squirmed in his hold and tried to tug the towel back down. Niklaus scoffed when he noticed.

"Nothing I haven't seen before, love," he commented, and the blush seemed to cover every inch of my skin. The fight left me as I realised this was nothing compared to last night's shame, and I went limp in his hold. Niklaus marched us down the hall to his room and kicked open the door with a thud. Once inside, the muscles in his chest bunched, and before I could consider protesting, he launched me towards the bed. I bounced against the mattress, and the knot of my towel came loose. It pooled about my hips, and I shrieked obscenities. I cursed him with every word I knew. My fingers scrambled for purchase on the plum-coloured duvet, and I ripped it up to cover my nudity.

"You can't just roam about this place in a towel, you absolute—" Niklaus' muttered tirade of reprimands faded as he disappeared into the bathroom. "*Visiting* people."

I could hear the sneer in his voice, and belatedly, I realised what he thought had been happening, and what sort of visit he had on his mind. It hadn't been that sort of visit... I wasn't tumbling in the sheet with Ophelia, but I liked that the idea had managed to get beneath his skin. A scowl twisted onto my lips and I sat a little straighter.

"So, what if I am?" I bit out. "It's not my fault you're a lonely, jealous prick."

Soft material slammed into my face and I gasped, startled. Niklaus Heira had approached the bed in the time it took me to reach for it and realise it was a shirt. He leaned over me with a hand planted on each side of my hips, his face far too close.

"As much as I love that you've found a bit of your spine—" he groaned. "It fucking infuriates me too, and I'm not in the mood, so shut the fuck up and get dressed."

"So, you *are* jealous?"

He scoffed. "Of you?"

"Of my *friend*," I pressed. He started laughing, and it was so unexpected to me as I thought I had been pushing the right buttons, that I flinched.

"In your dreams," Niklaus spat. "Now, get dressed or I'll dress you myself."

I blinked in shock as he dropped a pair of briefs into my lap, and then set a second pair of briefs and shirt to my left. I eyed the second set, and my throat bobbed as I considered that he might strip off to change. Instead, he grunted. "For tomorrow."

Niklaus Heira looked me up and down, his eyes lingering on the point where his duvet covered my chest before he folded his arms and turned his back on me. I waited a breath and eyed the back of his head to make sure he wasn't about to turn around.

"Hurry up!" he barked impatiently. I scrambled into action. I slid the briefs up over my hips and pulled the shirt over my head. Both were a little too big, so I knotted the elastic of the briefs at my bony hip and slid shakily to my feet. His shirt was black and covered in a strange bright print on the front. It fell all the way to my knees. I brushed my hands self-consciously down my front and realised it did nothing to help my figure. Not that it really mattered, I supposed.

"You can turn around." Niklaus turned slowly. Some of the tension in his body and the anger in his eyes lessened when he realised I was fully covered.

"Why are you doing this?" I asked when he bundled the second set of clothes into my arms and started pushing me back towards the door.

"I don't know," Niklaus admitted through clenched teeth.

"Sure, you do," I challenged. "You just don't want to admit it."

Niklaus stopped and fisted his hand in my shirt. The fire was back in his eyes. "Admit what?" His tone was icy, so angry that the hair on the back of my neck raised on end. I had the distinct feeling that I needed to tread carefully.

My voice was shaky. "Admit that you want—"

I hesitated.

"Want, what?" His tone indicated that there was truly a wrong answer to the question, and I could feel my courage in this conversation wilting like a flower without sunlight.

"Me? To survive? To be close to you?" I waved a hand at him. "Why else would you—"

"Have you ever thought—" Niklaus interrupted me as he placed a hand on my lower back and shoved me right out the door. His eyes burned wildly, and his upper lip curled with disgust that chilled me to my bones. "That I'm just waiting for the right time to rip out your heart myself?"

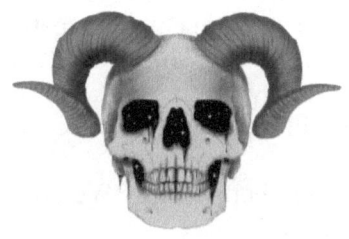

Chapter Thirty-Five

My heart raced long after I had returned to my room, which stank abhorrently. I stowed the fresh clothes beneath the bed and cleaned off my boots before I pulled them on. Eventually, I finally found myself in Phee's room, surrounded by tulle and bright colours. Phee, like Niklaus, looked far more put together than I would have expected. She yammered on and on about deciding what to wear, and I could almost have believed that the girl hadn't attended dinner the night before at all.

"Octavia?!"

"Huh?" I looked up at Phee. A flash of guilt crossed my face as the other girl caught my lack of attention. It didn't seem to faze her though. She flopped right down onto the bed beside me and sighed up at the ivy ruined roof.

"I said," Phee was much more patient than I deserved. "What will you be wearing to the feast? That shirt is fine for dinner, but you really must dress up for the celebrations. Something that will stand out and be noticed for the seven nights."

I chewed on my bottom lip. "We don't change clothes for the whole seven days?"

Phee gave me a funny look. "No. We don't leave the deep forest until the revelry is over. It's part of the tradition—seven days and seven nights, and the seven tiers."

"Seven tiers?"

"Yes, keep up!" Phee sat up. "I take it you don't have anything to wear. I'll loan you something. You'll have to come to me and we'll spend the day getting ready!" She ran her fingers through my dark hair. Then she nodded, mostly to herself. "We're going to look perfect and celebrate so hard that Samael won't be able to not notice us!"

I thought drawing the direct attention of the devil was a worse fate than Phee believed, but I still nodded to keep my new friend appeased. Phee beamed and consulted the delicate silver timepiece on her wrist.

"One hour to dinner," she announced. "Finally. I'm starving!"

I wasn't ready at all. The time had flown by, aided by the fact that I had slept away most of the day.

That night went not dissimilarly to the last, except that I managed to sit away from the flying remnants of Gluttony's meal, and I ended the night with much more of the food retained in my sore belly. I passed out, curled in the centre of my bed, and slept out most of the day. The next day was simply a blur. Then, before I knew it, I stood in Phee's room in only a pair of Niklaus' briefs. My arms were crossed over my chest for some semblance of modesty as Phee had changed her mind on a dress yet again and ordered that I strip and change. It was a pattern that had been repeating for over an hour before Phee was finally happy.

The result was a dress of deep green, not too far off the colour of the eyes of a certain set of twins, and it hugged my frame perfectly. Phee pursed her lips, then smacked them and squealed, finally happy with the result.

"Spin around," she demanded, and I complied. As I turned in a quick circle, the hem of the dress flared around my feet.

The dress was long and hung from thin straps at my shoulders, which crossed over at my back. Both the front and the back fell in a deep V, exposing no small amount of skin, and in turn, the soft pink of my healing scars. Phee had almost cried over the scars not ten minutes before. It pulled in tight at the slight curve of my waist, and snug beneath my breasts, before it fell to the floor. The bottom layer, in rich green, was a soft cotton, and the top layer was a darker green layer of tulle. The tulle had patterns etched into it, soft curls of ivy leaves, which became denser near the floor.

If I hadn't thought that voicing as much would hurt my friend, I would have said that Phee had dressed me to be the tithe—an offering to the forest and the devil himself. I supposed, in a way, the girl had. Especially when she emerged in a dress of coral, with billowing, translucent sleeves, and stated that she would be the one to catch Samael's eye this year.

We sat on the bed, surrounded by the floating material, and I pulled Phee's long hair into a plait that cascaded down her back before I took a few of the shining feathers from Phee's tight grasp and tucked them into her hair in various places. This was what it would have felt like to have a sister, I thought, and blanched when I thought of the sister I did have. A little girl who was a stranger due to my own selfish disregard—more unknown than the young woman I had met only a few days ago.

I stood then and raked my fingers through my own hair. I had not let Phee touch it, despite her begging, and it fell straight and blunt to brush against my collarbone. Nothing special, but I was less inclined to stand out. The thought was less appealing with every moment that Phee enthused about the attention we would gain. I reached for my boots, and Phee made a noise in the back of her throat.

"Don't wear those." For a second, I thought it was because they were ratty and worn. "You'll just lose them. The Feast of Samael is best attended barefoot, and—" Phee paused to glance at her timepiece again. "If we don't go now, we'll be late!"

As we bundled down the hall and joined other bodies—all dressed up for the true start of the trials—I thought being late and avoiding the whole affair may have been the superior option. The competitors walked together, and we thundered down the stairs and out of the front foyer of the mansion. The chill of the night air left me shivering and the ground was cold and slippery beneath my bare feet. I followed the slow march of my fellow participants as they led away from the city and into a deeper, darker part of the forest. Someone slammed hard into my left shoulder, and I went stumbling into Phee.

"Watch it!"

"Oh!" Phee caught my weight as I struggled not to slide in the soft mud that coated my toes. My head snapped to look at the person who had shoved me and blinked when I realised the soft figure with long dreadlocks was familiar.

"Nice to see you've replaced me so quickly," Helina sneered, looking us both up and down as she held her black skirts in one hand, the gauzy top she wore just brushing the base of her breasts and showing off her pale stomach. She looked so different to the Helina that I knew, and I couldn't stop staring.

"Hel," I uttered softly, one hand extended placatingly for the other woman, but Helina lifted her nose and sneered down at both of us.

"Don't." In a quick movement, Helina turned her back. "I didn't need you dragging me down anyway, Octavia. I always said I'd win, and it's better if I don't have to pull your weight too."

I flinched. "Hel," I whispered again, unsure of why I could find fire on my tongue when I spat words at a certain Heira twin, but Helina's haughty stare made me want to curl into a ball and disappear. "Come on," I whispered, my voice a little fractured— a small thread of hope still within it.

Helina shoved her way forward and ignored me completely. I swore under my breath, and Phee's fingers thread through my own. Her hand was soft and reassuring, even though she said nothing. We continued forward and climbed the ancient roots of a weeping willow before we all spilled out into a large clearing. A break in the canopy let the glow of the moon through, and if I craned my neck just right, I could see the half-smile of the moon itself. It, above all else, seemed like the first good sign of the night.

From their left and right, the residents of Gula flowed into the clearing as well, all of them dressed like they were attending a wedding or the grandest affair of their lives. I could not help but stare and drank in the sight of all of them as they stood beneath the light of the moon and waited, their faces a picture of serenity. It was the robe that caught my attention first, as a man moved smoothly into the centre of the clearing and raised his hand until everyone fell quiet. His outfit glittered like it was created of the midnight stars.

"Welcome," his voice echoed around the clearing. Deep and commanding, and the restlessness in my limbs finally settled. "I am Chancellor Cartwright. This year, we present to you seven days and seven emotions."

He waved a hand and the tree lit up with glittering lights. "Let us commence the Feast of Samael."

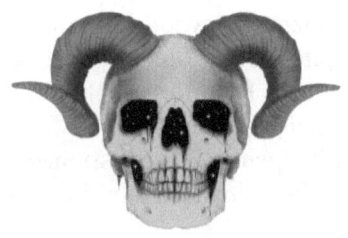

Chapter Thirty-Six

Phee clung tight to my hand—her grip nearly cut off the circulation to my fingers as she squeezed hard and squealed with just as much zeal. She shuffled close, and I was overwhelmed by the sweet undertones of her floral perfume.

"Last year, we did seven faces of the moon," she explained. "The food manifested as so many types of cheese; you wouldn't believe it! This year sounds so, so much better."

"I don't get it," I told Phee, craning my neck to look up at the bright orb. "The moon isn't made of cheese."

The look of utter perplexity on Phee's face would have been laughable had it not been so serious. "What?" she gasped. "Don't be silly! Of course, it is!"

I nodded and decided it was better not to argue. I watched as citizens ran forward first. Music picked up around us as they added sticks and pieces of wood into a big fire in the middle of the clearing. Despite the too-tight manner of Phee's grip, I didn't pull myself away as I felt more anchored by the blonde at my side than anything else.

"So, what is happening?" I questioned.

"Just watch," Phee insisted, and I could have groaned at the complete non-answer.

"For our first experience," the chancellor's voice carried across the clearing, and a hush fell across the crowd again. "We have granted you *happiness!*" He clapped his hands together like he was doing us all a great favour.

It ignited a round of applause, which rippled from one side of the clearing to the other. Cheers rose and people hugged. Behind him, flint struck, and sparks flew bright into the night air. The pile of leaves and twigs started to smoke, filling the air around them with a heady scent. The smoke was so thick that it left me breathless, and with that, a flare of panic squeezed at my heart. I had to remind myself that it would all be okay. I didn't know what this trial would bring, or how I was going to survive it, but I only needed to take it one day at a time. From the smoke, blue and orange flames started to flicker and grow. They greedily climbed the pile of branches and licked at the sky.

"Phee," I whispered in the shell of the blonde's ear and shook her shoulder to get her attention. "What's the battle of one bite, though?" I asked as apprehension fizzled through my veins at the idea that I could make one false move and fail instantly. That I might forfeit myself to Gluttony, tonight, in this very field. As if my thoughts of his name had conjured him, a wave of power shuddered from deep within the forest and swept through the clearing like a wind. The flames faltered, the grass rustled, and my dress tangled around my legs.

Gluttony's power was near-instantaneous, and my stomach growled in response to his call. My entire body trembled with a need for food, and I glanced over to Phee, watching as she battled with the same potent reaction. Thoughts of the trial fled my mind as long wooden tables appeared through the clearing and filled up with food. He had conjured them out of nothing. As I scrambled for the table and picked up the delicate and fancy hors d'oeuvres, I knew they were very real. It was tiny beneath my fingers, and my stomach twisted in demand as I surveyed the pink flesh of fish on the wafer-thin cracker, and the drop of creamy sauce on top. I lifted it to my lips, and Phee smacked it right out of my hand. The food tumbled into the mud, and my body violently flinched as I mourned the loss. Hunger ravaged my senses again, angry at the refusal to satiate it.

"Octavia!" The reprimand was sharp, and I spun to face my friend. My eyes were wide with guilt as I studied the blonde for any hint of what I might have done wrong. It must have been bad for Phee to slap food right from my fingers when I was so hungry. Phee's voice was hoarse like she was in physical pain when she spoke. "You need to pay the tithe."

"What?" I croaked.

"The tithe," Phee repeated. "For Samael... you'll bring us bad fortune if you don't."

I laughed. "All my fortune is bad."

Phee shook her head and stepped forward. In the light thrown from the flames, she looked fiercer than I had ever seen. Strands of blonde hair fell free from her plait, her eyes wild with magic-inflicted hunger, and her lips trembling like it took every drop of pure will to hold herself back.

"No!" Her full lips twisted into her signature pout, and Phee stamped her feet into the slick mud. It splattered further along the hem of my dress. "Pay. The. Tithe. Octavia."

Nothing, it seemed, not even the unsatiated hunger that had my knees buckling, would stop Phee Bell in her mission to be noticed by the most dangerous angel of them all. The blonde snatched up two of the little crackers, and with the utmost care not to break them, she turned towards the growing flames and jerked her head for me to follow. Unsteadiness rolled through my body, and every urge in my body screamed to turn back to the food, but somehow, I found the will to stumble after my friend. I slipped in her muddy footprints until we reached the edge of the fire. Phee turned, her chest heaving with rough breaths, and she carefully handed me one of the morsels. I cradled it gently between both hands. My entire body ached with the need to just taste it… just a small bite.

"Like this," Phee interrupted my thoughts and the subconscious movement of my hands towards my lips. "Place it down like this and offer it to him."

I watched, dazed, as the blonde settled the piece of food amongst the ashes of the fire and murmured something too soft for me to make out beneath the singing of the crowd. My movements were wooden as I followed suit, dropping to my knees. The ash from the fire smudged against my dress and splashed up my wrists. The food was settled in against the ground, and I bowed my head. I hoped the ash-sodden food tasted terrible for the devil.

I had never been one for prayers, or for the belief in things that could control your fortune—aside from my dice, or the moon, or the first Wednesday of every month… and I had believed that the devil, or Samael as he was called tonight, had been nothing more than a myth. He was a cursed tale, who only formed a real concept in my mind a week ago.

"Better the devil you know," my voice was rough, throaty as I inhaled the ash. "So, take it, but give me a secret in return, Samael." My chin lifted and I stared into the burning orange light as the flames devoured sticks with the same frenzy that Gluttony came for his meals. Sparks spat onto my offering, and it burned a fraction from my fingers. I hissed and snatched my hand back into my lap, but could not look away from the twisting, curling flames. My hunger momentarily forgotten as shadows formed within them. For a moment, they had a bony face, so real, so regal, that I could have sobbed; and a voice slithered through the shell of my ear.

'*I'm waiting for you,*' it whispered as intimately as soft kisses on bare skin. I shivered and searched the flames for the shadow face again—it was gone, and I felt strangely bereft in its absence. I shook my head, certain I had imagined the faces and voices. It was the ash, I decided, and a good lack of oxygen that left me hallucinating by the fire.

"Come on." Phee hooked a hand beneath my arm and pulled me to my feet. There was no more time left to think of the face in the shadows, and the fire in his eyes. No more time to wonder if the voice had been real or just fantasy because, as I staggered upright, the hunger returned. I reeled back from the fire as Phee held tight to my hand and dragged me back to the long tables of food. It never appeared to diminish, always full of the bite-sized starters, and the blonde squealed.

"Let's eat!"

This time, I didn't hesitate, and fuelled by the unimaginable hunger I felt, I fell into place beside Phee and started to take one of everything within my reach. I pushed each morsel past my tongue and barely chewed before swallowing them down. Right then, I realised what the chancellor had meant by being granted happiness in this first night of revelry. It flooded through my veins, this artificial elation, until my cheeks ached from the width of my grin. I felt giddy, and high on life.

Phee curled into my side and laughed brightly. I wrapped my arms around her body and squeezed, elated and affectionate. I could not help but join in. I laughed, and laughed, and laughed. Happiness spread from my head to my toes and pooled in every molecule of my body until I felt uncontrollable, wild, and completely and utterly manic. We climbed to our feet, food still clutched tightly in my fist and smeared against my lips. Phee and I took one look at each other and burst into giggles again.

"Let's dance!" Phee cried and I nodded jubilantly, all the while beaming at my friend.

We tumbled to the circle of people who surrounded the fire, and I felt so cheery that I couldn't remember to offer up the warning that I couldn't dance. Not that it mattered. Phee had already grasped my left hand, and the boy from the stairs grinned at her beneath his mop of wild, curled hair and held her right hand. He didn't seem to care about her sticky fingers, or the dirt that flicked up from the hem of her dress, and simply urged her on and on as we danced in a wide circle around the fire. We moved quickly and at a frenzied pace around and around the fire until dizziness claimed me, and my laughter was breathless. I felt like I was walking on air. My fingers tingled strangely, and every part of me felt alive tonight.

The fire crackled. It burned high and bright, right through the long hours as the moon crossed the sky. The stars watched on, their twinkling light encouraging all of us. I clung to Phee like she was life support as I drowned in the pure elation in my veins. I shrieked, I laughed, I danced, and I ate. Around and around the fire we spun, until the sun battled for dominance in the sky. It pierced over the horizon and stole the orange of the fire to paint the horizon. Gluttony let out a wild roar from deep within the forest.

Every single person shivered and fell unconscious at once. I stumbled and crashed into the mud, lashes pressed against my food-stained, dirty cheeks and succumbed to the darkness before I could register the impact of the ground.

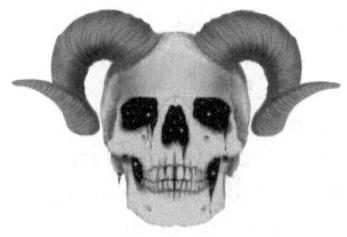

Chapter Thirty-Seven

A s the sun disappeared once more, we woke in unison to Gluttony's call. I opened my eyes slowly and exhaled a slow breath. Hunger curled and stabbed in my belly like a knife wound, and I surveyed the strangers beside me as they woke too. It took me a moment to pull myself up and find my equilibrium. In the dead embers of the fire, the chancellor stood proud and tall, waiting for us all to rise. The world felt unsteady as I found my feet. My eyes flickered around the clearing, but I couldn't see any sign of Phee, even though the blonde's clear eyes were the last thing I could remember from the night before.

"Sleep well?" the chancellor asked at large, without expectation of a response.

"Welcome to day two of our celebrations. Tonight, we delve further into the deep forest, along the banks of the sweet river," he announced and gestured to the right, where torches threw light onto a path for us to follow.

"Tonight, you must experience the antithetical adventure, and you will endure the pleasure of immense *sadness*," the chancellor said, and a few people gasped with delight. Dully, I wondered how there could be pleasure in sadness. My entire body ached, and I could remember little from the night before. I couldn't sort out my thoughts and focus on anything except how my stomach cramped with growing demand.

I needed to eat—hunger gnawed like a beast in my belly.

I wriggled my toes, and dried mud cracked along the top of my feet as I decided I would follow the others and find my friend along the way. The pace was slower than the day before, the pure happiness of the first night of the feast lost to lethargy. It quickly became apparent that the aches and bumps within my body came from sleeping the daylight hours on the ground and fresh bruises were blooming across my skin, beneath the smudged dirt and ash.

The torches led the way, and I followed each one like it would lead me to eternal salvation. I knew, deep within my soul, that it would at the very least lead me to food and the sweet relief that came with it. It was the food that made me pick up the pace as we all ventured further into the woods, our faces turned pale, and pain flickered across our expressions from the demand of hunger. The ground softened as we progressed, and the crowd of bodies thinned away from me as people started to spread out. It didn't take long for me to find myself walking along the side of the river, studying everything in a desperate search for something to eat. The torchlight flickered off the glassy top of the water, and I wondered if I would have to fish. I hoped not since I'd never tried before.

Gluttony's magic battered against me, insistent in his demand, and further increased responsiveness to fulfil his desires. The magic of an angel was heady, oppressive, and it could not be ignored.

Eat, feast, gorge!

It took me far too long to realise where the food was hidden. Hollowed knots in the trees, which might have normally been home to all manner of woodland creatures, instead held glass balls that contained delightful-looking sweets. Once the realisation dawned, I was practically hugging the rough bark of the tree. I scrambled up to reach and my hand darted into the tree. The glass orb was chilled as I pulled it free. It was smooth and shaped like an egg. Inside of it, I could see some sort of biscuit decorated with cream and plump, juicy strawberries. The sight of the bright fruit left my mouth watering. I swung my arm and the orb shattered against the tree. I barely managed to catch the biscuit, and as I did, cream smeared against my fingers. I lifted my finger for inspection. It was white with cream, tinged red with blood from a sharp piece of glass, and absently, I placed it in my mouth and sucked both off my skin.

I had the biscuit halfway to my lips when I thought of Phee. Sweet, innocent Phee who was wandering the woods somewhere, desperate for Samael to stake his claim. With a heavy sigh, I stumbled back to the edge of the river and sank to my knees again. Intuition warned me not to touch the water, in the same way I knew not to touch an open flame. My fingers scrabbled at the mud on the edge of the bank as I created a small well in the dirt and settled the biscuit within it. I rocked back until I sat on my heels and then glanced at my distorted reflection in the river.

I looked feral but alive.

"Come and get it, Samael." The impatience was stark in my tone. "I'm hungry, and I don't want to wait."

STEPHANIE GLUCK

Nothing happened for the longest time, or at least nothing that I noticed. Not until the temperature had dropped enough that I was shivering, and my breath puffed from my lips in white mist. I jolted surprise and breathed out slowly to watch it. As my eyes left the offering, it melted into the ground.

'Hmmm? No demands this time?' The voice was rough, and it pulled a deeper shudder from the depths of my body. I sucked in a sharp breath, and my palms fell to my thighs. Drops of blood from the cuts on my hands soaked into my dress.

"Not today, Samael," I whispered to the river, to the quiet, to the woods themselves. "Not today. Save me one for tomorrow."

The voice just chuckled in my ear, but the temperature rose as I snapped from my dazed inspection of the river. I crawled back up the bank and found my feet. I wondered if the time had come, and my brain had folded beneath the pressure of this entire foolish trial and these new cities and customs. I scrambled to the next available tree and ran my hands over the rough bark in search of a hole filled with food. Splinters slid sharply beneath my nails, though the pain dulled in comparison to the hunger that had returned after my offering.

There was nothing there, and my disappointment seemed tangible as I moved to the next tree, and the next, and the next, until I had seven glass eggs in my hands. Still, I wanted more. I found a space near the riverbank and settled in amongst the strange lilies that grew from the water, the same as the invasive pink flowers in my bathtub at Gluttony's palace. My fingers swept along the boggy ground in search of a rock, and when I found one, I shattered each of the eggs. I barely stopped to taste the sweets as they dissolved on my tongue. I shovelled each one past my lips and swallowed roughly.

The rough demand of magic eased just slightly. I was still hungry, but the compulsive feeling that if I didn't start eating I might die, abated just enough. With the glass shattered into

270

pieces around me, forming a dangerous nest of sharp edges, I rose to find more food. It became a successful hunt, but the more I ate, the more my mouth seemed to dry out, and the frenzy turned next into a hunt for water.

Each of the lush green lily pads were dry as a bone. Each one as dry as my mouth and tongue as I swiped it over my lips to attempt to steal moisture from the smudges of cream and chocolate I found there. It didn't help, so I found myself drifting closer and closer to the river. My body prickled with warning, but I ignored it as I knelt by the riverbank and stared into the crystalline depths of the river. It looked so clean, so untainted. Alarm pulsed through me as I leaned over the edge, and I ignored the warning that shivered through my body. I reached down and dragged my fingers through the water. It was so cool that it pulled a whine from the back of my throat. I licked my dry lips, but my tongue felt like sandpaper against them. I dipped my other hand in and watched as the river water pulled stickiness and dirt from my fingers. My hands formed a cup. My head dipped towards the water as I anticipated the sweet relief against my parched throat.

"Octavia!" My name echoed across the riverbank. The shout was loud and close—too close. Nash's normally hurried drawl was the snap of a tense rubber band.

"Don't! The others, they… they…" He ran at me. "Don't drink the water!"

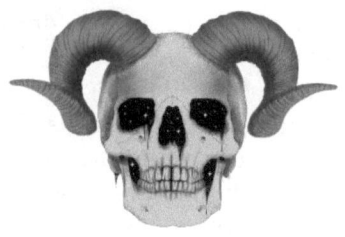

Chapter Thirty-Eight

I spun to face Nash, but my feet lost purchase against the slippery riverbank.

"Nash!" I cried, the world disappearing from beneath my feet. Panic spiked hot in my veins, and I reached for him with wild abandon. My fingers curled around a fistful of his shirt in hope that Nash would pull me free of the riverbank, but as I slid backwards, I took him down, too. We plunged beneath the glassy surface of the river, and where the bottom had looked so close, it now felt a world away. I sank blindly beneath the surface and let go of Nash as I thrashed and flailed to find my way back to the surface.

Where the water had been cool, it now felt frigid, and where I had been leaning in for a sip, I had swallowed a stomach full of the sweet-tasting water. It felt like my brain started spinning abruptly, and in my confusion, I had forgotten how to swim and tried to breathe. More water flowed into my lungs, and I choked on it, unable to find air. Unable to find the surface.

Not until Nash's hand wrapped around my dress and he ripped me from the depths of the river. We rolled onto the bank, mud dripping from our skin and hair after we had been washed clean. The impact of my body hitting the earth jolted me and my body convulsed. I vomited water onto the ground, repeatedly, until I was drawing in gasping breaths. My chest burned in reprimand of almost dying. Oxygen had become a bigger need than my hunger or my thirst, the latter of which was finally satiated. My soaked skin and the cold mud left me shivering, and my shivers turned to shudders as I realised I was sobbing aloud. The world spun in front of my eyes, and I pulled myself onto my hands and knees.

"Nash?" I croaked his name. The world seemed to shudder in front of my eyes. Two realities slipped in and out of place—I had almost killed him, and he had saved my life. Tears coursed down my face as two realities shuddered through my vision. One showed the blonde man on his knees in the mud, and he sobbed as hard as I did. His honeyed voice howled as he screamed a repetitive litany into the world.

"Alby! Alby! Alby! Alby!"

His complete and utter despair chilled me right through, but in the next blink, he was still. He looked strange, like he was there and not, all at once. His blonde hair stuck wet against his face. His skin had taken on a strange pale blue tinge, and he looked far too skinny, like the river had stolen his muscle and his strength. This reality flickered, but then settled firmly into place. Every time reality flickered between one scene and the next, it occurred to me that I was seeing things, but irrationally, I sunk emotionally into the moment before me.

Dread pooled in the pit of my belly, and I started hyperventilating. He was far too still, I realised a beat later. He wasn't moving at all. There was no curl of the left corner of his lips in wry amusement, and his throat didn't bob as he swallowed down comments he knew he shouldn't say. His fingers didn't move with a restless need to draw something or capture a moment, a colour, a memory in time. His chest didn't rise and fall with breaths.

Devastation swept hard through my body, and my entire torso wracked with deep sobs. My throat felt tight and scratchy as I struggled to breathe and accept the reality in front of me. I lifted a hand to my mouth and pressed my fingers to my lips to stifle my sobs. With my free hand, I reached tentatively for Nash's shoulder.

"Hey," I poked him. "Nash? Nash! Wake up!" I shook him harder, and harder, and on one shake, my world tipped sideways again and my reality changed. Nash was on his knees, sobbing for Alby to wake up, and before I could gasp in my next breath, he was dead once more. My brain couldn't work out what was true. Powerful grief rolled through me—a solid force intermingling with guilt as I remembered pulling him into the river with me. He had died, and I had killed him.

I knew it—I had seen a dead body before. Bloated and rotted with neglect, and at the time, I had wondered how someone could be so forgotten. Now I couldn't comprehend it at all, not when my chest felt like it had been cleaved in half at the fate of my friend. It occurred to me that if I had drowned and he had lived, maybe he would not feel the all-consuming sadness that I did. That didn't matter though, because I could feel the hole in my chest that his death left behind. The sadness that pulled wails of despair from my lips as I screamed and screamed in agonising grief, my fingers still wrapped into his shirt as I shook him and muttered demands for Nash to rise and to live.

I wailed aloud until my voice turned hoarse. I cried for Nash, who had died, and for myself, who had to live on as a murderer. It was only when my eyes burned as I ran out of tears that the loneliness joined the sadness occupying my soul. I scrambled away from Nash and attempted to climb the banks of the river, unable to sit beside the corpse any longer. I rolled into softer grass at the edge of the bank and tried once more to stifle the wracking sobs that started over and caused my entire chest to ache.

Fresh, hot tears rolled down my cheeks some fifteen minutes later, and I stood. The hunger in my belly raged for dominance against the strange hole in my heart. A hole that made no sense for the little that I knew Nash, but one I felt all the same, like a fragment of my world would never piece itself back together. Nothing would ever be the same again, and I would be lost to my wallowing and the knowledge that he had died too soon.

I ran forward and through the forest, and where the glimmer of a glass egg caught my eye. In any attempt to try and ignore the overwhelming despair that threatened to turn me numb, I feasted. In the moments I couldn't eat, I wailed. Until I realised the worst of it all... nobody else was wailing with me, nobody was dancing or cheering in celebration of the Feast of Samael, or of what they felt. The woodland creatures didn't titter and chip, there were no other sounds at all. The deep forest had turned deadly silent, and the only thing that I could hear was how my breath came too fast, and my blood thrummed in my ears—a drumbeat of doom that sparked in the depths of my very soul. A beat of judgement for my sins.

The world fractured and spun, I was dizzy and so worn out. I looked frantically for anyone else I knew. Phee or Helina, I would have even taken Niklaus' smirking face at that moment. I would have taken my brothers and the worried looks my father dished out. But fortune had never been good for me, and so not a soul made a sound, and no familiar faces surrounded me. I was completely and utterly alone. In the moments that I had been preoccupied with Nash and his lifeless body, they had all fled. They had left me to die with him, and they had not cared enough to come back and ensure I was alive.

Another piece of my heart fractured in my chest. I ached with unfathomable sadness, pain. The cracks in my heart fissured into something wild that I could not ignore. I was alone and unwanted, replaced and left behind. I wished I had died on the bank with Nash Wickham. I was better off dead and forgotten the way I had been when Scarlett was born. When, suddenly, my pre-teenage moods were all too much. Or later, when addiction led to theft and desperation, and I could see in the eyes of my family that they wanted me to just disappear forever. They would get their wish.

I would die here, choking on the palpable feeling of my own grief.

Nash had died, and everyone else had left me here alone to join him. I sobbed until the tears ran out again, and then long after that. Every time that I thought I could stop, stand, and move on, I was gripped by the gaping hole inside of my chest. It was jagged and it was ugly, like an Erlkang had tried to rip out my heart from beneath my ribs. It was invisible to the naked eye, but I felt it. I felt it every time I drew a breath, every time I opened my eyes, and each time I tried to move. This chasm that left me less of a person, destined to never be whole again. How could I keep going when so much of myself was missing? I felt it as it grew wider, until I was losing myself to the bone deep sadness that emanated from it.

I would look up, and the world would tilt on its axis for a moment. In the place of the deadly silent tree, I could see sprawled bodies and hear the echo of haunted, hopeless wails. It was the wind, I knew as much, just the forest itself taunting me with how alone I was. It teased me with the wails and screams of other people to feed into my desperation and hurt. I wanted so badly to be wanted, but I was here, alone and forgotten.

My chest ached and my muscles were worn out from the movement of constant chest wracking sobs. The sadness itself just wouldn't stop, and it echoed in the tremble of my lips and the pain in my eyes. I curled up on the ground and drew my feet to my chest. I sobbed and wailed, loud and violent, until the morning broke across the sky in coral orange and cotton candy pink. Until Gluttony's magic left the trees trembling and pulled me into a deep daytime sleep.

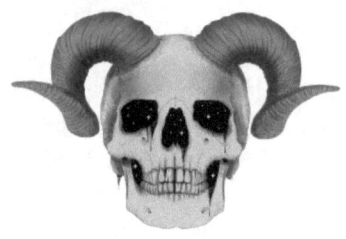

Chapter Thirty-Nine

Hazel eyes and a broken smile filled my vision after the night fell. I opened my eyes to Nash's lightly freckled face and reeled back so fast that he seemed immediately concerned. His hands raised in a placating manner—mouth puckered in a frown. I kept my eyes on him carefully as I skittered backwards and assessed every inch of the man.

"But—" My lower lip wobbled, and my gaze turned glassy. "You died."

A sob flowed from my throat, raw and reminiscent of the night before, and then I felt like I was too fragile for the world right now. "You died! And they all left me here with your body."

Nash flinched. "It wasn't real, Octavia, I'm alive," he spoke slowly, softly, like speaking too fast might spook me even more. "I tried to tell you not to drink the water. It was the river... the river made everyone cry."

My eyes flickered past him to the riverbed, and the water that flowed on like we had never disrupted it. My throat tightened and I pressed the pad of one of my fingers against Nash's face. It sunk into the soft flesh of his cheek, and he snorted.

"Alive," he reminded me, and I sighed.

"Are we?" I stared at my own hands now.

"Just barely," Nash replied. "But alive is a start, Octavia."

I scoffed. I couldn't quite shake the suspicion that had settled in my bones. The knowledge that some part of it might have been real, and I was truly alone in this world.

"Let's go," he whispered then and held out a hand to help me to my feet.

After a moment of deliberation, I took it. His skin was too warm for a corpse. "Where do we go?" I asked, and Nash pointed through the woods. It took me a moment to catch on and notice the same flickering torches from the night before. The same light in the path to usher us through.

We moved wearily and picked our way through the thick trees. The path was winding and steep before we came to a halt at the base of a second giant willow. The tree creaked and groaned, leaves swaying as the wind moved through the forest. People huddled together for warmth and human touch—a mixture of Gulan citizens and cuffed competitors. All were quiet until the chancellor shifted to stand at the base of the willow. He looked ever the same in his robes of starlight, and his expression impassive. I studied his face to ensure he didn't seem happy, in that moment, not after what I had been through the night before. Not when the dregs of sadness still lingered in the quiet hush of the moonlight.

"Day three of our celebrations," the chancellor did not hesitate in his announcement. He did not wait for our wholehearted attention, for our hearts had been shattered. "We come now to explore the mushroom caves beneath our oldest willow. Within this palace, you will experience the true depth of *fear*."

I felt my throat tighten, and my heart picked up in pace. After the last week, I wouldn't have been surprised if it was worn out completely and always beating off-kilter. As I glanced around the group, I saw that neither citizens nor competitors looked thrilled at the concept of our next experience. The amount of Gulans who were participating had dwindled, and I was sure that I, along with many other worn-out competitors, would have stopped too, if given the chance. Nobody had said when the trial was going to end, though, and I suspected I would need to face all seven days.

The chancellor cleared his throat. "Tonight, you may only travel in pairs, and once you enter together, the magic will bind you. You will not be able to move more than five feet apart," the chancellor added, and soft murmurs rose from the crowd. Someone even swore.

Already, citizens started to pair off. Magic pulsed from the centre of the forest and slammed into me so hard that I stumbled back a step. Despite eating so much lately that my belly had developed a softer edge, and I felt full even after waking, hunger roared to life within me. I was so emotionally drained that my body felt like it might give way to the feeling, and my knees shook. A moment too late, I realised that most people had a partner. I trudged to the base of the willow and watched as they passed the chancellor and slipped below the earth. I rubbed my stomach absently as I attempted to ignore Gluttony's influence, and spun on my heel to look for Nash.

"Oh." I breathed when I spotted Phee pressed against his side like a kitten hiding from the cold. Surprise must have shown on my face as Phee's expression turned uncertain, and she looked between us.

"You don't mind if I go in with Nashy, right?" Phee's lower lip wobbled, and I had the feeling it was a tried-and-true method of getting what she wanted. "It's just… fear, you know, I'd feel better going in with him…"

So would I—better Nash than a stranger—but he offered me a slow nod. I didn't know if it was the go-ahead to let him go with Phee, or the go-ahead to demand he be my partner. The loneliness from the night before still lingered in my bones and pushed me to think he'd rather go with Ophelia.

I shook my head and pushed hair from my face. "It's fine, it's fine."

"Thanks, Tav."

"I'm just thankful that you survived last night," I added. My eyes flickered to Nash's face, and I bypassed the haunted flicker in his gaze to study the edges of his lips to ensure they weren't still tinged blue. Dead man walking. I shivered.

"Us too." Phee's head bounced, and then she started pulling Nash towards the tunnels. He looked less than impressed at the thought of entering them. "Let's go, we still have to offer our tithe, and I'm so, so, *so* hungry."

At those words, my own feelings of hunger intensified. I cringed and wrapped an arm across my belly. With a resigned sigh, I turned to find a partner for the night. My gaze immediately found green eyes.

"Nik?" I stumbled towards him. The man's eyebrow rose and something dark and shadowy flickered in his eyes—dark enough to give me pause. I slowed, and my eyes dropped from his face to his full lips and strong jaw. His skin was marked with blood and dirt, but beneath it, I could not see the brightness of flowers against his throat.

"Mikhael!" I corrected softly. A fraction of the darkness in his eyes melted away as I added a quick apology. "I'm sorry, I knew that… I just… *sorry*."

I bit my lip and glanced away. As much as Mikhael had claimed the two were not so identical, if not for the markings that graced his brother's skin, I might never have been able to tell them apart. It would be a strange existence to investigate another's face and see your own staring back at you. Mikhael cleared his throat and his hand waved in an impatient gesture for me to join him.

"Be my partner, Octavia?" he asked, and his stomach growled in keen demand, loud enough for me to hear. I would have giggled had my entire body not ached with the need to follow in Gluttony's command again. I felt like my hunger was a beast beneath my skin, which grew worse and more temperamental with every night that passed. My chin jerked in a quick nod, and Mikhael let out a slow breath. I wondered if he had thought I would reject him.

Ever the leader, Mikhael Heira carved a path past the chancellor and to the base of the giant tree. It was here that I could see the wide, hollow opening, and the tunnel that dipped into the earth below us. Mikhael paused and I noticed the muscles in his shoulders bunch.

"I've never been underground before." I could hear the soft tremor of caution in my voice, and wondered if the tunnels, if not the tree itself, would collapse on top of us. Mikhael's back relaxed once I had spoken and broke his reverie.

"Me either," Mikhael admitted, and I nodded. It should have been obvious, since there hadn't been anywhere in Ilrea that extended beneath the rubble and dirt.

"Should we?" There were people pressed impatiently at my back now, and before I could say any more, Mikhael reached back to brace an arm around my shoulders. He pulled me firmly to his side and marched forward, dragging me, step by step, with him. Neither going first or last as we descended into the tunnels, and the ground swallowed us whole.

The tunnels created a strange network of crossing paths, which descended rapidly at first, and then joined into an enormous cavern. Pairs of people lingered within, and I could only see them because of the luminescent mushrooms that grew along the walls. They were fat, fleshy little spores that sprouted out in every direction and glowed in soft yellows and blues. As we passed, Mikhael lifted a hand and ripped the fungi from its place. By the time he turned to face me, he had them cupped in his hands and the soft glow of them threw shadows across the sharp angles of his face. He looked as otherworldly as Gluttony beneath their light. He pushed two of the plump little mushrooms into my grip and raised his hands to his face to eat.

"The tithe—" I gasped, even as Gluttony's power and the force of my ever-growing hunger caused tears to pool in my eyes and roll down my cheeks. Mikhael just grunted, chewed, swallowed, and turned for more. He shifted down a nearby hallway, and the magic shoved against me like a physical force. I stumbled after him as it forced me to stay close.

In the distance, people began to scream. Wild wails of utter terror. My knees wobbled and I dropped down into the dirt as my legs refused to hold me upright. Mikhael stuffed mushrooms into his mouth like a man possessed, and I crushed the fungi beneath my fingertips. The magic pushed at my body; Gluttony's influence slid beneath my skin, itchy and hard to ignore. I was hungry... so hungry that my hands shook. One of the mushrooms tumbled onto the dirt floor, and it crossed my mind to pick it up and have a taste. I could so easily follow

Mikhael into the reckless abandon of the magic. Slowly, though, I forced myself to think of Phee, and forced myself to whisper softly.

"Samael."

'Little one, you're back!' his voice slid against my senses, and like the other times, Gluttony's influence was suppressed as he spoke. I groaned with relief as the hunger abated.

"An offering," I murmured and took my eyes off the glowing mushroom on the ground. He laughed, a melody in my ear that left my blood singing in the strangest way. I wanted to make him laugh again. I wondered which depiction of the devil he truly looked like—the skull with twisted horns, the three-faced viper, or the charming man.

'Much appreciated.' The amusement in his voice was clear. *'Now, little one, did you want a secret tonight?'*

I did, and I didn't. I thought it might be a dangerous pastime to collect the secrets of the devil, but had I not already invited him right into my soul? It felt like I had, with the realisation that his voice didn't echo into my ear at all but passed through my mind like it was one of my own thoughts. I wanted to extend my reprieve from Gluttony, though, and that meant I had to converse with the devil a little longer.

I shuddered. "Yes," I finally agreed. "How do I survive this? This feast, we're not even halfway through and I feel like... I feel..." A sob rolled off my lips. There was a thud as Mikhael fell to his knees in front of me and let out a strangled scream. It was muffled from the devil's influence but still loud enough to roll off the cavern walls. Fear banded around my chest at the sound of it, but I couldn't move.

'Hmm,' the devil hummed, and that dark chuckle echoed through my mind again. It drowned out the sound of pure agony escaping Mikhael's lips. *'When the moment is right, find temperance. Then you will survive.'*

A strangled noise caught in my throat, and my thoughts raced. "That's not an answer! Who the fuck is Temperance?" I whispered, and the devil laughed thrice. I had the feeling that it was at my expense.

The feather-light pressure of his presence lifted before I could object. My stomach cramped around the sudden and intrusive feeling of emptiness that reappeared. It squeezed again, in hard demand, and I quickly shovelled the first of the luminous mushrooms into my mouth. It was chewy and tasted like dirt, but it would do the trick. As soon as the meal hit my stomach, I couldn't get enough. I stumbled towards the wall and plucked more mushrooms free. They grew back as fast as I managed to rip them free of the dirt, and I had two fistfuls pushed into the hollows of my cheeks before Mikhael let out another strangled yelp.

He shifted, too far away, and the magic tugged me backwards so forcefully that I landed in the dirt. "What are you doing?" I yelped as he pulled himself to his feet. I forced myself upright again. In the darkness of the cave, I could just see the hard grit of his teeth and the glazed look in his eyes. His pupils were blown wide, and the irises shone with the same glow as the mushrooms. I chewed and swallowed, and Mikhael stepped in beside me. He ate mindlessly, pushed by the magic, but I quickly realised he couldn't see me, only something else. Just like last night, the hallucinations had begun.

Mikhael's gaze flickered from side to side, witness to a conversation I could not hear. Stupidly, I pushed another mushroom to my lips to free my hand and reached out to touch him. It was a bad idea.

"Nik!" he growled and lurched forward. His entire body barrelled right into me. My back slammed against the wall and pieces of rock scraped against my skin. "Run, I have it in hand, Nik, get out of here!"

"No. I'm Octavia," I corrected him, even as Mikhael's strong fingers fisted in my hair, and his other hand found purchase at my throat. My scalp burned so badly that tears pooled in my eyes and he pinned me in place.

Stupidly, I realised I was *it* and not Nik in his hallucinations.

"I'll kill you before I let you take Nik from me! Do you hear me?!" Mikhael spat, and his fingers tightened around my throat. I grasped at his wrist, unable to stop myself from pushing another glowing mushroom past my lips at the same time. I was hungry, but I was in so much trouble.

"I'm—" I gasped as his nails pressed hard into the sides of my throat. "Not…" I tugged at his hand but couldn't find the right grip. Oh, devil, I was so hungry.

"I'm Octavia." I couldn't get enough air as he squeezed. The world spun.

A long time ago, I had been told it took ten seconds to pass out from strangulation, and these were the longest ten seconds of my life. My foot swung out, half-blind in the dark, and landed firmly between Mikhael's legs. A lucky shot. Through the haze of what he felt, the man yelped and let go as his hands dropped quickly to cradle his balls. We both slipped to the floor. I gasped for air and crawled to the side. As I moved, I reached for another mushroom, unable to stop eating them. As I chewed and chewed, something heady slipped through my veins. A slow and potent poison, and the shadows in the tunnel began to grow. The world flickered from one idea to the next as I lost my grip to a drugged reality.

I choked on mushrooms and fear as my nightmares came to life before my eyes.

286

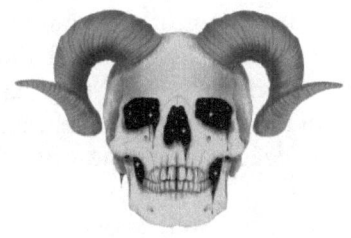

Chapter Forty

They slipped in and out of my vision, flickering into existence in the soft glow of the fungi-lined walls. With shadow for blood and bone, they were there, and they were not. My rational mind said something so incorporeal could not hurt me, but at the same time, the scars down my spine felt like they had ripped right open again—evidence of what these creatures could do. A strangled moan escaped my lips, equal parts hunger, and bone-deep distress. My back throbbed. My feet felt like they were wrought of bricks as I found them again. I fell against the wall; my fingers scraped against dirt to find enough leverage to keep myself upright.

"Stay away," I croaked and shuffled backwards. The giant Erlkang of my nightmares sucked in a deep, rattling breath. The sound caused me to whimper, and I stumbled over my own heavy feet as I tried to back down the tunnel.

The demon flickered out of sight but had moved two paces forward when it reformed. For the first time, I was given an unhindered look at the creatures that had featured in my nightmares every night for the past week. Each wisp of shadow looked pointed and deadly, from the tips of their claws to the sharp curl of their feet.

The Erlkang towered well above me, and I could see the glow of the fungi in between the flickering shadows of its ribs. How had I not known it would be twice as tall as me? The hair raised on the back of my neck as it slipped forward, and I realised it was hunting me. The worst part of all was its face. It was sharply angled like the rest of the creature, but the Erlkang had a mouth that seemed to open to a void. Sharp black teeth protruded in two rows from both the top and bottom jaw. It inhaled—a death rattle that I felt in my bones.

"No, no, no, no!" I cried and scrambled towards the other side of the tunnel. The back of my heel caught on the body of a man, and I hit the ground hard. I whimpered, my head bouncing so hard off the floor that dark spots floated in front of my eyes. My brain converted each spot into Erlkangs, which formed right in front of my eyes. That was how they must start out. Flickers of darkness on the edge of my consciousness, twisted into a bigger danger. I kicked out at them. Fear spiked so abruptly in my veins that I tasted copper on my tongue and felt warm urine slide down my legs and saturate my dress. I didn't have room outside of the overwhelming fear to feel embarrassed.

"Please," I wailed. My legs struck the man I had fallen over as I tried to use him for purchase to get away. "Eat him! Eat him! Leave my soul alone!"

In the next moment, Mikhael had rolled on top of me and pinned me into the dirt. "I'll kill you! Strike him again and I'll kill you," he seethed, and I thrashed beneath him.

"The Erlkang!" I screamed.

"Don't touch him!" Mikhael roared back.

"Mikhael! Mikhael!" I writhed in his grip. "It's coming! Move!"

"Better yet…" Mikhael roared. "I'll do it now."

We were trapped in separate nightmares. My wrists stung where he kept them pinned and he didn't budge an inch as I thrashed around. Behind him, the rattle of the Erlkang pierced through the air. All his weight pressed against my thighs to pin me down. He was making an offering out of me; I was sure of it.

"I'll kill you!" Mikhael roared again. He let go of my wrists, and both his hands circled a collar of flesh around my throat instead.

"Mikhael!" I cried as he squeezed hard and oxygen was lost. My lungs burned, and my fist flew at him. It bounced off his shoulders and he didn't even flinch. He squeezed tighter. Until my hands fell back to the dirt. The Erlkang crowded over Mikhael's shoulder. It leaned in close. Its pure white eyes seemed almost gleeful as the shadowy creature melded right into the man. Mikhael Heira morphed into my worst nightmare.

Suddenly, it wasn't thick fingers and blunt nails that cut off my air supply, but blackened claws that dug deep and painfully into my soft flesh. It tore through skin and muscle easily. I gasped, unable to find enough air to scream out loud. With a last burst of energy, my fists bounced off the dark, deadly creature. In a moment of desperation, I found a rock. Blunt, too smooth, and my only hope. I swung it as hard as I could. My eyes stayed closed, and I prayed to the devil with everything I had. I could only hope that the Erlkang would stay formed enough for me to do some damage. My hand fell back to the ground. My lungs burned and darkness flooded my vision.

The Erlkang toppled to the side with a human groan of pain. I sucked in a lung full of dusty air. The creature collapsed half atop of my body. Time slipped away as I lay there. I knew I needed to move, get out from under the creature before it moved again, but all I could think about was the fact that I was starving. So hungry that my stomach felt like it was a black hole. I wriggled my way out from beneath the creature. It was a slow process, and I couldn't breathe properly until the entire weight of it was free from my chest. I rolled onto my stomach and crawled across the floor of the tunnels; fingers outstretched to consume another mushroom.

"Fuck Temperance and fuck you," I whispered into the tunnel. "She didn't save me. I saved myself!"

Momentarily, the blind fear and constant hunger melted away as the devil laughed, a ripple of feeling and noise against my drugged mind. Time moved fast under the guise of fear, and in the world above, the sun began to appear over the mountains. Deep in the centre of the forest, Gluttony raged, bored and impatient with the night. With an impervious wave of his hand, we all fell still.

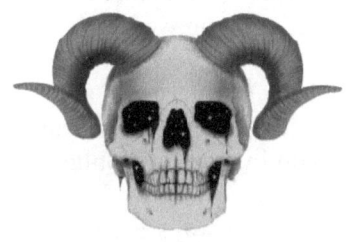

Chapter Forty-One

It was terrifying to wake in the pitch-black caves. The soft glow of the fungi had dimmed, and I could barely see in the low light left behind. As my eyes opened, I became profoundly aware of the pain in my throat and the stench of urine. It was smothering and unavoidable, causing me to gag as I sat up slowly.

"You're awake." Tendrils of fear snaked down my spine and I shuffled backwards.

"Stay away!" I gasped. The words sounded gravelly, and it hurt to speak.

"It's just me," Mikhael muttered softly. "Just me. Mikhael."

He edged closer, and in the soft light, I could see the familiar lines of his face. I rubbed at my throat and watched him suspiciously. "Last night, you were…"

"I know." He didn't voice that I had turned into his worst fear, and I didn't have the nerve to ask him what he had seen. Part of me thought it could be worse than my own fears, and I didn't know if I could live with two nightmares in my head. "Let me help you up."

Mikhael Heira was always the gentleman. A stark contrast to his brother. We both ignored the way I flinched when he took my hands and pulled me to my feet. I was unsteady, deeply tired despite the way I had slept the day away. This entire celebration had taken its toll on me.

The Feast of Samael was not for the faint of heart.

We made slow progress out of the tunnels and into the moonlight above. The moment light filtered through, I glanced toward Mikhael, just to make sure that it was truly him. A gasp rolled from my lips. "Your head!" Devil below, it hurt so badly to speak. He had a large gash at his temple and half his face was covered in dried blood. It flaked away from his skin, and he raised his brows, reaching to touch it before inspecting the blood on his fingers.

"No wonder it's killing me," he muttered. I nodded. "I think I remember you hitting me with a rock…" I wanted to protest that I had hit the demon with a rock to save my life. However, the unsettling reality was that what I thought had been a creature of shadows and death had simply been Mikhael, caught in the same miserable trap.

"Sorry," I whispered.

"Don't be." He waved the apology off.

"Why?"

"Apparently, I deserved it." Mikhael's voice turned rough as his eyes flickered to my throat. I lifted my hand to touch it, but couldn't feel the scratchy surface of dried blood, or the pinpricks of pain from an open wound.

"I'm fine." The grating edge of voice from my bruised vocal cords proved it a lie. We shared a look, and I knew we would never speak of what we had seen in those caves. Strangely, I felt an odd sense of trust in Mikhael Heira now, for enduring it with me.

Mikhael put distance between us, his hands slid into his pockets, and torment darkened in his eyes. "I'll make it up to you."

"It wasn't you," I insisted, and shivered because this trial was going to kill me. One way or another.

"I swear it," Mikhael muttered. He glanced around the crowd. "I need to find Nik." Without so much as a goodbye, he shouldered his way through the group, and I found myself very much alone again.

As I followed the crowd, I watched the bedraggled residents from the city glancing between each other and turning to walk the other way. They left without consequence, and my heart ached to follow them. Instead, I walked like a zombie along the low-lit path until we came to a halt. The fatigue in my bones pulled at me, so I dropped to sit on a nearby rock. My entire body ached like I had been beaten, and I buried my face in my hands. The chancellor took his time appearing that night. His dark hair was slicked back, and I noticed for the first time that his nose was crooked and slightly too hooked.

"Tonight," he smiled, all white teeth. "I give you *disgust!*"

He waved a hand towards a table filled with knives and other weapons. The crowd didn't cheer, there wasn't a whisper of noise, and the chancellor looked visibly upset at this reaction. "Tonight, you must hunt and make your own meal."

He knew his audience, and it showed. Aside from the few select chefs that were considered artists in their trade, the people of Gula did not cook, so I had no doubt that the few residents that were left would be shocked at the concept. If I was completely honest, I didn't think I could stomach the idea of it either. When it became clear that the chancellor would not continue until someone spoke, a voice rose from the crowd.

"Hunt what, exactly?" Helina's sharp tone was unmistakable in its derision. I turned to look for the woman but could not make her out from within the crowd.

The chancellor beamed and threw his arms wide. That was what he had been waiting to hear. "Wild hogs!" he announced. "In honour of our namesake emblem."

I thought of Gluttony's tattoo, the pig etched into his skin and the back of his currency, and my chest tightened. I didn't think I could manage to catch and hunt a soft-edged pig, let alone a tusked hog.

Nonetheless, I moved with everyone else and staggered towards the table of tools. It was loaded high, and as bodies crowded in front of it, the selection narrowed quickly. I looked over the meagre choices and snatched up a long, thin knife. As I turned away, the distinct shape of a box of matches caught my eye and I snaked my hand out to grasp them. Once they were in my hand, I followed all my instincts to run. I bolted into the forest to my left and ran through the undergrowth until I was sure I was alone. It didn't seem wise to linger when emotional people were in possession of weapons. I turned the knife in my hand and realised I'd never really used one. It felt heavy and awkward in my grip, but I hoped I would be okay.

Five minutes later, Gluttony woke, and the forest shuddered as the now-familiar hollow feeling slammed into my stomach. I gasped and doubled over. It felt like the feeling of famine grew stronger with every night, and I couldn't be half sure that my stomach wasn't beginning to eat away at itself in pure desperation. The distinct grunt of hogs floated through the air as they appeared in the forest. They were not quiet creatures—they ploughed noisily through the undergrowth with squeals of rage.

"Of course." I huffed and straightened. "Of course, they couldn't be happy little piglets."

The knife felt awkward in the too tight way that I held onto the worn handle. I angled it away from my body, careful of the sharp edges, and gripped the box of matches in my other hand. It took a long time to battle through the leafy undergrowth, even longer still until I came across a hog. It was a beastly thing, as large as my youngest sibling but with wild beady eyes and winding, dirty tusks. Its wiry, dark fur was twisted and matted. It came tearing towards me. Beady little eyes raged, a loud squeal tore from its bulking body. My entire body convulsed at the idea of having to kill it and then eat it.

Time seemed to stand still for a second, my heart hammering, but at the last minute, I threw myself out of the way. I crashed into a tree; the air rushed out of my lungs. The hog disappeared and my stomach complained sharply about the lack of food. The push of Gluttony's power caused me to cringe. I needed something to eat. Even though my stomach turned at the only option being the hog, I still wanted it.

I tried to stave off the never-ending hunger and deny the task that had been set. I wandered the forest in search of any other food. Berries or nuts, I'd even brave the river again for a fish. I plucked leaves from a tree and chewed on them slowly, but they turned bitter and acidic on my tongue. They burned in my mouth until I spat them back on the ground. I was faced with the inevitability of my situation. The hog needed to be found and killed, or I would fail. I could faintly smell smoke in the distance and heard the cries of hogs as their lives were cut brutally short. By the time I heard the telltale rustling and moved closer, the entire knife was trembling in my grip. Time moved slowly as I tried to ready myself, and with a raspy scream, I launched myself over the log and swung the knife wildly,

"What the fuck?!" The words cut through me. I stopped with the knife an inch from Helina Archer's gut. My eyes wide and wild, I looked up at my friend. I inhaled a shaky breath and let the knife drop onto the ground. The moment I did, Helina's entire weight shoved me off balance. My feet slipped on wet leaves, and I went sprawling to the ground. A place that I seemed to spend most of my time lately.

"You were going to kill me?!" Helina screeched.

"Hel—" I shook my head.

"Your stupid bitch!" Helina towered over me and sneered down the end of her nose. "Is that the only way you can think to win?"

"What?!" I pulled myself into a seated position and tried to edge away from her.

"First, you replace me with that idiot blonde." Helina sneered, and I wondered if she meant Nash or Phee. "And now you think you can gut me?"

Helina leaned down and I frowned back. "I thought you were a hog…"

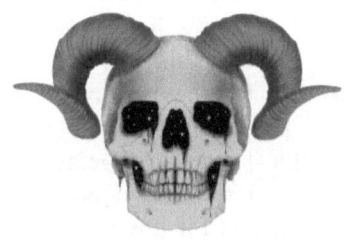

Chapter Forty-Two

Too late, I realised it was the wrong thing to say. Helina's face clouded over and turned stormy.

"Do you even think before you speak, Octavia?" She snarled. "I guess not because that would require having more than one working brain cell, and I'm fairly sure you don't even have that."

I flinched and raised my hands to placate her anger. My stomach was queasy with hunger, but Helina had become the more immediate threat. "I didn't mean it like that," I whispered, despite the way my throat ached. "Hel, you know me. You've known me forever, we're best friends... I wouldn't hurt you."

A sneer curled at the edges of Helina's lips and her eyes flickered with revulsion. Desperately, I hoped that the other woman had already eaten and that this was just the effects of the magic, like the fear had been, and the sadness before that. I ignored the sight of Helina's hands—too clean to have killed anything—and the fact that this was not a hallucination because they had never been a shared experience before.

"Best friends? Are you dumb?" Helina snapped in a tone that implied I shouldn't answer. "Octavia, me being your only friend doesn't make you my best friend."

I shook my head and bit down on my lip as I edged back once again. My fingers slipped closer to my knife and further from the danger that emanated from Helina.

"I kind of thought…" I whispered, and Helina glowered. The force of the disgust on her face as she looked right through me killed the explanations in my throat. Reminiscing of nights spent giggling over townsfolk or sharing food and secrets would do me no good.

"You entered this competition to take the prize from me and hold me back," Helina accused.

The splintered and stretched edges of my patience snapped. I reached for the knife and climbed unsteadily to my feet. My body felt strangely hot and cold at once as I stared at Helina. We had a history of her walking all over me, and I rarely, if ever, stood up to anything she said. Somehow, I found my voice.

"I hate to tell you, Hel." My throat protested vehemently against speaking with a sharp spike of pain. "While your head might be the size of a planet, the world doesn't revolve around you."

Helina scoffed. "Earth rotates around the sun, you uneducated Harpy."

"Who cares?" I asked and shook my head wildly. "Who the fuck cares!?"

Laughter rose in my throat, and I threw my hands up, the blade of the knife slicing through the air. "We're in a devils-damned forest hunting live animals to survive the night. I'm dirty and tired and you want to point out my lack of education?! Nobody here cares if you know your ABCs, Helina!"

Helina clenched her teeth and her nose lifted in the air. I had the distinct impression that I was nothing more than dirt under her foot. "You stink like piss, Octavia," was all she said, a low blow.

My eyes drifted through the treetops in search of the moon, and I shook my head. Helina Archer was a lost cause. "Nash was right," I said sadly. "You are a bad friend."

Helina's eyes darkened. "I'm not your friend at all."

I flinched when her words hit the mark. "Isn't that the truth."

All I could think of was the years of sitting in Helina's room as we talked well into the night of crushes, hurt feelings, and happiness. Now my friend looked at me like I was abhorrent.

"I'm your competition," Helina stated, oblivious to my inner turmoil about how she could forsake me so easily. "Of course, you don't get it, right? The devil doesn't want just anyone. He doesn't want all of us. He especially doesn't want you."

I knew what Helina was truly saying… he didn't want me in comparison to Helina. I wondered what things Samael whispered into Helina's ear, what feelings his words had twisted and brought to the surface. Did he whisper those sentiments?

"So, give up."

"*What*?"

"Give up, Octavia." Helina closed the space between us. We both jerked under the demand of the magic as it pulsed in demand that we feast. "You may as well put the knife through your own heart." Helina backed away, and she couldn't help but lash out with the last word. "You're already dead to me."

The sharp ache of betrayal in my chest matched the jarring sensation in my gut. An hour later, I clutched the knife like a lifeline and staggered to my right. It felt like Helina had opened a wound that might never heal. I could feel the magic of the evening pushing her on, and there was very little time to dwell on it. I needed to survive just out of spite. By the time I found a hog, it felt like I had taken the knife to my own stomach. It fissured and spasmed with intense hunger, and I knew now how old prisoners of war might have chewed off their own hands from starvation.

The hog was snuffling on the ground, large tusks ripping up the foliage. I tiptoed through the woods as quietly as possible and approached it. I fell still when it looked up, my heart hammering in my chest. My entire body trembled with the intense need to eat.

For a moment, I closed my eyes.

"You can do this," I whispered. "It's just like cutting up normal food." My gaze latched to the hog again. "If you ignore the fact that it's alive," I whispered to myself and dropped my chin to my chest. That was one element that was hard to ignore. The hog had spotted me, and my breathing hitched as its beady eyes seemed to narrow. It let out a wild squeal that echoed through my very soul. It came charging towards me in the next second, determined and wild. Its large tusks shined with wet blood and dirt beneath the moonlight.

The world narrowed to a point, and I realised that these hogs were more dangerous than I had expected, and it came down to a moment of my own survival or letting the hog live. The hog didn't slow. A pained shriek left my lips as I twisted to the left and blindly stabbed down with the knife. It found resistance against the hog's side, and filled with panic, I lifted my hand and stabbed at it again, and again, and again. Blood pooled, hot and slippery between my fingers. I sank the knife down again until the hog fell silent and still. Its pained and panicked squealing would echo in my ears for the rest of the night. The knife clattered to the ground, and I lifted my bloodstained hands to inspect them.

My angry belly churned, and I turned to the side, retching as I vomited up acidic bile. "I killed it." I felt numb. My fingers trembled as I offered the dead hog a long look. "Fuck, *fuck*! I killed it."

I had been hungry in the past, but never so hungry to kill food instead of stealing it. I had felt blood before and had staunched the flow of it on my own cuts and bruises, but it had never flowed so hot and free across my skin. The feeling was sickening, and there was no way to wash it off. My stomach churned in warning that I was about to vomit again, and I pressed a fist to my stomach to stop it. The growl of agony from my gut in response left me shaking. I stared down at the hog and tried to work out what to do next.

It took me ten minutes to pick up the knife again, and I cried the entire time. I mangled the creature as I attempted to carve the skin from its flesh, and then struggled further in my attempt to remove flesh from bone. My entire body ached from demand and the pressure of magic by the time I had fistfuls of dark flesh scattered in the dirt around me. Each one seemed a little more grotesque than the last. They were not dainty, well-sliced pieces like the dinner out with the Bell family. They were rough and ravaged, carved with pure desperation. I picked them up and brushed the leaves from each piece before I set them down on the hog, then turned my attention to the next issue.

Fire. The box of matches had scattered when I hit the ground, so I was left scrambling for the thin bits of wood and the box itself. In the end, I could only locate three unbroken matches. It felt like the entire night should have passed in the time it took me to build a pile of twigs and dry leaves. The first match hissed and fizzled before I could lower it to the leaves. My stomach twisted unpleasantly. The second match snapped in half. I held my breath and struck the matchbox a third time. I lowered it gently to the kindling. When it caught and flared with bright fire, I could have cried. I hurried to feed the fire and ensure it grew because I knew I couldn't stomach eating the hog raw.

"Come on, come on," I muttered as the flames danced, and threw off heat. Enough that some of my shivering stopped. It had been induced by the cooling blood on my skin and not the endurance of my never-ending hunger. Once the fire seemed content to stay lit, I sawed the knife through each piece of meat to cut it smaller and cook it faster, and tossed them into the crackling flames. The smell of roasting meat wafted through the air as I waited, and I pulled myself from the ground to search for a stick long enough to extract the meal without burning the flesh from my bones. When the charred meat sat in the dirt in front of me, I groaned and realised I had not yet paid the devil for my meal.

"Take it, Samael," I whispered, and reached for one of the other pieces, only to singe my fingers from the heat of it. "Ah! Take it so I can eat, *please*."

The pressure of Gluttony's magic was never so apparent as when it lifted. I realised it had been pushing at me from all directions. Squeezing me through an invisible tube.

'You're running out of time tonight, little one.' The piece of meat disappeared, and I stared into the fire.

"I'm forever running out of time," I admitted. "And chances."

'Time is a mortal construct. It exists not in Eternis.'

I laughed hollowly. "I am nothing if not mortal."

'Everyone is mortal compared to me.'

"What about your immortal souls?"

'Even them. All souls wear away, even if it takes an eternity. The devil continues on.' There was amusement in his low hum, which raised the hairs on the back of my arms. I had the distinct feeling we were nothing but a game for him, so I changed the subject quickly.

"I killed it." I studied my hands and the pieces of charred meat—one short as payment of my tithe. "I killed it."

'This will not be the last time you kill in my trials, little one.' I had nothing to say to that. A shudder worked violently down each knot in my spine.

'Eat,' the devil commanded then. I shivered at the bossiness of his tone. *'Eat quickly, or you will fail.'* His presence disappeared and the magic slammed back into me so hard that I cried out. When I looked up, I could see the first tinge of orange lighting the sky as the sun sought to rise above.

The dirt on the rapidly cooling meat was ignored, and I reached for the singed flesh and shovelled it in my mouth. I had barely swallowed my only bite of the night when my eyes rolled back in my head, and I fell into unconsciousness.

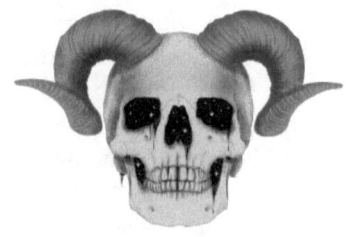

Chapter Forty-Three

The moon had fully risen by the time I woke again. The ash of the forgotten fire had blown across my body throughout the day. I could taste it, bitter on my tongue, as I swept it across my lips. As I staggered to my feet, I realised that for the first morning ever, I had woken with normal pangs of hunger instead of the feeling of over-fullness. After eating more than I realised every other night, my body rebelled against the single mouthful of hog.

A light flared in the distance, and I stumbled towards it. As I moved, I came across a body on the ground. A girl who lay unnaturally still, her eyes closed and her chest unmoving, an iridescent cuff secured around her wrist. She had not woken from the magically induced sleep, and when I pressed my fingers to her cold neck, I couldn't find a pulse. I wondered if that is what would have happened to me if I had not eaten.

My eyes flickered around the girl, but I couldn't find anything to cover her body with, so I stepped carefully over her limbs and continued towards the bright purple light in the distance. In the long walk that followed, I couldn't help but realise that, once again, I was so very alone. The forest came alive as I moved through it, creatures rustled in the trees, and the wind whispered. By the fifth day, we were so deep in the forest that I didn't think I would find my way back out again. As I closed in on the new destination, I could see it was some sort of old building.

The dark wooden walls were half-rotted and covered with a bright green moss. Soft light glowed from within, warm and inviting, but I didn't immediately enter. Instead, I studied the building and realised that, much like Gluttony's manor, the trees had grown right into and through it. Half of the roof lay in the tatters on the ground where the tree had grown up towards the run, its branches were stronger than the abandonment of the building. I blew out a long breath and suddenly realised how thirsty I was. I startled when someone appeared on my left. The band around their wrist indicated they were a competitor, too, but they paid no heed to me and slipped right through the doors of the building. Before I could follow, I was hit with an intense longing, and I turned to stare into the forest.

Vaguely, I wondered if I would make it out... if I just ran now and tried to leave the competition, whether sheer luck would lead me all the way back to Ilrea. It was a false hope, I knew. The magic, if not the forest itself, would swallow me whole before I made it through the night. With a soft sigh, I turned away and found my way to the door. There was no use indulging the idea that I could get out now. I was stuck in this forsaken competition whether I liked it or not.

The inside of the building was in utter contrast to the outside. It looked like it hailed from the fairy-tale stories my mother whispered to my younger sister at night. Long tables stretched from one side of the room to the other, laid out like we were dining with royalty, and perhaps in the eyes of the people, we were. My teeth caught my lower lip as I hoped Gluttony would not be in attendance tonight. The huge trunk of the tree dominated the middle of the room, and fireflies floated softly above everyone. If I had been in anything other than a dirty, bloodstained dress, I might have been able to imagine that I was a princess going to a ball.

I studied the room and mentally ticked off each person I knew. Niklaus and Mikhael, side by side again and surrounded by a group of men covered in blood. Nash with Phee still clinging to his side, both drenched in hog's blood. Helina, who, for a moment looked disappointed that I had survived. Smug satisfaction filled me at the sight of her disappointment. My weight shifted and I tried to decide where to sit. The area around Nash and Phee was full, and Niklaus had spotted me, his chin raised in silent demand to come his way. I watched him before my eyes flickered to the slice across his brother's temple, and I convinced myself to turn away. Instead, I told myself that I was better off with distance between us. I told myself that the loneliness that ached in my limbs was a figment of my imagination. I inhaled deeply and slipped into the closest spare seat.

Nobody spoke for a moment. I hid my dirtied hands in my lap self-consciously, but when I looked up, I realised that I was not alone in my state of complete dishevelment. We were all dirty, half covered in blood, with a too wild look in our eyes.

Like the forest—and by extension, Gluttony—had already claimed us. There were more competitors left than residents, I noticed, and belatedly realised this should not be unexpected. Phee had recalled the year before they had cheese and dancing, and this year, they revelled instead in some of the vilest of emotions known to man. If I'd had the ability to disappear back to my home, to my bed, I would have taken it two nights ago.

"So..." A body dropped into a seat on my left. His voice was jarring in the quiet of the room. "How are we feeling?"

I watched him closely out of the corner of my eye, and then jolted to realise I knew him. He was the boy from the stairs on my first night. The one who had wandered free of the house. It felt like he had been lingering in my peripheral vision, there but unacknowledged for the past week.

"Exhausted," I admitted, deigning to answer his question when I realised nobody else was going to speak. "And a little violated."

The smile I received back was crooked and lit up his entire face.

"I know, right?" He laughed, and I didn't know how he had the energy to do so. "I could sleep a solid month straight after this trial." He moved so close that his shoulder brushed against my own. "Who knew the Gulans were so damn wild? They'd give home a run for its money."

My interest was piqued, and the question came out in a rush. "Where's home?"

"Cupitidas Eylandt!" He grinned.

"The city of Lust?!"

"That very one. Land of all pleasure." He laughed. "Where the sun shines freely, and we actually enjoy the day. I've never been so cold as I am here, I tell you."

Somehow, I managed to laugh. He twisted in his seat then, and so did I, until our knees bumped beneath the table. I inhaled sharply, but when he didn't apologise, I stopped the one on my own lips. He raised his cuffed hand and held it out.

"Who are you?" he asked after we shook.

"Octavia Nox."

"Finley Nightingale. The second, incidentally." Finley introduced himself and bent forward like he was trying to bow. "Don't hold it against me though, I'm a much better version than the first."

My lips twitched. "Well, I can't really compare, can I?"

"I suppose not." Finley chuckled and reached for a pitcher of water in the middle of the table. He filled both of our glasses, and I drained mine dry. He refilled it, and I drank deeply again.

"What do you think the next one will be?" I asked as I twisted the glass between my fingers. Dirty fingerprints appeared on the clear glass, and then smudged with the next rotation.

"Devil's knees, I hope it's something on the positive side of the spectrum," Finley groaned. "I've had enough shaking in my boots to last a lifetime."

We lapsed into silence, and I stared at my empty plate. With six more trials after this, I knew it wasn't the last time we would be sad, fearful, or disgusted.

"Want to wager on it?" I asked him then, my eyes brightening. Finley perked up.

"Sure! What am I winning?" He sounded so self-assured, that I laughed again.

Only, that question posed a problem as I glanced down at my hands again.

"I don't have any coins." There was a tight pang in my chest, like it physically hurt to go without.

"The wager's a kiss," Finley decided. "I get a kiss when I win."

I spluttered. "What?!"

He grinned. "You can't take it back now... I already decided my prize."

"I didn't agree—"

"Too bad, how sad, Octavia Nox," he sang with a laugh.

"But I'll taste like hog and ashes," I told him. Finley shrugged, so I added, "And you'll taste like desperation."

"Oof," he pressed the palm of his hand to his heart in mock pain. "You've wounded me. If there's anything a Cupitidan man is, it's not desperate." His caramel-brown eyes were lit with good humour, and he rolled his sleeves up to his elbows, flashing more of his bronzed skin. "Pick your prize."

My mind spun, and it seemed to empty completely with the pressure applied to our childish bet. Whatever I picked needed to be as good as his prize. "A secret!" I blurted.

"Just any secret?" he sounded curious.

"A secret that'll help me pass the Lust trial!"

Finley didn't laugh this time, instead, his throat bobbed in a tight motion. Finley tugged at one of the tight coils in his shaggy hair. Neither of us voiced the concern that we may not make it that far. Hope was a powerful emotion.

"Deal. If you win, I'll pay up in Cupitidas. If I win, you pay up today," he said finally, and then the slow smile curled on the edges of his full lips. "Now, pick me an emotion, Octavia Nox?"

I was tempted to say hope because we all desperately needed it, but my mind snagged on another possibility then. "Failure," I whispered, and Finley's darkened skin paled just slightly as he considered it. He didn't miss a beat in countering my bet.

"I pick success."

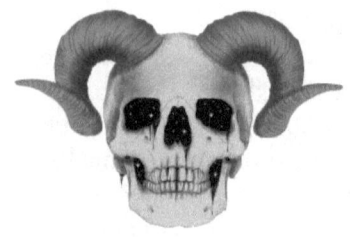

Chapter Forty-Four

inley pressed one long finger against my lips to cut off any argument that we couldn't do opposites. The pad of his finger was soft and dirty, and he only removed it when the chancellor swept into the room.

He was dressed up tonight, and his starlight robes were nowhere to be seen. He stood tall in a suit of black, which clung to his body, and I wondered if this was a sign of what was to come. My gaze dropped to the dress I wore, once in my lucky colour of emerald green and which was now torn and stained beyond recognition.

"Welcome back." When the chancellor smiled, my own dropped away. His smile was never a good sign. "You have succeeded on the fifth day of the Feast of Samael, and tonight, you need not work so hard."

I wondered what exactly that meant.

"Tonight," the chancellor crowed. "You will wine, dine, and taste the very best that Gula has to offer you. Beneath the fireflies, we give you Gluttony's Degustation."

As he spoke, pitchers of wine appeared on the table, each a rich, deep red reminiscent of the blood the night before. Bile burned on my tongue again at the sight, and Finley moved wordlessly to fill our glasses with it.

"Tonight," the chancellor repeated. "Your emotion is *confusion*."

He clapped his hands and magic pulsed through the room. The roar from Gluttony sounded much closer this time, and his influence swept through my body much quicker.

I leaned back in the chair as the gentle, hungry demands of my body increased tenfold. I glanced at Finley, and he looked like he was in actual pain.

"Guess we were both wrong," I whispered. The first plate of food appeared in front of me. "No kisses for you, Finley Nightingale."

His laugh was hollow, his fork already halfway to his mouth.

"No secrets for you, Octavia Nox."

With trembling hands, I reached for my knife and fork, and slowly dissected the first meal in half. I pushed one half to the side of the plate.

"Enjoy, Samael," I breathed ever so softly, and reached for the wine to satiate my belly.

The noise of the world and the pulse of hunger, which beat as ferociously as my heart, fell mercifully still for a moment.

'I do so like Quinn fish.'

The entire meal, not just half, disappeared. I whimpered aloud at the sight. "That was rude," I murmured to Samael and clutched at my glass. It rested against my lips before I swallowed all the deep red liquid.

'I am not well known for my manners, little one.'

"I suppose not. Tell me a secret," I demanded as I refilled my wine. I dipped a finger inside of the glass and rubbed the liquid between my finger and my thumb. It was thin, not like the blood of the night before. I lifted it to my nose and sniffed to get a hint of how it might taste It smelled as sweet as it tasted. For now, since it satiated Gluttony, wine was an indulgence.

'You will survive this night and the next.'

"That's not a secret!" I protested softly.

'No,' Samael agreed with a deep chuckle. The sound of which caused something inside of me to come alive. I leaned forward in my seat, anticipating the deep hum of his voice. *'It's a promise.'*

The world snapped back into focus as Finley prodded me hard in the shoulder.

"Are you listening to me?" he asked, and I shook my head. Dirty hair fell in front of my face, and I glanced up at him. Surprised to even see him there.

"What did you say?" I asked, dazed.

"You really weren't!" He laughed, and my inattention didn't faze him at all. "I said it's demonberry wine and it's delicious. You should finish that before I drink it for you."

"Oh!" I glanced down at my glass, and then at the table as the second course appeared. I drained the glass dry again and picked a fork. Soft meat and juicy vegetables slid over my tongue, and I devoured the entire meal in minutes.

A third plate appeared almost instantly, and the pattern repeated until we were twenty plates deep and it had not even put a dent in my hunger. I let out a whine of discontent, even as I dug into the next offering and let it melt against my tongue.

A platter appeared in the middle of the table to share, and I started as I realised that it was full of bugs. Little butterflies with brightly coloured wings. I reached for one and gasped as I picked it up, realising their little wings had been covered in a fragile layer of sugar.

"Oh!" There was a moan of delight from further down the table. "Candied butterflies."

They started rapidly disappearing and I turned it between my fingers.

Could I really eat a butterfly?

"Stick your tongue out and let it melt on it!" Finley advised and poked his tongue out in demonstration. A second later, he popped a bright blue butterfly on his tongue, and then it disappeared into his mouth. His eyes glazed over within an instant. I recognised the look and wondered if I could refuse the hallucinations that would come.

I thought of the girl left dead in the woods and decided that I couldn't risk it. I gathered my courage and trusted in the promise Samael had whispered in my ear. I would survive this… I would survive tonight and tomorrow. I tried not to think that he had not foretold my future for the seventh night and placed the butterfly on my tongue.

It was a burst of sugar with a hint of fruitiness.

A slow fog rolled across my mind, and a soft sigh pulled from my lips. I tucked into my next plate before a finger jammed into the side of my face. I blinked, dazed, and lifted a hand to touch my own face in confusion.

"Who are you?" Finley asked from my side, his voice uncertain and soft.

"I'm—" It was there, on the very top of my tongue, but I just couldn't reach it. My face crumbled into a frown, and my lower lip trembled. "I don't know."

"Are you sure?" He frowned.

"Uhhh," I opened my mouth, but no actual words came out.

"Where are we?" he asked.

"I don't know."

313

"Oh," Finley hummed.

"What are we doing here?" I asked him, and then answered before he could. "I don't know!"

"I don't know either!" Finley told me in between bites of food.

My head felt like we were underwater and disconnected from the world. I glanced around the room in a desperate search for answers. How did I get here? What was happening?

The only clear thought I could cling to was that I needed to keep eating, but otherwise, the world was a puzzle with missing pieces.

"If we—" My train of thought fizzled out on the end of my tongue and I frowned. "No, never mind."

A firefly settled in Finley's springy curls, and I gasped at the sight of the little creature.

"What?" he asked, his face a picture of pure confoundment. Wine spilled down his front as he drank deeply.

"I—" My voice came out as a stammer. "I can't remember. Who are you?"

What had I gasped at? I knew it, but I couldn't find the thought. It was slippery in my mind. Everything was slipping away. Finley pushed his face close to me, so close that I could count the freckles on his nose and couldn't help but gaze at his individual dark eyelashes.

Why did men always get longer eyelashes? It wasn't fair. A second later, I couldn't remember what was unfair.

"Who gave you those bruises?" he asked curiously as he inspected my neck.

I blinked. "What bruises?"

Finley shook his head and looked down at his wine-covered chest. "But I'm not bruised?"

His hands were raised in front of his face now as he inspected the length of his fingers, and I huffed out a sigh before I did the same. My gaze was caught on the specks of dirt and flecks of blood before I found myself distracted by the lines etched into my knuckles. I wondered if the soft folds of skin meant something. My hands fell back to the table as my stomach grumbled, and I remembered to eat and drink again. The fog on my mind didn't lift for the remainder of the night. I dropped glasses and they shattered at my feet. Pieces of glass bit into my soft skin. A plate fell from my fingers as I forgot that I was holding it, and then struggled to work out why it was on the ground. I stumbled in the middle of a dance as the movement fled from my mind.

By the time Gluttony tired of the night, I was lying on my back at the base of the tree. My head rested on Finley Nightingale's chest as I stared up into the ever-shifting glimmer of light provided by the glow worms and struggled to remember why I even existed at all. Sunrise was a blessing for my tired mind.

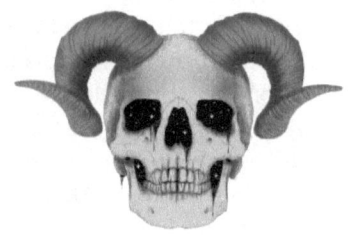

Chapter Forty-Five

On the sixth night, I awoke to hunger and unadulterated rage. I slammed into awareness long before I could comprehend the true nature of what I felt, and hunger clawed at my entire being—a beast birthed and demanding freedom. Before my eyes could focus on the fireflies drifting lazily above me, I was ripped from my place on the floor and pulled to my feet by the front of my dress.

The material ripped; the gauzy layer the offender had grasped tore free of the green cotton beneath, and I barely caught myself as I dropped towards the ground again. My fingers grasped at the edges of the broken fabric and I trembled with fiery rage that flooded inexplicably through my veins. It started as irritation and flared like a flame doused in alcohol. My gaze snapped up at the offender.

"Of course, it's you," I snarled as my gaze settled on Niklaus Heira. His eyes were flat and so dark that green irises looked back in his rage. "Of course, it's you," I sneered, unable to stop myself. "He who just can't fucking leave me alone."

Niklaus advanced a step on me. My toes curled against the dirt to force myself to keep my ground. I lifted my chin and looked down at him in the same way Helina looked at me. "Watch your fucking tongue, Octavia!" he growled, and I shivered. More the fool, I pushed myself forward until I was an inch from his face. I could feel his breath fanning against my lips.

"Or what?!" I challenged, mocking him with my tone. My hands fisted by my sides and my fingers blanched with the pressure. The growl of warning I received echoed from the very depth of his chest. Niklaus Heira had never taken after his supposed sin more than right then. A lethal, growling lion.

"Or what?" I snapped again and pressed forward. I expected him to back down, but Niklaus stood firm as I crashed into him.

"You're all bark and no bite," I taunted him. His eyes flickered and lit up, wild rage turned into unhindered abandon, a hunger stoked by Gluttony that twisted into something much more dangerous.

"I'll show you bite," Niklaus countered, and he grasped the back of my head, his hand fisted in my hair. My scalp burned as he anchored me in place. My head was jerked back, chin lifted, throat exposed. My breath hitched in my throat. My fists bounced off his chest as I inhaled deeply and prepared to scream.

"Freeze!" The chancellor of Gula could not be ignored. Magic slammed through the room. Suddenly, I couldn't move a muscle. I felt my heart thrashing in my chest, angry and impatient, and my lungs moving steadily to keep me alive, but I couldn't move any other muscle. My eyes stayed locked on Niklaus Heira, my head pulled back, the collar of black and blue bruises at my throat exposed. The jagged edges of my nails bit into the soft flesh of my palms and I couldn't remove them. I could only wait. I could only listen as the chancellor moved through the room and took his moment.

"On this sixth day, you will not eat," he said, and the room remained still with deadly silence. My vocal cords had frozen in place at his command, the protest from my belly silenced as well. "Competitors, you will not fall forfeit if you do not eat tonight, but you will feel. Feel your hunger, and feel your pain, and remember—" He paused for effect; dramatics that he did not need.

"The first person you see when I let you go is the reason you are so angry. They are the reason you are denied everything you want. Feel. That. *Anger*."

He shifted out of the way of us and snapped his fingers. My eyes remained on Niklaus Heira, and his on me in return. Throughout his entire speech, we had stared into one another's souls. Within seconds, I knew everything bad that had led me here was completely and utterly his fault.

"You bastard!" I snarled at him as pure hunger splintered through my body. The sight of the strong line of his jaw made me want to scream. "You absolute little—"

A scream dragged from my lungs. He snarled back and pulled sharply backwards, taking the fistful of hair with him as he used it to drag me out of the room. I spat every curse I could think of and struggled against him. My scalp burned and some of my hair ripped free. My protests were lost beneath the bellows of rage and agony from other competitors. Nobody was coming to save me, and I could barely keep myself upright with the pace that Niklaus dragged us away from everyone else. My heart skipped a beat as I realised, we were going somewhere secluded. I stumbled over roots and fallen branches as I pulled my weight to one side and tried to throw him off balance. I called him every name I could think of, shrieking them all at the top of my lungs, in a vain hope others would follow us. He didn't let go. Not until my fingers caught a tree branch and I swung it at him. Hard. The piece of wood bounced off ribs as he cried out in pain, and it was enough that his fingers loosened their hold in my hair and I could scramble free.

I ran to put space between us. I couldn't bring myself to flee, not when anger and hunger prodded against my senses. I turned to face him again, my hackles raised like a mangy, spitting cat.

"How dare you!" I screamed in fury. My fingers massaged my scalp, but the pain had already paled in comparison to the burning in my stomach and the blood I could taste in my mouth. "Who do you think you are?"

The tension in his powerful body was evident, and he surged forward to close the space between us again. My sense of self-preservation kicked in, and I backed up. Bark scraped against my shoulder blades, rough and abrasive, as he fisted the front of my dress and lifted me up off the ground. My feet swung in the air, so I kicked out at him. My heart lodged in my throat at the lack of purchase I had on the world. Splinters slid beneath the skin of my back as he pushed me against the tree and raised me higher. The pain reminded me that I was angry with him.

"Who gave you those bruises?" Niklaus roared in my face. Spittle landed on my cheek as he used his other hand to push my chin up and give him a better look at the marks on my skin. "Who the fuck touched you?!"

A beat of silence passed between us, and I laughed cruelly. "Well, they're your fingerprints, aren't they?"

His hand dropped from my chin and fit around my throat so quickly that I could have sworn that my heart skipped a beat.

The weakness of that reaction enraged me more than I could comprehend, and with another scream, I kicked out at him again. Niklaus said nothing. He merely shifted his position like my blows were an annoyance. He stared at the way his fingers lined up with the handprint around my throat. It was a perfect fit.

He snarled, so full of rage that goosebumps raised along my arms. His hand fell away from my throat and he used his hold on my dress to pull me away from the tree. He shook me so hard that my brain felt like it rattled within my skull.

"Oh." I breathed, as the world spun.

'Attack him now!' The devil suggested with glee.

"I never offered your tithe," I gasped.

Confusion flickered across Niklaus' expression. "What did you say?"

'You never needed to make payments, little one.' The devil laughed. It was not a toe-curling hum of delight this time, but something darker and richer. It stoked the flames of my anger until I felt possessed by it.

'Do it. NOW.' As the devil commanded, I threw my head forward with reckless abandon. The front part of my forehead felt like it split in half as it collided with Niklaus Heira's nose. A loud crunch of his face was a sickening sound. He screamed in agony; blood spurted down my face before he flung me brutally to the side. The force of his shove meant I staggered to the side and my legs failed to save me. I fell to the ground, dizzy as pain pulsed through my head, and rolled through the undergrowth. My gaze slipped out of focus and the world tilted as I struggled with the haziness from the impact with his skull.

"What was that for?" Niklaus cried out.

"Seriously?" I screeched back, holding my head. "How thick is your skull?"

"You broke my fucking nose!"

"You ripped out my hair!"

"Nobody cares about your fucking hair." A heartbeat later, he had the back of my dress in his grip, and he propelled me to my feet. I staggered away from him and held either side of my head until the world stopped spinning. When I looked up, his teeth were gritted, tension lining his bloodied face. His nose was a mess.

"You let Mikhael touch you!" Niklaus stomped forward and screamed in my face. I planted both hands on his chest and shoved him backwards as hard as I could. When he moved, I nearly fell flat on my face.

"Do you think I wanted to?" I spat, slamming my palms into him hard once more. "Do you think I wanted him to strangle the devil-damned life out of me?!" I sounded hysterical. When I shoved at him a third time, Niklaus caught hold of both of my wrists and pulled me with him. I stumbled and his hands tightened like manacles. A prisoner of war. With what looked like relative ease, he lifted me off the ground by my wrists. Panicked, I kicked out at him again.

"You probably bloody begged him to do it." Niklaus snarled. His gaze was an inferno within which I would burn alive, but I couldn't look away. "*And* you were lying on that little prick's chest."

Confusion twisted across my face. I had no idea what he was talking about. It didn't matter. Before I could register that it was a very bad idea, I spat in his face. Niklaus slammed me into the ground again as punishment. The breath rushed from my body, and my lungs spasmed at the loss of oxygen. He left me there for minutes before I could comprehend moving in my winded state. Everything in my body seemed to ache, everything felt broken at once as my lungs struggled for air. The fact that he left me alone told me only that he wanted me alive to torture and not dead at his feet.

Anger pulsed through me. Why couldn't he just kill me? I was better off dead than floundering through this ridiculous trial.

It was all his fault. All of it. Every bump, every bruise, every inch of my pain belonged to Niklaus Heira and his stupid little business in Ilrea. It was his beady-eyed man that had forced me off the bus and to the square the day of the sign-ups. If not, I would have slept through this fate. If I had hidden in that cold, metal container for a little while longer, I would have never joined the trial. I would never have been in this position. A groan rolled from my lips as I pulled myself onto my hands and knees. My scalp burned. There was a searing pain down my left side. My mouth tasted like copper and salt. I could hear my blood pounding in my ears. It became a violet drumbeat sending me to war. I staggered to my feet, and Niklaus offered up a look so dark, he may as well have been the devil himself.

"Why do you even care?" I snapped finally. There was a thread of weariness in my voice, for no matter how angry I felt, my energy was depleted, and I had little to nothing left to give him.

Niklaus stayed infuriatingly silent. Stubbornly, I staggered forward and closed the gap between us again. I was a glutton for punishment, it seemed. "Why?" I pushed myself into his face and screamed the single word on repeat. "Why? Why?! Why d—"

His fingers dug into my face so hard, I would be left with more fingerprint bruises. He stole my next question as Niklaus slammed his lips down against mine. The kiss was harsh and demanding. Lips bruised against lips, and he bit down hard enough to pull a cry from my throat. He punished me with his mouth like I was entirely at fault, like this whole moment had been of my own making. He kissed me until I whimpered against him and relaxed his hold. Some of the anger in my very bones melted away.

"Why are you under my skin?" Niklaus Heira snarled in my ear when he broke free. His breathing was rapid and his eyes tormented. Wrath sparked within his green gaze, and before I could answer him, he had shoved me backwards again. Niklaus threw me away with such fury that my ribs cracked, and my head snapped backwards. I slammed against the ground with such force that the world turned a blinding white before the darkness rushed in to claim me. I couldn't breathe, and a single tear rolled from the corner of my eye as I waited to die. My last thought was that Samael had lied when he said I would survive the night.

Never trust the devil.

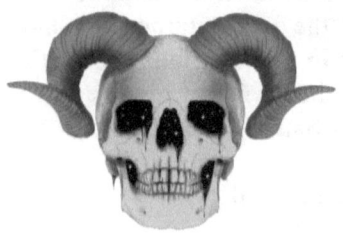

Chapter Forty-Six

The devil whispered in my ear.
'Wake up now, it's time to play.'
A groan rolled from my lips, and fleetingly, I thought that I didn't want to play his game anymore. My entire body ached with blinding pain, and the more I surfaced into consciousness, the more it hurt. I whimpered as I wished for darkness again. When my eyes opened, I saw double. Two faces in the field of my vision, near identical, and twisted into very identical frowns. I closed my eyes and exhaled slowly. After a minute, I couldn't help but take another look.

"Oh, thank the devil." One of the faces groaned and moved out of my field of vision. "I thought you'd fucking killed her, Nik. What would we have done?"

Dimly, I realised it was Mikhael, and that meant Niklaus was the face still hovering over my own. They weren't identical anymore, not with Niklaus' mangled nose. He looked conflicted, near tortured, and I let out a pained whimper. Every time I breathed, a new part of my body hurt. Mikhael's face reappeared and he frowned. I tried to focus on the cut I had created above his brow to centre the world as it spun. "Wiggle your toes, Octavia," he demanded. Slowly, I tried to follow that command. Niklaus sighed in relief, and the tension rolled from his shoulders.

"Now your fingers." I shifted my fingers in the dirt, and Mikhael nodded. "Good enough. Now get up."

No rest for the wicked nor the broken, apparently. A shake of my head left me dizzy, and I became acutely aware of the hollow pit in my stomach. It pulled at the rest of my body, all of which responded with more pain.

"I... can't..." I breathed, and Niklaus' relief turned into another frown. His eyes flickered over my body like he was trying to work out which part was causing me trouble.

"What hurts, love?" he asked.

"Don't call me that," I choked out, and he flinched. "You... you..."

"Nearly killed you?" Niklaus supplied. "Yes, I know. But the keyword is *nearly* and if you don't find your feet, Gluttony *will* kill you."

"Kissed me," I accused, and Mikhael risked removing his own head with the speed at which he turned it to look at his brother.

"You what?" Mikhael sounded genuinely amused. A moment later, he did laugh. "Nice to know you have your priorities straight, brother."

Niklaus looked like he could have murdered Mikhael on the spot. "Shut up."

I let out a breathy scoff and both turned back to me. Niklaus looked concerned and Mikhael frowned. "Baby steps. Nik's going to keep his tongue in his own mouth, and his entire mouth closed." He shot Niklaus a look—a warning not to argue. "You're going to take a deep breath and then we're going to get you sitting up."

It sounded like the worst idea he'd ever had, but Mikhael didn't wait for my protests or agreement. His warm hand slid beneath my back, and he held my gaze. There was no escaping what he wanted to do. "On the count of three?" Mikhael asked.

I barely managed a nod and exhaled slowly.

"Three." Mikhael and Niklaus pulled me into a seated position and a wail ripped from my throat. My entire body pulsed with a mixture of hunger and pain.

"Are you alright?" Mikhael asked. I glared at him.

"No," I muttered finally as I frowned. "Where was one and two?"

"They were unnecessary. Are you alright physically?"

"I'm sore and I'm hungry."

"Also, grumpy," Niklaus chimed in. Both his brother and I shot him a glare before Mikhael started picking leaves from the bare skin of my back. I whimpered as he ran his fingertips over the raw points in my skin.

"Hmm," he muttered. "I don't think I have time to try and get all of these splinters out right now." His fingers brushed against the sores again, and I pulled away with a sharp breath.

"Don't touch them!" It was Niklaus now as he pushed his brother's hands away and swept off the rest of the leaves brusquely. Distantly, I remembered his shout from the night before. The furious accusation about his brother touching me. My eyes flicked between them, and I wondered if there was more competition there than anyone knew.

"Let's just get her on her feet," Niklaus added, and they grasped my arms. They hauled me to my feet. No counting, no warning, just jarring pain. I breathed shallowly. As the world spun in glorious circles, it felt like the night of confusion all over again. What I wouldn't give to be back there instead of on this seventh night of the feast. Dread pooled in my stomach as I realised this trial was ending tonight.

"What are we supposed to be doing?" I asked when my voice came back, and I felt a little less like I was going to collapse on the spot. Both brothers kept hold of me though, like they didn't trust that it wouldn't happen.

"Well, the last day started an hour ago," Mikhael explained. "It took that long to wake you up. Seriously, we thought you were dead."

I blinked, confused. Every other day, I had roughly woken when Gluttony's power called. It was like he had worked his way beneath my skin and turned me into a marionette at his beck and call.

"Why did it take so long?" I whispered, and the twins shared a look over my head.

"We don't know," they answered in tandem, a disconcerting occurrence. I pulled free of their hands and took a tentative, wobbly step forward. It took all my willpower to swallow the whimper in my throat and pretend I was okay. Slowly, I took stock of myself. All in all, I was alive, even if my ribs seared with pain every time I inhaled, my scalp burned, and I felt like a building had fallen on top of my body. The main thing was that I was alive. Just as the devil had promised.

"Thank you," I whispered to Samael, and the world fell quiet for a moment. The devil said nothing, but his presence caressed against my mind. I felt the corner of my lips twitch just a touch. Not for the first time, I wondered what the devil whispered in everyone else's ears.

Mikhael moved into my line of vision. It was then that I realised he had been speaking and I had checked out completely, too focused on Samael. The world rushed back in, and I shook my head.

"What did you say?" I asked.

Mikhael shot Niklaus with an accusing glare. "How hard did you hit her, Nik?"

Niklaus didn't respond, but his jaw clenched so tightly that I was surprised that I couldn't hear his teeth grinding.

"Hard enough, I suppose," Mikhael muttered and watched wearily as I staggered forward another step. "This is progress."

"Just tell me what we're doing," I sighed, and he handed me a black rectangle. I blinked down at it and noted the metallic purple pig etched into the side. When I flipped it over though, the rest of the lines and symbols were unrecognisable. It was plucked from my fingers, and my head turned as I followed the path of the card, and Niklaus waved it at his brother.

"She can't bloody read, idiot," he told Mikhael, and I flushed. Mikhael looked nonplussed by the information though, and simply shrugged as if to ask how he should have known.

"It says the competitors have to make their way to the caves," he explained, without pausing to let me tell Niklaus off for sharing my secrets. There was a shift in Mikhael's gaze, a hardness, which said that he was done with our antics. "We can enter alone or in groups. Gluttony will explain when we're in."

I nodded and tried to find my equilibrium.

"I want Nash and Phee." I paused for a second, and my heart squeezed. Hesitancy gnawed at me as I wondered if I would regret this next choice. "And Helina."

The twins shared another long look. The muscles in Mikhael's neck tightened—more people meant more responsibility, but I was stubborn, and I would fight him on this decision. He took one look at my face and nodded.

"Fine," Mikhael said, and Nik grunted his agreement.

"Fine," I snarked back at them both. "Let's go then."

We were slow—mostly my fault—as we followed the soft glow of the torches that led us to the caves. After a while, I realised that Mikhael was limping and Niklaus was holding himself tense. We were all battered and broken. As we walked, my eyes flicked up to the thick canopy of trees above, in hopes of sighting the moon and getting an idea of how much time remained. The trees were so dense, and so unforgiving to my hopes, that I couldn't find any trace of the moon at all. We marched towards our last trial in silence.

It was a shriek from my left that drew my thoughts from the litany of colourful curses I was mentally raging at the devil. One for every part of my body that ached in protest of movement.

"Nash!" My heart pounded as I recognised the high pitch of the voice.

"Phee!" I screamed into the woods.

With energy I didn't have to spare, I took off at a run without offering the twins an explanation. I didn't even acknowledge them as I raced toward the noise. Behind me, I heard a low curse, and the crash of footsteps as the twins ran to catch up. My feet caught on the undergrowth, and I struggled to stay upright. The branches swatted at my aching, hungry body, but I was determined to keep moving, caught on a singular goal.

"Phee!" I yelled again. "Nash! Phee!"

"Octavia!" I twisted and followed the sound of my name, crashing back towards the river. My heart pounded as I remembered the last time, I had seen Nash there. I burst through the trees to find Nash spinning Phee in a full circle, his arms braced tight around her midsection. When he let go, Phee sagged back to the ground and I dropped to my knees in the dirt.

"You're alive," I whispered and rubbed my hands down my face. "Thank the devil."

They looked as broken as I felt. Nash looked like he'd had a run-in with a bear, his clothes shredded and hanging off his body. Phee was completely wild, a vicious woodland sprite. The lower half of her once-pink dress was dark and heavy with dirt. There was blood slicked up her arms and matted through her hair until it no longer looked blonde, and instead just hung limp and red against her face. Her eyes burned with an otherworldly hunger that caused my stomach to growl in a reminder that it too needed food.

Phee spun and gasped. A moment later, she was on her knees with me, her bloody forehead pressed against mine. We had known each other only a little over a week, and came from lives that felt a world apart, but we had endured a lifetime together in this trial. I studied each of her freckles, and the flicker in her eyes, determined to make sure that Ophelia Bell was okay. The night before, I realised, would have been the first time she had ever been denied food. Phee must have been starving.

"Are you okay?" I asked, my voice rough.

"Personally, I have been better," Nash chimed from behind Phee's head, and the laugh that barked from my chest was the most surprising thing of all. Ten minutes ago, I would have said I would never laugh again. Not after the emotional turmoil of the past week.

"Me too." I carefully extracted myself from Phee's tight grip and stood. My knees wobbled, and it was Mikhael's hand on my shoulder that stopped my fall back down. I shook off my fatigue and quietly took stock that we were not the same people that had entered the forest. We would never be those people again. Ravaged by emotion and fuelled by magically amplified hunger, we had lost the polished masks society saw days ago. Now we stood as a collection of jagged edges that showed the truth of humanity. We would do anything at all to survive—kill, revel, bow down to the angels. We were no better than the men and women of old. No wonder the angels had won when they arrived on our earth.

"Let's go and find Gluttony," Mikhael's voice carried as he stepped into the lead again. "Let's end this trial."

He walked away, and I felt helpless to do anything but follow. The path wound up a steep slope and the trees and roots faded. I found myself tripping over rocks instead of roots, and the higher we moved, the thinner the air felt. We climbed higher and higher until I looked over my shoulder and realised, we were standing just above the treetops. In the distance, I could see the soft lights of the city, alive at night. My chest felt tight when I realised, we weren't all that far from Gula itself, not anymore, and as I gazed out over the trees, I thought we never really had been. We debased ourselves on the outskirts of our city. They wined and dined, and I walked closer to my own doom. The citizens of Gula had slipped away from the trials of this week so easily. Content to find their beds after the emotions left them weary and cold. Or maybe they believed they had paid their dues to the devil already.

There were a handful of competitors still standing at the wide mouth of the darkened cave when we approached. The chancellor stood to the left like a sentry, and I watched him wearily. He seemed to delight in what we had been through without participating himself. Mikhael approached him, and the chancellor held out his hand in the universal signal to stop. It worked and we all fell still. My stomach cramped painfully, and I wished we were still moving, with distractions from the hunger.

"Your party must wait their turn," the chancellor told us. With an imperious flick of his fingers, he dismissed us. Mikhael nodded, although the tension on his jaw betrayed his unhappiness at the chancellor's attitude.

We scattered about the rocks, and I dropped to sit against Nash, his arm wrapped around my shoulder like he needed me to anchor him as much as I needed him. My eyes swept straight over Helina the first time I inspected the crowd. When I realised, she was there, a sense of relief washed through my body. I was a fool for still caring if she lived, but I couldn't help it. The effects of the emotional toll of this celebration were evident in the slump of Helina's shoulders and the gore that spilled over her clothes. The hard and prideful expression Helina wore said that she had survived the mental burden better than most.

"Hey, Helina," I called as Nash helped me to my feet. Helina's head turned, and her eyes narrowed as she took me in. Then, she looked away like I didn't exist. My stomach churned unpleasantly, and I rocked on my heels. I was too tired to fight. I blew a slow breath from between my lips to try and staunch the strike of pain I felt at her dismissal.

"Come in the cave with us?" I asked, determined to at least try. I had told the twins I wanted her with us, and it was true. Helina might have given up on me, but she had been my first and only friend for a long time. It wasn't something I could give up so easily. Helina had been an over-eager child who sat next to me through every class and whispered answers that I never had. Even when it wasn't her time to speak. She had been a teenager who grumbled about how we should abide by the rules, even as we broke into the chancellor's offices to try and steal a fabled can of peaches. She grew into a woman who liked to show off her position and had bought our first ever piece of steak with the whole of her first pay, only to realise that neither of us knew how to cook it properly, and we had had to swallow down chewy overdone meat. Now, she pretended we were nothing. I knew better.

"Come on, Hel." I could hear the pleading edge in my voice as I was reduced to nothing more than a beggar for my friend's attention. "Please?" Helina pretended she couldn't hear me. Her jaw hardened as she stared into the distance.

A group of two stumbled out of the cave, and a group of four shuffled in. Helina didn't join them. Mikhael roughly pulled me backwards and ordered me to sit next to Phee before I fell. I complied and curled next to the blonde with my knees drawn to my chest. I watched Helina the whole time and retained the hope that she would come with us—that her hunger to win, and the powerful hunger to consume that had grown in her belly, would merge enough for her to put aside her pride and walk in as a group. Of the four people who entered the cave, only one returned. His face had lost all colour and was stark with horror. He said nothing as he stumbled to the side and retched loudly.

Helina strode right past him and entered the cave alone.

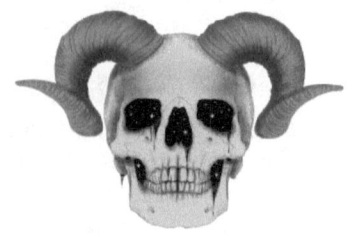

Chapter Forty-Seven

Impatience ravaged me as I waited for Helina to return. When she did, she marched past my bedraggled group and into the forest without a word, her mouth pursed into a thin, tight line.

Nash caught my eye, and he looked grim. "Of course, she didn't tell us what we'll be going in there for," he drawled. "Not a lick of loyalty, that one."

Our entire group shuffled with unease. Not even I could deny it.

"I'm so hungry!" Phee moaned. Our bellies roared in unison. I pressed my fist to my gut to silence it. This hunger felt so different, after nights of a magically induced need to eat and indulge, this one felt a little hollower around the edges. It felt a little deadlier. Despite the new, soft curve to my belly, which said I had been eating for days, I felt like the food of the feast had not sustained me at all. I wondered if we had been hallucinating the food along with the emotions. That thought caused me to cringe. Had the others not come back because they hadn't eaten inside that cave? Would we die without real sustenance? I wrapped my arms around my body and curled into a ball. Faced with the concept of my mortality, I wanted to flee as far and as fast I could. My fingers rubbed at the edge of the cuff around my wrist, and I wondered what the devil would have to say tonight.

"We're going to be okay." I don't know how I found the words and my voice lacked conviction, but Phee leaned gratefully into my shoulder all the same. By the end of the night, the first trial would be over, and I'd either survive or be too dead to care.

"I really, truly hope so… if I don't eat soon," Phee whined, and I brushed matted hair from her eyes, "I'm going to die."

I nudged her and frowned. "Nobody is going to die tonight."

"Promise?" Phee whispered.

"I double swear on the devil."

We waited until the chancellor cleared his throat and indicated with a sweep of his hand that we were holding up the line. My ribs ached sharply as I pulled myself up, and the world spun violently as I battled to stay on my feet.

"You're good, love." Niklaus had a hand beneath my arm for balance. His palm was warm against my cold skin. I pushed at him.

"I told you not to call me that."

"Since when do I listen to you?" Niklaus commented. Out of the corner of my eye, I watched a smirk tug at his lips. "*Love*."

We entered the cave in a single line, side by side, and completely equal. Privileged twins, a daughter of Gula, and two people who had been offered little chance in the world. We were a hopeless, hungry group. Covered in blood, grime, and the evidence of our sins, we approached Gluttony's table. He sat behind it on a throne of fruit-laden vines.

As the angel rose from his chair, I could see in the soft candle lighting that he had changed. He had been fed by power and not food. His strong muscles could not be denied now that the softness of his belly had faded. His dark hair was swept back, displaying the powerful angles in his face and the deep power that flashed in his eyes. Phee had called him a forgetful angel, but it felt like he remembered every ounce of our judgement of him. He knew our sins better than we did. His wings rustled and stretched wide, proving that he had gained a lot from the Feast of Samael. He was revitalised in the pure indulgence of his citizens. For seven nights, he had fed on the gluttonous natures of humanity. Although the Gulans thought they honoured the devil alone, their base nature had brought their sovereign angel back to life. The sight of him took my breath away. His wings folded tightly against his back, and he stalked forward on bare feet. A piece of fruit crushed beneath his foot. We all became statuesque as we realised the danger was close, and I reached down to hold Niklaus' hand tightly before I could think better of it.

"Welcome." Gluttony did not shout this time. He did not need to project when he knew we were listening. His words echoed off the walls of the cave, anyway. "To your moment of damnation."

Gluttony gestured to the table, where five place settings had appeared. It had a pristine white tablecloth and rich purple plates. Glass goblets of wine sat in front of each space. A single gold fork beside each plate. There was a simplicity here that contrasted to this angel's usual excess.

"Sit," he commanded. We hurried to follow his order. I let go of Niklaus and stumbled forward. Sticky liquid pulled at the soles of my feet as I approached a chair. When I glanced down, I saw blood. Bile burned at the back of my throat, and I pressed my lips together to stop myself from gagging. It was Niklaus' guiding hand on my lower back that kept me moving, and I sat in the seat second from the end—a Heira twin on either side of me. I dared not touch the pristine white tablecloth with my grimy hands, or the golden fork. My hands fell to my lap, and I focused on reducing the tightness of panic that squeezed around my chest. I felt eerily like I had walked right into a trap, and there was no way out.

"Do you feel hungry?" Gluttony asked, and it was Phee who answered eagerly.

"Yes!" she moaned.

"You need not wait much longer," Gluttony assured us, and his eyes flared brightly for a second in appreciation of her enthusiasm. My stomach curled with hunger as I stared at the plate and imagined it laden with food. Crusty bread, soft pieces of fish… I would even eat the strange green tree-like vegetables that seemed to appear so often but tasted bitter on my tongue. Tonight, I would have even taken one of my family's burnt whole potatoes.

"We angels have seen into the hearts of men, and we know the trials you bear," Gluttony told us. He smiled like we were pets who had pleased them with our indulgences each night. "We know how hard this feels."

Phee was nodding, and I tried to stop the shaking in my fingers.

"This one last meal," Gluttony continued, "will erase all the hunger you feel. You will finally find satiation. You will never feel so ravenous again."

As he spoke, his eyes flared in hues of royal plum, and my belly growled back in salute of his power. The feeling of hunger I felt was indescribable. I had not been so famished in my entire life.

"Please," someone whimpered, but I was too hungry to pay attention to who spoke. Need pounded in my ears in violent demand, and I gritted my teeth at the way my body shook.

"Your final meal," Gluttony announced. As with every other course, it appeared from nothing more than a pulse of magic. The final meal contained a single cubed piece of meat in the centre of the plate. I couldn't place what sort of meat it was, and I didn't really care. It was tempting. The sound of my blood pounding in my ears fell away as I focused on the task at hand. Mikhael's erratic breathing left me nervous.

A throat cleared, but it was not my own. It was a sound that slipped against my mind with an intrusive presence and left me shivering. Samael had come to play.

"*Wait*." The word caught in my throat, hard and demanding. "Don't eat yet." The twins froze like I wielded magic and not the angel. My body screamed at me to eat but I forced myself to ignore it. I waited, feeling faint, but the devil said nothing more, he had merely wanted me to stop and think.

"What is it?" I asked Gluttony in a stall for time as I tried to work out what the devil wanted from me. Tears began to roll down my cheeks as I denied the burning need in my body. "What are we eating?"

Gluttony grinned widely—he had wanted us to ask. His expression twisted into something otherworldly and terrifying. His eyes glowed as he answered.

"Human heart."

My own heart thumped harshly in my chest. Despite the hunger, my stomach curled with disgust. Could I eat part of a human being? Only the worst of humanity did that. It had never crossed my mind before to eat another human. Now, I was so hungry, and it looked to be only a single bite, that I considered it. I didn't have to taste it, just swallow it, and live.

"Devil's green knickers, you're kidding us?" Nash sounded appalled, and Niklaus looked sick, a faint green tinge colouring his skin. Awareness prickled at the back of my neck as we all battled with this new knowledge, and my toes curled in the blood on the floor. I was missing something, but I couldn't work out what.

For six nights, I had spoken to Samael, and for six nights, he had indulged me with useless secrets. Another form of power for the angel in front of me, I supposed. Another indulgence I hadn't realised I had participated in. The devil had offered me information for a cost I didn't understand since the tithe had never been necessary. I picked apart everything he had said and realised he had not lied to me yet.

"Mikhael?" my voice shook. Suddenly, I realised I had picked up the fork. Mikhael grunted like he couldn't quite form words.

"Who is Temperance?" I whispered. Samael had told me that when the time was right, I needed to find Temperance. No time had seemed more important than it did right then. The name was so familiar that I could have sworn I'd heard it before. I couldn't help but hope that Helina had forsaken us to make room in our group for someone who could save us. Temperance would appear and become our hero.

A vein throbbed in Mikhael's neck as he stared at his plate—a man possessed by need. Gluttony had gone very, very still, a ripe green pear held tight in his fist.

Mikhael found the strength to answer. "Temperance isn't a who, it's a word."

I frowned. "What do you mean?"

"It's a word," he repeated.

Rich men were idiots, I decided.

"What does it mean?" I pressed. There was a hint of urgency in my voice as I watched Nash pick up the piece of human heart and turn it between his fingers. I had been so sure that Temperance was a person.

"It means…" Mikhael's fork clattered to the plate loudly. His hand flew past my face and I pressed back into my chair. He grasped at his brother's wrist and caught him with the piece of heart just at his lips.

"It means…" Mikhael squeezed tightly at his brother's wrist until Niklaus' hand spasmed, and he dropped the fork. The piece of heart rolled onto the white tablecloth and splattered blood across the surface.

"Abstinence."

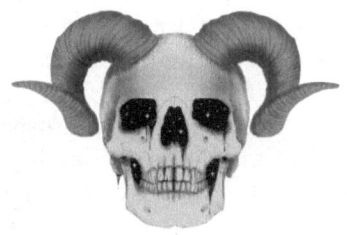

Chapter Forty-Eight

This word was just as foreign as the last. Temperance, which was abstinence, meant nothing at all to a woman with no literacy skills. Frustration and hunger gnawed at my soul in equal measure. The word meant something to the Heira twins, though. Niklaus grabbed his abandoned fork and my plate and shoved them towards the angel. They clattered forward loudly enough that it distracted him before he could place his portion in his mouth.

"We refuse." Mikhael shoved his own plate away. His fingers pulled the heart from Nash's hand to discard it as well. I could see the faint smudge of blood on his lips where he had almost eaten it.

"We refuse to eat the heart," he repeated, even as hunger howled in my ears and a sob burst from my lips. I felt like a child throwing a tantrum. I was going to die of hunger or be forfeited to Gluttony for failing the challenge. I had no idea what a beast of his nature would want from humans, but my life forfeited to his service seemed a bleak prospect.

"We abstain," Mikhael gasped like it pained him to say it. Tension melted from the room as the magic fell away. It had been pressing against us, urging us to eat the entire time. Gluttony began to laugh, a booming and maniacal sound.

"Not all of you," he practically purred. I glanced at my discarded plate, and at the stabbed piece of heart at the end of Niklaus' fork. Mikhael's and Nash's were accounted for too, but it was Phee's plate that was bare. Her blue eyes were wide and flared with the same violet hue as Gluttony, her fingers pressed inside her mouth as she sucked the juices of the single bite off the tips of her fingers. Horror pooled in my belly as Gluttony smiled down at the girl.

"I'm not hungry anymore, Nashy," Phee hummed to the man on her right, her face bright and finally satisfied. The same ravishing need within the rest of us had disappeared in the blonde. She looked so content that I could have cried. "It feels so good. It's the best feeling in the whole world." Phee sighed and smiled softly.

"Your trial has ended," Gluttony declared. The angel approached us. His influence dropped away and I sagged in my seat. Hunger still gnawed at me, but it was less intense. I felt hollow, empty, and ready for the consequences of my actions.

It was waiting that felt the worst, waiting for the mercy of an angel. At the last moment, I lifted my chin and pushed greasy hair from my face. I would keep my head held high and face my death with any tattered scraps of my dignity intact. Gluttony stalked along the length of the table. His all-powerful eyes assessed us one by one. Four refusals, and one acceptance.

When he took his place in front of Phee, he smiled indulgently, and the angel reached out and caressed her jaw. The daughter of Gula, his favoured child.

Phee came alive beneath his indulgence. She inhaled and sat straighter. Her skin glowed with energy. His power flickered in her eyes, and a content smile twisted onto her full lips.

"Oh, little one... Ophelia Bell, my little glutton," the angel purred. At the nickname, I was reminded of the devil himself, and of how we were all so little in comparison to these angels from the last world. Just flickers of existence in time, and they could snuff us out with ease.

It happened so quickly, that my brain struggled to process it. Gluttony's grip tightened around Phee's jaw. His hand was too firm, and she flinched beneath his fingers. She struggled just a touch but couldn't manage to move herself away from him. Gluttony's free hand slammed into her chest, and before I could expel the breath that caught in my throat, he had ripped out her heart. Time stood still, and the angel stood before us with my friend's heart held in the palm of his hand, blood slick across his fingers and wrist. Phee's body slumped onto the table, limp and lifeless.

Gluttony lifted the heart to his lips and took a bite.

Screams echoed off the cave walls. High-pitched and keening, they rang in my ears. I shoved backwards from the table. Distantly, I was aware that the screams were mine. My chair broke with a crash as it slammed into the ground, and I scrambled onto the table to try and get to Phee. The commotion caused Nash and the twins to startle from their horror. A plate cracked beneath my knee, and my palm slipped on a piece of heart as I crawled across the table to the blonde and reached for her desperately. Face-down on her plate, I willed her to just be sleeping, willed this to just be another hallucination in the Feast of Samael. Strong hands gripped my biceps and the twins wrenched me backwards. I thrashed in their hold to get closer to my friend.

"Phee?!" I shrieked. "No. NO! Let me go! *Phee*!?" The blonde had been so full of life, so vivacious, and it had all been lost in the blink of an eye. My nails bit into Mikhael's hand, and I gained a few inches towards the blonde before Niklaus Heira jerked me backwards by a fistful of my dress and picked me up. He hooked his hands beneath my knees and bundled me tight against his chest.

I flailed against him. "Let me go!" I wailed and sunk my teeth into the muscle of his chest wildly. He grunted with pain but held me tight. I screamed for Phee long after we fled the cave.

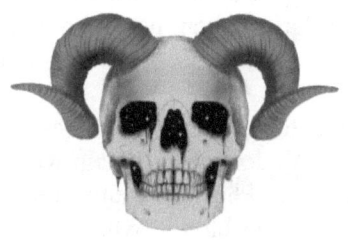

Chapter Forty-Nine

We crashed through the forest and ran towards the city of Gula. As the lights grew closer, we veered away from the city and the patrons who dined throughout the night. We turned through the trees until we reached Gluttony's decrepit mansion. I didn't bother to raise my head from Niklaus' chest as we climbed the stairs. Harsh sobs rolled off my lips as he entered a bedroom, and Niklaus lowered me onto the mattress. I didn't thank him, only pulled my knees into my chest and curled into a tight ball. Phee's name was a murmur on my lips.

Niklaus disappeared, but I didn't move to follow. When he returned, I realised he was holding my boots and a fistful of Phee's clothing. It was the sight of her dresses that spurred me into motion. He had been in her room. I sat up so fast that my head spun, and a ragged breath pulled from my lungs.

"We should have taken her with us," I told Niklaus in nothing short of accusation. He shook his head in quick rejection.

"She belongs to Gluttony now, remember?" He sounded angry. "Silly girl. We forfeit to the sin we failed." I wasn't sure if he was calling me or Phee silly, and I felt angry at the idea that he could be judging the blonde when he hadn't known a thing about her. Niklaus placed a hand beneath my arm and dragged me off the bed as Mikhael appeared in the doorway. He had washed, and now wore a clean, soft navy shirt, and had a backpack in his fist.

Mikhael looked between Niklaus and I. "Hurry up. I'll find Nash."

"Five minutes," Niklaus grunted, and Mikhael nodded.

Before I could breathe a word of protest, Niklaus had whisked me into the bathroom and turned on a tap. Water rushed noisily into the tub. Niklaus pushed at the ruined material at my hips to gather it in his fists. Awareness kicked in, and I slapped at his fingers, pushing his hands from my body.

"Don't touch me!" I hissed.

"Have it your way," Niklaus grunted as his patience hit an end. He picked me up and dropped me in the tub of cold water. Water was coughed from my lungs as I surfaced.

"You bastard!"

"There you are," Niklaus sounded relieved. "Keep cursing. Sobbing won't keep you alive."

"What if I don't want to stay alive?"

"Well, too bad, how sad. Nobody else is dying today," he snapped, and I flinched. Before I knew it, he had stripped all his clothes off. Despite the frigid water, my body flushed hot, and I closed my eyes quickly. My face was level with his waist, and now I'd seen just how far his ink extended.

"What are you doing?" I asked in half a sob. He answered by sliding into the other side of the tub. The water sloshed high against my chest and then cascaded onto the floor. My eyes snapped open, and I scrambled back as much as possible. Our legs tangled—the tub was too small for both of us. I ended up perched on the rim with my arms folded across my chest and my dress tangled around my legs. The water was murky, filled with grime, and I watched as Niklaus picked up a bar of soap from the tiled floor and began viciously lathering it against his skin.

"Nik?" I whispered.

He glanced up and his gaze flared with something feral. "What?"

"Get out."

"Clean yourself up, Octavia." He ignored my request.

"But—"

"Now!" His voice was hard. With two hands, he snapped the soap in half and passed me a piece. I stared at it. "We have to get out of here before Gluttony comes back." The thought of what would happen when the power-drunk angel returned hadn't occurred to me. Nothing had, except the brief glimpse of the cavern in Phee's chest before she fell. The flatness of her eyes before she landed on her plate. I took the soap and leaned down to wet the soap and start lathering it up.

"She ate the food," I said dully. "I thought… I thought…"

"Stop thinking." Niklaus reached over and pulled the straps of my dress down my shoulders roughly. The once-green garment pooled around my waist and bared my chest to him. I shrieked. His rough hands caught my calves, and he pulled them forcefully into his lap and began tugging the material down my body. The result was that I slipped beneath the surface of the water again.

When I surfaced, spitting and sputtering, he offered a look that said I needed to get moving. I kicked out to get him to let go. He glared until I rubbed the soap across my skin. Once I did, he relaxed enough to speak.

"We had to eat to survive in the lead-up. It was designed to be a frenzy of indulging our hunger and then denying it so that the desire to eat was at an all-time high, but..." Niklaus shrugged and more dirty water spilled to the floor. He ran the soap through his cropped hair roughly. I watched for a moment, and I did the same, sliding it against my dirty scalp.

"But...?" I prompted him to keep talking and scrubbed at my face until it felt sore.

"But the real challenge was temperance, not indulgence. We needed to abstain of our own free will."

"Oh." I stared into the dirty water, at the murky edges of my reflection. "I don't know what that means," I admitted. "Abstain."

Niklaus didn't miss a beat. "It means we had to stop ourselves from eating, from indulging the gluttonous part of our soul. We had to deny even the one bite we desperately wanted, even if we thought it was the only way to live."

Suddenly, I felt foolish. I should have been able to work that out myself. That was why Phee had failed—she had indulged in the moment and proved her loyalty to Gluttony and, as a result, he had taken her from us. Niklaus stepped out of the bathtub. I fought not to look at the lean muscles of his body, and instead, kicked at my saturated dress and tried to scrub the remnants of the feast off the rest of my legs. He held out a towel after he had wrapped one around his waist. My head dunked underwater, and I rubbed at my scalp before I was up and wrapped the towel quickly around my naked flesh.

The cool air of the night left me shivering as I picked my way back out to the pile of clothes Niklaus had brought into the room. They all belonged to the dead blonde, and that turned my stomach. I couldn't complain when I had nothing else to wear. I pulled a soft pair of lined leather pants over my thighs; they were warm after days of freezing in the forest. I deliberately kept my eyes down as I found a black shirt to wear. I couldn't bring myself to pick up the shimmering pink top that reminded me so much of Phee. In the seven days of oblivion, my tattoo had lost its redness and no longer itched. I brushed my fingers over the lucky dice as I pulled the shirt down.

I was lacing my boots when Mikhael reappeared in the doorway. By his side, Nash looked exhausted. I felt it too—the bone-deep ache of fatigue that may as well have shaved years off my life. I stood and ran the towel brusquely over my dark hair. It kinked with a gentle wave when I stood upright. Both twins surveyed me quickly, like they thought I would crumble, emotionally or physically.

"Jacket," Mikhael snapped, and I wondered if he had always been so bossy. Niklaus shoved a tan leather jacket with the silky inner lining in my direction. It wasn't the right size, but I pushed my arms into it and rolled up the sleeves.

My fingers shoved into the pockets and voiced the most important question. "What now?"

"Now we get the hell out of here." Niklaus herded us towards the door. Mikhael nodded in agreement. "I don't think Gluttony will be too fond of us sticking around after we've completed the trial."

We were halfway out of the house before I twisted back to look at what we were leaving behind. "Where do we go next, then?"

Nobody had an answer.

We marched back towards the city, and I hurried to fall into step with Mikhael. "Wherever we're going, I need to make a stop in Gula."

Mikhael considered the request. "What do you need?"

I shrugged awkwardly. "I want to go and see Phee's mum."

"Why?"

"You know why…" My throat bobbed with another wave of emotion that threatened to overwhelm me. "She deserves to know. You'd want me to tell your mother if you died just outside of Ilrea." Mikhael's jaw tightened. I thought he would object but he nodded in a sharp, jerky movement.

"We'll split up," he announced to the four of us at large. Mikhael ran his hand over his scalp, and for a startling second, I could see the stark resemblance to Chancellor Heira. He was worn out and aged with responsibility like his father. "Two of us will go for supplies, and two of us will go to Phee's house."

He didn't wait for protests or agreement. Much like his father, he thought his word was law.

"We'll meet at the train platform in an hour and a half," Mikhael continued.

"I'll go with Octavia," Niklaus said, almost instantly.

"No." Nash spoke for the first time since we left the caves. "I'll go with her to see them. I've met them before, and I knew Phee just as well as Tav did. Phee and I, we did fear and anger together, and she…" He swallowed roughly. "That girl didn't deserve that. She had a bright life, and so much room to grow."

Nash looked like he might cry and I shuffled over to nudge his hip with my own. I nodded softly. "Let's go, then." There was no more discussion as I took a hold of Nash's hand.

It took a good part of an hour, and two sets of mumbled directions to find the right door. On the doorstep, I hesitated and shared a long glance with Nash. My chest felt tight as I raised a hand and banged my fist against the door.

"You know." I sighed softly. "We got through that whole load of fuckery, and I think this might actually be the bravest thing we've ever done. And the hardest."

Nash sighed. "She deserves to know."

"I know… I just wish… I feel responsible…"

"Me too."

Nash scuffed the toe of his boot on the ground, and I knocked again. A body shuffled behind the door, and one of Phee's sister's faces appeared in the crack that opened. Without her makeup and hair done, the woman looked much younger, and so much more like Phee. It felt like a punch in the gut.

"Hi," I greeted her and suddenly became self-conscious. I wasn't sure what to do with my hands. "I'm Octavia… we went to dinner with you the other night?"

The woman blinked. "I know. I'm Claudia, you sat next to me."

"Oh, right. Well…"

"Did you need something?" Claudia asked and glanced over her shoulder at a man who had appeared at the base of the stairs. "We were just turning in for the day."

My throat tightened. "Yeah. Um, is your mother home?" I asked. "It's about Phee."

Claudia glanced over her shoulder at the man again and shook her head. He stamped back up the stairs. Then she pushed the door a little wider and motioned to the sitting area we had bypassed the other day. I bundled inside with Nash close on my heels. Neither of us sat. Instead, I found myself staring at pictures of Phee and her siblings on the wall. It was a collection of their growth from muddied children to beautiful adults. Three eerily similar girls and one boy. Phee was the brightly smiling energy in the later photos, with two plaited pigtails and a gap in her teeth.

"Hello?"

When I turned back, Fiona was on the bottom step. There was a daughter on either side of her, and her son standing on the step above. "You're Ophelia's friends?"

"Yes, Mrs Bell," Nash answered slowly. We shared a look, and Fiona caught it. The woman's brow pulled together.

"Where is she?" Fiona asked, her voice strident with urgency.

"Well..."

"Where's Ophelia?" She came so close, so quickly, that I wondered if she was about to slap me. Instead, the woman scooped up Nash's hand in both of hers and held them tightly. "Where's my baby girl?"

"Mrs Bell..." Nash's voice was soft and so full of apology that understanding crossed the woman's face and shattered the perfection there.

"No!" She dropped Nash's hands and pressed her fingers to her mouth to stifle a gasp. "No! Ophelia is..." Benji stepped forward and wrapped his arms around his mother's shoulders. He squeezed tight, and his sisters joined in as their mother began to wail.

"Not my Ophelia! Not my baby!"

"I..." Nash's voice broke.

I felt compelled to say something, anything at all, in the wake of their grief. "I'm so sorry," I whispered. "So, so sorry."

It was Claudia who looked up, her eyes brimming with tears and cheeks wet. "What happened?" she asked. I glanced at Nash, who shook his head the tiniest amount. He was right, of course, there was no pleasant way to describe the macabre moment when Gluttony had stolen her heart. I didn't like the idea of lying to them, in fact, I had never been a great liar. So, I attempted to stay as close to the truth as I could.

"The final test... we had to dine with Gluttony," I whispered. "One of the foods, it... it shouldn't have been eaten. But... but you know Phee, she's all about traditions and manners and you try every course..."

My voice broke and Nash intercepted. "She ate the food, ma'am." His fingers curled around mine in a show of support.

"Was it painful?" Phee's mother croaked. "Did my baby die in pain?"

I thought of the way Phee had flinched back in Gluttony's strong hold, and the split-second twist of pure terror in her expression as his hand sped towards her chest. I thought of how it would feel to have an angel's fist tear through flesh and bone and rip the most vital of organs from its home.

"No," I lied outright this time, and then added some truth. "It was quick."

"Thank the devil," the Bell family prayed as one, and I flinched. Could I really thank the devil when Ophelia Bell had adored him, paid all his needless tithes, nevertheless, she died in his ridiculous games? No, he didn't deserve their thanks, or mine.

"Ma'am." Nash tapped me on the arm and nodded at the clock on the wall. "We need to hurry on, I'm sorry to rush. We just wanted to let you know so you didn't spend an eternity wondering..." Nash hesitated. "We wanted to tell you how sorry we are."

"We really are." I sobbed.

Fiona burst forward in a flurry of action and hugged us both tightly. Her arms were so tight around my shoulders that it felt like my ribs were cracking. In the woman's arms, I felt like I was drowning in guilt. I should have died in Phee's place. When we shuffled to the door and I glanced back at the broken Bell family, I breathed out slowly, gathering my courage.

"Gluttony," I started, and they all looked up. "He has her body, if you wanted to..." I trailed off and shrugged, unsure of how to say any more. Nash grasped my arm and pulled me out the door.

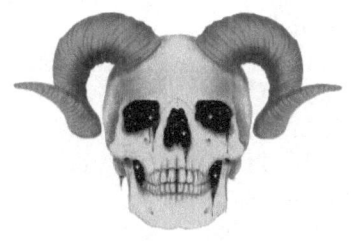

Chapter Fifty

A train waited beside the platform. The twins stood in wait for us to arrive.

"You're late," Mikhael commented as he pushed a bottle of water into my hands. My hands were surprisingly steady as I held onto it tightly.

"Yeah, well, you try telling someone their baby died," I muttered bitterly. I felt overwhelmingly like the twins just didn't care enough about the loss of Ophelia. Rationally, I knew they didn't know her well, if at all, but it still stung that they could carry on like they hadn't been witnesses to the horror of her death. I opened my mouth to call them out when an unfamiliar voice interrupted.

"Pay your toll," Charon's smooth voice was melodic in my ears, and when I turned, his single diamond earring glittered in the early morning sun.

"We don't know where we're going," I informed him stupidly. He raised a singular brow and held out a hand expectantly. He didn't care.

"Give me a devil's coin," Charon said silkily, his strong chin lifting as he caught the gaze of the man behind me. "One for each of you, and I shall refund you the balance when you decide to exit the train."

It sounded like a scam, but I had no room to argue. We couldn't stay in Gula any longer. My eyes narrowed as I realised, I was left with a familiar predicament. A severe lack of money. I had silvers hidden in my shoes, stolen from the purse of a now-dead girl, but I didn't have a single gold piece to my name.

"Here." It was Nash who flicked two coins dismissively at the man. They bounced off his chest and tumbled to the platform. Charon did not move to retrieve them. Nash placed his hand in the centre of my back to guide me onto the train.

"Thanks," I whispered my gratitude.

"Don't thank me." Nash sighed. "We're a bit beyond that now, don't you think?" I grimaced because he was right, but I still couldn't stop thinking of what I might do to get my hands on some of the devil's gold. I wondered if Phee's packed purse still lay abandoned beneath her bed in Gluttony's mansion. I resented Niklaus for not taking it, too.

The train carriage we entered wasn't empty. It was occupied by one other person. It took a long moment, during which the man in the seat offered me a quirked grin, to realise it was Finley. He who had wagered kisses on the night of confusion. He looked different, with his curly hair washed and the dirt cleared from his sun-darkened skin. He wore a blue shirt with white dots, buttoned up high beneath his chin. A style that should have looked ridiculous if he hadn't carried it with so much swagger. He was a man who knew he looked good, and it showed.

"Finley Nightingale the second," I remembered his name.

"Octavia Nox." He planted his hands on the back of the seat in front of him. He looked us over as the twins appeared at my back. "I'm glad you survived."

"Me too," I answered honestly and took a seat. Much to my frustration, I was crowded in by the twins as they forced their way onto the seat beside and across from me. They had no concept of personal space, so I huffed at both and turned to curl up against the window. It was the movement of the train that lulled me to sleep, and the nudge of Niklaus Heira's foot that snapped me out of it an hour later. I blinked slowly and peered into the bright train carriage. I found two identical pairs of deep green eyes staring right back.

"What?" I muttered groggily. Hair stuck to my face, and I tucked it behind my ear, twisting absently at each of the ringed piercings. The back of my hand swiped at the drool on the corner of my mouth.

"We have a question," Mikhael announced.

"And?" I reached for the bottle of water and unscrewed the cap quickly. "It couldn't have waited until after I slept properly?"

The twins looked at each other, and I felt awfully like they were having a full conversation without words. I frowned at them and leaned my head against the cool glass. We had passed a trial and fled a city without any proper plan, and the world outside moved by like a blur. I felt apprehensive about what might come next, and wished I was still asleep.

"Look." Mikhael leaned forward, and I got the feeling he was trying to be approachable. The bulk of him felt so intimidating as I remembered the feeling of being choked in the caves, that I flinched back. My hand automatically moved defensively to my throat. Mikhael looked horrified and sat back abruptly. His hands fell to his sides. "I wasn't going to hurt you."

"I know," I whispered. "I'm sorry."

"Don't apologise," Niklaus interrupted. "You apologise for everything. It makes you seem weak. You can't afford to be weak anymore."

I flinched again. It sounded like something Helina would have said. One of her little harsh truths that she believed made others stronger if they acknowledged them. I was weak though, that was the truth of it. I wanted to crawl beneath a seat and hide.

"I feel weak," I admitted. "I feel like I've died more than once. I feel like I've lost everything that was important." The twins glanced at each other again—another conversation I wasn't privy to.

"I wouldn't be surprised. I'm pretty sure we were dead and not sleeping each day that Gluttony knocked us out," Niklaus said and rubbed at his jaw.

"No, we weren't." The denial was automatic.

"Prove it," Niklaus challenged. It couldn't be true. I gaped and tried to process that I might have died several times over. Mikhael nodded in my peripheral vision.

"It's the only reason we can think of that we didn't wake up feeling in any way revitalised," he added, and I pulled a face at him. They were putting far too much thought into it.

"I want to sleep," I told them and rubbed my hand over my face. I was tired. "What was your question?"

"Temperance. How did you know the answer to the trial was temperance?" he asked, and it was the first time I had heard him so bewildered. "I can't work it out. You went through everything we went through, but somehow; you found the answer and I didn't."

My eyes rolled. "Maybe I'm smarter than you, Heira."

"That's doubtful."

I was close to pointing out that others also found the answer. Finley, Helina, and every other competitor that had walked free of those caves. Somehow, they too had learned that it was a test of refusal and self-control.

"Well…" It was on the tip of my tongue to confess and tell the twins of the secrets shared with Samael, but the rumble of the train fell away, and a feather-light touch brushed against my mind.

'Shhh!' The devil whispered wickedly. *'Secrets, secrets, little one.'*

The use of the nickname turned my stomach. My lips pinched together and killed the confession before it poured out. Instead, I awkwardly shrugged and lied for the second time that day. A little lie, with some truth mixed in for good measure.

"I heard someone talking about it," I muttered and glanced down at my hands because I couldn't look the twins in the eye and lie at the same time. "During the night when we hunted down the boars. I… I thought Temperance was a person, not a thing."

'Good girl,' the devil praised, and reflexively, I smiled. There was something about Samael's praise that sent warmth right down to the end of my fingertips. I curled my fingers into my palms and glanced up at the twins. Mikhael looked contemplative, but there was a suspicion in Niklaus' eye that hinted that he didn't believe I was being truthful. He didn't call me out on it though, instead, he glanced at his brother and folded his arms firmly across his chest. The fact that they accepted it—accepted that I couldn't work out the answer and had stolen it from someone else—should have hurt, but I was too tired to care. I curled deeper into the seat and succumbed to sleep again.

The next time I woke, it was because the lights inside of the train carriage brightened. I jolted in my seat, and Nash cursed as he smacked his head on a nearby seat in his haste to get up. Both twins looked like they were on high alert, tense, with the muscles in their forearms bunched. Finley merely leaned on the back of the next chair, again. When he caught my eye, I pulled a face. He raised a single brow in a smooth movement, and then blew a cheeky kiss.

I flipped him off.

It was Finley's laugh that had Niklaus turning in his seat, a frown twisting his features. He started to say something, but it was cut short as Charon entered the carriage. The man walked proudly and stood in the middle of the aisle. All five of us fell silent, our eyes dropping to the crisp, gold envelopes in his hand.

Charon dipped his head and studied us each. "Finley Nightingale, Nash Wickham, Mikhael Heira, Niklaus Heira, and Octavia Nox," he named us, and it felt like a curse. I shivered, but with each name, he offered a golden envelope. I gripped the chair tightly, but Charon was not done. He lifted his chin and cleared his throat. His fingers smoothed at the lapels of his grey suit, and his mouth curved into a full smile.

"Lord Envy requests your immediate presence."

Acknowledgements

Thank you to everyone who supported me throughout the process of writing this novel. To my beta readers Addie, Michelle, and Nikki, who provided invaluable feedback and insight to an admittedly raw draft. To Laura, for all your editing expertise. To Aamna and team, for your patience at my thousand questions and cover design tweaks.

Thank you to my RP buddies Alex, Caz, Jes, Tori, and many more. I appreciate that you let me rely heavily on your expertise as lovers of books and magical worlds.

Rhys, who cooked more than his fair share of dinners because I just wanted to just write a little longer. You have been my sounding board and support while I verbalised every plot and characterisation struggle until I had them solved. I'm sorry for all the chores I neglected for you to do, and for the date nights where I talked more about this book than anything else. I couldn't have done it without your ever-lasting support.

Ira, who put up with only half of my attention while I wrote, but still curled up on the couch beside me while I edited.

Emily & Amy, who were my consistent cheerleaders in times of self-doubt.

Lastly, thank you to the readers who have come to the end of this book. Thank you for allowing me to take you on a journey through Kaida and face the first of the deadly sins. I hope you enjoyed reading it as much as I enjoyed writing it.

About the Author

Stephanie Gluck writes on the traditional lands of the Larrakia people and pays her respects to Elders past, present and emerging. Thank you for allowing me to express my creativity on your lands.

Stephanie is the author of The Devil's Trials series, with debut novel Feast of Samael. When not writing she avidly feeds her coffee addiction and adds to her ever-growing collection of books. She is a registered nurse and lives with her husband Rhys, and Great Dane, Ira.

You can keep up to date with The Devil's Trials series and what Stephanie is writing next at www.stephaniegluck.com or via social media at @stephaniegluckbooks